DESPERATE DESIRE

Jenny knew what was coming. She could have stopped him when she felt the soft butterfly touch of his lips on her shoulders, but she leaned into him, letting his lips travel up her neck to her earlobe. Such sweet desire coursed through her. Such wanting that she thought she would go mad if he spurned her again.

But, when Travis turned her around to face him she saw her own passion mirrored in his eyes. He loved her, and she knew no greater happiness.

A slow fire filled Jenny's body until she thought she would surely burn through the floorboards. She could feel the heat of his flesh radiate with a pulse, a life of its own. They stood apart yet together in a way neither had ever experience͟

Travis's hand ca͟ her cheek. "You are a͟

Jenny's eyes clos͟ in his embrace. She k͟ he groaned in ecstasy ͟ying her to the berth. Nothing could have prepa͟ her for the incredible night of love that lay ahead. . . .

RAPTURE'S RAINBOW

Toni Gardner

ZEBRA BOOKS
KENSINGTON PUBLISHING CORP.

ZEBRA BOOKS

are published by

Kensington Publishing Corp.
475 Park Avenue South
New York, NY 10016

First printing: May 1986

Printed in the United States of America

To Mom
For being there
To Bill
For sharing your knowledge, your love and your life
with me

Chapter One

The ocean was alive, brought to life by winds that whipped the waves into frothing demons of incredible heights only to disappear into hellish depths. Lightning resounded from the heavens, making the very ghoulish light upon the gray clouds look like patchwork that constantly changed and moved to the devil's beat. God had abandoned the world to the devil just long enough for satan to unleash his fury upon the earth, and he was destroying everything in his way.

For three days the storm raged, and on the morning of the fourth day the sea calmed as if by magic. An azure blue sky heralded the beginning of the new day with huge white clouds scudding across its color. A grand and glorious day, washed crystal clear and fresh by the past storm.

Only one had survived. How, she didn't know but she did. God was not done with her yet. Surely He had something else in mind for her.

For three days she had clung to the bit of wreckage, not knowing if it was day or night. She was battered, her nightgown torn. She was exhausted, cold, so cold she prayed desperately for the strength to die.

Jenny Grayson was eighteen, beautiful and pos-

7

sessed an indomitable spirit that had never waivered during the harshness her life had brought. She looked about her, wondering how she had survived.

Bits and pieces of wreckage were scattered on the surface of the sea. She grabbed at a seaman's cap to protect her face from the sun that now burned her skin, almost losing her perch on the hatch cover that she clung to for safety. With the cap pulled low over her brow, Jenny scanned the sea from horizon to horizon hoping to find other items that might help her survive, but she could see nothing worth the trouble of reaching out for.

Thinking about Lady Elaine and her watery grave gave Jenny a moment of sadness. The lady had been good to her under less than auspicious circumstances. Jenny remembered those circumstances now with the same bitter taste of betrayal she had had two years earlier and since the beginning of her life.

Her mother had died giving birth to her, and her father, a gambler and a dreamer, had abandoned her to the care of a stranger, a kind woman but a woman who worked hard for every penny they had. She could give Jenny nothing but the one thing she had possessed and that was a knowledge of literature, music, and numbers. Jenny's bright mind had learned everything Connie Darrow could teach her and more. But, when Jenny was fourteen, the father she had never seen returned and took her away to London, away from the only home she had ever known. He filled her head full of tales of riches to be had and of handsome princes and carriages trimmed in gold. The fourteen-year-old Jenny sat entranced all the way to London dreaming of rich velvet and brocade gowns. Tall, elegant gentlemen in periwigs and ruffles and a castle to live within.

The dreams came to a swift end when they had

arrived at what Gregory Grayson said was to be their temporary residence. As Jenny walked up the creaking, rotting stairs, beady yellow eyes stared up at her through the cracks and missing steps. The smell of rotting garbage and human defecation assailed her senses. Feeling faint from the odors, Jenny made her way up the rickety stairs to the room she and her newfound father would share for the next two years. It had only one window, and when Jenny wet her finger to trace across its surface, her finger came away black with soot and grease. The small, airless room had but one narrow pallet, a wooden chair, and an aged chifforobe that was being propped up on one corner by a book without a cover. The floor was littered with discarded clothing and empty bottles. A slop jar in the corner needed tending to, for the smell was about to overpower the smell of vomit and excretion from the hall.

Looking about her, Jenny wondered how she would live in this room. Connie's cottage had been small but it was neat and clean. This room needed a good cleaning and most importantly, somewhere for her to sleep.

Gregory rushed to pick up the clothes from the one chair in the room, telling Jenny about a cot he could get for her to sleep on. But, without getting a cot or food for the evening meal, that night he had left her, telling her he had an appointment and not to wait up for him. He had not returned until dawn, when he came stumbling into the room reeking from spirits and looking much the worse for wear. He didn't seem to notice Jenny as she leaped from the bed to stand in a corner, afraid of this stranger who was her father. He simply sat down and removed his shoes before stumbling to the bed and passing out with loud snores reverberating throughout the room.

Thus began Jenny's life with her father. A life that saw her reduced to working as a scullery maid in order for them to eat and live in the rat-infested flat that they called home.

And now, as Jenny drifted aimlessly on her bit of wreckage, she relived the night her life with her father had ended, an ending that still had the power to torment her and reduce her spirit to ashes if she would let it. Now, two years later, she still could not believe it had happened. It had been a cruel farce, a nightmare that she had relived over and over again. The night her father had betrayed her.

She had been surprised to find her father at home as she came in, exhausted and hungry from her day of grueling, backbreaking work. He had turned to her looking like a dandy in dark green velvet breeches and waistcoat, white hose, and black, shiny shoes. The sight of him made her stop in mid-stride.

"Jenny, me love, come see what I've brought ye." Gregory had preened with a broad smile that showed his blackened teeth in the thin light coming from the lantern.

Stepping to the corner, where she had placed her cot, she saw the most beautiful emerald green gown she had ever seen. "Father, what—where did—"

But Gregory rushed to her, saying, "Just you get ready, me dear. You and me is steppin' out this night."

The dreams of riches and gowns that had sustained her for years came back. "Father are we rich?" she asked in awed hope.

Gregory Grayson threw back his head with ribald laughter. "Not yet, me darlin', but tonight will see us out of this dump." He indicated with a sweep of his hand the room they shared. "We'll have proper digs and proper gowns for ye, me beauty." He patted her cheek then grew serious. "Now hurry up and put on that gown. Times a wastin' and so's me chances."

Blindly following her father, Jenny had washed the grime of her day's work from her and slipped the heavy gown over her shining white-blond hair and onto her body. The gown hid the torn chemise she wore underneath and the hole in her stocking. She stroked the soft fabric for a moment before turning to her father.

"Ah, me darlin', you will cause a stir this night or me name's not Gregory Grayson. You look like a princess."

She *had* felt like a princess as her father escorted her from the little room, down the rotting steps and out onto the lamplit street. And, when they walked into a bright gaming hall, Jenny felt none of the fear that should have prepared her for what would follow.

She had gone with her father as he examined the tables of chance that were everywhere about the huge, elegantly furnished rooms. Red damask wall hangings and crystal chandeliers reflected light on the gentlemen seated at the tables playing their games of chance.

Gregory seemed to pause, then stood erect and walked toward a table that had one empty chair. "You gents mind if I sit in for a few hands?"

The eyes of the men sitting at the table went from Gregory to Jenny. One gentleman looked Jenny over from head to toe, making her feel as though he were undressing her. The feeling of revulsion she had was quickly stemmed when Gregory started introducing her and each gentleman came forward to kiss her hand.

"Gentlemen, may I introduce me daughter, Jennifer." He indicated her, then introduced each man in turn. "Jennifer, this be Sir Miles Seaton." Sir Miles came forward and kissed her hand all the while holding her eyes with his dark, sinister ones. An involuntary shudder crept up Jenny's back for no apparent reason as Gregory continued the introductions. "Sir Reginald Wenthrop," her father intoned as the tall, thin man stepped forward. He had the lightest eyes Jenny had ever seen, and they were devouring her like they had when she had first noticed him at the table. He bowed, taking her hand in his, but when he placed her work-roughened hand to his thin red lips, Jenny gave an audible gasp. She could not believe it but his tongue was tracing each finger before he stood and let his gaze linger on the cleavage that was exposed by the low bodice of her gown.

The other introductions were a blur as Jenny tried to regain her composure, all the while knowing that the gentleman, introduced as Sir Reginald, was eyeing her in a fashion that made her skin crawl.

Her father sat down at the table, leaving Jenny to stand awkwardly behind his chair. She noticed the stack of bills Gregory placed before him on the table, and her eyes grew large with surprise. She could not believe the amount the pile represented. The thought that she had worked so hard while her father had such riches made her stand straighter with indignation. But after two hours of playing, Gregory was left with but a farthing. He asked and received a small loan from Sir Miles, never realizing the price he would pay in the future.

The cards were dealt and Gregory knew this was the turning point. His hand was so good he knew he couldn't lose.

The betting started with Sir Miles. "One hundred pounds," he said while placing the wager in the middle of the table.

Sir Reginald met and raised Sir Miles's wager, making the bet two hundred pounds for Gregory.

Gregory looked at his hand and then up to Sir Miles who was watching Jenny with a lustful expression.

"Sir Miles, will you extend me the two hundred pounds to meet this bet?" Gregory begged.

Miles's gaze moved from Jenny's stricken expression to the fawning simp who was her father. "What do you have for collateral, Grayson?"

Gregory pulled his hand through his thin gray hair. Sweat beaded his brow and a tic moved his left eyelid when he looked back at Sir Miles. "You can have anything, milord," he said quietly.

Miles lifted an eyebrow, "Anything?" His gaze moved back to Jenny, the lust so evident even her innocent eyes discerned their meaning.

Gregory saw the look and knew what Sir Miles wanted. He looked again at the cards he held in his shaking, sweat-drenched hands, then back to Miles. "I'll put me daughter up as collateral." He heard the gasp from behind him but he couldn't or wouldn't turn to his daughter.

Miles grinned evilly before saying, "Your daughter doesn't seem too eager to be placed as a wager."

Gregory withdrew a handkerchief and mopped his brow. "Don't matter what she wants. *You* can see how comely the lass is. She would more than cover the wager."

Jenny heard her father begging this lecherous man to take her as a wager. She was sure this was a nightmare when Sir Miles Seaton said, "Are you willing to sign a document of indenture should you lose?"

Jenny quickly moved to her father's side. "Father, no! Come, let us go." She pulled on his arm.

Gregory Grayson had been a loser all his life. This was his chance to recoup, to be avenged for all the bad luck that had plagued his life. He turned to his daughter, completely devoid of any feelings he might have had toward her, saying, "Stay out of this, Jenny. I know what I'm doing." He turned back to Sir Miles. "Aye, I'll sign the document *if* I lose, but I won't."

Miles Seaton nodded his head, and Gregory lay down his hand. Three treys and two deuces. But, when Gregory gave a whoop of joy and moved to rake in his winnings, Sir Miles placed one elegant, bejeweled hand over his.

"Not so fast, Grayson."

Gregory's expression of glee faded to one of horror as Sir Miles laid down his four fives.

Smiling, Miles looked up at Jenny's horror-stricken face. "I believe this hand wins the grand prize."

Jenny remembered the way she had swayed and the blackness that had briefly blocked out the scene before her. The next thing she remembered was awakening to see Sir Miles standing over her, holding a piece of parchment in his hand.

"You are mine now, little one. I plan to ride you *this* night." He leaned down and pulled her to her feet. As she cowered before him, Sir Reginald came to stand beside him.

"Remember that we are friends, Miles," he said with a lecherous grin. "We could share this one's favors."

Miles simply laughed. "Not tonight we won't. I plan on using her myself. You can try her out after I tire of her charms." He snapped his fingers in the air, and a servant rushed to his side. "Take this wench to my townhouse. Watch her closely. I would be most distressed if something happened to her."

Reginald looked surprised and said, "You mean

14

you're going to stay here when you have that." He pointed to Jenny. "To warm your bed?"

Miles signaled a waiter for his cloak and then looked around the gaming hall as though looking for someone in particular. "I have an appointment that I must keep. She will be there waiting for my eager return though, won't you, my dear?" He placed his hand under Jenny's chin, making her look up into his steely black eyes. "It's been so long since I've taken a virgin, and my dear, you are a beauty."

Jenny wanted to scratch his eyes out. "You will never touch me!"

Miles lifted an eyebrow, then squeezed her chin between his fingers. "I will do anything I want with you, my beauty, for you see, you do belong to me, body and soul."

He pushed her away from him, making her fall against the servant who was charged with taking her away. When she noticed that people were staring at her, she squared her shoulders and lifted her head before turning and walking out of the gaming hall.

Standing outside, waiting for a carriage, Jenny felt someone pull on her sleeve. She turned to see Gregory Grayson standing beside her with slumped shoulders and a pleading expression on his face. Jenny turned away from his eyes, feeling she never wanted to set eyes on him again. He had sold her for a hand of cards.

The night would remain in Jenny's memory forever for her father had not only lost Jenny her freedom but his as well.

She had paced the room she had been shown to for hours. Feelings she had never experienced before coursed through her veins. Hatred, anger, humiliation, but the most frightening emotion Jenny felt was that of betrayal. She had tried to make her father's life easier by working hard to put food on the table and to

15

have a roof over their heads and all for this? She found herself in the frightening position of being owned by that blackguard Seaton. He would try to take the only thing that remained hers: her womanhood.

"Never!" She had screamed out loud into the silence around her. She decided to keep that most prized possession if it meant death. What had she to live for anyway? Indentured to a man who would use her until he tired of her, then hand her over to a man like Sir Reginald Wenthrop! A shiver shook her when she thought of the pale blue eyes that had looked upon her with such lust.

And, as if her thinking of him made him more real, the door opened and *he* walked in.

He stood before her with a hand still holding the door. He had removed his periwig, showing thinning reddish-blond hair pulled back with a blue satin ribbon.

Jenny stood watching him, waiting for an opportunity to run away should he advance on her. But, she was not prepared for his announcement when he spoke.

"Miles is dead," he said rather matter-of-factly. "Your father ran him through before my very eyes. You will remain here until the authorities are finished." He turned abruptly and closed the doors once again.

What surprised Jenny was her lack of feeling. She felt nothing. No sadness for her father's deed. No gladness that the man who would have taken her was dead. Nothing.

Trying to get in a more comfortable position, Jenny almost fell off the hatch cover. Her foot slipped into the water, hitting a soft, cold object in her search for better footing. Turning to see what she had touched, Jenny let out a scream that seemed to come from her very soul. Floating away from the hatch cover was the body of Lady Elaine Seaton. The jeweled hand that floated to the surface looked like a claw coming up from the dark depths of the ocean floor.

Covering her face with her hands, Jenny cried for all the injustice in the world. She cried for Elaine who had been as much a prisoner as she. Elaine, who had never been happy or content but had tried to be a friend to Jenny, did not deserve this death. She had finally been free of Miles and his sadistic treatment of her only to perish in this watery tomb.

The day after Sir Miles's death at her father's hands, she was summoned to the library. Sir Reginald was seated behind a massive oak desk, dressed in a charcoal gray waistcoat over a black vest and white ruffled shirt. His powdered wig, with its elaborate curls and waves, was once again adorning his head. His light blue eyes were scanning a parchment on the desk, but he looked up as she came into the room and casually looked her over before saying, "sit," while indicating a chair.

Taking the indicated seat, Jenny sat demurely on the edge. She was still clad in the green gown from the night before, having no other clothing.

Sir Reginald leaned back in his chair and looked down his long, thin nose at Jenny. Picking up the piece of parchment he had been perusing, he said in a slow, precise manner, "This is your indenture document, Jenny. It is quite binding and legally witnessed. In lieu of Miles, you will now become the property of his heir and widow, Lady Elaine Seaton. She has been summoned from her country estate and should arrive shortly."

He stood up and came around the desk toward Jenny. Sitting on the edge of the desk, he let the parchment fall back on the desktop before leaning toward her. "Now, my dear, I feel that since poor Miles is no longer with us, I should ready you for some of your duties." He pulled her to him and was struggling to hold her when they were interrupted by a spitfire of a woman advancing on them with a vengeance.

"Is this the way you act in my home, Reggie? I would say I have arrived in the knick of time." The woman then asked, "And who is this may I ask? One of Miles's doxies or is this one of yours, Reggie?"

Reginald seemed to shrink before the fire of this woman, and he abruptly let Jenny go to stagger to the chair she had used only moments before.

Standing up straighter, Reginald pulled at his waist vest and attempted to regain his composure. "This, Elaine, is the reason Miles lost his life. Her father wagered her to Miles and lost. He was most distressed and as Miles left the club last night, this gent just came upon him and ran him through with a wicked-looking rapier. She was indentured to Miles before all this happened and, of course, will now be indentured to you in lieu of Miles."

Lady Elaine Seaton was only a couple of years older than Jenny but carried herself with as much grace and aplomb as a woman twice her age. She was looking at Jenny now with an expression of compassion on her face. "Come here, girl," she commanded. She waited until Jenny approached her before asking, "What's your name?"

"Jennifer Grayson, my lady," Jenny answered in a whispered reply.

"How old are you?" Elaine asked as though trying to see what Miles had seen in her.

"Sixteen, my lady."

Turning to Reginald, Elaine said with a sneer, "Had Miles taken to violating babes? Nevermind." She waved away the question. "I don't wish to know." Turning back to the child before her, Elaine seemed to make a decision. "You will stay with me and become my personal maid. Is that all right with you?"

Reginald stepped quickly toward Elaine. "Elaine, I was so hoping to buy her indenture from you. You really don't wish to have one of Miles's conquests under your very nose, do you?"

Elaine turned back to Jenny. "Did my husband violate you?"

Jenny held her head high and answered, "No, he did not, my lady."

Reginald saw the smile on Elaine's face and rushed to stem her desire to keep the chit. "Elaine, her father is the one responsible for Miles's death. Surely," he begged, "you cannot mean to—"

"That's enough, Reggie. Miles got exactly what he deserved. I'm only surprised someone hadn't done it before this. No, Miles's death was a fitting end to a faithless husband." She walked around the desk and looked at the papers scattered on the surface. "Go make the arrangements for the funeral and leave me to get to know my new maid. Now go!" she commanded him.

With one last look at the woman he had been wild to possess, Reginald took his leave.

Jenny remembered seeing him again at the funeral, but she did not see him again for the next year. That year had been spent at the country estate, Eden Hall. The year dragged by but Elaine was kind to her and did not demand much of her, but Jenny was constantly aware of her status as an indentured servant. She was not free to come and go. She was not free to

19

plan a life for herself, at least for the next seven years that Elaine would own her. At least, Jenny would console herself, she was not abused or violated as she was sure she would have been had Sir Miles been her master.

Reginald arrived one day the next year, and it was obvious to one and all he had come to stay. He began courting Elaine on the first day, carefully avoiding Jenny at all times, which Jenny could only hope would continue. The man still made her nervous, but she could stand if it he kept his distance.

Then Jenny remembered the reason she now found herself floating to nowhere on a bit of a ship that had been heading to Charleston in the Colonies.

Sir Reginald had asked for Elaine's hand in marriage in the fall of the second year of Jenny's indenture, and Elaine had accepted. He began running the vast estate of Eden Hall, making Elaine more and more dependent on his opinions. But Jenny was uneasy with his obtaining so much power over Lady Elaine. She had felt him gaze at her on more than one occasion, making her shiver when she realized it was the same look of lust she had seen that night two years before.

In the two years since her indenture, Jenny had become an exquisite beauty: flawless skin, fine arched brows over huge luminous blue-green eyes fringed by dark brown lashes that swept her cheeks when she closed them. At eighteen she was still an innocent, but she could feel Reginald's eyes undress her when she would come upon him. He never touched her, but Jenny was sure that once he married Elaine this would change. She let him know at every opportunity that she was not going to be easy. He would have a fight on his hands if he ever touched her. Hopefully, he would think twice before trying to force his way on her.

Just after New Years, a package had arrived from the American Colonies. It was a family Bible from a man claiming to be Elaine's uncle. He was inviting her to come to Charleston for a visit.

"I don't remember my father's ever mentioning relatives in the Colonies." She perused the letter and then took the Bible from Jenny. "Why, it says here that Jules Colby is my father's younger brother, born three years after Father." She squinted her brown eyes as though trying to remember something her father had said that would shed some light on this mystery, but nothing came to her.

When she handed Jenny the Bible, Jenny looked over the entries written in a bold script in blue-black ink. Jenny remembered that Elaine had told her her father had died only three months before Miles's death. Jenny wondered that the Bible listed Jerome Colby's date of death. If, as Elaine had just stated, she didn't know of this uncle, how did he know his brother had died and the exact date. Jenny felt a foreboding, but it was quickly forgotten when Elaine told Jenny that if she did go she would take Jenny along as her maid. Elaine thought the trip would make a wonderful wedding trip for herself and Reginald, but Reginald seemed reluctant to go.

"Elaine, I think you should go before the wedding. A last bit of pleasure, so to speak. I will stay here and oversee the affairs of Eden Hall."

Elaine had pouted and whined for days before Reginald had convinced her that the trip would be good for her.

When she finally acquiesced to his wishes, he rushed to obtain passage on the H.M.S. *Himes* bound for the Carolinas in a fortnight.

He found Elaine and Jenny in the great hall when he returned. "All set, my love," he said fawning over

Elaine. "Two berths have been secured. I do hope Wilma does not tend to seasickness." He smiled.

"Wilma?" Elaine questioned, for the old woman had been Elaine's maid before Jenny and was of a sour disposition. "I'm taking Jenny. Wilma is too old to be going on such a journey."

Reginald seemed to pale but covered his discomfort by walking to a sideboard and pouring himself some brandy. "Whatever you say, my pet."

Jenny had been sure he had been angered by Elaine's decision, but she was just happy to be going on an adventure and quickly lost interest in Sir Reginald's pique. The Colonies were much noted as a wild, untamed land where savages roamed and civilization had not yet been cultivated.

As Reginald had been to the Colonies only last year, Elaine plied him for information on the people. How they dressed, talked, lived and so on.

Reginald seemed pleased to tell them of the quaint communities he had visited but said he had never been to Charleston, so he could not tell them what to expect.

The day before Jenny and Elaine's departure, Elaine came to her room in a worried state. Jenny noticed her agitation while she placed the last of the vast wardrobe for her mistress in a trunk.

Elaine paced her bedchamber, knitting her brow and chewing on her lower lip. She seemed distressed and concerned more than angry.

Glancing up at Elaine while she bent over the trunk lid, Jenny wondered what had happened to cause the usually impassive lady such anxiety. "My lady, would you care for some tea?" Jenny asked.

Elaine stopped her pacing and looked at Jenny without really seeing her, then turned to stare out the window. "He wants me to sign over power of attorney

22

to him. He wants to have control, in case of emergency, while I'm away. I'm not sure but I felt, just for a minute, that Miles was alive and well in the body of Reggie." Elaine turned to Jenny, a pleading expression on her face. "God, what should I do? I've promised to marry him! The man who accompanied Miles on all his sordid little forays around London. I was so sure he had changed but then, just for that one instance, that one fraction of a moment, it was as though a mask had been taken away and his evil, vile soul had been brought to light." Elaine wrung her hands in anguish. "Have I been so blind as to not see him as he really is? I'm so afraid that if I refuse him he will do some injury to me."

Giving a sigh of relief, Jenny wondered how much she should say about her own fears concerning Sir Reginald but decided it could wait until they were on board the *Himes* and away from him.

"When are you supposed to sign this power of attorney, my lady?"

Again pacing and wringing her dainty white hands, Elaine seemed about to lose her tightly held control. "Tomorrow. He is to leave early tomorrow for London. He said he would go to my solicitor and have the documents drawn up. I am merely to go by the solicitor's office before going to the docks."

Jenny smiled. "My lady, why not just go to the docks and forget about meeting him."

"Maybe I'm just having second thoughts. I don't wish to anger him without cause. I plan now on using this voyage as a time to think about this step I'm about to make. Could I be so lonely for a man I would take Reggie, knowing of his past?" She asked this last question more of herself than of Jenny.

Thinking of ways to be delayed, Jenny smiled. "Leave it to me. Just pretend everything will be fine

23

and—"

Again having a change of mind, Elaine interrupted: "Why are we doing this? He will still be here when we return. I must end the engagement."

Frightened at Elaine's determined stand, Jenny felt a wave of fear go through her. "My lady, I think it would be wiser to wait. Send him a missive from the Colonies but don't confront him openly. He wants Eden Hall. I'm afraid—"

Having her own fears voiced by this girl brought the nightmare of Elaine's marriage to Miles come upon her once more. If denied what he wanted, Elaine was positive that Reginald would *take* just as Miles had.

Elaine came closer to Jenny. "What can we do?"

"We will just leave so late from here that time will not permit us to stop until we reach the ship. We can think of a number of crises to keep us from leaving." Jenny smiled and took Elaine's hand. "Don't worry. It could take hours to prepare your coiffure."

Putting her hand under her head, Jenny gazed up at the darkening sky. Poor Elaine was never going to have to worry about Sir Reginald again. She didn't know who would now own Eden Hall, but Sir Reginald wouldn't. At least Elaine could rest in that bit of knowledge.

Chapter Two

The sun was a large orange ball that seemed to kiss the water before slowly sinking beneath the sea. Darkness seemed to descend in the blink of an eye. Seeing the first star of the evening light up in the eastern sky, Jenny closed her eyes to make her wish.

"I wish to live. I wish to live to smell the heather and see the wild flowers of spring. I want to watch a magnificent stallion run free across the fields. I want to hold a kitten, as soft as silk, to my cheek and hear its purr. I want to love and be loved in return and to have a child and know it to be a part of that love. Oh, God! Please let me live to know these joys."

A tear rolled gently down her cheek as a wave of loneliness and desperation at her plight rushed over her. She wasn't going to live much longer. If God were going to save her, He had better hurry.

She felt her limbs relax and a kind of melancholy invade her senses. Was this the way her life would end? It was so peaceful. Her eyes closed while she let the feelings wash her spirit. Maybe it was close now. Maybe she would just go to sleep, never to awaken again.

Suddenly her tired body tensed. "Did I hear a

sound or is it my mind wanting for this to be so?" A bell. She had heard a bell. Lying on her side, she opened her eyes to search the horizon as far as she could see. Nothing. Was she to lose her mind now, too? Then she heard it again, only louder this time. She carefully unwrapped her arms from about her and tentatively sat up to see. Her eyes caught sight of a sail on the opposite horizon, with moonlight reflecting off the sails, making it look like an apparition. The ghostly ship was coming closer as she watched. Her heart started to pound in her chest. She must get the attention of someone on board. She heard the sails flap in the gentle breeze, and she knew this was no ghost ship as another thought entered her mind. She remembered Elaine's telling her that the captain of the *Himes* had said they were now in waters frequented by pirates. What if this ship proved to be a pirate ship? Jenny was lost in indecision. A voice inside told her what did she have to lose. She could either die alone out here in the water or she could take a chance and signal the ship. Making the only decision she could, Jenny quickly tore a section from the hem of her nightgown. It was white and would be easily seen in the moonlight. She grabbed hold firmly with one hand on the hatch and with the other hand waved the piece of cloth and shouted, "Over here! Over here!"

Captain Travis Gardiner was on watch aboard his hip, the *Sea Breeze*. All was quiet on board. His men had fought against the storm for days and were all exhausted. They had lost one man to the mighty sea, but the ship had suffered only minor damage. He would effect repairs in Barbados before going home.

Home, thought Travis. Home for good. How I'll miss the sea and you my beautiful *Sea Breeze*.

He was watching the stars to get his bearings. The

storm had pulled them off course, and he searched the night sky for the star that would bring him back on course for home. As his eyes raked the horizon, he thought he saw something moving. He looked again. Something was there to starboard. He called to a little man who had just come on deck. "Darby, what do you make of that movement off starboard?"

Darby Combs, first mate on the *Sea Breeze* and Travis Gardiner's best friend, held a glass to his eye and searched for the movement the captain was talking about. He spotted it about a mile to starboard. "Cap'n, I can't rightly be sure, but I think it's a woman a floatin' on somethin'." He continued to look through the eyeglass, squinting his one eye to bring the subject into a clearer view.

Travis thought the old man had finally lost his mind. What would a woman be doing out in the middle of the ocean?

A thought crossed Travis's mind and he smiled. "Darby you don't suppose it's— It couldn't be," he said shaking his head.

Darby dropped the glass from his eye and looked at the captain. "What?"

"Why, you don't suppose it's a mermaid, do you?" Travis grinned.

Darby cocked his eye at the captain and then returned the glass to his eye. "Nay, it be a woman," he stated with certainty.

Travis continued to bait the old man, still thinking what they were seeing was a reflection of some kind. "Well, Darby, whatever shall we do with her?"

Darby picked up the game as he scratched his chin whiskers and looked at the captain with something akin to a thoughtful expression. "Well, cap'n, I think the only thing to do is sail on by her and if'n she's pretty, we'll bring her on board."

27

Travis hid a grin. "And what if she's and old crone with a wart on her nose?"

Darby looked at Travis with a lopsided grin. "Well, we'll just throw her a rope and let her ride the wake."

Travis threw back his head and laughed. "Darby, you are a prince."

"Aye, cap'n," Darby replied, and he was already calling some mates to get the dingy ready to put over the side.

While Travis changed course to intercept Darby's woman, he thought of how good it felt to best the sea yet again and on his last voyage to be hero to some damsel in distress. He thought again how much he would miss the feelings of exhilaration that accompanied these tests of skill for all men of the sea. But, he had made the decision to leave his ship and become the "landlubber," as Darby would say. He had been gone a long time. A lot of changes had taken place, and a feeling of loss threatened to overwhelm him. He would not dwell on that again. He had fought the demons of hell for three days and nights but no more. What's done is done.

They were headed on an intercept course for Darby's mermaid. Travis could barely make out the child or woman who was bobbing in the gentle waves. The moonlight reflected off her gown but did little to illuminate her features. However, Travis was able to see long golden hair that seemed to halo her face. Darby had been right. It was a woman.

He wondered why this solitary woman was adrift. The storm was fierce but they survived. Travis silently thanked Darby again for his bunion which gave warning of the coming storm. Travis realized that if it hadn't been for Darby, the fate of his beloved *Sea Breeze* might have been different.

As they neared the castaway, Travis called out

orders to trim the sail and set to.

Darby lowered the dingy and started from the ship to rescue his mermaid.

Jenny saw the ship change course and was saying a prayer to thank God for saving her life. "Dear God, thank you for this ship. Thank you for sparing my life. But, would you please make sure that this is a friendly ship. If it is a pirate ship, please make them treat me kindly. Thank you, God."

Darby sat in the bow of the dingy as it came up to the hatch cover. He couldn't believe his eyes. Why this must be a mermaid!, he thought. She's just a wisp of a thing and as pretty as any woman I've ever laid eyes on.

He called to her, "Don't be scared, darlin', we'll get you safe in just a minute." At her silence, Darby added, "You do speak English, don't ya?"

Jenny shrank from him to the far corner of the cover. With eyes wide with fright, she asked in a whisper, "Are you a pirate?"

Darby laughed. He had forgotten what a picture he must make with a patch over one eye and a peg leg to boot. "No, darlin'. Me names Darby Combs and I'm first mate on the *Sea Breeze* out of Charleston in the Carolinas. Come on now. Give me your hand and I'll get you nice and safe on board."

Jenny didn't know what to do. The man before her seemed friendly and kind, but he certainly did look like a pirate. He was small of stature; a bright red bandana covered his head, with gray wisps of hair hanging down his neck in straggling disorder. His white shirt was covered by a black leather vest that was left unbuttoned. His gray knee breeches with a vivid stain on the thigh didn't escape her attention. His left calf and foot were bare. She noticed his smile and although still wary, she stretched her hand to his and let him pull her over to the dingy.

Darby gasped when he touched her ice-cold hand. "My lord, child. You're as cold as ice and wet, too! Here, let me put me vest over ye 'til we get ye on board."

Jenny was grateful for the warmth of this man's vest on her back but as her body continued to shake, she didn't think she would ever be warm again.

The dingy pulled up by the *Sea Breeze*, and Darby helped her climb aboard. When she set foot on deck, she found she couldn't stand. An arm was around her, but she fainted before she knew whose.

Travis held on to the girl with an expression of wonder. How beautiful she was. He scooped her up in his arms and, making a quick decision, he walked to his cabin and gently laid the girl on his bunk. He turned to Darby, who had followed closely behind. "Bring me a blanket and some of your clothes. They will probably fit her."

Darby bristled at the reference to his stature. He walked over and drew a soft, worn, wool blanket from the cupboard, handed it to Travis and then left quietly to get some of his clothes for the girl.

Travis eased the soggy nightgown off Jenny's shoulders and gave a short gasp. Travis had seen plenty of women in his thirty-five years, but this girl was perfection: translucent white skin that he longed to touch; gently rounded breasts; a tiny waist that he was sure he could span with his hands; full, sensual hips, and long shapely legs. His gaze went to her face. In its relaxed expression, he noticed her lips were a little cracked, which he could understand. Her nose was sunburned, which could cause her some pain, but even so, he thought her a vision to his travel-weary eyes. She was young. Travis guessed not more than seventeen or eighteen. What had she gone through out there, all alone? On what ship had she been on and where was it bound? What had been its fate? Questions. So many questions.

He heard Darby approaching and quickly threw the blanket over her.

Darby walked in with several garments thrown over his shoulder and said, "Cap'n, this be the only decent thing I have for the young lady."

Taking the garments from Darby, Travis told him he could leave. Darby spotted the wet nightgown lying on the floor and bent to pick it up, looking from Travis to the girl and back to Travis.

Seeing Darby's expression, Travis quickly said, "Well, you didn't expect me to put her in bed with that wet nightgown on, did you?"

Darby gave a shrug of his shoulders and turned before Travis could see the grin on his face.

Travis could not understand how this beautiful girl could have survived alone, floating in the middle of the Atlantic Ocean, but he knew he would have to wait until later to find out. He stood up and turned to his desk to work on some charts. It was hours before he noticed movement coming from the bunk.

Awaking slowly, her mind still in a haze, Jenny thought at first she was still on the hatch cover. Then she remembered the little man who had saved her. What was his name? Darby.

She felt so warm. So warm and safe from harm. She wanted to sleep a while longer but found she was so hungry and thirsty that she must wake up.

Stretching her long limbs before opening her eyes, Jenny let her hands trail down her body only to find herself naked beneath the warm blanket. Her eyes flew open as the realization came to her that someone had taken her nightgown from her. She saw his broad back across the room and pulled the blanket up high beneath her neck. Angrily, she asked, "Excuse me, but where am I and who took my clothes?"

The captain of the *Sea Breeze* turned around to stare into the bluest eyes he had ever seen, fringed with a double row of thick dark brown lashes. He stood up and walked over to the bunk.

Jenny noticed how very tall this stranger was. He had to hunch his shoulders in the confining space of the cabin.

Pulling a chair up beside the bunk, Travis sat down beside the steely blue eyes that blazed up at him with angry indignation. "My lady, you were brought on board my ship, the *Sea Breeze*, after we rescued you. You were sodden with dampness, and I only meant to make you as comfortable as possible."

A flush of embarrassment arose to color Jenny's cheeks at the realization that this handsome stranger had obviously seen her naked body. Then anger, an unusual ally, replaced her discomfort. "And just what kind of liberties were taken while I was unable to defend myself?" she demanded in a huff.

Travis cocked his head and valiantly hid a smile that threatened to cross his face. "My lady, I assure you that no impropriety occurred during your sleep. Only your comfort and health prompted me to divest you of your nightgown. Please be assured that your virtue is safe while on board my ship." Seeing her eyes lose some of the angry sparkle, Travis asked gently, "Now, may I ask a few questions of you, or would you like to sleep a while longer?"

Jenny tried to swallow and again was reminded of how hungry and thirsty she was. "Could I have a drink of water first?"

While he walked to the table and poured her some water, Jenny tried to think. This could be her chance. He didn't know about her or the fact that she was only an indentured servant. He had called her "my lady," hadn't he? Could she make this handsome man think her a lady? Besides, what would he do if he knew her to be only a lowly servant? He might return her to London and Eden Hall or worse: He might demand she serve him, not only as a servant but as a harlot also. A shiver ran down her spine at that thought. But could she lie and make him believe her?

Travis sat on the side of the bunk, leaned over and lifted her head to accept the cup of cool, sweet water he held to her lips. "You are a very lucky woman. It was only a miracle we spotted you." He spoke softly as if to a child.

He let her head gently down onto the pillow, noticing again her beautiful eyes. "You must be hungry. Darby will be here shortly with some food. Until then could you answer some questions?"

Instantly alert, Jenny nodded her head. "Of course, captain. What would you like to know?"

"Well, first, I would like to know your name."

Jenny stared intently into his eyes for several moments before answering, "Lady Elaine Seaton."

Travis cocked his head a moment as though in thought.

Jenny looked away from his probing eyes as she wondered why she had decided to tell the lie. She knew why. Sir Reginald. He would make her life a living hell when he found out about Elaine's death. Jenny remembered the lustful looks directed at her. How could she ever let such a revolting, vulgar person touch her. He would use her like a whore. How long would she be spared the demands of Sir Reginald Wenthrop if she were forced to return to Eden Hall? Maybe if she continued this charade, she could save herself that humiliation a while longer.

She looked back at the captain. She would be

Elaine, at least until they docked in the Colonies. Maybe it would insure this captain's treating her with a little more respect.

Travis interrupted her reverie with his next question. "Well, my lady, what happened to find you alone in the ocean?"

Jenny couldn't look him in the eye. After informing him that she was a widow, she said, "I was traveling on the H.M.S. *Himes* with— with my maid." She stumbled over the reversal of roles but continued. "We had been at sea for five days with nothing to note, when on the evening of the fifth day we were hit by a storm. It came with no warning. The ship seemed to be tossed about like a toy." Her eyes took on a hazy aspect, as she seemed to relive the horror of that night again. "I tried to get her out of the cabin. She was hysterical. I had to slap her." Tears welled in her eyes but her voice droned on. "I just knew we should get out of the cabin. I was so scared but I knew she wouldn't or couldn't go without help. I dragged her up the steps of the companionway. She was there one minute but when I turned, she was gone."

She was weeping softly, still seemingly unaware of Travis who sat beside her. He couldn't stand to see a woman cry and said, "My lady, I'm sure your maid did not suffer."

His voice brought Jenny back to the present. "I pray she did not."

Travis noted the way her small, pink tongue licked her chapped lips. "Is there anything else?"

Jenny looked up at him again. "I am terribly sorry, but I am truly too hungry to think. Do you suppose you might find something for me to eat now?" she asked hopefully.

Travis stood up and apologized to her, saying, "My word, I imagine you are ravenous. I'll go see what's taking so long. You may wish to put on some of these clothes." He indicated the breeches and shirt at the end of the bunk. "I'm sorry, but a woman on board is rather new to us, and we are ill equipped to supply you with gowns." At the thought of her naked body under the blanket, his speech became erratic as he continued: "These will—have—to do until something—else can be found. I shall return with food and tea—shortly. Please—make yourself at home." He walked quickly out of the cabin, closing the door behind him. My God! I was as nervous as a schoolboy in her presence, he told himself.

When the door to the cabin closed, Jenny again thought back to the shipwreck. Only this time it was the real memory that came to her.

The days had moved slowly on board the *Himes* for Jenny. She spent most of her time in the cabin, mending, washing out various items and pressing the many different gowns Lady Elaine wore. It was nothing for Elaine to change clothes four times a day. Jenny was up late every evening awaiting the return of Elaine from the captain's cabin, and up early every day to see to the lady's breakfast. She became thinner, and her eyes lost some of their brilliant color.

On the night that Jenny would remember for the rest of her days, Elaine had just returned from her evening meal with the captain, and Jenny was combing out Elaine's hair, preparing for bed, when the ship gave a lurch that sent Jenny reeling. She couldn't remember which had been louder: the screams that came from the lady or the sounds of the wind ripping the sails above them. To Jenny it sounded like the sounds of hell.

Jenny managed to reach Elaine, who was by this time lying on the floor. Elaine grasped Jenny's arm in a death grip and continued to scream as Jenny tried to

35

comfort her.

The ship was being tossed this way and that. Jenny didn't know what to do. She felt, instinctively, that they should get out of the cabin and up on deck. She dragged Elaine to the door and tried to stand up as a crashing sound came to them from above. Jenny managed to release the grasp Elaine had on her arm just enough to permit her to get to her feet. Grabbing a hold of the door handle, she opened the door to a wall of water that had settled in the companionway. Elaine held her arms around Jenny's legs, making any progress impossible. Jenny bent down, and with strength she hadn't known she possessed, lifted Elaine up to stand beside her. Elaine was hysterical and Jenny slapped her face several times before sanity returned to Elaine's eyes. She yelled over the sounds around them, "We have to get out of here. Let's try to get to the deck."

The ship seemed to turn on its side just as Jenny walked through the doorway. She was thrown up against the doorjam, feeling a searing pain go through her back. Elaine held on to Jenny's arm while they fought their way up the companionway. That was when the ship gave another lurch and Elaine was gone. The ship was tossed up in the air and what happened after that Jenny couldn't remember.

She pushed back the blanket and went through the clothes lying at the foot of the bunk. She found a long pair of underdraws, men's breeches, and a long-sleeved white shirt. "This outfit would definitely be a picture," she said out loud. She put on the underdraws, then thought better of it. They would be entirely too hot, as she noticed the sun was high in the sky. She slipped the breeches up her legs and then

36

pulled the shirt over her shoulders. She had no camisole to wear underneath the shirt but at least she was clothed. She decided not to put on the stockings since she had no shoes. Sitting on the bunk, with the knee-high breeches exposing half her shapely legs, she wondered what her only friend Hannah would say if she could see her now. Thinking of Hannah gave Jenny a sad feeling. The old woman had befriended her when she needed a friend the most. She made the days bearable at Eden Hall with her kindness and sweet treats. Would she ever see Hannah again? Would she ever walk into the little house, smelling the fresh scones that were Hannah's treat for her? Now that she had taken on Lady Elaine's identity, what would become of her?

Looking at herself, she was surprised at how well the clothes fit. Then she remembered the little man with the eye patch and peg leg. "These are probably his." Jenny wondered about Darby Combs and what had happened to him. Then she thought about Captain Gardiner. He was a handsome man. Tall, well built with midnight black hair and the darkest eyes Jenny had ever seen. They reminded her of a portrait she had seen at Eden Hall that had captivated her. She also remembered that the captain had been kind, which helped dispel any feelings of apprehension she had had earlier. At least the captain didn't look like a pirate.

There was a knock on the cabin door before it was pushed open by Darby who carried a tray with food and a pot of tea.

Jenny sat down and consumed the food without looking up or taking an occasional breath. Darby stared at this spectacle, wondering why the *lady* had abandoned all forms of good manners, even if she were starving. Darby shrugged his shoulders and

37

discarded the thought, attributing her lack of manners to her ordeal.

After what seemed like only minutes, Jenny pushed herself back from the table and only then realized Darby was still in the room. "My, Mr. Combs, that was good. I guess I was hungrier than I thought."

Darby simply smiled and said, "Aye." He took the tray, leaving only the teapot and a mug. When he got to the door, he turned around and looked at the girl standing by the window and thought that she looked adorable in his breeches and shirt.

Darby walked on out into the passageway where he met the captain coming down the steps. "Hey there, cap'n. You shoulda seen the young lady gobble down these vittles. She acted like she hadn't eaten in a month." Darby shook his balding head and smiled. "Cap'n, wait 'til you see her in me duds. She looks sweet as can be."

Travis looked on the little man and smiled. "Darby, if I didn't know you for the reprobate you are, I would swear the girl has gotten to you."

Darby looked up at Travis with a wicked grin. "Just me, cap'n?"

Travis scowled at the little man while Darby whistled and limped up the steps to the deck above. Turning to his cabin door, Travis knocked and asked, "May I come in?"

From behind the door, Jenny called, "Why of course, captain."

Travis opened the door and stopped dead in his tracks. She stood before him dressed in Darby's shirt, which fit a little loosely about her shoulders but defined the firm, round breasts underneath; a pair of breeches that fit rather snugly around her hips and came down only to just below the knees. And with her golden hair flowing freely about her shoulders, she did present a rather sensuous, although innocent, poise.

Not realizing what her appearance was doing to Travis, Jenny walked up to stand before him. "Captain, I want to thank you for rescuing me. I rather thought I was going to die out there all alone."

Travis was having a problem breathing. Sweat appeared on his upper lip. My God! Didn't this woman realize he hadn't been with or even seen a woman in months? He swallowed hard while the woman looked closely up at him with those enormous blue eyes of hers. He turned abruptly and walked through the door, saying in a curt manner as he looked over his shoulder, "You are entirely welcome."

Jenny stared at the closed door in confusion. She thought the man may have a fever, the way he looked and acted. Confused by his abrupt departure, she felt a little hurt. After all the attention he had displayed toward her earlier, she couldn't fathom his conduct.

Travis leaned up against the wall of the passageway, trying to steady his heart to beat at a normal rate. "This chit has gotten me so flustered, I can't breathe. I must get control of myself or I'll bed her before she'll know what hit her."

Darby was carrying a large tub down the companionway when he saw Travis by his cabin door. At what Darby felt was a confused expression on the captain's face, he said, "Thought the little lady would like to get some of the sea off her back, cap'n."

This brought thoughts of the Lady Elaine Seaton naked in a tub to Travis's mind. He groaned and ran up the stairs to the deck, leaving a thoroughly perplexed Darby staring after him.

Darby couldn't imagine what had happened in the short time since he had seen the captain to dispel his good humor. Maybe the lady could tell him something. After all, the captain in a bad humor boded ill for the entire crew.

He knocked on the cabin door and was asked to enter. Jenny looked at the tub and immediately forgot the effect of the captain's departure.

"My lady, I thought you might want to wash some of the sea off ye."

"Oh! Darby you were sent from heaven," she said as she walked over to him and kissed his whiskered cheek.

"Well, ma'am, maybe not heaven but just a wee short distance from it." He grinned at her. He was suddenly very glad he had thought to bring her the tub. He watched her smile and again thought how beautiful she was. Then he remembered the captain's strange behavior and asked, "My lady, do you know why the cap'n was so strange actin' when he come from here a minute ago?"

The smile left Jenny's face. She turned to look at Darby. "Why no. He came in here and just stood staring at me. I tried to thank him for rescuing me and he just turned around and left."

Darby looked at the girl to see what could have upset the captain. Ah, he thought while a smile formed on his lips, the cap'n must a been in agony.

He put the tub down and, turning to Jenny, he said, "Never you mind 'bout him. Let me get you some hot water for this here tub." And he left.

After several trips to the galley and back, he filled the tub full of hot rainwater. Jenny thanked Darby again as he left, then quickly took off her clothes and eased down into the tub. Laying back, she felt the tiredness once again envelop her body. The water was so warm, it made her just want to relax. Before she knew it, she had fallen asleep.

On deck, Travis was wondering what to do about Lady Seaton. He felt something was not as it should be. She was certainly beautiful but was she who she said she was? He had noticed the nightgown was not of silk or satin but of a heavy cotton. Even allowing for the exposure of sun and sea the gown was threadbare. He also noticed her hands. Some of those calluses had been there for a while. No *lady* he had ever met had calluses on their hands.

He drew his hand through his thick black hair. There was no denying the effect she was having on him. He could feel those ripe firm breasts under his hands. Feel the secret place between her thighs. "God! What am I doing?" he said. "This chit isn't here a day and all I can think about is bedding her." He couldn't explain the anger he felt. Travis Gardiner prided himself on his lack of emotional commitment to the opposite sex. He looked at women as good for one purpose, and he had decided long ago that he would never let a woman control his emotions. Although a number had tried to ply him with their charms, he had always been able to step back and analyze the situation before any harm to his independence could be done.

The girl in his cabin was beautiful and had an innocent air that left him wondering. For some reason he sensed that the girl was a threat to him. He would be in constant contact with her for at least the next few months. He wondered again at her story. A young woman alone, except for a servant, bound for the Carolinas. If she was to be married on her return to England, what was the man she was to marry thinking of? The conflict between England and America had left a scar between the two nations that had not yet healed. A young Engligh woman would not be safe alone, especially in Charleston where the British had occupied the city and threatened the citizens. Something about the young woman's story did not ring true.

Not realizing his true intent, he decided to go speak to her again and try to put some of his nagging doubts aside. With that idea firmly planted in his thoughts, he left the bridge and headed for his cabin.

He was about to knock, when the anger seized him again. Why should he have to knock on the door of his own cabin? He opened the door, realizing what he hoped he would find would be there.

There she was in the tub, fast asleep. Her face looked so innocent. She was absolutely breathtaking. She looked so young, so vulnerable and so beguiling. All his resolve and anger vanished as he stared at this creature before him, with her breasts out of the water and her hand resting on the rim of the tub.

He decided not to disturb her, but as the anger came again, he thought he would be damned if he would leave, and went to his desk. As he looked up from his charts, the image of the girl was before him, reflected off the mirror over his desk. While he watched, her hand fell into the tub, splashing her face and effectively waking her.

Jenny brushed the water out of her eyes and became aware of a presence. She turned her head slightly and saw the captain sitting in his chair. At the same time, she became aware of eyes watching her and then noticed the mirror. She let out a gasp and sank as low as she could under the water. Indignation at being so observed rankled Jenny. "Captain, may I ask what you are doing in here while I am taking my bath?" Crimson stained her cheeks at her embarrassing predicament.

The captain slowly turned and looked directly into

the clear, blue eyes. "Why, my lady, I'm sorry but I thought this was my cabin."

Choking back tears of humiliation, Jenny sputtered, "But—but you put me here, and I was told to make myself comfortable. If you want me somewhere else, I will be only too happy to concur with your wishes."

"You may, by all means, make yourself at home in my cabin, my lady, but I will also be in residence." He stood up, walked to a cabinet and poured himself a glass of wine. "I'm sorry. Would you like a glass? No? All right. Let's see, where was I? Oh, yes, anyway this is not a large ship, as you have no doubt observed, and accommodations are hard to come by."

Jenny felt threatened for the first time. "But you can't possibly be serious, captain. What would your crew think if you slept in here with me? I'm sorry, but that is out of the question. I will be happy to move to another cabin if you must stay in this one."

"As I said before, my lady—there is no other place for you to sleep. I'm afraid we will just have to make the best of a, shall I say, bad situation."

Thinking he hadn't heard the last of this, Jenny looked up, and asked, "If you will be so kind as to leave me so I may finish my bath, I would be grateful."

The captain turned back to his charts, replying over his shoulder, "I must see to the log book. I'm afraid my time is valuable, and I must get this work done."

Angry at the captain's obvious lack of chivalry, Jenny glared at his back. "Well, if you will promise to keep your back turned, I will finish and be done with it."

Travis did not even answer but just turned to his book.

With a furtive glance at his back, Jenny took a

cloth Darby had given her and rubbed the huge bar of soap until a lather formed. She washed and then dunked her head under the water to rinse the salt water from it. Coming up, she noticed a movement from the corner of her eye. The captain was running his hand through his hair in a gesture of, she felt sure, contemplation over his work.

Actually Travis was trying unsuccessfully to control the rise of his manhood. He had watched Jenny in the mirror as she bathed. He saw the way the soap glistened on her skin; the way she cocked her head this way and that, as she held up one shapely leg to slide the rag over its contours. As she had tilted her head back in the water, he had seen the twin peaks rise from the water as though begging for him to touch them. When she had rose to a sitting position again, with her long golden hair cascading down her back in long, wet tendrils, he was reminded of the mermaid that he had jested about to Darby. She was the loveliest woman he had ever seen. God, he needed a woman! He was controlling himself by sheer force of will while she finished her bath, and looked down to his books, not seeing the pages before him but the soft white skin of the woman.

Jenny glanced again at this back and decided he was too engrossed in his papers to pay her any attention. She stood up with her back to him. Leaning over to the table, she lifted the big towel Darby had left for her use. Wrapping the towel around her, she could feel eyes upon her once again. She turned to see herself reflecting off the mirror and the black eyes of Travis Gardiner staring at her.

He asked her with his brows drawn down into a scowl, "Where did you get that bruise on your back?"

Embarrassment rose from Jenny's toes to the top of her head. "Captain, please. I need some privacy."

Travis stood and walked up to her, putting his hands on her shoulders, and turned her around to look at the bruise running in a diagonal line across her otherwise flawless back. "How did this happen?" he asked softly.

Jenny remembered hitting the doorjamb when she and Elaine had tried to get out of their room on the *Himes*. Quietly, she told him of the accident, eliminating Elaine's part.

Travis wanted to touch the ugly mark and make it go away, but common sense prevailed, and he left her to return to his work. "I will have Darby bring you something to put on it."

Jenny quickly turned around, "That is not necessary, captain. It doesn't hurt."

Travis merely lowered his head and started writing.

Jenny moved to the far corner, where she felt sure he couldn't see her in the mirror, and quickly dressed again in the breeches and shirt. She tried to think of what she would do about this situation. Nothing came to mind so she decided to calm her anger and trepidation by being busy. Looking for something to do, she picked up the bucket and filled it with her bath water. She looked around the cabin for some place to dump it, then started for the door, intent on disposing of the water up on deck.

Travis turned and asked, "Can I be of service, my lady?"

Turning to face him, Jenny looked down at the bucket and back to him. "If you will just tell me where to dispose of the bath water, I would be eternally grateful." Her voice dripped with sarcasm.

Standing up quickly, Travis hid the smile that threatened to break over his face. "Why, my lady, I wouldn't think of letting you do such work. I will call Darby to fetch it."

Exasperated by his attitude, Jenny replied, "I am perfectly capable of carrying a bucket of water, *captain*," she said, sneering at the title.

"But, my lady, you must have had a cruel life with Lord Seaton if he expected you to do such work."

Jenny's anger grew to new heights as she realized that this pompous ass was not only going to invade her privacy but would stand there and demean her supposed husband as well. Without stopping to think, she threw the bucket of soapy water at the towering figure of the captain, effectively drenching him from head to toe.

She had done what she had set out to do and had wiped the smile from his face, but the look he was leveling at her now was by no means a comfort. His black eyes were narrowed slits of coal. His lips were pulled back in a sneer across his white, even teeth.

The two stood rooted to their places, each ready to do battle with the other. Each more angry than they had ever been. Travis had never come so close to physical retribution on a woman, and Jenny had never dared show her defiance in quite so dramatic a manner. Each leered at the other while they breathed heavily in the silence around them.

Then suddenly, Travis started to laugh. He bent over, putting his hands on his soggy knees and laughed.

Jenny's own anger left abruptly when she saw the reaction of this man, and she too began to laugh at their situation.

Looking up through his tears of laughter, Travis said, "By God, you've got spirit."

Jenny stood up and wiped at her eyes, growing suddenly serious once more. "And pride, captain, so be warned. I'll not be made a fool."

Travis looked closely at this slip of a girl who had

had the nerve to throw a bucket of water at him. She was determined to have his respect and grudgingly he gave it. "I am truly sorry for my lack of manners. It has been so long since I've been made to use them that I fear they are rusty. I will, in the future, respect your privacy."

"Thank you, captain," she said as though it were her due and nothing less would have been tolerated.

Grabbing the towel she had used, the dripping captain of the *Sea Breeze* dried his face before turning to the door. "I will call Darby to fetch the water now."

"If you wish, captain, by all means call Darby. I merely wanted to show my gratitude for all the kindnesses—you—have shown me." After she said this she realized, after what he had just witnessed, Lady Elaine would have scratched his eyes out and not tell him of her gratitude. *How stupid*. She had better not talk at all or seriously consider every word she said if she wanted to continue in this charade.

Travis went out the door and called for Darby. The little man hobbled in and Travis told him, "The lady is finished with her bath. You may take away the water and tub now."

"Aye, aye, cap'n," Darby said then glanced from the captain's wet clothes to the lady. He wondered about the captain's state but decided not to ask. As he walked over to the tub, he nodded to Jenny and asked, "I trust the bath was to your likin', my lady? I'm only sorry we didn't have the fancy soaps and oils I know you're used to.,"

Jenny smiled at the kindness of the old man. "The soap was just delightful, Darby."

Travis knew that soap. It was one of Darby's concoctions. It would take the hair off a bear and smelled awful. Darby swore it would cure all skin problems, but what Travis needed a cure for was

47

Darby's soap. This was another thought to ponder about this *lady* who was before him.

When Darby came back for the now empty tub, Jenny asked him casually, "Darby, would you please direct me to somewhere else where I may sleep?"

Darby looked from the captain's scowling face back to the lady's. "Well, my lady, there be only the two cabins and the other be for the crew. I really think you'll be more comfortable here."

Jenny turned back to the window to watch the sunlight fade into pinks and golds, effectively hiding her disappointment and chagrin.

Darby looked again at the captain, only to see a smug look of satisfaction replace his earlier scowl. He pulled the tub out into the passageway and quietly closed the door. I wonder what the cap'n has up his sleeve now? he thought. I been with him long enough to know he's cookin' up somethin'. He better not try nothin' wid that wee bit of a girl or he'll have me to deal with. He lifted the heavy tub over his shoulder and decided to keep an eye on the captain and the lady.

Travis walked up behind Jenny. "I guess you're not willing to believe what I say, my lady."

Startled out of her reverie, Jenny turned to find the captain bending over her. She didn't know what to do. She saw only one bunk, and it was not big enough to accommodate two people even if she would allow that, which she wouldn't. She spied a narrow ledge running under the stern galley window. "I'll just sleep over there if you have no objections?"

Looking to where she had indicated, Travis smiled and looked back into her wide blue eyes. "As you wish." He bowed then turned and walked back to his desk to begin mopping up the water around his charts. He knew she would never be able to sleep on

48

that narrow ledge, especially once the night air started to seep in.

Jenny went over to the bunk and took a blanket over to the ledge. She looked down at the narrow plank and questioned her wisdom at such a decision while she spread the soft blanket out to make as much padding as she could.

Over his shoulder, Travis called, "Don't get too cozy. Darby will be here with supper in a few minutes."

Jenny ignored his sarcasm, grateful at not having to test her bed of boards just yet, and stood up. "Then I think I will go up on deck for a breath of fresh air." She started for the door when Travis halted her.

"I wouldn't do that if I were you."

"And just *why* not!" she demanded with hands on hips. "Am I to be held prisoner in your cabin, captain?" She was breathing heavily in her anger.

"No. You are not being held prisoner. I simply will not take the responsibility for your safety on deck unless you are escorted."

Jenny felt rage again fill her being. "I am not a child, captain. I can find my way around such a *small* ship, and I assure you I won't fall overboard."

Travis didn't miss the reference to the size of his ship. He put his pen down and turned to her, noticing the fiery flecks of light in her eyes. "Lady Elaine." He sounded like a disgruntled parent trying to reason with a spoiled child. "I was not afraid of your falling overboard. My men have been at sea for some time without the benefit of a woman. That in itself would be reason for some for the more foolhardy to throw caution to the wind. Your *virtue* may be in jeopardy."

Jenny didn't catch the reference to her state of virtue but looked about the cabin in some agitation. Sharing this confining cabin with a man was posing

49

more problems than she realized. "But—captain, I need somewhere to go for a personal reason." She implored him with a look.

He saw a trace of embarrassment and rose immediately. "Oh, well, you will find what you require in that cabinet over there." He walked over to a small window in the stern galley. This window opens to dispose of—garbage. I'll go see what is keeping Darby." With that, the captain walked to the door. He paused. "I will knock before I come in." He walked out before she could see the smile on his face.

Jenny watched the door close and went to complete her business. She thought of the captain's obvious arrogance. Why did he continually bait her? Heat rose in her when she thought of his witnessing her bath. What make of a man was this captain who thought nothing of her modesty? It was bad enough that she must walk before him in this limited outfit. Her legs were exposed and with no chemise, she felt positively naked under the billowing shirt. What would it be like for him to be constantly at hand, both awake and asleep? She had to admit that he was the most devastatingly handsome man she had ever seen. "He probably expects me to fawn over him and leap to do his bidding. I will not give him that to laud over me. I will not give him the opportunity of witnessing my shame again. I will play the haughty lady and bring him to his knees. He will be begging to do *my* bidding." A slow smile appeared when she thought of him bowing and scraping to her every whim. Yes, she would see the callous Captain Gardiner do as she wished.

When Travis had closed the door and turned around to leave, he saw someone at the far end of the passageway. "Who goes there? he called into the darkness. He squinted his eyes to see better as a big, haulking man approached him. It was Tim Hawkins. Travis had signed him on in Singapore. "What are you doing down here, Tim? I thought you had watch tonight?"

The big man appeared nervous and twitched a great deal before saying, "Well, cap'n, I was feeling a might poorly and thought I would look for Darby and his cure-all I heard so much about."

"Darby will be in the galley at this time of day and you have no business in this area of the ship. From now on my cabin is off limits. Understand?"

"Aye, cap'n," the man choked, before adding, "By the way, how's the little lady doin'?"

"She's doing just fine, but she is exhausted from her ordeal," Travis stated with wariness in his voice.

Tim smiled and licked his lips. "I bet she's really somethin' in bed, heh?"

Travis spun with such violent fury that Tim retreated, stumbling up the steps in his haste, "Captain, I just wanted to see the little lady. Surely you don't plan on keepin' her all to yourself?"

Between clenched teeth, Travis threatened, "Hawkins, the *lady* is under my protection. If I so much as see you looking toward my cabin again, I'll keelhaul you!" Travis's voice had risen as his reason fought with his temper. "Now, get back to your post and don't let me see you off it. Understood?"

"Understood, cap'n."

Travis barely heard his response through the sound of blood rushing in his ears.

Upset at looking the fool, Tim went to his post. He seethed at the way the captain had talked to him. He knew what was going on in the captain's cabin. The captain might be able to fool the rest of this scurvy crew but not him. Tim saw the Lady come on board. He saw the wet nightgown cling to the ripe, full breasts that just begged to be felt.

As Tim thought of the lady lying in the captain's bunk, his manhood rose. Turning to a darkened corner of the deck, he put his hand down the front of his pants to try to relieve some of the pressure. When he looked out to sea, he didn't see the wake of the ship or the moon rising in the clear night sky. Tim saw himself lowering over the lady and pumping her, hard. His breathing increased to match his hand. When the flow was released inside his pants, the vision he had created vanished. He felt unsatisfied. He needed the real thing and was determined to get it.

He was thinking of a way to get to the captain's cabin when he walked up on a group of men, sitting in a circle, mending sails. He sat among them, taking up a hook and began stitching along with them.

Looking casually around the group, he said, "It seems to me that the captain is keepin' the little lady all to hisself. Got her all snug in his cabin. Bet he's had her more than once today. Ain't seen much of him." He waited for some comment but none came. "Did you see those teats when she come aboard? Yea, I'd give a whole month's pay to have that one."

None of the men liked Tim Hawkins. They didn't trust him and would have been happy if he had been the one lost during the storm instead of Hendricks.

John Rabun saw trouble brewing in the way Tim was trying to get a rise out of the men. He decided it would be a good thing to get this over with before any real damage could be done, for he knew what Tim was getting at.

John stood up, catching Tim's eye, and indicated with his head to follow him. As they stood in a dark corner of the deck, John whispered, "I'll tell you what, Tim. When the cap'n comes up for his watch tonight, I'll keep an eye on him for you, so's you can go visit with the little lady."

Tim looked at John skeptically and with a wary expression asked, "Why would you do that for me?"

Looking around the deck as if to be sure that they were not being overheard, John leaned closer to Tim. "Because I'm hopin' you'll do the same for me. I sure would love to have that girl." He looked out to sea as he continued: "It's been so long since I got any snatch, I just hope I remember what to do with it."

Tim laughed, which made John reach up and place his hand over Tim's mouth until he quieted. Leaning still closer to John, Tim whispered, "You got a deal, friend. I'll watch for your signal when the captain comes on watch." He turned and walked back to the men still mending the torn sails.

John leaned an elbow on the rail as he followed Tim's progress across the deck with narrowed eyes. "You scum, I'll see you in hell before you touch that girl." He walked back and joined the group, with Tim's demise on his mind.

Chapter Three

The captain of the *Sea Breeze* knocked on his cabin door, then called, "May we come in?"

"Of course," Jenny responded in a now composed voice.

Darby walked in followed by Travis. He placed a tray laden with fish, boiled potatoes, a green-looking concoction, and ale in mugs on the table. He set everything up and indicated a chair for Jenny. She sat down demurely and waited for Travis to take his seat before helping herself to each of the dishes presented. She ate a spoonful of the green dish and looked up at Darby. "Why this is delicious, Darby. Whatever is it?"

Darby smiled down at her. "Glad you like it, my lady. It's just some things I throws together."

Jenny tasted another spoonful. "Why I bet I can guess what this is." She smiled. "Spinach!"

Travis choked on his fish and leaned over to her, saying, "Why, of course it is. We have an acre plowed up on deck for fresh vegetables." He laughed until tears came to his eyes.

Darby thought the captain was being rather hard-hearted to the lady and attempted to set things right. "No, my lady, 'tis seaweed."

Jenny was so upset at being made the fool again that she didn't hear what Darby had said. "I'm sorry,

Darby. What did you say it was?" She risked a furtive glance at the captain who only an hour before had told her she needn't worry about his manners any longer.

Darby leaned closer and repeated, " 'tis seaweed, my lady."

Jenny looked up at Darby with surprise written all over her. "Seaweed!" She wrinkled her nose in obvious disgust.

Darby leaned back, folding his arms over his chest and, frowning at Travis, said, "Aye. But it does taste a little like *spinach* if you cook it long enough." Darby poked Travis with his peg leg to try to get him to stop laughing.

Travis looked up at the old man and simply laughed harder. "Spinach!"

Jenny had had enough of his laughter and stood up, pushing her chair back with so much force it tipped over. She walked to the ledge and sat facing the sea. How dare he laugh at me, she thought.

Darby walked out of the room in silence, throwing a scowl at the captain.

Travis settled down quickly as he had been left alone to finish his meal. He looked up at the girl with just a hint of a smile on his face. "You had better come eat your supper. We don't waste food on my ship."

Jenny didn't turn around but said through clenched teeth, "I'm not hungry." She was silently thinking she would wait until he left. Then she would be able to eat in peace.

The man was insufferable. How dare he treat her like a child. First to come in while she was bathing and then not to have the decency to leave when she requested it. On top of that to treat her as an imbecile in front of Darby. How did he expect her to know

55

what a ship's fare consisted of? They had fresh vegetables on the *Himes*. Then, Jenny thought back to what Elaine had told her just before the shipwreck: In a few days they would no longer have fresh vegetables as there was no way of adequately preserving them.

She was absolutely sure now that if she told this man the truth about herself, her life on board this ship would be another nightmare. If he would treat a *lady* with so much callousness, how would he treat a servant? Visions of mopping and scrubbing for him came to her mind's eye. She would jump overboard before she would give this pompous ass the satisfaction of seeing her in that state. She just wished he would hurry and finish so she could eat in peace.

Travis made no more attempts at conversation. He ate his meal, knowing he had been a little unkind to her, but he would be hanged if he would apologize. After all, *spinach*. He started to chuckle to himself again as he finished his ale.

While he watched her ramrod stiff shoulders, he contemplated the changes this girl would cause on board his ship. Tim Hawkins being by his cabin was a bad sign. He didn't trust Tim and wouldn't have signed him on if he hadn't been shorthanded when they were leaving Singapore. He decided to keep a watchful eye on Mr. Hawkins.

With that resolved, he stood up and picked up the tray. "Well, it has been a wonderful, fun-filled evening. If you will excuse me, I will go up on watch." With the tray in his hands, he turned and walked to the door, only turning back to see she hadn't even turned around.

Her stomach growling, Jenny finally turned at the sound of the door closing. She got up and went to the new empty table "Why that big oaf! I'll just starve to

56

death and let my death be on his shoulders!"

She decided the best thing to do would be to go to sleep. She lay down on the ledge but soon realized this was no good, as everytime the ship lurched, she fell off. Then she tried lying on her back, and with half of her off the ledge, the ship lurched, and again she landed on the floor. She gave up and curled herself into a ball on the floor with the blanket pulled over her. "Let him see me like this on the floor, the big ox." The last thing she remembered was the bell striking ten bells.

Travis was a little chagrined at making the lady miss her supper. After all, Darby had outdone himself on tonight's fare. For a meal at sea, it was delicious.

He thought about the sleeping arrangements they had settled on. It really was best that Lady Elaine remain in his cabin. His men were hungry for feminine companionship. Lord knows what would happen if she weren't under my protection, he thought.

Tim watched the captain take the wheel for his watch. He noticed John Rabun go up to talk to him. "This is my chance," he said under his breath. Without waiting for any signal from John, Tim carefully crept to the companionway leading to the captains cabin. As he approached the door, he kept looking back to make sure he hadn't been spotted. He eased down the steps and silently walked to the cabin door. He listened outside but heard nothing. Carefully, he opened the door with no sound to be heard except his breathing and saw her lying on the floor with the moonlight spilling over her in the mantle of silver. "God, but you're a pretty wench," he whispered.

He stalked Jenny like a cat, spying her calves and

feet sticking out from under the blanket. Curled on her side, she looked like a kitten, and Tim knelt down to softly touch the spun gold hair that was falling over her shoulder.

Jenny moaned in her sleep and shifted positions but when she did, the blanket fell from her shoulder to expose the gape in the neck of the shirt.

Tim caught his breath and with a groan of long suppressed desire, he jerked the blanket off and ripped the shirt down the front.

Startled, Jenny came awake but could not see her attacker. She started to hit at the face of the man she didn't see, but he easily pulled her hands up over her head and held them in one powerful fist, while he started to rip away at the buttons on the front of the breeches she wore.

Jenny fought by kicking and turning. She found the soft, underside of his forearm and bit down as hard as she could.

Tim, so intent on her breeches, paid her thrashing no mind until the sharp little teeth found their mark and sank into his flesh. With an oath, he backhanded her across the face with so much force, she thought she would faint.

It was this scene that greeted the eyes of Travis Gardiner when he stormed into his cabin. With two strides, he reached Tim and pulled him into the air.

When Tim felt himself being pulled up and away from the girl, he struck out at the intruder with all his might. He searched for the person who would dare to interrupt him with wild, passion-crazed eyes. When he was finally set free, he spun around and faced the rage of Travis Gardiner. Tim had, of course, heard all the tales about Gardiner but had not thought the man capable of living up to the legend his men had tried to make of him. Looking at the man who now faced him,

Tim believed.

The man standing in front of him with legs slightly apart, his back hunched and both hands forming tight fists, was enough to convince Tim he didn't want this madman after him. He tried the only weapon he had. "Now cap'n, surely you can't mean nothin' 'bout this chit. Why not share her with your crew? I wasn't mean to her. I could a showed her a good time. She would a enjoyed it, cap'n."

All the while he had spoken, Tim had moved backward to the door, but Travis had advanced with every step. When Tim got to the door, he quickly turned to run out, only to find his way blocked by John Rabun.

He looked up at Rabun with terror-filled eyes that quickly changed to anger. "You bastard. You betrayed me! I'll get you for this."

"You will get no one for this, mister. You are going off my ship." The words were whispered through Travis's clenched jaw.

Tim turned to get a view of the captain. "You mean you're goin' to put me off in Barbados?"

"No. I mean you are getting off now, tonight," Travis said with a snarl.

"But—but—we're three weeks from land. You can't put me out in the middle of the ocean," Tim implored.

"I, Mr. Hawkins, can do anything I wish. I *am* the captain of this ship."

"But that's the same as murder. I'll never make it out there." He started to perspire and his hands were shaking when he extended them in front of Travis in a pleading gesture.

"That is precisely what I am counting on."

"You'll be sorry you did this, cap'n. That wench ain't worth what you're doing," Tim stated.

"That, Mr. Hawkins, is one man's opinion." Travis's eyes never looked away from Tim's face when he addressed his next remark to John. "John, get this garbage up on deck. I'll be up presently."

"Aye, captain." John led the trembling form of Tim Hawkins away.

Travis closed the door and turned to find a wide-eyed child in the corner between his bunk and the ledge, holding her shirt together with a shaking hand. Her eyes looked like two pools in the desert. Tears could be seen in the corners, ready to spill over and down her satiny cheeks.

At the moment, he had the strongest desire to protect her. To be so young and to have been thrown in amongst his love-starved crew would have given a harlot pause. As spunky as this girl was, he was sure that what almost happened had effected her greatly.

He thanked God again for John Rabun's sense of duty, informing him of what was to take place here in his cabin. A shudder wracked Travis's body. He could have come down here and found something entirely different than the woman-child staring up at him with eyes that didn't understand.

He knelt down and tenderly brushed a tear from her face, but at his touch she recoiled as though his touch had burned her. Gently, he said. "I'm so sorry this happened. Did he hurt you?"

Jenny shrank from him, seemingly fading into the wall.

"Don't be afraid Elaine—I mean, my lady. I won't hurt you, and I will make sure this does not happen again." With a smile on his handsome face, he held out a hand to her, careful not to touch her. He wanted her to come to him.

After several seconds of indecision, Jenny tentatively placed her hand in his, but when he pulled her up, she felt her legs go numb and she started to fall.

Travis grabbed her around the waist and held her close to him. Thinking she would faint, he carefully picked her up and laid her gently on the bunk.

When he moved to leave her, she pulled him closer and whispered in his ear, "Please, don't leave me alone."

Travis was at a loss to describe this scene and told her, "All right, but I must go up on deck for a few minutes. Let me go find Darby to sit with you while I'm gone." He gently took her arms from around his neck and stepped to the door. He hollered down the passageway for Darby to come to his cabin, then looked back at the girl on his bunk, who looked so frightened and fragile. He was surprised at the amount of concern she had brought out in him. She really looked so innocent and vulnerable lying there staring at him with those big blue eyes. She probably just brought out the fatherly instinct in him, he thought.

He tried to reassure her. "You will not be bothered again, that I promise you. I will keep a guard outside from now on if that will make you feel safer."

Darby appeared before Jenny could answer, and Travis explained the situation as gently as possible and told the old man, "Do not leave her until I return."

"Aye, cap'n. You can count on me. I'll make sure the lady is safe." Then Darby watched the expression on his captain's face and hoped he would never have to defend the lady from the captain.

Travis walked up on deck, dreading the next few minutes. He found John Rabun and a few others holding Tim with his hands tied behind his back.

61

Travis looked at Rodney Daniels, an old sailor who had traveled many miles with Travis, and said, "Rodney, lower the dingy."

"Aye, cap'n."

Travis then turned to Tim. "Mr. Hawkin, this is the last time I wish to lay eyes on you. If, by some stroke of luck, you do survive this punishment, I trust you will never cross my path again. For if you should, I will finish what I have started this night. Now over the side with you and may God have mercy on your soul."

John led Tim to the side and cut the ropes that bound him. Tim turned to the captain, raising a fist in front of him. "Don't worry 'bout me, cap'n. I'll survive this and when I'm able, I'll get you and that slut down there in your cabin." He shook his fist with each word, then slowly went over the side into the small dingy that would be home or coffin to him.

While Travis watched the small dingy drift away from the ship, the men gathered at the rail throwing taunts at the imprisoned man. They all knew justice had been served. The captain had left no one with the slightest doubt as to what would happen if they accosted the young woman they had rescued.

They were mostly family men out for the treasure a good voyage would net them. They had been together for more than a year working against the sea and with her. They were building new lives for themselves and their families after the war with Britain.

Noticing their captain staring out at the man drifting away, the men moved away from the rail and back to their duties in silence. They all knew this man who led them. They respected him and were all honored to be with him. But not one of them wanted to cross him. Travis Gardiner was revered as an honest man who expected honesty in return, but lie to him or cheat him of his due and the Almighty could not save you from the captain's wrath.

When Travis walked into his cabin, he saw Darby sitting on the side of the bunk with a tray on his lap, feeding the Lady Elaine. Travis could not define the resentment he felt welling up in his chest and said without thinking, "What's this, Darby? Taken to being a Mammy in your old age?"

Darby, his own resentment building at being called a mammy, looked up. Why was the captain baiting him? He was just making sure of the lady's comfort. The poor thing was still in shock at being so viciously attacked. Couldn't the captain see this? "Cap'n, I was just helpin' the lady with the broth I had Kirby bring up from the galley." He looked at Travis with as stern an expression as he could muster and continued, "After all, cap'n, she didn't eat much at supper. I thought she'd like some broth and tea to calm her." He hoped the implication that Travis was responsible for the lady's not eating was apparent.

Travis understood Darby's meaning and immediately regretted his outburst. "I know you're just thinking of the lady's comfort, Darby, and I thank you for staying with her. Now I'm exhausted. Call me at seven bells."

"Aye, cap'n." Darby turned to Jenny. "And you don't worry none. The cap'n won't let nothin' more happen to you while you're on *his* ship." He patted her arm and stood up to leave.

Jenny gave Darby a tentative smile and sank down in the bunk, pulling the blanket up under her chin. She stared at Travis with big watery eyes.

Travis looked at the bunk and the girl in it. She looked so frail staring up at him. Should I ask her to

63

share the bunk? No, she's been through enough already for one night. I may add to her fright for I'm sure I would possess her if we lay together. Turning, he opened a cabinet next to his desk and withdrew a hammock. He hung it from the rafters, silently wondering what a night's sleep in this thing would do to his already sour nature.

Jenny watched him until she was sure he intended to sleep elsewhere, then turned on her side facing the wall, immediately falling into an exhausted sleep.

When Travis heard her even breathing, he thought it curious she didn't have trouble falling asleep. He gazed at the slow rise and fall of her shoulders and wondered about her obvious calm. She certainly mustn't be as upset as I thought previously, he thought piously.

He climbed up into the hammock, using his arm behind his head for a pillow. He was exhausted but sleep eluded him. What was he to do about this girl? She had already caused him trouble, and they were three weeks from Barbados.

He wondered about her story again. So young and seemingly innocent of men. A smile appeared on his ruggedly handsome face when he remembered her throwing the bucket of water at him. She certainly didn't cower in his presence, something he liked in anyone, not just his women. *His women?* This is a child, not a woman and certainly not *his* woman. But, she was beautiful, and he couldn't wait to see the fire in her eyes as they went about baiting each other. Face it, he told himself, he wanted her but he wanted her willing, not kicking and screaming. He couldnt' bear it if he caused her to look up at him like she had looked at Hawkins. He wanted her purring in his arms. Eager for his kisses and joyous with his lovemaking.

Enough! He would never get any rest if he thought of her as he had seen her earlier: naked and vulnerable to his every whim.

He was not comfortable in the makeshift bed and squirmed to get a more comfortable arrangement. He silently cursed the foolishness of even attempting a night's rest in this contraption. Folding his six foot, two inch frame into a small hammock was not his idea of rest.

He could not find a better position and was about ready to give up and go on deck to rest when the girl moaned in her sleep. She tossed her head from side to side, thrashing about and tearing the covers from her as though they held her captive. Travis swung from the hammock to sit beside her perspiring body, trying to calm her troubled sleep.

"Sssh, Lady Elaine. It's over now," he crooned but to no avail. The moaning turned into a long piercing scream of agonized terror until Travis was forced to slap her across the face to awaken her.

Jenny's eyes opened, revealing the stark terror her dreams had provided her. The sight of Travis so close to her seemed like an anchor. His face held no menace or threats. His touch was not vile or loathsome as the other's had been. All she wanted right at this moment was for someone to hold her and chase the demons away.

Sensing her need, Travis drew her to him with her face to his chest as he gently stroked the back of her head and continued to croon in her ear. "It's over now. You need never be afraid again. No one is going to hurt you on my ship." He continued to rub his hand over her silken hair and murmured words of comfort.

Jenny held on to him even tighter, reliving the scene with Tim in her mind. His face was blank as he kept coming at her. Choking back sobs, she pulled back to look Travis in the eye. "Will he be able to get to me again?"

Seeing the terror in her eyes, he pulled her again up against him. "No. He's off my ship for good. He will never accost you again."

After a time, Jenny sniffled, and Travis reached into a side compartment and retrieved a handkerchief for her to use. She blew her nose noisily and wiped at her eyes.

"I'm sorry to be such a bother. I'm usually more in control than this."

"I know. I was the recipient of your control earlier. I always admired fish and their freedom until today." He grinned. "Being wet has its disadvantages."

Jenny returned his smile until she remembered why she had thrown the water. "You deserved it, you know?"

"Yes, I guess I did," he answered softly. He reached up and brushed the hair from her cheek. The contact was electric. Before he could stop himself, he bent forward, drawing her lips to his.

Jenny took only a moment to realize what was happening as his lips captured her's in a soft, tender kiss. When he held her tighter, she submitted and put her arms around his neck to touch the hairs falling over his collar. Feelings she had never before experienced cascaded over her. Strange, erotic sensations that at once frightened and thrilled her.

Travis felt her nipples harden through the thin fabric of her shift when he tightened his embrace. Felt the light, almost featherlike touch of her fingers on the nape of his neck. Felt the blood in his own veins pulse like he hadn't felt in years. A burning passion was being kindled, but for some reason he was holding back. Waiting. He would not force her. Besides, he had a feeling that this was all new to her. What would be the ramifications of such an act? Would she demand he marry her? That was something to consider. Travis was not about to marry anyone, especially a woman he continued to have doubts about.

Ready to abandon all caution, Jenny was surprised when Travis broke off the kiss and sat back, away from her, looking at her with a troubled expression. She wanted his kiss to continue, sure that something wonderful would happen if it did.

He gently lowered her back down on the bunk, saying, "You had better get some sleep, my lady. I must go check the watch but will return shortly." At seeing the terror return to her eyes, he added, "Don't worry. There's a guard outside. No one but Darby or myself will enter this cabin. Now lie down and go to sleep." He pulled the blanket up under her chin then rose to go to the door. When he opened the door, he made sure she heard him: "Kirby, guard her well." Then he shut the door on the face that would haunt his every waking and sleeping moment from this time on.

Jenny heard the door close softly. Embarrassment rose in her when she thought back to the kiss and the way she had molded her body to him. He must think me a harlot. Why would I enjoy a kiss from him? She certainly had enjoyed it, but she felt unsatisfied, as though there was something more that her body cried out for. She had no idea what that something was. She knew, or thought she knew the act between men and women, but actual experience was lacking. She had kissed the butcher's son back in Salford, but that had only left her with a bad impression. His breath had smelled of garlic and his kiss had been wet. She drew up her knees and hugged them as she thought back to Travis's kiss. He had kissed her with tenderness and his was a kiss to remember as something special. He was definitely handsome and had an air of authority she had never seen. Not in her father, surely, and not in the arrogant authority of Sir Reginald or Sir Miles. Why would he treat her like he had at supper, then turn into such a concerned and, yes, tender man? She had seen his anger and rage directed at the man who had attacked her and the sarcastic arrogance he had directed at her. This was no man to cross. She would have to rethink her earlier wish to make him crawl before her. She couldn't see him bowing to anyone. He was his own man and knew what he was doing at every turn.

Why had he kissed her? What should she have done when he did? Should she have slapped his face instead of molding her body to his? "Oh! Why must everything be so complicated?" she said aloud into the empty room. How was the best way to get along with him? Should she continue acting out her spite at his unscrupulous behavior or should she try in every way possible to not get in his way or bait him to anger? A sudden thought intruded in her mind. What if he were married or engaged? She had seen no evidence of such, but the thought was something to consider. A blush stained her cheeks when she once again thought of his kiss and thought she would like him to kiss her again. With this thought in mind, she relaxed and finally fell asleep with no more thought of her attacker but of the tall, handsome sea captain going through her mind.

Travis eased back into the cabin and stood silently beside the bunk gazing at the now sleeping woman. Satisfied that she was in a peaceful sleep, he climbed back up into what would become his torture chamber.

Chapter Four

The sun was just peaking over the horizon when Jenny stretched and gave a contented sigh. She opened her eyes to see Travis, draping one leg over the side of the hammock and one leg folded into it. His face wore a scowl in sleep and his head and neck looked out of position to his body. She eased the blanket back and threw her legs over the side of the bunk. She must have made a noise, as Travis's eyes flew open to leer at her.

"I'm terribly sorry if I disturbed you, captain," Jenny murmured, suddenly feeling shy.

With a grimace, Travis swung out of the hammock. His right leg was asleep, his neck ached and he had been up most of the night. Needless to say, his disposition, never very good in the morning, was rotten this particular morning. "You didn't disturb me half as much as that infernal contraption."

Jenny looked at the man bending over in the cramped confines of the cabin and then to the small hammock he had tried to sleep in. Compassion overcame her good sense and she said, "Why don't you let me take the hammock from now on. It looks to be more my size than yours."

Travis leaned down to her. "Why how very kind of you, my lady. Allowing me the pleasure of sleeping in my own bed!" he shouted at her.

She retreated to the ledge and abruptly sat down. What have I done now? She decided to make herself as inconspicuous as possible and maybe he would go away and take his poor disposition with him.

Travis walked over to the washbasin and poured water into it. He threw water into his face and prepared to shave. He had lathered his face when there was a knock on the door.

Jenny didn't dare get up and answer the summons for fear of being pushy. After all, it was his cabin.

The knock sounded again and with an oath, Travis turned to go to the door, nearly hanging himself on the hammock strings in his haste.

Jenny stifled a giggle when he all but tore the hammock off the hooks, then reached the door and flung it open.

Darby was sagging under the weight of a huge tray laden with food. "Beggin' your pardon, cap'n, but I couldn't reach the handle to open the door."

"Obviously," Travis said with a scowl. "Tell me, Darby, are we to entertain the crew for breakfast? If you had only told me, I could have had more chairs brought in."

Darby noticed the captain's mood at once. "No, cap'n, I just thought the lady would enjoy a nice breakfast after last night."

"Well, Darby, obviously you have taken a liking to the lady." He paused for effect. "So *you* eat with her!" He rubbed the lather from his face, grabbed a shirt out of the cabinet and stalked through the door.

Still holding the heavy tray, Darby followed the captain's movements until he was staring at an empty doorway. Slowly, he turned around to Jenny and shrugged his shoulders with a sheepish grin on his bewhiskered face. "A mite touchy this mornin', heh?"

"Just a mite," Jenny said with a shrug and grin to match Darby's.

"Well, we'll pay him no never mind, my lady. Here, you set yourself down and eat some of this here grub."

Jenny found she was ravenous and proceeded to put a small dent in the piles of cornbread, grits, fish, and some more of Darby's seaweed. "Darby, what is this bread and this white dish, here?" She pointed.

"Well, ma'am, the bread there is cornbread and this here is grits."

"Grits and cornbread. Darby you are giving me a real education. Are these dishes standard ship's fare?"

"Don't know for sure, my lady. All I knows is that on this here ship we eats good."

Licking her lips, Jenny said, "You sure do."

Seeing the lady push away from the table, Darby began gathering up the dishes. "I'll take this back to the galley and bring you some nice, hot tea."

"Thank you, Darby, but before you go—" She waited until he turned back to her. "Could you answer a question for me?"

"Sure, my lady, if I can. What you want to know?"

Not knowing how to broach the subject without coming right out and asking, Jenny gazed up at Darby with a questioning expression. "Is the captain married?"

Darby almost doubled over with laughter. "The cap'n married, heh! Why, my lady, the cap'n says he'll have to be dead before he would marry. Says most women are all soft and sweet until they land a husband and then they aren't satisfied with a ring on

71

their finger but want one through the poor fool's nose."

The elation she felt was quickly replaced by embarrassment.

Jenny didn't want Darby to think she was inquiring for herself, so she hurriedly explained, "I just didn't want any trouble about my sleeping in his cabin."

Darby knew the arrangements were not to her liking and tried to calm her fears. "Why, my lady, we all know there's no help for the way things have to be. You're much better off here."

"I know. After last night—" She let the rest go.

Darby tried to make her forget the happenings of last night and said, "How would you like to go up on deck for a breath of fresh air?"

Her eyes took on an excited look that quickly vanished when she remembered the captain's orders. "I would love to, but the captain told me to stay here."

"He just meant not to go on deck by yourself. He won't mind me takin' ya. You just wait here and I'll make sure the boys know you're 'bout. Don't want to surprise someone takin' a leak—Oh, I beg your pardon, my lady, but we ain't used to havin' ladies on board." Embarrassed at his indiscretion, Darby didn't look at her but down at his boot.

Taking pity on the sweet, old man, Jenny raised her hand and touched his sleeve. "That's all right, Darby. I wouldn't want to surprise anyone."

With a smile, Darby picked up the tray. "I'll be back in a jiffy." He hobbled out the door, leaving Jenny to get ready for her first outing on board the *Sea Breeze*.

She walked over to the mirror over Travis's desk to see if she needed to do anything about her appearance. She looked at her reflection and started pulling her fingers through her tangled hair. She wasn't doing a very good job of it and looked around for something to use. On the shelf, she spied a hairbrush, obviously the captain's. She debated using it, then decided if she hurried and put it back quickly, he would never know and could not accuse her of using his brush along with his bed. She ran the brush though the mass of golden strands until they shone with silky highlights. After putting the brush back where she had found it, she pinched her cheeks and wet her lips, like she had seen Lady Elaine do many times.

She stepped back to get a view of the rest of her. She saw the shirt which had been torn and quickly crossed the two sections in front of her, tucking the ends into the breeches more securely. By crisscrossing the shirt, her breasts were accentuated rather than hidden as before. Since no one had thought to give her another shirt, she decided to wrap the blanket around her like a shawl. This would at least give her some protection against the stares she knew would follow her progress on deck.

She looked again in the mirror, turning this way and that. She did look peculiar, dressed like a boy from the docks. She started to giggle then laughed until tears came to her eyes. "I can't go up on deck looking like this. It would be like holding a red flag before a bull." Realizing the folly in her walking before these love-starved men like she was a tempting little morsel to be stared at but not touched, she looked around the cabin to see if there wasn't something she could find to make a skirt out of. She was about to give up, when she saw a box under the bunk with a bit of blue velvet caught under the lid and exposed. Bending down, she pulled the box from under the bunk and lifted the lid. Inside was a bolt of beautiful, peacock blue velvet and a bolt of fine white, Irish lace. She smoothed her hand over the material and thought this had to be the most beautiful color she had ever seen. What would the stern captain of the *Sea Breeze*, who was not the least bit concerned about getting married, be doing with such material in his cabin? So absorbed in her discovery, she did not hear the door open.

Travis took a step into the room then stopped dead in his tracks. "Just what do you think you are doing?" he asked angrily.

Jenny jerked her hand away as if burned. Looking up at Travis's scowling face, she whispered, "Why, I just saw a bit of this material sticking out of the box, and I just wanted to touch it. I wouldn't hurt it."

Travis looked at her on her knees with the soles of her dainty feet sticking out from under her bottom. Turning his gaze back to her eyes, he softly told her, "That color matches your eyes."

Sensing a softening of his mood, Jenny decided to press her luck. "Would you let me have some of this to make a skirt or dress from?"

Travis started to say no, but thought again: What do I need it for now. Looking at her, a sadness came upon him that nearly overwhelmed him. "I no longer need it. By all means, make what you wish." He turned to his desk, saying, "I'll send Darby to bring you thread and needle. You do sew?"

Overwhelmed at his generosity, Jenny smiled. "Why yes. I learned from Con—my maid, as a child."

"Then you had a liberal education as far as the gentry go. Most ladies of my acquaintance would not know about such things as sewing." He turned to his desk with charts piled high and said under his breath, "Just the stupid needlepoint that clutters their parlors."

Jenny didn't want to bother him for more but needed to ask another question: "Captain, I am also in need of a change of shirt. I'm afraid this one will need mending."

Travis took note of the crisscross effort she had used to hide the tear. He also noted the way her breasts pointed and saw their taut peaks pressed against the fabric. "In my second cabinet you'll find several shirts. I'm only afraid mine will be entirely too big for you." He almost regretted giving her another as he watched her walk to the cabinet, her breasts bobbing to her steps.

"I'll make do, captain, and thank you very much for the shirt and especially the velvet." She returned to the bunk and again rubbed her hand across the fabric as though mesmerized by the touch.

Seeing her joy, Travis remarked, "Think nothing of it. I'm just happy to be able to accommodate you."

Looking up at him, Jenny couldn't read the expression on his handsome face. Deciding not to press her luck with this complicated man, she bent down and pulled the box up to the bunk. She was smoothing the material out when Darby knocked and came in the cabin.

"Ready for your walk, my lady?"

"Oh, Darby, come see what the captain has given me. Isn't it just beautiful?"

Having seen the blue velvet before, Darby turned toward the captain's back with a quizzical look on his whiskered face. Looking back to the lady, he said, "It matches your eyes."

Embarrassed at so much attention given to her eyes, Jenny asked. "Do you think you could find a pair of scissors, some thread, and a needle for me?"

"Aye, my lady. I'll bring them when we're done with our walk."

"Oh, Darby, I can't go up on deck looking like this. Would you mind if we waited a day or two until I can make a dress from this?" Her eyes found the velvet again while her hand continued to rub it.

Thinking maybe the lady was right about going up on deck with half her legs showing, Darby nodded. "All right, my lady, whatever you wish. I'll just be a minute with the things you be wantin'."

Travis watched the old geezer walk from the cabin. She's really bewitched you, you old fool, he thought. He turned to watch her from the corner of his eye. She seemed enchanted with the velvet. Why? Surely she had had many gowns made from the soft fabric. She continued to rub her small hand across the nap as though under a spell. Her face, in profile, presented an alluring sight to his travel-weary eyes. Her eyes were closed and the thick lashes seemed to veil her cheeks. Her nose tilted just the correct amount to 'be an attractive feature over her slightly parted, sensuous lips. Her gold hair spilled down her back to almost her waist, flowing in rich lustrous waves. Seeing her hair had been brushed to silky softness, he scowled, then his eyes went to the brush he kept on the shelf. On seeing a few bright gold strands caught in the bristles, he almost said something but, turning quickly back to her, he noted she had picked up a corner of the folded bolt and with eyes closed, she was rubbing it against her satiny cheek. Not wanting to break her enchantment, he remained silent.

While he continued to watch, he examined his obvious fascination with her. She appeared to be so innocent and unaware of her beauty. He longed to take a wisp of her hair and twine it around his fingers to feel its softness. He shook himself mentally as he felt arousal begin. This was something else he would have to deal with. His constant urge to bed her. What would her reaction be if he pursued his lust? She seemed to enjoy his kiss of last night. Yet he had noted the almost chaste way she had kept her lips tightly closed, as though the act was foreign to her. Somehow that thought pleased him.

He thought back to all the women he had ever had. Not one had been a virgin. Although, *one* led him to believe she was. If this one were a widow, as she claimed, then she couldn't be as innocent and chaste as she seemed. Unless—he chuckled—unless he had died on their wedding night before. . .

Jenny snapped out of her reverie when she heard a laugh come from his lips. Thinking him pleased with her joy at his gift, she favored him with a brilliant smile. "How can I ever thank you, captain? This is indeed an unexpected find. I hope whomever you purchased this for will not be upset at your giving it to me?"

The look of pain he had worn before came back to replace his laughter. "I told you I no longer needed it. I'm only too happy to have it come to some use." He turned back to his desk, leaving Jenny to ponder again his swift and sometimes frightening mood swings.

After last night, she thought he had finally warmed to her, but now it seemed he was only tolerating a bad situation. What was it Darby had said about why he would never marry? Something about women putting rings through men's noses. Somehow Jenny couldn't see this tall, good-looking man being cockholded by a woman. His insults still rankled her, and she knew that whoever did finally wed this man would have a hard time of it. She then remembered his kiss from last night. Maybe he did have some attributes that would please a woman. However, it was the time spent out of his arms that concerned her. Always having to watch what one said to him would become a very tedious task.

Jenny rose from the floor and sat on the bunk. At seeing Travis's attention centered on her once again, she spoke to break the tension. "Captain, I was wondering what had happened to Darby to cause him his injuries?"

Travis leaned back in his chair and folded his arms across his wide chest. "What do you want to know?"

"Well, he has obviously been in some kind of accident. He's lost a leg and an eye. I just wondered how it came about?"

Travis stood up and walked to the window, looking out at the sea he loved. Turning back to stare down at her, he decided to tell her. "You must promise me not to let on to Darby I have told you. He's a mite touchy about the whole incident."

At her nod, he continued. "Darby has had a rather colorful background. I met him fifteen years ago at an inn in Malaga, Spain." He started pacing the small confines of the cabin with his arms behind his back. "Actually when I walked into that inn, so long ago, a rather spectacular fight was in progress. Not wanting to involve myself in someone else's squabbles, I retired to a safe corner and watched as the two combatants threw punches at each other. The fight was progressing fine until the man, who at that point was losing the battle, produced a rather wicked-looking knife. Before anyone knew what was up, the man poked Darby in the eye, and when Darby put his hands up, the man sliced his leg to the bone behind his knee.

I'm afraid that is how he lost both his eye and his leg."

"But how did you get involved?"

Seeing her with her legs crossed up under her body, her hands clasped, he continued: "Well, as you no doubt noticed, Darby is small of stature. The other man was quite large, and as Darby had gotten the best of the larger man up until the knife was produced, I felt the little man had spunk and the other had used unfair tactics to win. After the man fled, I tried to help Darby stop the flow of blood. As I had a rather renowned ship's surgeon, I took him to my ship where the surgeon did everything he could to save Darby's leg, but I'm afraid the arteries were too badly damaged. As Darby couldn't get around by himself, he set sail with us to France, where a carpenter made his wooden leg for him."

He bent down and asked, "Is there anything else I can explain to you?"

Jenny thought for a moment, then looked at the velvet again. "Who did you buy this for?"

He stood up quickly and with a scowl on his handsome face, told her, "Did anyone ever tell you you ask too many damned questions?" He pulled a jacket off a peg on the wall and slammed the door as he stormed out.

Jenny sat in stunned silence. She had pressed too hard. When he had been so willing to talk to her, she thought maybe they would be able to really talk together. She found that she really wanted to be able to tell this man of her troubles. Why? She had only met him a few days ago, and she surely had seen his anger, his temper, his insults and his pain. She wondered why this captain had made her want so much to erase the pain she had seen in his eyes and why she longed to see him smile instead of scowl at her. She longed to have him kiss her like he had done last night. Maybe, just maybe, she could make him forget his troubles like she hoped he would make her forget hers.

Darby went about gathering the items the lady had requested, muttering to himself as he did. "He bought the velvet for Celeste, so why's he given it away to the lady? The way he tore up Hong Kong to find it, I woulda thought no one woulda got it from him. Damned if I can figger out what he be a doin' again. Don't matter to me that he done give Miss Celeste's goods away. I'm just me and she jest be his sister."

He jabbed his finger with the needle and cursed himself for getting so upset. He put his finger in his mouth to suck at the wound and then he remembered Singapore.

They had been loading the last of the cargo when a man came on board and asked to see the captain. Darby had led the man to the captain's cabin and had heard him introduce himself as the British Consulate of Singapore, before he had closed the door and gone back to his duties. The man had only stayed a few moments then had left, showing himself from the ship. Darby remembered thinking it odd that the captain hadn't escorted his visitor himself and was too busy to give it much thought at the time. That is, until they were prepared to sail on the evening tide, and still, Travis had not emerged from his cabin.

Darby had gone to the captain's cabin and knocked on the door. At receiving no answer to his summons and fearing some harm had befallen Travis, Darby had opened the door. The cabin was in shadow, not even a candle burning to give light, but Darby saw the captain, silhouetted against the fantail window. The lights of the harbor outlined him.

"Excuse me, cap'n, but we's ready to set sail."

Receiving no response, Darby had walked closer to the man standing as though alone in the world. "Cap'n? Cap'n is somethin' the matter?"

Travis had lowered his head and turned to Darby saying, "I just need some time Darby. Can you handle the crew?"

"Aye, cap'n, but are ya ill?"

"No, but I need to be alone for a while. You set sail for Madagascar." He placed his hand on the old man's shoulder and quietly added, "I'll be all right, Darby."

Darby wondered now if the captain's giving away Miss Celeste's goods was somehow tied in with his peculiar behavior so many months ago. "I hope it weren't bad news 'bout Miss Celeste."

That evening, Jenny sat at the table sewing with delicate stitches on the velvet. While she sewed, she hummed a sweet song from her childhood.

Travis, working at his desk, was conscious of her presence and was thinking what a nice sound it was and that all they needed was a hearth, a dog, and some soft candlelight to be a domesticated couple. He shook his head to dissolve the thought. I'll never be stupid enough to hogtie myself to a woman for the rest of my life, he thought as he stretched his arms over his head and stood up from his desk. "Well, it's been another exhausting day, and I would really like to get some sleep."

Jenny started to put her sewing away quickly as these were the first words he had spoken to her since coming back to the cabin. "Of course, captain. Would you be so kind as to hang that, whatever you call it, up for me?"

He gazed at her with the hint of a smile on his lips. "Are you sure you'll be able to sleep in a hammock? It takes a little getting used to."

Thinking he was trying to bait her again, she stuck out her chin and stood up straighter. "Well, I'm sure if *you* can do it, I'll be able to."

His grin widened as he bent to take the hammock out of the cabinet. "All right, my lady." His earlier hurt and anger was completely gone from his demeanor.

Jenny watched him tie the ropes securely to the rafters. It was terribly high off the ground, but seeing the mirthful expression on his face, she was determined to do it. She looked around for something to stand on to get up to the roped hammock. Pulling a chair up under the sagging canvas, she stood on it, turning around to place her backside up against the sagging sides. She put her hands behind her and grabbed hold of the side, leaning back slightly to test the strength. Pushing down, she was able to pull it under her and gingerly sit down. Satisfied that the contraption would indeed hold her, she placed one foot up and over the side. Then she turned slightly to put the other foot up and as she did the hammock started to swing. Trying to stop it, she overcorrected and set the thing in violent motion. The next thing she knew, she was staring up at it from the floor.

Looking over at Travis with an "I dare you to laugh" look, she climbed back up, only this time tempering the original technique, and she was finally able to lie down on the swinging contraption.

When it dawned on her that she had forgotten to

bring her blanket up with her, she debated asking Travis to hand it to her. But seeing him smiling up at her with an "I told you so" expression on his face, she lay down again. The night isn't that cold, she told herself.

Travis took one last look at her, then turned down the lamp and went to sleep.

Afraid to move or breathe for fear of putting the thing into motion again, Jenny lay like a board, stiff and unyielding. After what seemed like hours to her, she finally relaxed enough to fall into an exhausted sleep.

Never a very heavy sleeper, Travis woke about four bells to the sound of a *thud* followed by a *groan*. He reached over to turn up the lamp and saw Jenny on the floor rubbing her shoulder.

Forgetting her intention to camouflage her anger, Jenny swore: "I wish the burning fires of hell on whoever invented that damned contraption."

Travis looked amused as he leaned toward her. "Spoken like a true blue-blood."

Jenny caught her breath when she realized what she had said but decided not to remark on his comment.

Travis climbed out of the bunk and reached a hand to help her up. She extended her arm and when he pulled, she screamed in pain.

Kneeling down, Travis slipped her shirt from her shoulder and examined her arm. He looked at her pain-filled eyes. "I don't think it's broken, but you'll probably have some pain for a while. There's a nasty bruise taking shape up here." He touched the already blackening spot. Looking into her eyes with a grin on his face, he lifted her up. "That must be what you fell on first."

Favoring her arm, she grimaced. "It really hurts.

Are you sure it's not broken?''

"No, I'm not sure, but I have seen a lot of breaks and this doesn't look like one to me. But if it will calm your nerves, I'll have Darby look at it. He's our resident doctor. I think he could cure the plague if he put his mind to it." He paused when he saw the pain registering again on her face. Thinking his holding her was aggravating the condition, he lowered her onto a chair. When he took his arms from her, his hand brushed her breast, and the contact caused a sensation in his loins. He stepped back hurriedly from her. My God. I'm no better than a rutting stud. I can't seem to touch her without wanting to bed her.

He walked over to the washbasin and splashed cold water in his face. "Ah, that's better."

A blush stained Jenny's face when Travis shed his shirt, revealing his broad shoulders and muscular chest. He turned, bending down to wash, and Jenny marveled at the way the muscles across his back moved and rippled with pulsing life. Almost as though her fingers had a mind of their own, they reached out and almost touched him. Realizing what she was doing at the last moment, she jerked her hand back to her lap. She wanted this man to hold her like before. Kiss her like before and make this ache she felt go away.

She had to stop this. She was feeling things that she could not define and had no knowledge of. She had never wanted to know of these things in the past. Sir Reginald had made all desire seem evil and sordid to her. She could remember the way Sir Reginald had looked at her. She also remembered the sounds coming from Lady Elaine's room as she would lie on her cot in the next room. What they did, she didn't know, but she had decided she wanted no part of something that sounded so frightful.

Removing a clean shirt out of the cabinet and putting it over his massive shoulders, Travis turned to Jenny and said, "I'll go roust Darby and have him come take a look at your shoulder."

"Thank you," Jenny answered as a blush stained her cheeks. Could he tell what she had been thinking? She hoped not.

She sat on a chair, rubbing her sore shoulder for what seemed like only a moment, when the door opened to admit Darby. He was tucking in his shirt as he approached her. "What in the world have you been up to, lass? Can't take me eyes off of you for a minute now, can I?" His grin erased the sternness of his statement.

Jenny smiled at him, thinking he was the sweetest man she had ever met, and then she let out a screech as Darby poked and prodded her shoulder.

"I'm sorry, my lady, but I've got to make sure nothin' be broken."

"I'm all right, Darby," she said. "Is anything broken?"

"Not that I can see, but let's just put you in a sling for a few days to take some of the pressure off it."

"But I'm not done with my dress yet, Darby. I think I can still sew if I don't move around too much. If you put it in a sling, I won't be able to finish my gown." Looking up at him with wide, pleading eyes, she continued, "I do so want to get out of this cabin. Please Darby?"

Darby couldn't resist the look she directed at him, but he was concerned about her shoulder. "Now, now. 'Tis better to be safe than sorry, I always say." As he wrapped a kerchief around her arm and tied it around her neck, he noticed her look of disappointment. "I'll finish your gown for you, and I'll be able to keep an eye on you at the same time."

Jenny looked skeptically at him. She would never hurt his feelings, but she didn't want her dress ruined, either. Not knowing what to say, she lowered her head.

Darby noticed the dismay she displayed and quickly said to reassure her, "Don't be a worryin' 'bout your gown. If you promise not to tell, I'll show you somethin'." At her renewed interest Darby pointed to the shirt she was wearing. "I sewed up that shirt and them breeches you be wearing. But you've got to promise not to tell any of the mates. The captain thinks me the next best thing to a wife, and I sure don't want the lads to know I do the sewing, too. I'd never live it down."

Jenny looked surprised as she looked down at the delicate little stitches on the shirt front. "Why Darby, you are amazing."

Pride getting the better of him, he puffed out his cheeks. "Just a little talent I picked up workin' for the cap'n. Like I said, he never had no woman to do for him, and I'm the next best thing." He then went about tidying up the cabin, making up the bunk, taking down the hammock that Jenny silently cursed, and putting everything away. He then got the needle and thread and started to work on the blue velvet gown.

Jenny watched him for a while and marveled at the speed with which Darby worked. After a time, she became bored and got up and walked over to the book shelves above the captain's desk. She reached, with her good arm, and pulled out a book of verse to read. As she slid the book off the shelf, a piece of paper floated to the floor. Bending to retrieve it, she couldn't help but read the lines written in a bold pen.

Captain Travis Gardiner
Sea Breeze, *Singapore*
*It pains me to inform you of the death of your
sister, Celeste, this 29th day of September, 1817.
She died in her sleep and did not suffer. My
deepest condolences.*
Marvin Simples

Gardiner and Simples, Attorneys at Law

Jenny gasped and said, "Oh, no." Then she looked
toward Darby.

Darby looked up from his sewing to see the
expression on her face. "Why, what's the matter,
lass?" He then noticed the paper she held in her
hand.

Jenny didn't know what to say, so she handed the
paper to Darby.

He glanced over the paper, then put the sheet down
and simply stared at the floor.

"Darby, you didn't know?"

The sound of Jenny's voice brought Darby back to
reality. He slowly turned his head to Jenny to reply.
"What? Er—er—no, but I thought somethin' like this
had happened. She was so frail after the accident. She
was such a lovely young woman. The cap'n cherished
her. Their mother had died givin' birth to Miss
Celeste. The cap'n's been both mother and father to
her for so long."

"Accident?" Jenny asked.

"Aye. She couldn't walk. The cap'n took her all the
way to Paris, France to find a doctor what could help
her but no one could. Poor lass."

87

"But, where was their father?"

"He was lost at sea the same year their mother died. He never even knew he had a daughter or that his wife had died."

"Oh, how sad," Jenny said with tears threatening to spill.

"Aye, but the cap'n, he took both Celeste and Jeff under his wing and they both turned out to be two fine people."

"The captain has a brother, then?"

"Oh, I should say he does. Jeff is a lawyer in Charleston. He's the Gardiner in the message. Simples be his partner. I bet Celeste's dying near tore Jeff up. It's odd that Simples wrote to the cap'n and not Jeff."

As Darby contemplated that thought, Jenny thought of something else and asked, "Darby, this material, was it for Celeste?"

"Aye. The cap'n took to every shop in Hong Kong to find just the right color."

"Then that's what he meant when he said he didn't need it anymore. It must be very painful for him to see it and remind him of her." She paused, thinking again how she longed to erase the pain from his face. "Darby, let's put it away and forget about the gown. It would be too much to put him thorugh everytime he looked at it."

"But what are ya goin' to wear, my lady?"

"Oh, I'll make something out of that shirt that got torn. Maybe I'll use some of the lace and make a shirt or something.

She didn't elaborate, but Darby saw the shame wash over her as she picked up the shirt and saw again the rip in the front. He knew that shirt would bring back painful memories of her own.

He carefully folded the velvet and laid it in the box. As he did, Jenny carefully placed the sheet of paper back where she had found it. The captain would tell everyone when he felt like it. Anyway, she didn't think he would appreciate her reading his private papers.

"My lady," Darby suddenly said. "I just remembered. I have some bleached muslin in me quarters. We could make a decent skirt and maybe a blouse for ye from that. It wouldn't feel too good, but at least you could go up on deck."

"Why, Darby that's marvelous. Let's do it." Jenny did so want to breathe the fresh air that would surely be up on deck. The cabin was getting smaller by the minute.

Darby left to get the muslin, and Jenny sat down to take apart the shirt as best she could. Maybe she could fashion a camisole from it.

She was startled by the sound of someone who was kicking the door. She froze in her chair, remembering her attacker of the other night. The kick sounded again, and then she heard Travis's voice coming from the hall. "Come on, open the door. My hands are full."

Relief flooding through her, she jumped up and ran to the door, opening it to see Travis standing there holding a tray filled with dishes and a teapot. He came in and sat the tray on the table. With a grin, he turned to her.

"I knew Darby would be too busy with his doctoring to get our breakfast so I got it myself."

Jenny noticed how he seemed so pleased with himself over such a mundane gesture.

He continued talking while uncovering each dish. "I must say the cook was a little shocked to see me walking into his galley at this hour for a breakfast tray."

Jenny felt some praise was being asked for and could only think to say, "You did a splendid job, too." Then she thought about this man's sister and the heartache he had gone through. She wanted to console him, but then she remembered that he didn't know that she knew about Celeste.

Travis pulled out a chair for her, and she sat down to the same type breakfast as yesterday. She ate slowly and quietly. She really wasn't hungry and simply moved the food about on her plate. She felt strange sitting next to him, knowing that she knew something about him that he obviously didn't want anyone to know. Why hadn't he told Darby about his sister's death? She looked up at him, unobserved. The subject was probably too painful to bring up, even to his closest friend.

When Travis finished his breakfast, he noted the amount of food still on her plate. "Aren't you hungry this morning? You have certainly had a good appetite up until now." He paused and looked at the sad expression on her pretty face before she realized he was watching her, and she put a smile on. Travis was puzzled by the change of expression and asked, "Is everything all right? You seem sad."

Not wanting him to think something amiss, Jenny smiled at him again and shrugged her shoulders, wincing at the pain that shot through her arm. "I'm just tired. I didn't sleep very well last night."

He smiled at her. "Speaking from experience, I can well imagine. That brings me to an apology I owe you." Seeing her confused expression, he continued: "Yesterday I was aching all over and tired for the same reason. I let my poor disposition lead me into treating you abominably. I'm sorry for being such a bear."

Jenny had not expected this and was not sure how to react. She whispered, "Apology accepted, captain."

"Good. Now why don't you eat some of the dried figs. They are very good and you need to eat something."

Jenny took a bite of the figs and found they were indeed delicious. As she was finishing her bowl, Darby backed into the room carrying the bleached muslin. Without turning around he said, "This will be better than the outfit you're wearing, my lady." He then turned to find Travis's questioning gaze on him.

"What's this? I thought you were going to make a gown out of the blue velvet?"

"Oh! Cap'n—I thought you were on the bridge. You see, the little lady, well— she— that is, we— thought the velvet would be— too— hot, yes, hot." Darby stammered in his surprise.

Travis looked at Jenny for confirmation. She met his gaze then hung her head, not wanting him to see the pain in her eyes.

Standing up, Travis walked over to the bunk, bent down and pulled out the box holding the pieces of velvet that had already been cut and partially sewn. His hand touched the soft material, then he spoke without looking at either of them, "You know, don't you?"

Darby looked at Jenny, and they both knew that they should tell him the truth. "Aye, cap'n. The letter just dropped to the floor when the lady went to get a book. I'm sorry 'bout Miss Celeste, cap'n. She was a beautiful child."

Still touching the velvet, Travis felt their eyes on his back. "She was such a beautiful *woman*, Darby. She could have had such a wonderful life, if only—"

91

Darby walked over to him and placed a worn, old hand on his arm. "Cap'n, you can't live on *if onlys*. She was happy. She never blamed you for the accident."

Travis dropped the velvet and looked at the little man who had been like a father and was a friend to him for so long. "She never did, did she?" Turning to the window, Travis walked over and gazed at the lightening sky. "Has Darby told you about Celeste, my lady?" he asked softly.

Jenny looked to Darby. He nodded and she turned to Travis. "He told me she suffered an accident and was not in good health since then."

"Yes, she suffered an accident. An accident I caused!"

Darby heard the pain and guilt that lined the captain's voice and quickly said, "Cap'n, you couldn't have known. Don't keep blamin' yourself," he begged.

"If I hadn't bought her that stallion for her birthday, she would be alive today."

Jenny looked at his slumping shoulders and walked over to place her hand on his arm.

He turned to stare down at her and said, "You see, I bought her a horse in England as a surprise. It was a magnificant animal, or so I thought. Celeste was thrilled with my gift. She ordered it saddled and before I could saddle my own horse, she was off like the wind, her blond hair blowing behind her. It was a sight." He looked through Jenny as though seeing Celeste riding again in his memory. "She seemed to float in the saddle. She was so quickly out of my sight. I followed her but when I found her—" He closed his eyes as though the pain was too much to bear. "She was lying on the ground with a gash over her eye and her legs crumpled under her." He moved away from

Jenny and placed his hands over his face for a moment. "I shot the horse on sight."

He looked back at the sea and Jenny knew he was reliving every agonizing moment of the day over and over again in his mind.

Darby came up beside him. "Cap'n, she never blamed you. She was always tellin' you she thought somethin' had spooked the horse. Don't blame yourself."

Travis looked down at the little man, shook his shoulders like he was trying to dispel the image, and walked over to the box holding the velvet. He turned to Jenny and with almost a pleading expression, he said, "My lady, please use the velvet. It will only go to waste if you leave it, for I have no one else to give it to."

"But, captain, won't it bring back painful memories for you?"

"No. I will have no unpleasant memories of Celeste. She was beautiful of both mind and spirit. All my memories of her will be happy ones."

For some reason, which Jenny could not discern, she wanted to please this man more than anything. She walked up to him and looked into his dark eyes. "All right, captain, and thank you." She smiled sweetly up at him.

He returned a slight smile, saying, "My lady, I haven't asked, but how is your arm?"

Knowing the subject of Celeste to be closed, she indicated the sling. "Darby, the doctor," she said gazing at the old man affectionately, "made me wear this sling, but I am beginning to feel much better."

"Was I correct in my humble diagnosis of no broken bones?"

"Aye, cap'n. I just suggested she wear the sling for

93

a few days to make sure."

"Suggested!" Jenny scowled playfully at him, then turned back to Travis. "He demanded I wear this. Suggested indeed!"

Travis started for the door, saying, "Well, I will leave you two to your domesticity. I must go check the bridge. I don't think I will be able to come back before nightfall. Darby, you will stay with her, won't you?"

"Of course, cap'n."

"Good. Maybe you can finish her dress for her." He grinned and quickly ducked out of the cabin.

Darby watched as the door closed. "Seems he's resigned himself to the death."

Jenny nodded and sat in a chair, beginning to remove some more stitches from the shift. Darby pulled out the velvet again and started sewing in his quick, precise manner. They spent the rest of the day in companionable silence, each with their own thoughts of Travis Gardiner.

Chapter Five

The sun was sinking below the western horizon, making vivid streaks of pinks and golds, highlighting the end of Travis's day. He was agitated and constantly swept the horizon with his eyes. He couldn't explain the feelings he was having. He knew he should have told Darby about Celeste's death, but somehow he had felt that if he told of the tragedy, it would become more real. By keeping the news to himself, he could think on it as a mistake. Some grotesque joke perpetrated by someone's morbid sense of humor. His logic told him it was no mistake and that Darby should have been told sooner. It was probably for the best that Elaine had found the missive.

Elaine. The very thought of her sent his heart pounding. He had purposely stayed away from his cabin the entire day. She had looked at him with such concern and tenderness at his loss that he had wanted to comfort himself in her arms and touch that spun gold hair. She was a mystery to him. Her wide, innocent eyes contained no malice or haughty disdain for her predicament at being forced to wear the breeches and billowing shirt, yet she was willing to put the velvet aside to spare his feelings. He hadn't met many women who would forego their own comfort for the sake of someone else.

He noticed the eyes of his crew on him and stared at John Rabun's smile. "What's everyone staring at me for?"

John came away from the railing and approached his captain. "Cap'n, you been pacin' a hole in this here deck all day. The lads just thought it strange you stayin' up on deck and not sayin' a word."

Travis realized he had done just that as his mind had been on other things. "I've been going over the repairs we will need to have done in Barbados." He turned to look at the main mast. "I think we had better take the main mast down and check it."

John nodded, even though he had checked the mast himself only a few days before and could find no weakness in its massive strength. "That will take a while to do, cap'n. We'll have to stay in port fer 'bout nigh onta a week."

Travis's mind whirled as he wondered again of his purpose. "That can't be helped. I would hate to have it crack as we come in to Charleston Harbor."

John noticed the agitation come back to Travis, so he nodded and left the bridge to the Captain and his thoughts.

Travis was unconscious of his true motives for spending the extra time in Barbados. He didn't want this voyage to end, for when it did, it would be an ending to his way of life and the end of his freedom. He would be a plantation owner and forced to remain on the land. He didn't blame Jeff for his career which took him away from Moss Grove. Travis had been so pleased when Jeff had announced his intent to become a lawyer. Jeff had made Travis proud, and he could not deny him his opportunities.

The sky had turned to deep purples with a faint

streak here and there of brilliant red. The lanterns were being lit on deck while Travis continued to pace. He knew he would have to go to his cabin soon and again be assailed with wanting the woman who was sharing his quarters. He thought of the hammock he had been forced to endure the other night. He couldn't put her in it again, not with her arm in a sling. He would be forced to suffer through another night in the damned contraption while she slept peacefully in his bunk. He wondered again what her reaction would be if he asked to share the berth with her.

He saw Darby coming across the deck and rushed to intercept him. "Is the lady all right?"

"Aye, Cap'n. I just left her so's she could put on the gown. It turned out pretty good, if'n I do say so meself." He puffed out his chest in pride.

"I'm sure it did, Darby. Why don't you send some supper to my cabin in say—about an hour. I'll go see how she's coming along."

Darby watched as the captain almost ran across the deck in his haste to see the lady. He smiled and thought that the captain just might not walk away from this one. "Yes sir, he might not."

Travis went down the companionway and knocked on his door.

"Oh! Come in," Jenny called from within the cabin.

Taking a deep breath, he opened the door and couldn't believe his eyes. The gown was a masterpiece. It was square necked with lace sewn into the bodice. Long puffed sleeves had lace ruffles that spilled over her wrists. The skirt was full but with the lack of a petticoat, it molded to her slim hips. She was looking at him with a brilliant smile transforming her face. He couldn't remember seeing her smile just that way

97

before, but he was determined to see it more often. She looked beautiful. No longer a waif but definitely a woman.

She didn't know what she had hoped when he saw her, but the light in his eyes and the way he just stood there staring at her gave her a sense of power she had never felt before. His eyes took in the gown and then came up to meet her eyes. They held her spellbound in their dark depths until she realized that she hadn't taken a breath since he had walked in the door. With her heart pounding in her chest and her hands shaking, she turned and asked, "Captain, I'm afraid I can't reach the hooks in the back. Could you do them up for me?"

She turned around, presenting her back to him and waited for what seemed an eternity for his touch. When it came she was aghast at the dynamic power that seemed to go from his body to hers.

The back of his hand barely brushed her skin, but the contact generated feelings and sensations she had never known. For some reasons she longed to experience what she knew would be complete fulfillment. How she knew this she didn't know, but it became an all-driving force within her.

She was in love with this man. She didn't know when it had happened or why but she suddenly realized that she wanted him. Wanted him in a way that was all consuming. All powerful. There was nothing, she knew, that she would not do for him. She would kill or be killed to insure his well being. She would lie, cheat, or steal to make his life bearable. All these characteristics were not Jenny's. They were those of a woman desparately, completely committed to a man who, at best, was an enigma. His quicksilver moods, his demanding presence, his quick assessments, all contributed to his power and charisma.

Jenny knew what was coming. She could have stopped him when she felt the soft butterfly touch of his lips on her shoulder, but she leaned into him, letting his lips travel up her neck to her earlobe. Such sweet desire coursed through her. Such wanting that she thought she would go mad if he spurned her again.

But when he turned her around to face him and she saw her own passion mirrored in his eyes, she knew no greater happiness. He loved her. She saw it there in the dark depths of passion so like her own desire.

She stood proud when he slowly slipped the gown from her shoulders to fall in a blue heap at her feet. The camisole she had fashioned from parts of the ruined shirt and bits of lace clung to her hardened nipples. Slowly, so slowly, he lifted the camisole up and over her head. His eyes never left hers as his hands found her tiny waist and began the gentle pursuit of her flesh.

And when she was finally naked, he groaned and held her to him as though afraid she would disappear before his eyes. Gently his hands roamed over her back and then searched out her buttocks to cup and lift her into him.

She pulled at the back of his shirt until she could reach under the coarse material and feel the rippling muscles across his back. She felt the power and strength of him. The gentleness and softness of him. She felt his warmth and tried to pull him into her to become one, but he pulled away from her, making her feel a loss so profound that she wanted to cry out her hurt. Then he cupped her face within his large hands, looking deeply into her eyes before kissing her gently.

He stepped away to quickly shed his own clothing, then stood close to her without touching. It was almost like a ceremony to her: each letting the other sense the magnetism of the other without physical contact; as though their spirits were melting into one.

A heat slowly filled Jenny's body until she thought she would surely burn through the floorboards. She could feel the heat of his body radiate with a pulse, a life of its own. They stood apart yet together in a way neither had ever experienced before.

Travis's hand came up and lightly touched her cheek. "You are a very beautiful woman."

Jenny's eyes closed at the praise, and she leaned into his arms, letting the feel of his naked flesh touching her go all the way from her head to her toes. She wanted this feeling, this sensation to last forever. She kissed him with such passion that he groaned deep in his throat before picking her up and carrying her to the berth. When he put her down, she clung to him, pulling him closer to her as he stretched his body out to lie beside her.

His hands roamed all over her body, making her wither with the need of him. But nothing prepared her for the incredible passion he evoked in her when he touched the entrance to her maidenhead. Spasms of erotic feeling coursed through her until she could feel every nerve in her body. Sounds became muted and colors became brighter. Not knowing what she was doing, Jenny pulled and tugged at Travis, raking her nails down his back in her anxiety to have him complete the pleasant torture, yet unsure as to what would come next.

In her frenzy, her hand came in contact with his manhood. The rigid rod pulsed beneath her grasping fingers. He gave a gasp of unrestrained desire and quickly moved on top of her straining body to complete the act.

She felt his weight and the probing of his member into her flesh. Moving up with her hips in her desire

100

to subdue the pulsing, thrilling pain she was experiencing, she let out a cry of such agony that he momentarily stopped his thrusting to stare into her wide, surprised eyes. But the pain quickly was replaced by the return of passion, and the wild thrusting and pumping continued with no more thought of the past but only of the savage climb to heights neither had ever been to before until it exploded in a kaleidoscope of pleasure.

Their bodies slick with perspiration, they lay silently together as one, letting the sensations of the aftermath of loving wash their spirits.

His weight on her increased as his whole body seemed to relax into her, but she didn't care. She just wanted him to stay within her; feel their bodies together and know she was loved.

When he did withdraw from her and rolled to the side, she gave an involuntary cry of regret until he kissed her and cradled her to him to lay within the embrace of his arms. Finally she had someone to love her. Someone who would take care of her so she would not have to take care of herself.

Travis tried to sort out his feelings. She *was* a virgin. He was shocked at what the knowledge meant to him. Not so much that she had lied to him about a previous marriage but that he was the first to taste her sweet nectar. The thought pleased him immensely.

Jenny had imagined nothing like what she had just experienced. The feelings that had gone through her were too wondrous to think about. She closed her eyes and continued rubbing her fingers over his chest, while listening to the now steady beat of his heart. She opened her eyes and wondered what his reaction would be if she confessed to him, but she dismissed the thought. She wasn't quite sure and decided to wait a while longer. Whatever happened between them, from this moment on, would bring no regrets. The experience was marked in her memory forever.

Travis continued to wonder about this woman beside him. What would all this mean to him? The feeling of wanting to protect her, of wanting to see her smile and be happy, of wanting to hold her like this in the sweet afterglow of their love play? Contentment was what he was feeling now. Contentment as pure as a new kitten. He didn't even care about her deception at this point. He was remembering his other conquests and how when he was done with them, he would usually just up and leave with no regrets, with no compunction to stay. But somehow this girl was different. He wanted only to keep her here beside him and make her safe. Why, he wondered? Could I be falling in love with this one. Never, the common sense part of his mind told him. I will enjoy her for the voyage then get on to my new life. When we get to Charleston, I will simply say good-bye to the sea and to the Lady Elaine Seaton. A slow smile spread across his handsome face as he thought of the many hours before Charleston Harbor would be reached.

They were both startled out of their separate thoughts by a knock on the door. Jumping out of the bunk, Travis started to put on his breeches. "Oh, damn. That's Darby with supper." Throwing Jenny's dress to her, he whispered, "Here, get dressed."

Travis had just pulled on his shirt when they heard Darby from outside the door. "Cap'n! Lady Elaine! Could one of you open the door? I've got a load here and I can't reach the handle."

Trying to fasten the hooks in the back of her gown, Jenny looked to the door and called, "Just a minute." Turning to Travis, she presented her back. "Hook me, please."

Travis was doing up the top hook as the door

opened and Darby backed in.

"Jest let me stand out there holdin' this darn food 'til it gets cold, would you!" He sat the tray on the table and turned to look upon the two very guilty people standing before him.

Jenny's hair was mussed and her gown looked rumpled. Travis had one shirt tail hanging out and no shoes on.

Grinning from ear to ear, Darby bowed to them and walked toward the door. "I'll be back later for the tray," he called over his shoulder, then stopped and turned, seeing again the two faces that spoke volumes. "Aye, 'tis goin' to be a glorious voyage."

As the door closed, Jenny felt a rush of blood to her face. What will poor Darby think of me? It was obvious what had taken place here in this cabin only moments before. How could she ever face him again?

Travis noticed her embarrassment and touched her shoulder. She did not look at him but quietly said, "Captain, I don't know what came over me. I'm afraid you must think me a harlot."

Travis gently placed his hand to her chin and waited for her eyes to look upon him before saying, "Please, call me Travis. Captain sounds too impersonal, and, my lady, as far as what just happened, it in no way makes me think of you as anything but the most desirable woman I have ever met. I seem to be a schoolboy in your presence."

Jenny noticed he hadn't said he loved her, but she was sure he did. Didn't he? All of a sudden she wasn't sure of anything and felt foolish for giving herself so completely and with so much abandonment. Then she saw his eyes take on a wanting look again, and she quickly moved from him to the table. "Can we eat now? I seem to be ravenous tonight."

Travis, wearing a bemused expression, walked over

and pulled out a chair for her. Jenny piled her plate full of baked flounder, fried potatoes, some of Darby's seaweed, and some small round bread that looked fried. She held one on her fork and tasted it. "This is delicious. What is it?"

"Those are hush puppies and it's a treat when we have them. Darby guards his cornmeal like it was gold."

"Darby really is a jack-of-all-trades, isn't he? Is this another of his special dishes?"

"Sure is. The cook gets a little put out when Darby fixes my meals, but Darby knows what I like. Great, right?" He smiled at her.

"Sure is!" They both laughed again.

Jenny felt, for the first time in her life, love. She did not analyze the feeling or the emotion. She loved this man and that was that. She felt safe and secure, something she hadn't felt for a long, long time. She gazed at the man across from her, knowing happiness was finally hers. It didn't even matter that he did not tell her he loved her. She just knew he did.

They hadn't spoken during dinner except to ask that this or that item be passed. Each was feeling the unease as to what this evening had meant to them.

Travis took the teapot and poured her a cup. "That gown becomes you. Although I like you out of it as much as in it."

Jenny felt herself blush but returned his gaze without flinching. "Might I say the same for you?"

"You may." He smiled, then leaned back in his chair. "Hurry up and drink your tea. I have a surprise for you."

"A surprise! What?"

"Well, you have been so anxious to go up on deck, I thought I would show you around."

Her eyes showed her excitement but then all of a

sudden they showed fear. "Maybe we could just stay here."

Confused by her change of mood, Travis leaned forward and took her hand. "I thought you were so desperate to get some fresh air?"

"I am— I mean I was," she whispered.

"What's changed your mind, Elaine?"

"I—I don't—" She stuttered, unable to finish.

"Elaine, you know you will be safe, don't you?"

She looked down at his large brown hands covering hers. "Will I?"

"I told you no one would ever accost you again. Especially now that—" He seemed to search for the right words. "Now that we are lovers."

"Lovers." She repeated the word. Not that he loved her but that they were *lovers*. But wasn't that the same thing? You only gave yourself to the one you loved.

He interrupted her thoughts. "Come on, my *lady* and I will show you my kingdom." He bowed before her and extended his hand.

He looked so funny that she laughed, then she took his hand. "Of course, I will tour your kingdom with you, milord."

And, hand in hand, Travis showed her his ship. He had been correct about its size, and whatever space was available was used for cargo. The deck was clean and the jumble of rope overhead looked well tended. He tried to explain the importance of each item, but Jenny couldn't follow all the names and uses for so many items.

After touring the deck they stopped to watch the moon rise and the stars twinkle in the cloudless night.

Jenny breathed deeply of the balmy air then smiled to herself.

"You're happy about something. What is it?"

Travis asked.

She turned to him with her eyes reflecting the moonlight. "I was just thinking about the night you rescued me. I had just prayed to God that you weren't a pirate ship, when I saw Darby and was sure I had run into Black Beard's lair."

Travis laughed. "I had forgotten but Darby said you had asked him if he was a pirate."

They continued to stand by the railing for a while longer until the evening breeze grew chilly, then Travis led her back to the cabin.

"I had better go check on everything. I'll be back in a while," he said to her before closing the door on her pretty face.

Jenny stared at the closed door and suddenly became fearful when she thought about the coming night. Would they share the berth or would he hang the hammock up? Should she go along with his desires without his stating his intentions? Of course he loved her and would marry her, she only needed to show him how much he meant to her.

She put it from her mind and began to straighten up around the cabin. She had cleared the table and was straightening the bed sheets when Travis walked into the cabin and overheard her gasp.

"What's the matter?"

Grabbing the sheet from the bed and balling it behind her back, Jenny turned to him and tried to pretend nothing was amiss. "Oh, nothing. I just wondered where the clean sheets were kept."

Travis thought he knew the reason for her panic and did not try to embarrass her further. It was enough that he had proof of her virginity. "Under the bunk, there are some fresh sheets." He looked around the cabin and commented, "I see you've been busy." He walked over to slip his arms about her like it was a common practice of his. "You sure feel good." He nuzzled her neck. "As soon as Darby picks up the dishes, we'll go to bed, all right?"

Feeling a slight quiver of consciousness that she quickly pushed aside, Jenny leaned against him, feeling his heart pounding against her. This is where she really wanted to spend the rest of her life. Right here in Travis Gardiner's arms.

That night they made love again. Although it lacked the mystery of the first time for Jenny, it was more exciting because of the anticipation. Her body tingled with passion and sexual pleasure. Travis led her through the things that pleased him, and they gave to each other until each screamed out their release.

They slept then, wrapped in each others arms, dreaming of the tomorrows to come, and before the sun peaked above the horizon, they once again joined their bodies in the act of love, each marveling at the way they felt.

Chapter Six

The next few weeks went by with Jenny and Travis making love at night and acting like two young lovers by day. They would walk hand in hand along the deck and look at the stars, while Travis would show her interesting sights on board his ship and regale her with tales of the sea. Jenny noticed the pride and love he held for his ship and could only hope that someday he would feel the same toward her.

She wanted to believe that this was the fulfillment of her dreams: that her life would be by Travis's side as his wife and the terror of her past would be at an end. She tried to deny her doubts, and the fact that he had never said he loved her or talked about their future was only a nagging flicker that she quickly pushed to the furthest recesses of her mind. She took one day at a time, falling under the spell of love and contentment that she had never experienced before in her life. She prayed every night that this would not be an end but a beginning for all her dreams.

Jenny saved the blue velvet gown for the excursions up on deck. When she was in the cabin, she dressed in the shirt and breeches. Travis was looking at her one day while she sat mending one of his shirts and said,

"I think when we get to Barbados, I'll take you shopping."

Jenny looked up from the mending. "Shopping for what?"

"Although I love seeing you walk around half naked, my dear, I do believe you could use some new clothes. I will buy you some in a little shop I know of in town."

"I suppose I could use another gown to make do until we reach Charleston."

"We'll see about that. We will be there for several days, anyway. Some repairs I've been putting off can be done, and we will have some time to explore the islands."

Jenny smiled at him, thinking about warm moonlit nights and the feeling of firm land under her feet again. "That sounds like heaven."

"Wait until you see it. You will really think it is." He smiled at her. He wished again, for the thousandth time, that she would trust him enough to tell him the truth about herself. He felt as long as she kept secrets from him, he would never be able to give her his heart.

When they dropped anchor off the coast of Barbados, Jenny was completely captivated by what she saw: mountains, white, sandy beaches, and the most beautiful of all, the crystal clear blue water. Standing by the railing and looking down into the clear depths below her, she saw fish of every size and shape swim beneath the ship.

Travis walked up behind her and placed his hands on her waist, leaning over the railing to see what she was looking at. He put his lips close to her ear and whispered, "I'm a little sorry your shoulder has healed."

Jenny looked up at him in shocked surprise. "Why, what a terrible thing to say. Why do you say that?"

Chuckling into her ear, he replied, "Because I don't get to hook up this gown any longer. I did so like to do that."

Jenny giggled and whispered back to him, "But you never hooked this gown. All you know how to do is unhook it." She kissed his temple then turned back to watch the marine life that changed every second.

Darby was coiling a rope close by and saw them together. He smiled as he always did when catching sight of the two of them. I think there'll be a new mistress for Moss Grove any time now. He chuckled and turned back to his task.

Travis gave orders and then placed Jenny in a dingy and rowed them to the beach. He helped her out and they walked hand in hand up the path to the city of Barbados.

Jenny was mesmerized by the sights and sounds of this magical city. She looked in shop windows and ran to a man selling scones and tea in the square. Travis bought her whatever she wanted, which wasn't very much. A scone, some tea, a pear from an old woman, and lastly a big cherry tart. He laughed as she finished the tart and leaned over to wipe a bit of juice from her chin. He kept thinking about her pure innocence. To be so completely captivated by these small items. Who is this girl? Someday, he hoped to find out.

"Are you ready to go or would you like another tart?" he asked her with a grin on his handsome face.

Jenny giggled and stood up regally, saying, "I could probably eat another, but I must watch my figure."

Travis perused her as she walked out of the cafe. He certainly would watch her figure.

He led her to a small shop off the main street. Here he chose fabrics and various items for gowns. Jenny was in awe of the number of different colors and textures he chose. The little woman measured Jenny from every conceivable angle and when she was finally through, she left Jenny to dress and came out to where Travis stood waiting in the front.

Travis asked about something she had already sewn up, and the old woman produced three gowns that she explained were made for a lady who had recently died, and therefore she would give him a good price for them. Travis handed over the coins and informed her he expected the rest to be delivered to his ship within the week. The lady assured him she could guarantee delivery.

Jenny could not understand a word they spoke as she knew no Spanish. When she again joined them after getting into her gown, she was surprised to see so many packages in his arms. The first thing she thought of was maybe he had bought something to take home to someone else. Oh, why can't I feel safe and secure with him when we are not making love? she thought. Why do I have this feeling that when we are making love, he is only using me?

They didn't say much to each other while they were returning to the ship that evening. Travis attributed her quietness to being tired. When they reached the ship, Travis called to Darby, "Take these to my cabin and escort the lady, will you?"

"Of course, cap'n," Darby replied. Looking at Jenny's pensive mood, he continued: "Was it too much walkin' you made the lass do? She looks 'bout ready to fall down."

Travis looked at her slumping shoulders as she

descended the stairs to his cabin. "Maybe she is tired. Anyway, tell her she may open the packages and select the gowns she wants. If she doesn't want any of them, I'll take them back." He turned and went to inspect the repairs that had begun.

Darby caught up with Jenny as she walked through the cabin door. "I'll get you some hot tea while you select the gowns you want from these." He laid the packages on the table.

Jenny turned to look at the bundles. "What do you mean? Are those for me?"

"Aye, my lady. The cap'n says if you don't fancy one or all of them, he can take them back. He bought these for you."

Jenny's face lit up and she ran to Darby and hugged him. She tore open the boxes one at a time. The gowns were beautiful and she loved each one in turn. She opened a small box and saw gloves and a lace shawl inside. Another big box held a straw bonnet. Still another, a pair of shoes. She couldn't believe these were all for her. She put the shoes on her feet and was surprised at how well they fit. The last box contained a tortoise shell brush, comb, and mirror. Travis never failed to notice what she needed. A thrill ran through her at his thoughtfulness.

Darby, glad to see her smile again, wondered who she thought these things were for. He began to wonder if he had jumped to the wrong conclusions as to the captain's motives toward her. She didn't seem too sure of her relationship with him.

When Travis came down from the deck, he couldn't believe her change in mood. She was dressed in a tan day dress that was piped in chocolate-brown braiding.

When she saw him, she ran to him and hugged him tightly. "Oh! Travis. These clothes and all the rest, they're just wonderful. Thank you so much."

He circled her waist and drew her lips to his. "You've already thanked me, little one."

Jenny thought this an odd statement but contented herself in his arms.

Travis looked over her head at the items spread about his cabin. The cakes of perfumed soap he couldn't resist. The brush, comb, and mirror set he had bought her to spare his own. The small bottle of toilet water he purchased while she was talking to a small boy with a puppy. She was becoming a fixture in his life which he couldn't understand. He wondered how much time he could stay here in Barbados without his crew's threatening him with mutiny.

A knock sounded at the cabin door, and Travis whispered into her ear, "I asked Darby to bring down the tub. I thought you might like a bath with your new soaps."

Jenny stood up on her toes and kissed his cheek. "Oh, Travis, you are so good to me."

Travis smiled and watched her run to admit Darby with the tub and the first of many buckets of hot rain water.

When Darby left a short time later, Jenny quickly undressed and eased her body slowly into the steaming water.

Travis watched her body relax and the hot water put a rosy glow in her cheeks. "You are very beautiful," he said softly.

Jenny opened her eyes slowly to see the undeniable expression he wore. She smiled sweetly at him which seemed to be an invitation.

He wished the tub were bigger so he could join her in her bath, but he knew it just wouldn't work. He stood and picking up a small cake of the perfumed soap, brought it to the tub. "Would you like me to scrub your back for you?"

"That would be nice." Her eyes never left his. He knelt, picked up the cloth and applied soap until a rich fragrant lather formed. Jenny sat up, and he slowly moved the cloth over her back, noting the way her eyes closed at his touch. He gave a low rumbling laugh which brought her attention to him in fiery blue inquiry. "Is something funny?"

He leaned over to her and kissed her moist brow. "I was just thinking that if someone would have told me a year ago that I would be kneeling beside a tub washing a wench's back, I would have told them they had lost their mind. But somehow I think I like this little task—as long as it's your little back I'm scrubbing." He dropped the cloth in the water and stood up. "Now, hurry up. I'd like a bath before the water cools."

Jenny quickly scrubbed the rest of her and stepped out of the tub. She smiled to herself, thinking he had just spoked the first words of love to her even though he hadn't actually said the words she longed to hear. Her spirits rose while she watched him out of the corner of her eye as he stripped the shirt and breeches from his body. He was magnificent: long, lean legs with swelling calf and thigh muscles and a broad chest and back that she loved to touch. As he eased into the tub, she wrapped a towel around her. Then, kneeling down beside the tub, she began to search for the cloth. "Travis, if you will hand me the cloth, I will scrub your back for you."

Travis opened one eye and an amused grin spread across his face. "It's on the bottom. Would you mind getting it? I just want to lie back and relax for a minute."

Jenny looked up to see he had closed his eyes and leaned his head back to rest on the rim. She put her arm into the water and started to search. She couldn't

114

find it on her side of the tub, so she leaned over to search the other side. She gave a small squeak when Travis pulled the towel from around her and let the sensation of her firm, round breasts brush his chest. He reached up and grasped her under the arms to pull her into the tub with him. Her legs were hanging over the side as her bottom settled on his stomach.

"Travis, what are you doing?" She giggled as she tried to get out of his grasp but only made the water splash over the sides of the tub.

"Be still, Elaine, and enjoy the moment." He pulled her to his chest, and she laid her head on his shoulder as the warmth and closeness made them feel very content.

They were quiet, each in their own thoughts. Travis was finding Elaine a joy. She was not adverse to any new experience. He rubbed his hand on her thigh and noted again the silky texture of her skin. He was enjoying her presence more every day. He was going to hate to have to say good-bye to her.

Jenny was thinking back to her childhood and the dreams she had had of her handsome prince. She had finally found him, only he surpassed any dream she had ever had. Lying here in his arms made her feel so safe and secure; so wanted and cherished. She was sorry Elaine had died but so happy that she had survived to be rescued by her knight in shining armor.

The next morning Travis poked Jenny to wake up early. "Come on, wench. I have a surprise for you. Come on, wake up. You'll love it."

Jenny groaned and tried to bury her head under the blanket. Travis ripped the blanket from the bunk and tickled her feet. She threw the pillow at him, but he ducked and began dressing.

"If you're not ready in *fifteen minutes*, I'll leave you."

She sat up and rubbed the sleep from her eyes. All right, but this better be worth it. The sun's just coming up."

As she stretched getting out of bed, he swatted her behind. "Don't worry. I think you'll love where I'm taking you."

They ate a hurried breakfast and then Travis put her in a dingy and rowed toward shore. He didn't go the same way as yesterday but veered to the right. She saw a small cove appear when he turned back toward shore. It was charming. He beached the boat and helped her out. She noticed on a branch a parrot that had so many colors she couldn't count them. While Travis pulled the boat up higher on the shore, she quietly approached this wondrous bird to get a closer look, but when she got too close, the bird squawked and flew away. Turning back to Travis, she saw him leaning against the boat with his legs crossed and his arms folded over his chest, smiling at her.

"Well, what do you think of my surprise?"

Walking up to stand before him, she said, "Oh, Travis, this is a beautiful spot. However did you find it?"

"We stop in Barbados every time we come home. This is, I guess you could say, my favorite place in the world."

"I can understand why." She giggled and placed one delicate white hand on his chest. "Do you know what I feel like doing?"

Smiling at her conspiratorial look, he said, "No, what?"

"I would love to kick off my shoes and go walking in the surf." She looked at the waves lapping the beach. "Do you think anyone would see me?"

Travis had something else in mind. He had thought about it last night when the smallness of the tub disturbed him. In fact, he had thought of nothing else but this day. "My lady, why don't we go swimming." He walked her to the trees that lined the cove. "No one is about, and I've never seen anyone here for as long as I've been coming. No one would see us."

She caught his meaning as he started to unbutton her gown. "But, Travis, you can't be serious. Not out here. You don't know who might come by and see us."

He never stopped his task even though she tried to bat his hands away. "I want to go swimming with you, and, my lady, I usually get what I want."

"But I don't even know how to swim." She laughed with a hint of fear in her voice.

"I'll teach you." He slipped the gown off her and stepped back to take off his own clothes.

Jenny tried to hide herself with her arms and hands and then gave up and ran to the surf, quickly submerged herself up to her neck in the warm water.

Travis joined her just as a wave receded, leaving her bare to the waist. "If Darby could see you now, he would think you really were a mermaid."

"Oh, Travis, don't joke. I feel positively sinful."

"Well, my lady, you look positively delicious to me."

He held her around the waist when a wave almost pushed her over.

The contact made little pinpricks of sensation run along her stomach. She no longer cared who might happen by as they played like two children in the warm sunshine. She dunked him under the water and then ran to the shore when he came up sputtering and coughing.

He quickly regained his footing, wiping the salt water from his eyes, when he saw her running out of the water. He started chasing her and soon caught her from behind, where he tripped her. She went down onto the soft white sand, laughing, and turned over to see his face. He kissed her fiercely while a wave washed over them in foaming abandon.

"You are so beautiful, Elaine." He stroked her wet cheek then let his hand slide down her body that looked like pure alabaster on the still whiter sand.

She lay before his eyes feeling like a queen and began to feel beautiful in his presence. "This is such a beautiful place," she whispered. "Are you sure no one will come upon us?" She touched his cheek with her passion-filled eyes watching him.

"No one. Besides, if someone does, I will be willing to wager they will think it a dream, for you are what dreams are made of this day." He kissed her while another wave almost washed over them, then he quickly picked her up and carried her to his cloak that he had spread on the sand.

He kissed her mouth then moved his lips to capture one pink nipple between his teeth. Gently, he pulled on the taut peak, making her groan and gasp in ecstasy. But when his lips moved on to her stomach and his tongue drew circles around the flat contours and traced one protruding hip bone, she gasped, pulling on his hair, wanting him to stop, yet at the same time wanting to experience everything he could teach her. She began to tingle with new sensations and yearnings.

"My God! Oh, my God, Travis. Travis. You must—stop!" She wailed as she climaxed not once but twice in succession.

He rose up and eased into her then, and she grabbed his buttocks, pulling him into her in rapid drives until he too was panting in the afterglow of climax.

They lay side by side, each feeling the sun on their

flesh and the sand at their backs. The sound of the waves lapping on the shore seemed to beckon them, and again they walked into the sea.

They spent the rest of the day lying on the beach, swimming and eating the picnic lunch Darby had fixed for them.

As the sun was going down, Travis reluctantly suggested they had better get back to the ship. Jenny started to get dressed, feeling that she had just spent the most wonderful day of her life, when she gave a groan of pain as the material touched her sunburned skin.

Travis rushed over to see what had happened, knowing immediately what the matter was. He cursed himself for the fool. She would be in agony for days until the burn healed. "I will get you something to put on that when we get back."

Jenny looked up at him and laughed. "You had better get enough for two. You are as red as I."

He looked at his chest and arms. She was right. He dreaded putting on the tight-fitting breeches but knew they couldn't go back to the ship naked. He gritted his teeth and eased the breeches over his sunburned thighs and buttocks. What a fool I am, he thought.

He helped Jenny into the dingy and pushed them out to sea, groaning everytime he pulled on the oars.

He helped Jenny up the rope ladder, carefully trying not to touch her too roughly. He called Darby over to him and whispered something in the old man's ear, then walked slowly with Jenny to his cabin.

Darby came in a while later with a jar of what appeared to Jenny to be a dark ooze. He put it on the table and turned to them with a roguish grin. "You goin' ta need any help with this?"

Travis scowled at him. "I think we can handle it from here."

Darby rocked back and forth, with his arms folded over his chest. He saw the red, sunburned faces and correctly surmised that the rest of them was in the same shade.

Travis picked up the jar, indicating with a wave of his hand that Darby could leave. Darby ignored the gesture, which did nothing to improve Travis's already sour nature. "Darby, you may leave us now."

Darby stood up straighter and turned to the door. "You'll be wantin' some food. I'll be sure an' knock before I come in." He closed the door, smiling to himself. He could imagine what happened to them. "I would love to've seen it," he mumbled to himself and then slapped himself for such lurid thoughts as he went whistling to the galley.

In a few days Jenny was starting to feel like her old self again. The burn had turned to a rich golden tan. Very unstylish for a woman, but she thought it looked healthier than the pasty white complexions on the *ladies* she had seen.

The clothes arrived from the shop, and Jenny tried every piece on at least twice. Once for herself and again for Travis.

Travis liked watching her change from one outfit to another but wondered at her excitement. He thought it strange for a person of Elaine's breeding and wealth to become so excited over a few rather moderately priced gowns. Eventually, he cast the thought aside and attributed her excitement to her childlike sweetness.

They set sail on the last leg of their journey on a balmy, clear morning in late April. Jenny was so happy and contented, she almost wished this trip would last forever. She had not given any thought about the conclusion of the voyage. In her mind, the natural scheme of events would be for Travis to marry her and they would live happily ever after. She no longer thought about his voicing his love to her. She knew to the depth of her being that he loved her as much as she loved him. The happiness she had felt for the last weeks was so comforting that she never imagined the misery she had endured for so long ever coming back into her life.

Chapter Seven

They were a day outside of Charleston Harbor when Travis came down from the watch to find Jenny standing over three gowns spread across the bunk. "Is there a problem, Elaine?"

Jenny glanced up at him with a look of consternation, which was evident by the way she knitted her brow with one hand holding her chin. "I just can't make up my mind about which outfit to wear tomorrow."

Travis walked over and pointed, saying, "I like this one the best. The dark blue brings out the little sparks of light in your eyes." He pinched her nose, then walked to his desk and sat down.

Pleased with his choice, she folded the other two neatly and laid them in an open trunk. "What time do you think we will get in to Charleston tomorrow?"

Over his shoulder, he replied, "Around two o'clock I would imagine." He wrote something in his ledger and without stoping, asked, "By the way, where do you want your trunks delivered?"

Thinking he was playing with her again, Jenny said, "Oh, the local nunnery would be nice."

Travis laughed then said more seriously, "No, really, I'll be very busy tomorrow so it would help me to know where to send your trunks. Do you have someplace to go or would you like me to get you a room?"

Jenny played along with his game, not yet realizing the full import of his statement. "Oh, I have some-place in mind."

Travis wrote something else in his log, then said, "Well, I wish you would let me in on it. I will need to know before we dock so I can arrange everything."

Jenny turned to stare at his back and realized that he was serious. Turning back around, she held her hand to her breaking heart. If he had slapped her he could not have inflicted a more sudden or heart-wrenching hurt to her.

He is going to dispose of me as he will dispose of his cargo. My God! What will I do? Tears of pain and humiliation stung her eyes. She hadn't thought about her destination since the night she and Travis had become lovers. She had assumed she would be going with him.

Jenny's mind whirled with thoughts. Why should I have assumed anything? He has never said that he loved me. He bought all these beautiful clothes for me as payment for services rendered. What was it he had said when I thanked him for the gowns. "You've already thanked me." My God! He paid me for my services with these clothes. I walked into his arms and let him into my heart, knowing of his vow never to marry. What should I have expected?

Not getting an answer to his question, Travis turned to see her straight back. "Elaine, I asked where you are to go tomorrow so I can make arrange-ments for your trunks to be delivered. Are you listen-ing?"

Pretending to fold the garment she held, she whis-pered, "I'll be staying with my uncle—Col. Jules Colby and his family. I'm afraid I have lost the address, but I am sure someone will know of their

123

whereabouts."

"I know exactly where they live. You should have told me you were the colonel's niece," he stated angrily.

She judged his tone to be directed at her and not at the fact that her living arrangements were unsatisfactory to him. Hanging her head and trying not to let him see the tears that threatened to spill over, she replied, "I guess the subject never came up."

"Well, the colonel and I go back a long way. My plantation is only six miles from his. We share a common border on one side." Travis frowned, not liking this news at all.

Her hurt turned to anger when she thought of him just casting her aside once they reached shore. She looked over at him and declared, "Well *captain*, I'm sure the colonel will repay you for the clothing and the many *kindnesses* you have shown to me. Now, if you will excuse me, I will finish packing."

"I don't want nor expect payment for the things I have given you, Elaine. What's the matter with you, anyway?" Travis did not understand her swift change of mood, and the bitterness that her voice imparted was completely foreign to him. What the devil had he done now to make her upset and obviously angry at him. He marched out of the cabin muttering, "Women!"

Jenny sat down on the bunk and stared at all the trunks. He thinks me a whore. These clothes were my payment. She put her hands over her eyes and cried as she hadn't since the night her father had betrayed her. What will I do now? Go to the colonel's where I must keep up this charade? She felt frightened and alone. She wanted only to be back in the small cottage in Salford with Connie, where she had always felt wanted and loved. Her father hadn't wanted her, except as his good luck charm, and then he still put her up for a wager when he wanted a pot. Now the captain was discarding her, along with his cargo. "Even though I love him with all my heart and soul, he is no different than any other man," she said aloud into the empty cabin.

She cried until there were no more tears or self-pity left in her. Angry with what she thought to be the truth, she sat up with a look of determination on her tear-streaked face. She would go through with this charade, and she would be a constant reminder to the captain of what he could have had. She would get this colonel to give a ball in her honor and invite the captain. She would waltz with every man in town. She would make him remember the days and nights they had spent together. She stood up and threw her shoulders back. She would show him she wasn't the cowering female he thought she was.

With that resolved, she started folding her new gowns, petticoats, chemises, and stays into nice, neat piles to be placed into the trunks. She kept out the smart, navy blue gown Travis had picked. It had closely fitted sleeves with a low neckline. She picked up the saucy little hat that went with the gown and walked to the mirror. How would she make him take her with him tomorrow when they docked? She had a thoughtful expression on her puffy, tear-streaked face when she remembered Travis had said they would only be six miles apart. She would make him want her or she would make him hate her.

She heard footsteps in the passageway and quickly dried her eyes and stood with her back to the door.

Darby knocked on the door and came in. "The cap'n says I'm ta help you get your things together, my lady."

"Thank you, Darby, but as you can see, I'm almost

finished."

Darby had been upset with the captain. He did not appreciate the captain's telling him to make arrangements for the lady's trunks to be delivered to the colonel's. He thought for sure the captain would marry the wee lass when they arrived in Charleston. How could he have been so wrong about him?

"My lady," he said with his hands behind his back and looking down at his boot, "I just wanted to tell you it's been me pleasure to serve you, and if you need any assistance in the future, please call on me."

Jenny felt tears again threaten to spill as she rushed over to him and kissed his cheek. "Thank you, Darby. You have been a true friend, and I will never forget all the things you have done for me."

Darby, a little embarrassed by her show of affection, started to shift his weight, then wiped his nose with the back of his sleeve. "Gee, my lady, I was only doin' the decent thing by ye. You being all alone and stranded like you was. It was me pleasure to make you feel safe aboard the *Sea Breeze*. Besides, I'll be seein' you again. The cap'n tells me you're goin' ta the colonel's. That's just a hop, skip and a jump from Moss Grove."

"Moss Grove? Is that the name of the captain's home?" she asked.

"Aye and it's the most lovely plantation around," Darby answered with pride.

"Darby, would you tell me something about Travis's home?"

"Ah, my lady." He smiled and looked into his memory to the home he now thought of as his own. " 'Tis a grand place. Sits up on a hill with oak trees that seem to grow into the sky. It has a wide portico with six huge white columns facing the Ashley River. The cap'n's father had it built back in 1776. Some say it were to commemorate the winning of the War of Independence—" He suddenly realized the *lady* was British. "Sorry for the reference, my lady."

"That's quite all right, Darby. Please go on."

"Well, Mammy says he built it to celebrate his fathering a fine son to carry on the Gardiner name. I hear tell it was a proud day when Cap'n Gardiner, the first that is, brought his family to Moss Grove for the first time. Mammy will tell stories of those first years at Moss Grove. Perhaps you will meet her while you're in Charleston. You'll like her. Everybody does. And she helped me a lot when I first come to this country with the cap'n."

"I would like to meet her very much, Darby. Do you think I will get a chance?" Such sadness was in her eyes when she looked up at him, but seeing Darby's anguished expression made Jenny hurry to remedy his uneasiness, and she asked, "How did the plantation become known as Moss Grove?"

Relief at not having to commit himself, he said, "Well, Miss Ellen, that be the cap'n's mum, she took one look at the Spanish moss hangin' from all those old oaks and she says, 'Why, it's just like livin' in a moss grove,' and so the cap'n's father says, 'Why that's it. That's the name of our new home.' And it's been Moss Grove ever since."

Jenny thought for a moment, then asked, "Could you tell me anything of Colonel Colby? I've never met him."

"Aye, my lady. 'Tis said, he be a stern man, but I only knows this from others. He and his wife and daughter come over here 'bout twenty years ago from what I heard. He bought some land near Moss Grove and built a huge monstrosity of a house, if you ask me."

"Why do you call it that?" Jenny asked with a

puzzled expression.

" 'Cause it's big and dark and sits on the edge of a swamp. Nobody ever sees anyone 'bout. No one seems to know what the colonel does, either. He don't farm and he don't have no business that anyone can see. The Nigra's, they say his place is haunted and none, save one, will go near his place. Has a big black workin' for him. I can tell you that black man do scare me to death just to think of him."

"What about his wife and daughter?" She thought a minute and then repeated, "I mean my aunt and cousin."

Darby thought this peculiar but made no comment. "Well, no one seems to know much 'bout Mistress Colby. She be a mystery to the women around. Don't socialize much and never goes to town. Their daughter, she does most of the socializin'. I'll see her sometimes struttin' round town."

"You don't like them very much, do you?" Jenny asked quietly.

"Oh, my lady, I don't want you to get the wrong impression. I know they be kin but I don't know much 'bout them is all. Everybody knows just 'bout everything that goes on round Charleston, and it's just queer that no one seems to know nothin' 'bout them is all. They probably just fine people." He patted her shoulder like he was trying to soothe a child.

"You said the Negroes think the colonel's house is haunted. Why?"

Darby didn't know whether to continue or not but decided she should know as much as possible to prepare herself. "The Nigras are a superstitious lot. They hear things at night and see things, then they put meanings to them. Some years back a young mulatto from Moss Grove was seen pickin' berries close to the colonel's. She was never seen again. The

128

town people just put it down as a runaway." Darby scratched his chin whiskers. "The Nigras say she stepped over the boundary, and the colonel's ghosts got her."

"Why that's nonsense. There's no such thing as ghosts." Jenny couldn't imagine that kind of thinking. "What's the name of the colonel's—my uncle's plantation?"

"It be Salford Manor. Named after the part of England the colonel come from."

"Salford!" Jenny's excitement turned to puzzled consternation. She had lived in Salford for fourteen years. She didn't remember any Colby, but the name Salford Manor brought back many happy memories for her and she was glad they had picked it. "So, Salford Manor is my destination."

"Well, it be the social season in Charleston, so you may find the colonel in residence at his townhouse in Charleston."

Standing up to place a gown in a trunk, Jenny smiled at the little man. "We'll just have to find out when we get there, I guess."

Seeing the bravery on the girl's face, Darby quickly added, "Don't you worry none. We'll find the colonel for you."

"Thank you, Darby. I don't know how I will ever repay you for all you have done for me."

"Don't think nothin' of it. I'm sure we'll be seeing you once the cap'n becomes a *landlubber*."

"What do you mean?" Jenny asked quickly.

"Why this be the cap'n's last voyage. Jeff, the cap'n's brother, is living in Charleston now, and the cap'n needs to stay at Moss Grove to oversee the plantation."

"He never told me that."

"The cap'n don't talk much 'bout himself. He's

had a hard road before him most of his life, what with takin' care of Jeff and Celeste for most of his life."

"How old was Travis when his mother and father died?"

"Jest fifteen, but he took hold and did a fine job raisin' those two, and he has the respect and admiration of all the people in Charleston."

Jenny looked up into the friendly face before her. "Darby, thank you for telling me all this. It helps me understand him better."

"The cap'n's not easy but he is fair, and he has had to fight his way himself with no help. This is probably why he is like he is. Independent he is!"

"Yes, I have found that out." With a look of embarrassment, Jenny told of her heartbreak. "Darby, I was so hoping something would come of the captain and myself. I guess he doesn't feel for me the way I feel for him and just used—" She hung her head and cried softly in her misery.

Darby didn't know what to do. He had never been around a lot of women but he couldn't stand to see one cry. "My lady, here, here. Don't cry. I know the cap'n and he'd never hurt you. I *do* believe he has feelings for you but he's just too stubborn or—*stupid* to realize it. You'll see. You'll be close by, and this might not be the end but a beginning for you."

Jenny looked up with hope in her tear-filled eyes. "Do you really think so?"

Darby patted her shoulder again, "Aye. Now you just dry those tears and we'll work somethin' out."

Jenny sniffed and dried her eyes. "Thank you, Darby. I only hope that you are right and something can be worked out." She knew she would never be happy without Travis.

Darby stared at this lovely child. He had such hopes for her and the captain. It wasn't right what the

130

captain was doing. Darby knew they had become lovers and thought the captain would do the honorable thing and marry the child. He knew the captain had said he would never marry but that was before. Travis never had such a lasting relationship with a woman. Of course, Darby realized there was no way he could have gotten away from this one at sea, but the captain was sure different since she came on board.

He left Jenny to her own planning and walked up on deck muttering, "He's so damned stubborn." He hated to see the lady being thrown to the colonel. Darby didn't know that much about Jules Colby but what he did know was enough to make him wonder.

He spotted Travis up on the foredeck and watched him. How could he get the captain and the little lady together? He sensed that the captain was in love with her. Such a change had come over him. It just had to be love. The captain had been pensive and moody most of his life. The last few weeks had seen him whistling and smiling, something the crew was not used to. The little lady had certainly made the captain happy.

The lady . . Darby couldn't quite figure her out either. She sure wasn't snotty like most of the highborn he had run up against. Something in the back of his mind told him she wasn't quite what she represented herself to be. But he knew her to be sweet and kind and full of life which meant more than a title to Darby.

"Yes, I'll have to get those two together somehow," he murmured as he walked toward Travis.

Jenny was sitting at the table later that evening, reading a book of verse Travis had gotten her. She had

131

already determined that tonight would be one Travis Gardiner would not soon forget.

She had taken a long, hot bath and washed her hair with the perfumed soap. She had put on the creamy silk nightgown that was cut extremely low in the front and dabbed perfume behind her ears.

When she heard footsteps in the passageway, she quickly closed the book and went to stand provocatively by the window.

Travis was tired and wet from the spray of the ocean. All he wanted was to go to bed. He hoped Elaine wouldn't be in the mood he had left her. He would like to make their last night together pleasant for each of them.

When he approached the door, he stood momentarily with his hand on the handle. Straightening his shoulders and taking a deep breath, he opened the door. When he came in the cabin, she turned. He smelled the perfume and saw the nightgown he had especially liked molded to her body. She was smiling a seductive smile when she came up to him and started taking off his jacket. She said nothing as her hands unbuttoned and unhooked in a slow, contrived pace.

Travis was breathing heavily by the time she slid his breeches down his muscular legs. When she stood up, he grabbed her by the shoulders and brought her to him. He kissed her with such passion and longing that Jenny's heart soared.

Travis broke his kiss and stepped away to lean down and slowly pull the gown up and over her head. He looked at her golden tanned body for what seemed an eternity, imprinting every detail in his memory.

She was trembling with a burning passion that could only be quenched by him. She went to him as he pulled gently on her hand. She touched his face and his shoulders as though trying to memorize each subtle swell of muscle. When her hands went around to trace the muscles rippling down his back, he lowered his head to plant feathery little kisses on her neck.

She couldn't stand the wanting she felt. She pulled his head down lower to have his lips capture her hardened peak. With a groan, he picked her up and laid her on the bunk where he lay on top of her and quickly directed his shaft into the moist part of her being. They came together in a frenzy, a fast-paced climax of passion and emotions.

He could not seem to get enough of her. His manhood rose within her, and this time he took his time to bring her to a height of ecstasy she had never known before. When she trembled beneath him and screamed for him to take her again, he obliged with a pounding heart and an overwhelming feeling of loss that he could not explain.

Afterward, she lay exhausted beside him. The usual contentment did not come to her as she brushed her hand over the fine spray of hair on his chest. All Jenny could think about was this was it. It was over. He had not said the words she had longed to hear. In fact, he had not said a word to her as their movements had spoken for them. Jenny had almost told him she loved him but held back, the humiliation of his possible rejection making the words freeze on her lips.

As the watch struck four bells, Jenny finally fell into a troubled sleep.

Before first light, Travis was up and directing his crew. The coast of Carolina lay to port, and the day promised to be glorious.

Jenny came up on deck dressed in the blue gown with the little hat perched on top of her now perfectly coiffed hair. She looked beautiful and received more than one baleful stare from the members of the crew.

She stood with her back straight and her head held high while they maneuvered into Charleston Harbor. Jenny was concerned to see so many guns and cannons, which were positioned on both sides of the harbor. To her left she saw majestic trees. Ash, birch, oaks, and towering pines rose to the sky. They sailed through the opening into a natural bay. She could see a river to her left and one almost directly ahead of them. She caught a sense of wonder on seeing the little town emerge in front of her. Church spires, houses, warehouses, and people. Sea gulls swooped and darted above the sails that flapped in the breeze. White clouds moved across the deep blue sky. Colors were so vivid with the blue sky, green trees, and whitewashed buildings. The excitement of her first glimpse of this new land vanished when she thought about what her life would be like from this day forward. What would happen to her? Would this man, Colonel Colby, accept her lie? A tear appeared in her clear blue eyes when she thought of Travis and the way he so casually was dismissing her from his mind, his heart, and his life. Again the dreams of happiness were floating away from her, like smoke billowing into the wind to dissipate in the air.

How she loved this man. She would take the memories of the past two months with her to her new life. She would revel in the thoughts that only she would know.

They were getting close to the wharf, and the people were taking on faces that could finally be discerned. A sadness ran through Jenny as she saw men running along the docks ready to help the *Sea Breeze* rest next to the busy wharf. She stood straighter and, with a determination she had been born with, said to herself, "Lady Seaton, you are about to meet your uncle."

The ship pulled up to the wharf, and Travis came up beside Jenny. "If you will allow me, I will send some men into Charleston to seek out your uncle's whereabouts."

Jenny looked up to his strong face, noticing the uneasiness he exhibited. She reached up and tenderly brushed a hair off his forehead. She fully realized that if she were going to tell him the truth about herself, then now was the time. If she didn't she would be forced to play a role she didn't want to play; fool people who were Elaine's family into thinking she was the lady they thought. But she couldn't tell him now. She couldn't bear to see the disappointment or even rage at being duped which she was sure he would exhibit. So she said instead, "Please and—" She looked away from his eyes. "Will I see you after you are settled?"

He looked at her downturned head. "I'll be busy for a while but I will get in touch with you sooner or later." Why does it hurt so much to know I might never see her again? he thought.

Jenny felt his rejection to the bottom of her soul as he turned from her. He won't get in touch with me. He will take up his old life, forgetting me and our little affair as easily as he had probably done with countless others. I am just another conquest of his, nothing more.

Travis called out to some tars and told them to go ashore and find Colonel Colby. As they ran off, he turned back to Jenny. "I must see to the unloading of my cargo. If I don't see you before you leave—" He looked deeply into her wide blue eyes and pulled her to him for a last kiss. He broke it off and abruptly turned and walked away from her, leaving her feeling confused and alone.

Travis did not want to admit to himself that Elaine was now an important part of his life and that he would actually miss her. He remembered the nights of love and playful wrestling that had preceeded a particularly lively evening. He imagined his hand stroking her soft creamy white skin and the way her hair looked with the moonlight reflecting off its golden shafts. He smiled when he remembered the deserted beach. The way she had looked when she realized he wanted to swim in the nude and how she had eventually abandoned all fears as they played like children in the sea. He remembered her joy at picking out fabrics and hats as if it were something she had never experienced before.

He was so lost in his memories that Darby had called his name three times before touching Travis's sleeve to get his attention.

"Cap'n, the lady's trunks be on the dock."

"All right, Darby, and thank you."

Jenny had walked back to the cabin to make sure she hadn't left anything, and for one last remembrance. She looked at the bunk where she had found love and spent so many beautiful nights in Travis's arms. She spotted a conch shell that Travis had found on the beach. There, in the corner, was where Travis had hung the hammock. She smiled at the memories that contraption brought to her. She remembered the hours she and Darby had spent together, sewing on the blue velvet gown. A tear slowly rolled down her cheek but was quickly wiped away. Today, she would not cry.

She walked back up the companionway and saw Travis talking to a huge black man dressed as a coachman. She then saw a coach at the end of the gangway.

When she approached, Travis turned and introduced her. "Your uncle's servant, Cicero. He will take you to the colonel's residence in Charleston. The colonel is away but is expected this evening. Cicero will tend you until your uncle returns."

Cicero turned to Jenny with a stern, ebony face and said with an equally stern voice, "Your trunks will have to be delivered later. Follow me." He turned and walked down the gangway leaving Jenny to stare after him.

Jenny knew why Darby had said he scared him to death. He was having the same effect on her.

She turned to look at Travis with a smile but said with a tone of a small child saying good-bye to a loved one, "I hope to be seeing you soon." Then she quickly turned so that Travis would not see the tears welling in her eyes and followed Cicero to her new life.

Travis watched her and felt his heart lurch as they drove away. He tried to convince himself that he had done the right thing. He then turned and quickly became engrossed in getting his cargo ashore.

Chapter Eight

Jenny could not remember the drive to the colonel's house. She never noticed the cobblestoned streets, the huge mansions that faced the bay or the intricate designs that separated this city from all others. The tangy salt air and freshness of this city were lost to the girl who was riding in a coach in a strange city to play a role of a great lady. Jenny's thoughts were back on the high seas with her lover and the many moments of happiness that now seemed like only a dream.

When the coach stopped, she sat up straight and prepared for her new role as Lady Elaine Seaton. She would have to put Travis from her mind in order to play this farce out.

The door was opened by Cicero, and she stepped out of the coach and looked around. The house was four stories high but didn't look very wide. She could not see the rest of the house from her vantage point. They walked up the steps to the front door and into a vaulted entrance hall that was so dark she could barely make out stairs and doorways. Cicero lit a taper and proceeded to another room.

"You may wait in here," he said with the same sternness evident in his voice.

She walked into what appeared to be a library. He entered before her and lit some candles, revealing a long narrow room that was filled with bookshelves from floor to ceiling, but they contained only a few books. Small odds and ends of mismatched furniture were scattered about in no apparent order. There were several long windows, but they were covered by heavy velvet drapes. Jenny walked over and began to open them, to let in some of the bright sunshine, when Cicero came up behind her and jerked them closed again.

Looking down at her, he stated, "The colonel don't want these open."

Jenny was perturbed and a little frightened by this man's manner. "But, it's so dark in here."

"I am following the master's orders and you," he said, pointing a finger at her, "had better do the same."

Shocked, she sat down on a velvet settee. Cicero walked out, closing the doors behind him. She thought about what Lady Elaine would do in this situation and decided she would do what she wanted and *hang* Cicero. She stood up and walked over to the windows, throwing back the drapes.

The window faced a small garden in an overgrown, mismatch of color. It was obviously not cared for with azaleas of various shades allowed to grow into each other. Tulips and daffodils looked strangled, but Jenny had the feeling that once this had been a lovely place to enjoy. The thought was somehow soothing to Jenny's jangled nerves.

She did not hear the door open behind her and was startled when a black hand came in front of her and pulled the drapes closed with a jerk.

Cicero stood before her and declared with a scowl on his face, "I done told you, the colonel don' want dese open."

Jenny looked him in the eye, noting his speech was changed from his precise diction to a more slurred one. "Do you treat all the colonel's guests this way?"

Again, using the precise diction, he looked down his wide nose at her. "The colonel doesn't have any *guests*." He turned and walked to a table in front of the velvet settee. He poured tea out of a chipped teapot into a mismatched cup and saucer. He gazed up at her with what Jenny assumed to be a daring expression, then stood up, throwing back his huge shoulders. "I hope this will be enough for you. I will tell the colonel you are here when he returns."

Jenny decided to test her authority over this man. "Cicero, I would like to be shown to my room. I feel like a nap." She removed her gloves, not looking at him.

"You will have to wait until the colonel returns." He closed the door behind him, effectively cutting off any further conversation.

Jenny marched to the door, determined to tell the big oaf just what she thought of him. She turned the handle and discovered she was locked in. Pounding on the door with all her might did nothing to summon him. She listened as silence filled the room.

What was happening here? Was she being held a prisoner in this house? But that was absurd. Why would a servant take it upon himself to lock her into a room? She knew nothing of this Jules Colby, but if he were related to Elaine he must be at least civilized.

She paced the room, her shadow becoming distorted everytime she passed the candle, sending the flame dancing in all directions. If she were a prisoner, what could possibly be the purpose of locking her in here? Was it to keep her in or keep something out? What about the windows and keeping them closed up?

"This is crazy," she said aloud in her frustration. She looked around the decaying room and said, "If he wants a fight, I'll give him one."

Determined that this man would not get the best of her, she turned and once again went to the windows to throw open the drapes. "I'll show you, you big ox." She walked to the other window and threw those drapes aside as well. This window faced the direction of the front where they had originally arrived. She saw Cicero moving the carriage into a side entrance. He looked up and saw her face in the window so she smiled and waved to him. "You think you can get the best of me? Hah!" She turned and went back to the settee and drank some of the tea, hoping this would calm her. She had never been so angry.

She felt eyes on her and looked up to see Cicero's face outside staring at her with a grin on his black face. He leaned to his left then his right and closed the outside shutters with a bang. He then went to the other window that faced the garden and did likewise.

"Why you!" Jenny screamed and jumped up to run to the window. She tried to push up the sash but discovered the windows had been nailed shut. What could she do? "When the colonel comes in, I will tell him what Cicero has done and have him discharged. He obviously has overstepped his authority. To treat a guest in this manner is outrageous! He won't get away with this!" She was breathing heavily as she returned to the settee and drank some more of the tea. The tea tasted bitter but it seemed to be helping. She noticed the way her breathing had calmed and her hands were no longer shaking. She felt sleepy. So sleepy. She

141

decided she would just close her eyes for a moment. That was the last she knew.

Travis was overseeing his men and watching the unloading of the cargo when he heard his name shouted and turned. Up the gangway came a young man with dark brown hair and black eyes. His waistcoat was dark brown over tan knee breeches with white stockings. He ran to Travis and embraced him as a long lost friend.

"Jeff, you look prosperous and well." Travis gleamed while his young brother smiled and pumped his hand.

"I'm so glad to see you. We've had some pretty bad storms lately, and I was afraid you would get caught in one."

"We did, but we only suffered minor damages. We did encounter the remains of the H.M.S. *Himes* that unfortunately did not fare as well."

"Everyone lost?" Jeff asked with concern evident in his voice.

"No, we picked up one survivor. A lady." Travis's expression turned to one of longing that did not escape Jeff's attention.

"What was this *lady* like, Travis? An old hag with a wart on her nose?"

Travis smiled at Jeff and changed the subject. "How about a brandy? I'm almost finished here and Darby can handle the rest."

"Where is that old geezer anyway?" Jeff looked around with a devilish grin on his handsome face.

Looking around for Darby, Travis smiled at the reference to the old man. "Oh, he's here somewhere." Travis then saw Darby down by the wharf personally seeing to the loading of Elaine's trunks on an open dray. His happy mood at seeing his brother again vanished at the sight of Elaine's trunks. Again, the memories assailed him.

Jeff leaned over the railing and called to Darby.

Darby turned to see Travis and Jeff standing side by side up on deck. He told the driver the address and turned to hobble up the gangway. Jeff met him and hugged the old man with affection. Darby hugged Jeff tightly and overwhelmed himself at the depth of feeling he had acquired for the boy. He quickly stepped back from Jeff's embrace. "Mr. Jeff, how you been? You look good."

"Darby, you old coot, you haven't changed since the day I met you. Let's see—why it's been fifteen years."

Darby gazed up at Jeff. "Aye, but you, you young scalawag, have done enough changin' fer both of us. Why when I first saw you, you was a skinny little clabber-headed kid with too much bull in you." Darby stepped back and put his hand to his chin as he gazed at Jeff and grinned. "Why now you are a *big* clabber-headed kid."

Jeff laughed and put his arm across Darby's shoulder telling the man, "Darby, don't ever change. You are the only thing I can count on to remind me of my past indiscretions."

Travis recovered from his memories in time to hear this last remark and smiled at the bantering twosome. "If you two are quite through insulting each other—" He smiled. "Darby would you finish up here? Jeff and I have some things to discuss in my cabin."

"Aye, cap'n. I'll take care of everythin for ye."

"I'll see you later, you banty rooster you." Jeff said over his shoulder while he followed Travis to the companionway.

Darby watched the two brothers descend the stairs.

They looked so much alike, yet they were so different. Travis was all seriousness while Jeff had always been fun loving and a scrapper. Darby remembered more than one occasion when Travis was rousted out of bed to come get Jeff out of one scrap or another. To think with all the trouble that boy had with the law that he would become a lawyer. Darby shook his head and turned to yell at a sailor to get cracking.

In the process of pouring brandy into the glasses, Travis asked Jeff quietly, "How'd it happen, Jeff?"

Jeff's smile vanished and he lowered his head, knowing exactly what Travis was talking about. "It happened so fast, Travis. We didn't know what to do."

"Tell me everything. When I set sail she was fine."

Jeff hung his head and started to tell Travis the anguishing facts surrounding Celeste's death. "We had come into town so Celeste could see a new doctor who had just arrived from Philadelphia. I took her but he concurred with everyone else that nothing could be done about her legs. We came back to the Tradd Street house, and I left her with that Negress, Lulu, while I went to my office to catch up on some paperwork. Anyway, you know how Celeste loved the garden? Well, she talked Lulu into taking her out to sit among the flowers. It was cool but there wasn't much wind. Lulu evidently left Celeste out there while she went to buy some food or something. Anyway, while she was gone a shower came up. Celeste was left out in the rain for an hour. She was soaked through when I found her sitting there."

"Didn't she call for help? Where the hell was Lulu for an hour?" Travis asked in exasperated pain.

"Celeste said she had called until her voice was raw." Jeff swallowed the lump in his throat and

144

continued. "She developed a fever that night. I called a doctor but he said it was consumption and he could do nothing. She opened her eyes and smiled at me, then just closed them and went to sleep. She never woke up. As for Lulu, she never returned. Simples made several inquiries but it was as if she just vanished. The stupid girl is probably afraid to show her face but if I ever find her I swear I'll put the lash to her like no one has ever seen before!" Jeff put his head on his hands. "It's all my fault, Travis."

Travis walked over to Jeff and placed his hand on his brother's shoulder. "Of course it wasn't your fault, Jeff. She wouldn't want you to tear yourself up like this."

Jeff looked up at his brother with tear-filled eyes. "I went off the deep end after she died. I was drunk for a week."

"Is that why Simples wrote me the news?"

"Yes. He took care of everything. I was no good to anyone."

Travis walked over and poured another brandy and gave it to Jeff. "Drink this and then we will talk no more of it." He smiled reassuringly at his once carefree brother, feeling Jeff's pain along with his own.

Jeff drank the burning liquor in one gulp and rubbed his eyes. "What are your plans now that you're determined to settle down?"

"I just received a note from my agent saying he has a prospective buyer for the *Sea Breeze*. I'm supposed to meet with him sometime this afternoon. After that's finished I plan to go to Moss Grove and see what's left after your managing." He smiled at his brother.

Jeff sat up straighter and with a show of pride, said, "I think you will be pleasantly surprised at how I've handled Moss Grove in your absence. I have implemented a few changes and I have a proposition to offer to you."

Travis looked dubious. "What kind of changes?"

"Well—" Jeff's chest blew out and he put his thumbs in his waistvest pockets." You know that old barn down by the river that we used to cure tobacco in?"

Travis nodded.

"Well, I patched up the holes and put a new floor in it—"

"Why would you fix up that old thing?" Travis interrupted in obvious confusion.

"I put a cotton gin in it."

"A cotton gin!" Travis scowled. "But, why?"

"Settle down and hear me out. I figured we were losing money by shipping raw cotton down the river to have someone else gin it and then shipping it back up river for processing. After all, Travis, you're the one who won't own slaves, and our free men didn't like pickin' the seeds out by hand. It was only natural to pay someone to do it. My idea took that payment away. Now we gin it ourselves and can ship directly to the mills up river in Columbia and Greenville."

Travis still looked skeptical. "And just how much did this idea of yours cost me?"

Standing up, Jeff walked over and picked up a conch shell from the cabinet and put it to his ear. Turning to Travis once again with smugness in his expression, he said with pride, "That's the beauty of my plan. I have already recouped our original investment and now we're making a profit."

"How's that possible? You've only had one season to do it in."

"Well, the other plantation owners around us were so impressed that I have contracted with them to gin their cotton, too. After it's ginned I make the arrangements to have it shipped to the mills."

"Are you telling me you've become a factor?"

"Yes, and that brings me to my proposition. I would like to handle all your cotton deals personally all the way to the mills." Jeff smiled, awaiting Travis's decision.

Travis watched the play of emotions on Jeff's face, so like his own. "Well, Jeff, if what you tell me is true, I would be a dolt not to hire you."

Jeff extended his hand and the brothers shook on it. "How about meeting me for dinner tonight, and we'll celebrate our new business arrangements?"

"All right. Let me finish up here and I'll meet you back at the Tradd Street house, shall we say—" He looked at the clock on the wall. "About seven?"

Jeff stood up and walked to the door. "You've got it, big brother. Should I arrange for some female companionship?" Jeff's smile turned down when he saw the sad expression on Travis's face.

"No, I don't think so. Just you and me, all right?"

Jeff couldn't understand what was with Travis but decided not to push it. "All right, you're the boss." He waved before he walked up on deck.

Jeff saw Darby standing by the railing, watching the crew unload the cargo. He walked over and placed his hand on the old man's shoulder. "Darby, what's with Travis? He just turned down an evening with a woman. I know how he usually is when he comes home from one of his voyages. What's with him?" He looked at the little man, but when Darby didn't make a comment, Jeff added, "Listen here, old man, I remember the days when the good ladies of Charleston would lock their daughter in their rooms when they heard the *Sea Breeze* was back in port."

Darby looked up into Jeff's puzzled face. "Me thinks the cap'n don't want no one, 'ceptin' maybe the lady he just said good-bye to."

"You mean the lady you rescued?"

"Aye. She be the prettiest, sweetest woman I ever did see."

Jeff looked back to the companionway with an all-knowing look. "So Travis has finally been bitten by old lady love. Who'd a guessed it?"

"I don't think the cap'n knows it," Darby stated.

"Well, maybe we should help him to realize it." Jeff gazed at Darby with a conspiratorial grin.

Darby saw the old Jeff coming to the surface and quickly said to dispel any shenanigans, "Maybe we should just let matters run their course. I'd hate to do anything that might hurt the lady."

Jeff realized that his brother wasn't the only one smitten and clapped Darby on the back. "Just let me know if I can help. I have to go now, but I'll see you later." He walked with a bouncy step while he left the deck and started down the gangway. He stopped midway down and turned to Darby with a broad smile. "I'll sure have to meet this wonderous lady who had turned old sea dogs like you into persian kittens."

Darby watched him leave, hoping Jeff wouldn't do anything stupid.

Just as Jeff's coach departed, Darby noted another carriage pull up beside the ship. Darby was surprised to see Colonel Colby get out and walk up the gangway.

The colonel spotted Darby and came up to him, saying, "I'm here to see Captain Gardiner. Please inform him I have arrived." He turned as though Darby were of no significance and looked about the deck.

Darby looked the fat man up and down, then turned to Rodney Daniels and asked him to fetch the captain.

The colonel was walking around the deck inspecting this and that when Travis came up on deck. "Colonel Colby? To what do I owe this visit?"

The colonel turned and said, "Gardiner, I understand you were informed by your agent that I would be coming by this afternoon to negotiate the sale of your ship."

"I was informed that *someone* was coming, but I'm afraid my agent didn't specify *who* it would be."

"Well, I'm here to buy your ship. Is there somewhere we could go to settle this matter promptly?"

Travis indicated the direction of the companionway. "My cabin. Would you follow me?"

Colby walked behind Travis as Travis led the way to his cabin. Colby's small eyes darted right and left, making notes in his mind as to the changes that would be required.

Inside the cabin, Travis offered his guest a drink. "No, thank you. This won't take long." Colby took some papers out of his breast pocket. "I believe the price you are asking is twenty-five thousand. You will find a bank draft for that amount in here. If you will sign the bill of sale, I will trouble you no longer."

Travis was anxious to have this obnoxious fop off his ship and glanced quickly at the papers. He could not decline as the colonel had met his terms. He picked up the quill and quickly signed his name. He wondered what the colonel was planning to do with the *Sea Breeze* but knew it was none of his business. Besides, it wouldn't take long to find out if the information became necessary.

The colonel gave Travis the bank draft and walked out the door. When they reached the deck, he turned to Travis and with a perfunctory wave, said, "I trust you will vacate the ship promptly. I must have it ready to sail quickly."

Travis glared at the pompous man, whom Elaine

was to live with, and felt a wave of apprehension that almost overwhelmed him. "I will be off the ship this afternoon. You may do whatever you wish after that."

As the man walked down the gangway, Darby approached the captain. "Did he know about the lady?"

Still watching the progress of the colonel, Travis shook his head. "No, at least he didn't mention it, and I didn't say anything to him." He turned and walked back to his cabin to collect his belongings.

Late that same afternoon, with his crew paid and dispatched, Darby and Travis were about to leave the *Sea Breeze* for the last time, when a grim, bewhiskered man came up the gangway, ordering some men on the dock to bring his trunks on board. Travis knew this man. He had run up against him before. "Capt. Nathaniel Quartermaine. I'm afraid this ship has been sold or are you just visiting?" Travis did not try to hide the contempt he felt for this man.

The foul-smelling man approached them. "This ain't no visit, Gardiner. I be the new cap'n of this here tub." He wrinkled his hairy nose while he looked around the clean deck.

Surprise registered on Travis's face. Quartermaine was known to be an unscrupulous man. Travis hoped Colby knew what he was doing hiring a blackguard like Quartermaine to captain his ship.

Travis leaned away from the man, asking, "What are you going to be doing with the *Sea Breeze*?"

"That's no longer any concern of yours, Gardiner." He spat tobacco juice onto the deck, then continued: "I was told you'd be gone this afternoon. Why are you still here askin' questions?"

"I was just leaving." Travis turned and swept the

decks with his eyes one last time. Turning back to the man who was to command his beloved ship in his place, he gave a mocking bow and said, "Good-bye, Quartermaine." He then turned and left his ship with an uneasy stride.

Darby was concerned, too. Quartermaine had run a ship a ground, full of Nigras he had been smuggling in. All had perished except Quartermaine and a few of his crew. The man was evil. Darby felt a chill run up his spine when he looked back to the *Sea Breeze* for the last time. To think she would become a slave ship; for Darby knew that would become her fate.

Just as the carriage started to move away from the wharf, he turned and gazed one last time at the ship that had been his home for all these years, a foreboding in his spirit.

Their carriage pulled up in front of the Tradd Street house, and Travis was surprised at the lack of light coming from the windows in the late afternoon gloom. "Where are the servants?" he said to no one in particular.

Opening the door with his key and stepping into the foyer, he noticed the dust covers on the furniture. The house looked bleak until Darby went around opening the drapes. Travis walked up the stairs and entered Celeste's room where he found everything exactly as he remembered it. Her clothes were still in the press. Her perfume bottles still sat on the dresser. He walked over and opened a delicate bottle that contained her favorite scent and let the fragrance assail his senses. All the memories of her rushed in on him. He walked to the window and turned to look back at the bed-chamber. The canopied bed was covered with a drab muslin spread to save the white organdy counterpane. He sat down on a small chair, the scent of the perfume he held in his hand again assailing him.

He thought about the Christmas when he had given Celeste her first bottle of perfume. She had been twelve and skinny but with a bloom about her big dark brown eyes. Although her hair was light and his and Jeff's was dark, they all had the same dark brown eyes. He remembered Mammy scolding him for giving her baby perfume at such an early age, but Celeste had been thrilled with her gift, knowing that Travis felt her to be old enough.

A smile touched his lips when he remembered her first cotillion. She had looked so beautiful in the white gown that he had brought back from Paris. Mammy had only to take up a little in the bodice to make it fit. He remembered staring up at her as she slowly came down the stairs, trying so hard to look sophisticated. He had been so proud of her. And that night he had stood by while she had danced every dance with one boy after another. He remembered the feeling he had when she came up to him for the last waltz and told him, "I have saved this dance for you." He had felt like her father, brother, and friend in that one moment.

One memory seemed to make another. He couldn't quite grasp the reality of her death. She had been so full of life, so caring.

The day he saw her coming up from the river with her skirt held out in front of her.

"What have you got there, Celeste?" He had noticed the tears in her eyes.

"Oh! Travis," she had wailed, "someone tied these poor little kittens in a sack and threw them in the river." She had opened her skirt to show him five tiny kittens nestled within the confines of her skirt.

Travis had gotten down from his horse and gone to inspect her find. "Why, Celeste, they're only a few days old. How will you feed them?"

With a look of determination on her pretty face, she had answered, "I will find a way and I will not lose a one of them!"

She hadn't either. She had kept them in the barn and fed them goat's milk from the tips of her fingers until her fingers would wrinkle like dried plums.

Travis's thoughts turned to the day of the accident and all the happy times seemed to fade when he remembered her valiant effort to regain the use of her legs.

Darby found him sitting there on the small chair by the window. "Cap'n?" He walked in, feeling Celeste's presence around him. Tentatively, so as not to disturb her, he walked over and placed a hand on Travis's shoulder. "Cap'n, you shouldn't be sittin' up here in the dark."

Travis gave no indication he had heard him. Darby was about to leave when Travis looked up and said softly, "She was so beautiful. I hope she can be happy now."

Darby didn't like the vacant look Travis presented him. "Cap'n, 'course she is. Now come on out of here. Miss Celeste won't be happy if'n she sees you broodin' like this." Darby put his hand under Travis's arm and pulled him up.

Travis looked down at the worried man before him. "You are so right, Darby. She wouldn't." He walked out to the hallway, leaving Darby to close the door gently behind him.

As Darby was about to do just that, he looked again into the room. He gasped when he saw Celeste's smiling face looking at him. He closed his eyes, and when he looked again, the face was gone.

Jenny awoke with a start. Someone was in the

room. She sat up and looked around but saw no one. She looked toward the window and saw the drapes had once again been drawn closed. Getting up, she walked over to the window, pulling the drapes apart slightly., She saw the night sky filled with brilliant stars. She turned and walked slowly back to the settee. "Why, I must have slept for hours."

She heard voices coming from just outside the door. She was just standing up again when the door opened to admit a little man with a rotund belly coming toward her. He stretched out his arms and gave her a hug.

"Why, Elaine, what a beauty you are."

Jenny knew this man must be the colonel and offered her cheek to his kiss. "Thank you, uncle. I must thank you for the kind invitation."

He smiled at her, saying, "Think nothing of it, my dear. It is the least I could do for my favorite brother's daughter."

Favorite, Jenny wondered, but her concern at being accepted as Elaine began to vanish as the man preened in front of her. Holding her hand the colonel stood back, an if in appraisal of her worth.

"I think you favor Jerome. Yes, especially the mouth. I would have known you anywhere, my dear."

Jenny gave an inaudible sigh of relief at his words. She quickly decided this man did not remotely favor Lady Elaine, but she felt safe, at least for the time being.

Jules Colby was small in height but his protruding belly told Jenny he enjoyed the finer things in life. He was dressed in gray knee breeches with white stockings and black, shiny shoes. His expansive waist was skirted by a bright red cummerbund and a darker gray waistcoat fit snugly over a ruffled shirt. His hair was long for the style Jenny was used to, and his side whiskers were closely cropped to his jawline. His puffy cheeks were rosy and his smile was, to Jenny, a little forced.

Jenny decided to tell this man of the treatment she had received while he had been absent. "Uncle, I hate to bring this up at this time, but do you know I have been a prisoner in this room since my arrival this afternoon?"

"Nonsense, my dear. Cicero just wanted to be sure of your comfort. The rooms upstairs are rather in disarray, and he wasn't sure which room I had picked out for you."

"So he locks me in this room?" She felt her anger rise. "I am sure some other form of constraint could have been found, like telling me he didn't know which room I was to use. Really, I think he should be reprimanded."

"Of course, my dear, but Cicero is a very conscientious servant, and I'm sure he only wanted you to be comfortable."

"But he wouldn't even let me open the drapes to bring in some light and when I did, he shut the outside shutters."

"Come, come, Elaine. You must realize that these Nigras do exactly what they are told. They don't have the wherewithall to differentiate tasks. I told him that I didn't want the drapes open because the sun damages the furniture and of course he took it to mean ever. I will talk to him about it."

Jenny wasn't sure if she believed his explanation but could only hope the colonel was right. The Colonel continued: "My dear, I know you must be tired after your long journey, so I will show you to your room and have a tray sent up. We will catch up on all the news tomorrow." He held the door for her and picked up the candelabra from a side table in the entrance hall. On the second floor, he showed her to what would be her room. Her trunks were perched by the window, and her valise was on the bed.

As he lit a candle, the colonel said, "This is Eudora's room."

From what Jenny could see, Eudora was not a frivolous person. There was a small bed with a plain counterpane, a small bedside table with a candelabra on it which the colonel had lit, and a plain desk with no mirror. A chifforobe stood in a corner with a washbasin and pitcher on a stand next to it. The only feminine part of the room were the frilly white organdy curtains covering the closely shuttered window.

The colonel interrupted her perusal. "Will you need assistance with your toilette, my dear?"

"No, thank you, uncle, but I would like someone to move the trunks so I may open the window. It is rather stuffy in here."

"Of course, I'll send Cicero at once. Now I will say good night." He closed the door, and Jenny thought again what an odd decor for a girl's room.

She went to her valise and pulled out the nightgown and slippers she had packed this morning. Pulling out the tortoise shell brush and mirror that Travis had surprised her with, saying, "So you won't have to use mine," gave Jenny a sad, wistful feeling. Maybe he will come to take me away. "Please God, make him come for me," she whispered.

She laid the brush and mirror by the washbasin and sat on the bed. There was a knock on the door, and a little black woman with wrinkled skin and a slit of a mouth came into the room carrying a tray. She said nothing as she put the tray on the desk and backed out of the room.

Jenny stood up quickly and called to the woman but the woman didn't seem to hear her, closing the door on Jenny.

She had wanted to ask if Cicero would be up shortly to move the trunks. She would have to see about that later.

She was surprised to discover she was really hungry, not having eaten since breakfast that morning. She went over to the desk to inspect the tray and saw a piece of meat that looked boiled, potatoes and peas mixed together in some type of sauce, and a piece of dry, crusty bread. Nothing looked very appetizing but Jenny ate the entire meal.

Pouring a cup of steaming hot tea, she decided to get ready for bed while it cooled, but she really wasn't tired after her long nap this afternoon.

She pulled the counterpane down and then walked over to the desk, picking up the now slightly cooled tea. She brought it back to the bed and sat the cup on the bedside table. As she adjusted the pillows so she could sit up in bed, she discovered a bedbug in the sheets. She quickly brushed it off the bed and stepped on it, then ripped the sheets from the bed. She saw nothing and decided it was the only bug, so she made up the bed and sipped her tea.

She was thinking how she would probably never sleep tonight. The eccentricity of this house and its occupants caused Jenny to feel a wave of apprehension. The servant, Cicero, was menacing and seemed to like his role as guardian of this house and its contents. He didn't seem to be witless like the colonel tried to picture him.

Jenny perused the room she was now occupying. Nothing of Eudora's personality was seen in the austere furnishings. This room, like the library, was just taking up space in this house. It seemed no one had given the slightest amount of thought to the inside. *Functional* was the only word that came to mind. Chairs to sit on, beds to sleep on, and tables to eat and write at. No pictures adorned the cracked, plaster walls. No statuary or other bric-a-brac to give some clue as to the personality of its occupants.

Jenny recollected the meeting with the colonel: a man of probably two score and ten who reminded Jenny of a robin with his expansive girth encompassed in its red cummerbund. He seemed genuinely pleased to have her here but the forcefulness of his smile and actions seemed a bit overstaged. What would her stay here be like? What would have been Elaine's reaction to this house and its residents.

Jenny knew her role to be tenuous. She had made several blunders on board the *Sea Breeze* that Travis hadn't caught. Jenny began to question the wisdom of taking Elaine's role as her own. If someone found out, what would they do to her? Would they send her back to Eden Hall?

Her mind whirled in different directions as the possibilities of her predicament were brought home to her.

With shaking hands, Jenny picked up the cup of tea and sipped at the strong, bitter brew, hoping it would calm her troubled heart. She was in a most difficult position.

Why hadn't she been brave enough to tell Travis the truth from the beginning? She couldn't see his throwing her overboard or taking advantage of her status. He had dismissed her easily enough when thinking her a *lady*. She could only assume it would have been thus if he had known the truth. She gave a sigh as her body started to relax of its own accord. She had started this charade to keep form going back to Sir Reginald. She knew that with all aspects of her situation before her, she was too much of a coward to tell the truth. If she received a modicum of freedom with this ruse, then she would take it.

While her mind whirled with all the possibilities of her fate, her eyes grew heavy, her head slumped, and her tea cup rolled off the bed with a crash. A crash she never heard. She never heard her door open or the footsteps as someone came in and took the tray and the shattered cup away.

Chapter Nine

The next morning, Jenny awoke with an aching head and a rather sluggish spirit. She went to get out of bed and, finding her legs unable to support her, she fell back on the bed. "What's the matter with me?" she wondered aloud. She had never felt like this before. She felt herself about to become ill and reached for the chamberpot. After losing the contents of her stomach, she felt instantly better. "It was probably that awful food from last night," she muttered. Getting up, she did indeed feel much improved.

She opened a trunk on the top of a pile, noting that they had never been moved, and pulled out a tan gown piped in dark brown. It was a day dress, suitable for morning wear. It would be better than the blue traveling gown that still lay in a chair where she had placed it last night. After completing her morning toilette, she walked to the door. About to open it, she heard a key turn in the lock and pulled it open to find Cicero outside in the hall.

"What are you doing lurking outside my bedchamber?" Jenny felt instantly defensive, noticing the big, hulking man perusing her state.

"The master wants you to come down for break-

160

fast." He turned and walked away from her without a backward glance.

Looking at the door from the outside and inside, Jenny noticed something peculiar. The door could only be locked from the outside. "How strange." She had been locked into the bedchamber last night. Why? All the feelings of apprehension returned as she slowly descended the stairs.

Arriving in the dining room, she noticed the servants entering with dishes of steaming eggs and plump round sausages, baked bread that gave off an aroma of yeast and steaming pots of freshly brewed tea. This room, like her bedchamber of last night and the library, was sparsely furnished.

The colonel was already seated and rose to help Jenny to her chair. The servant, the woman of last night, offered her each dish with a scowl on her face. Jenny was at least relieved to see this meal was more attractive and flavorful than the one of last night.

The colonel talked with his mouth full of food and gestured with a fork in one hand and a knife in the other. "Your aunt and cousin will be so happy to have you at last. The crossing took longer that I expected. From your message, I assumed you would have been here a month ago." He stuffed another sausage into his already filled mouth and added, "I trust you had a pleasant trip on the *Himes?*"

Jenny sat back, not looking at the disgusting spectacle of this man spitting food in all directions. She wondered why Cicero hadn't informed him of her arrival on the *Sea Breeze*. "I did not arrive on the H.M.S. *Himes*, uncle, but on a ship out of Charleston, the *Sea Breeze*."

"What's this? Your message said passage had been arranged on the *Himes*."

Jenny lowered her head as she said, "The H.M.S.

161

Himes is at the bottom of the ocean, and I was its only survivor. The *Sea Breeze* rescued me from certain death a few days afterward."

"But how unfortunate for you, my dear." He seemed to be thinking of other problems than hers.

Jenny noted the disappointment he displayed rather than the shocked horror or even concern at her predicament she had expected.

He looked up at her with expectation evident. "That is why you are unaccompanied. I had thought it rather odd that you arrived with no servant to take care of you."

Again, Jenny noted the disappointment in his manner.

He continued: "So you have met the invincible Capt. Travis Gardiner, heh?" He thought it odd that Gardiner hadn't mentioned this when he saw him yesterday. "It is a small world. I trust he treated you well and that he did not try any indiscretions?" At her look, he knew something was amiss. His fork and knife poised in expectation as he looked at her, awaiting her response.

Jenny took note of the wide eyes and poised manner, almost as if he were waiting to hear a bit of juicy gossip. "The captain treated me well and I look forward to seeing him again, so that I may repay him for the items he purchased for me in Barbados."

"What items are you talking about?"

"Why all my clothing and possessions were lost with the sinking of the *Himes*. The captain graciously bought everything I have with me."

The colonel resumed eating and as if in dismissal, continued, "You won't have to bother the captain, Elaine. I will send a messenger over with the funds to repay him."

Jenny didn't want this man to ruin her chance to

see Travis again and quickly said, "I would prefer to do it in person, uncle. He was very kind to me, and a personal thank you would be better than to have a stranger handle it."

"Don't you worry your pretty little head about such matters. *We* are going to take care of you from now on."

Jenny didn't like the sound of this and, putting on her best air of the lady, stated, "Uncle, if you will be so kind as to send a message to my banker in London, I am sure you will be amply repaid for all your trouble." She paused, trying to decide how best to test her position, then said, "After all, I will *not* be staying here that long. And, I really don't need to have you take care of me. I have been taking care of myself quite well for many years."

He smiled, showing bits of sausage between his teeth. "My dear, I am your only living relative, and I think I know better than you how to handle your affairs."

Jenny felt a wave of panic rise in her. This man was trying to control her, run her life, make her decisions. She started to deny this man's relationship to her when out of the corner of her eye she saw movement in the hall. Looking over, she was surprised to see that Cicero was carrying one of her trunks outside.

"Are we to leave for your plantation today?" she asked, hoping that this aunt would be a better ally.

Jules Colby looked up in the direction her eyes had traveled. "I thought that it would be best. I have to remain here a few days, but Cicero will take you there as soon as you finish breakfast. After all, your aunt and cousin are so looking forward to your visit, and I'm sure you will be more comfortable there."

A little unsettled by these latest developments and feeling she was being rushed, Jenny replied, "I wish

163

you had told me so I could have prepared. This gown is not suitable for traveling."

"The gown you're wearing is just fine, Elaine," he said without looked at her.

Seeing the woman carrying her valise outside, she got up out of her chair, "Wait!" she called to the woman, but the woman didn't seem to hear her.

"What's the matter, Elaine?" Jules asked.

Jenny looked down at him, feeling herself being propelled into the eye of a storm. What was happening around here? "I—I have to get my gloves and hat out of those trunks."

"You will be in a closed carriage, Elaine, No one will see you." Jules whined like he was talking to a disagreeable child.

Jenny sat down, holding her shaking hands in her lap so he wouldn't notice. I am being held prisoner. Why?

Jenny jumped when Jules placed his pudgy hand on her shoulder, saying, "It's time to go, my dear."

Looking up, she saw his smiling, almost comical face which seemed a mask. She stood, allowing him to lead her into the hall and out of the door. Cicero was already seated on the driver's seat. The door was barely closed before the carriage started on its way to Salford Manor and an uncertain future for Jenny.

Jenny turned to look at the outside of the house, just as the carriage started to move. The house was beautiful on the outside. The hedges were manicured and the grounds kept up. She remembered the enclosed garden that she had viewed yesterday which was overgrown in its confinement. The inside of the massive house was sparsely furnished with odds and ends. Nothing seemed to be right. It was almost as if the house itself were a cover for something. What was the reason for all the darkness and the locked doors?

Jenny hung her head and tried to think of what Elaine would do if she had been put in this situation. Would she sit here in this carriage and shake with fright as Jenny was doing now? "No!" Jenny said aloud as her shoulders straightened, and her head came up with a snap. She was just having a reaction to her own lies. Her conscience was bothering her, making her see these people from a dark side. She would have to be strong, like Elaine. She would demand her rights as Lady Elaine Seaton and would laugh in the face of Jules Colby and his peculiar ways.

While Jenny was leaving Charleston, Travis was eating breakfast with Jeff.

"Jeff, I forgot to mention last night something I found disturbing yesterday."

"What's that?" Jeff spooned in another bite of Darby's hot apple cobbler.

"When we arrived here last night, this house was vacant as though no one had lived here for quite sometime. Aren't you using the house?"

Jeff put his spoon down and looked up at Travis. "This house is too big for me, Travis. I have taken a room at the Colony House. It's worked out well for me."

Travis looked into Jeff's eyes and knew the reason for his absence but did not press it. "Well, I hope you will continue to come over and stay with us while we are in town. I get tired of Darby's face all the time." He chuckled as Darby glanced over his shoulder.

"You don't got nothin' to gripe 'bout. I at least change me eye patch colors to match me dress." He huffed good-naturedly.

Jeff and Travis both laughed.

Jeff looked back at Travis with a gleam in his black

eyes. "What are you going to do today?"

Travis put down his cup before saying, "Well, I'm going to the bank to deposit this bank draft. Then I'm going to Moss Grove."

Jeff looked at him with merriment in his dark brown eyes. "So soon? I thought we could get a couple of girls and go steppin' tonight."

Travis laughed. "Is that all you think about? Stepping out with a woman draped across your arm?"

Jeff looked at Travis with a thoughtful expression crossing his handsome face. "I seem to remember you as a ladies' man, old boy. What's the matter? Has the wind died in your sails?" He leaned closer. "Or is it that you're too old to enjoy the favors of a woman?"

Travis felt Darby's eyes on him and turned to scowl back at him. Turning back to Jeff, he said, "I'm not too old to show you, you young pup. All right, go out and get two willing young ladies and I'll show you how old I am."

Pleased, Jeff stood, saying, "You've got a deal brother. I will see you tonight." As he reached the door, he turned back to face his brother. "Better take a nap." He grinned then rushed out the door with Travis's angry retort ringing in his ears and a balled up napkin sailing through the air at him.

The trip to Salford Manor was uneventful and went slowly for Jenny. She found the passing scenery breathtaking, her nerves easing with each mile. They went from marshland to fertile soil to swampland. They had just come through a stretch of dank, dark swamp when the coach pulled up before an immense house.

Jenny felt the carriage sway as Cicero climbed down from his perch. She waited for him to open the door and adjusted her gown as best she could. She thought she should have had a hat and a pair of gloves for this first meeting with the female Colbys. She looked out of the carriage portal to see what was taking Cicero so long to open the door for her and spied him on the front portico talking to someone.

"Why the big oaf," she hissed. He didn't even have the manners to help her down. She opened the door and stepped down from the coach with little difficulty, and as she was ascending the steps to the front door, she heard conversation up ahead. She couldn't see who Cicero was conversing with until she came up beside him.

A small woman with a turned-down mouth and faded green eyes stared at her. She wore a mop cap and a black dress with long sleeves, with her bodice buttoned up to the neck. Jenny took a deep breath and again assumed the poise of Lady Elaine.

"Pardon me, but I am Lady Elaine Seaton and I wish you to inform my aunt that I have arrived."

The woman said nothing, so Jenny repeated herself, only louder, fearing this woman was deaf.

The woman pursed her lips and said in a squeaky voice, "You needn't shout." She turned from the door. "Just come in."

Jenny followed the woman into a dark entrance hall. She must be in the right place, she thought as she looked around. This place was just as dark and unfriendly as the Charleston house. Jenny didn't know how she could live in a house with no sunshine.

The woman stood by the doorway leading into another room. She looked Jenny up and down in a disdainful manner and said, "Follow me." Then she walked ahead of Jenny into the room.

Jenny assumed this to be some sort of music room when she saw an old spinet piano and a harp that had evidently seen a lot of use or no care. Jenny was sure, as her eyes found dust motes under the piano and cobwebs in the corners, that the latter was the case.

The woman stood before a settee and motioned Jenny to sit down. Walking to the small seat, Jenny decided to sit only on the front portion, if possible. The woman continued standing, and Jenny began to feel uneasy with the woman staring at her. "I beg your pardon, but where, may I ask, is my aunt?"

The woman simply turned and walked to the mantle, flicking a bug from its dusty surface. Without looking at Jenny, the woman began speaking. "I will make this short and to the point. I would advise you to listen." She turned and stared again at Jenny. "My husband invited you to come here."

Jenny sat up straighter as she realized this woman was, Katherine Colby.

"I understand you are without funds due to your untimely shipwreck." Her lips pulled back in a sneer and the hate that radiated from her was an almost physical force when she continued: "Well, my dear, I do not run a charity house here. If you are to stay with us, you will be expected to perform certain duties to pay for your room and board. If you do not like this arrangement, you may leave at once. Cicero is waiting for your decision before unloading the carriage. This arrangement would, of course, be terminated when and—" she looked down her nose at Jenny, "if your funds arrive from England."

Jenny looked up at the woman with wide blue eyes, then asked, "Are you telling me that you invited me here with the idea of charging me rent for my visit? That's absurd."

"Maybe you expected to come here and eat our food and take our hospitality for nothing? Well, my dear Lady Seaton, you must pay your way in this country and that includes the nobility."

Jenny could not believe this austere woman to be Katherine Colby. What would Elaine have done? Would she humble herself and do as this woman suggested? Jenny looked the woman straight in the eye and asked, "Just what duties are you referring to?"

The woman turned again to the mantle and rearranged a dying bouquet of flowers, which somehow went with the room. "The usual: mending, ironing, cleaning."

Jenny was aghast. She had assumed she'd take on the responsibilities of running the house but not this. She stood up abruptly. "But, that's servants work." Lady Elaine Seaton would *never* do the work of servants.

Katherine Colby gave a sneer and walked closer to Jenny. "Exactly, my *lady*." The title was obviously a thorn in this woman's side.

Jenny looked around the room. "But, don't you have servants? You have some in the Charleston house."

The woman threw back her head, folding her gnarled, white hand in front of her and said with a laugh of contempt, "We do not have house servants here. I won't have the filthy black creatures in my home. What my husband does and who he employs is his business. As I do not go to Charleston, I do not care what he does with the house there, but as far as this house goes, I prefer white, and they're hard to find on a—permanent basis."

Jenny looked again around the gloomy room. She had done this work before, it wasn't beneath her. But what about Lady Elaine? Would she do this work? No, Jenny realized, but Jenny wasn't Elaine and she had nowhere to go. Maybe if she could just stay until something else came along.

"All right, I will help you, but just until my funds arrive from England. After that I will make other living arrangements."

"Fine. You can start by fixing Eudora's and my lunch. And mind, I expect no waste. Fix only enough for one meal. Follow me and I will show you the cook house."

Jenny looked down at the fine, light tan gown she was wearing and said, "But, I can't fix a meal in this gown. If you will show me the way to my trunks, I will change. It will only take me a moment."

The woman turned again with such scorn marking her already wrinkled face that hatred and evil could once again be seen in the pale green depths of her eyes. "You can wear the rag you have on." She walked out the door barring any further discussion of the matter.

Jenny found the cook house in as much disarray as the music room. She did manage to find some ham and potatoes that looked as if they could be eaten. She cut a thick slice of the ham and put it in a skillet to fry. It would be enough for the three of them. Cutting up the potatoes, she knicked her finger. As she sucked the blood, she wondered what her stay with these people would be like. Uncle Jules was rather an enigma. He seemed friendly, but Jenny had the feeling he was covering up his true identity. She would have to watch him. She then thought of Katherine. This woman's nature was foreign to Jenny. Why would she react as she had to her, supposedly her only niece? What would Jenny's life be like with this woman ordering her about? What of Eudora? Jenny hadn't met this cousin of Elaine's but was curious to find out about her.

She put the potatoes on to boil and cut up some

vegetables. When she finished, she was rather proud of her efforts. Fried ham, boiled potatoes in a delicate white sauce, sprinkled with fresh parsley and greens flavored with thyme and rosemary. She put the dishes on a tray she had found in a cabinet and walked back the way she had come to the main hall. Hearing conversation to her right, she walked into the dining hall. She noted the silence that her presence had brought. Katherine was staring straight ahead. She didn't even deign to acknowledge Jenny's presence. The other woman present, who Jenny assumed to be Eudora, watched her closely behind lowered lids.

While Jenny put the tray down, she said in as friendly a way as she could, "You must be cousin Eudora. I'm Elaine and I am so pleased to finally meet you." The girl simply stared at her. As Jenny took her place, she noticed Katherine's attention directed at her.

Katherine spoke slowly and distinctly. "You will eat in the cook house, not at my table."

Jenny sat, shocked by the venomous gaze the woman directed to her. Not only does this woman expect the Lady Elaine Seaton to wait on her, but she will also deny her her table. Jenny was furious. "Madam, I will not be treated as some poor relation begging favors. If my being at your table displeases you, I will take my leave of you and this wretched house." She arose with all the dignity she knew Elaine would have shown and walked to the door with her head held high.

As she walked down the front steps, she noticed Cicero sitting on the stoop. She hailed him. "Cicero, get me a carriage. I will be returning to Charleston after all."

He didn't move or even indicate he had heard her. He just watched her with a smile on his ebony face.

The feeling of humiliation and hot anger was not new to Jenny but her pride and the honor of Lady Elaine were the objects of her mind as she gazed at the man smiling smugly at her. When he did not move, Jenny understood she would be alone in her escape from this manse. Pulling her skirt up, she descended the steps with her back straight and her head held high. She headed in the direction they had come from only a few hours before.

The swamp loomed before her in its quiet mystery. She knew the road went through the darkness and while her determination mounted, she stepped briskly along with the darkness quickly encompassing her with every step. She turned to look back to the house, sitting forlornly on the fringe of this bog. As her attention was directed once again to the road ahead, her foot slipped on a wet stone and she fell to her knees, scraping her hands as she sought to brake her fall. Tears of pain filled her eyes as she rubbed her palms against her skirt to dislodge the small stones and clinging moss that stuck to her raw, bleeding hands. Seeing the blood stains, vividly standing out on the tan skirt, seemed to break the spell of dignity she had tried so hard to create. Kneeling in the middle of the road, she wept. She was alone. Alone in a far country with no money and no prospects. The feelings of betrayal she had felt at her father's hand and now Travis's was like a weight on her shoulders that threatened to hold her down in this quagmire of despair. What would happen to her alone in a strange city and with no clothes except what she was wearing? She could imagine her reception upon arriving with no wrap, no hat and blood stains on her gown.

A name came to mind: Travis. Would he help her out of this nightmare? If she went to him, would he hold her and love her again as he had on the ship?

No! A voice inside her said. He wanted to be rid of her. He didn't want a woman putting a ring through his nose. He had dismissed her from his ship and probably from his mind. She was alone and as such must make her own way in this hostile land.

Her shoulders slumping, she pushed herself up and gazed about her. A faint light filtered through the twisted trees. She felt eyes upon her as she turned slowly, trying to penetrate the dark interior around her. She caught sight of a movement, not ten paces from her, on the road. A strangled scream froze in her throat when she recognized a snake, slithering slowly toward her. Slowly, with a hand to her heart, she stepped backward. After a few more hesitant steps, the snake lost interest in his hunt and slithered to the murky waters on the side of the road and quickly was lost to Jenny's sight. She realized she hadn't drawn a breath until her lungs felt near to bursting. Closing her eyes, her chest heaving, her body seeking air, her torment extended to the limit of her pride. She could do nothing but go back to the uncle and aunt of her dead mistress and complete this charade. She had only the slim hope of Elaine's solicitor, in London, sending the funds that would somehow see her out of this abyss.

Another thought came to her, as she slowly retraced her steps to the manor. Travis knew where she was and might come to her. At the thought of him, her senses rushed to liven her steps. She wondered how she could still feel the rising pulse and quickening heartbeat at just the thought of him. He had abandoned her just as her father had, to her own devices. But he thought she was going to her family and would have no way of knowing what her reception would have been. Maybe he would come to call and she could tell him of her predicament. No! Again the voice halted her steps. If he came, she would have to pretend to be well. She could not live with his pity. If he wanted her, it would have to be because he loved her and for no other reason.

As her steps brought her to the front of Salford Manor, Jenny raised her eyes to stare into the black orbs of Cicero. His smirk told her that he had expected her return, but she wouldn't let this beast know of her turmoil. She squared her shoulders and glared at him, then she walked up the steps and into the dark, dismal hall of her prison.

She noted the dining hall was now empty and walked in to gather up the remains of the luncheon.

While she slowly loaded the tray, Katherine came in without the slightest evidence of surprise at Jenny's return. "I had Cicero put a pallet in the cook house for you. I trust you will be comfortable." With a nod, she turned and walked out leaving Jenny alone in her humiliation.

How long would she be able to manage this charade, she asked herself while she watched the straight back leave the room. She almost smiled as she thought: What charade? I was better off as an indentured servant than I am as Lady Elaine Seaton.

The sun had disappeared in the western sky as Charleston's night life came alive. The streets were a bustle with shopkeepers' closing up and hurrying home for a blessed respite from their busy day. Men were heading to the saloons for a drink of ale before heading to the restaurants and meetings with the more notable citizens.

Travis had had a busy day. The banker had insisted

Travis listen to his endless chatter on how best to invest his sizable profit from the sale of his ship and cargo. He had met some friends who had insisted on celebrating his return by toasting his health at a local pub. All in all, Travis wished he had gone on to the peace and quiet of Moss Grove instead of letting Jeff bait him into going out tonight.

While he fussed with his cravat, a vision of long, golden hair and deep blue eyes confronted him; the way the moonlight made her hair look almost silver and her skin a luminous sheen of perfection.

He shook his head to dispel the image. What was the matter with him? He had thought about her almost to the point of looking addle-minded in the eyes of his friends and associates. They had had to repeat themselves more than once as his mind constantly remembered her, and he would lose the attention their conversation demanded.

He tried to analyze his preoccupation with her. She was gentle and timid, easy to please and so quick to hurt. She could be as fragile as a newborn and as determined as a she-cat. Her beauty was beyond comparison, but there was always the nagging doubt about who she really was. If she wasn't the Lady Elaine Seaton, then who was she? A poor relation perhaps or a companion to the lady. But, why the charade? Why would her true identity be so much worse than the lady's? If she were, in fact, the Lady Seaton, could it be an aged title with little funds to back up the premise? His mind gave little help to his constant thoughts of her. Where was she now? He somehow couldn't see the fragile Elaine having a comfortable visit with Katherine or Eudora. Eudora Colby was a simpering cow of a woman. Always putting on airs while she strolled along the streets of Charleston. Travis could not remember ever seeing

Katherine in town. She would stay in that swamp house and relegate authority to Jules and Eudora. As the Colbys were never, to his recollection, ever present at any of the innumerable social functions he had attended, he rather doubted the chance meeting at a ball or play with Elaine.

Successfully tying the obstinate cravat, he determined it was probably better if he didn't see her again. He had a new way of life ahead of him, and all his energies would be needed to forget the sea and become the plantation owner in earnest.

He heard Jeff downstairs and, with determination in his step, walked down the stairs to meet his brother and get this evening over with.

Jeff saw him and with a twinkle in his eyes, exclaimed, "Why, Travis, I am impressed. You actually look good!"

Travis scowled. "Don't start with me, Jeff," Tugging at his waistcoat, he continued into the room. "Where are our companions for this evening, or weren't you able to find anyone who would go out with you?"

"Oh, mine was no problem. It was finding someone who would go out with *you* that took some time." He grinned at the scowl Travis presented him. "You're certainly in a party mood. What's the matter? Have you suddenly realized you have forgotten what to do?"

Travis started for the door, ignoring the prodding of his brother. "Let's just get this over with." He turned. "Where did you say the young ladies were?"

Jeff laughed and walked up to the door and opened it. "In the carriage, just waiting for you to make their every dream come true."

Travis climbed into the carriage and was sure he should have returned to Moss Grove. Alicia Adams sat in a seat, patting the one next to her. "Travis," she drawled, "y'all sit heah next to me. Ah'm so happy y'all came home."

Travis nodded and noticed the mousy girl sitting beside Jeff. Jeff did the introductions while the carriage pulled into the street.

"Travis, this is Betty Jane McNaulty. Betty Jane, my brother, Travis Gardiner,"

Travis nodded then turned to level a stony stare at his brother. Of all the women in Charleston, Jeff just had to pick Alicia Adams. She had made no secret of her attempted conquest of Travis. She had used every ploy in the book the last time Travis had seen her. She had chased him to the point of making him leave early on his last voyage. He had hoped to get back to Moss Grove before she knew he had returned.

Alicia placed her leg next to Travis's and placed her hand on his knee. "Ah missed you, Travis," she whispered in his ear, then looked coyly into his eyes.

Travis was quite perturbed with Jeff as he scowled, looking at his brother. "It's good to be home," he said.

Jeff smothered a grin and turned to the young lady next to him. He had known exactly what he was doing by asking Alicia this evening. She was his brother's nemesis. She had made Travis's life miserable the last time he had been home. She clung to him and put forth the most brazen displays of affection. He couldn't wait to see what she would do this evening.

Alicia had set her cap for Travis a long time ago and had made no bones about it. She could see herself as mistress of Moss Grove, and if she had to marry the most eligible bachelor in Charleston to get there, that was so much the better. She had declined numerous proposals, and now that she was twenty-two years old, spinsterhood was looking her in the eye. She knew time was running out for her and decided a bolder approach was necessary. She had planned this evening with infinite care. If she could get him to her bed, she could demand he make a decent woman out of her. She knew Travis, as a gentleman, would never back down from his obligations. She set forth on a path to the altar as she gazed lovingly into his eyes.

Travis started to perspire when Alicia's hand came closer up his thigh. He couldn't believe she would be so bold and in front of Jeff and the other girl. He covered her hand with his and gently removed it from his leg. "Where are we going Jeff? Someplace lively, I hope."

Jeff looked up into the wild eyes of his thoroughly perplexed brother. "I thought we would go down to the wharf and have some shrimp and clams." He looked to each of the ladies for approval. "Of course, we could go somewhere where there aren't so many people?" He smiled.

Travis responded before Alicia had a chance. "The shrimp and clams sound good to me," he shouted. "Haven't had shrimp or clams for a long time."

Alicia leaned over to Travis, brushing her nearly exposed breast on his arm. "Afterward, we can go back to my house. My parents are still on the plantation." She looked up at Travis with desire written all over her face, all the while rubbing her breast into his arm. "We could get to know each other again, Travis."

As she leaned up against him, her low-cut bodice gaped open, and Travis swallowed when he saw the obviously rouged crest hang in all its glory. She whispered in his ear, following his gaze. "If y'all think that's somethin', Ah have some more surprises in store for you."

Travis was in agony. She was coming on to him like a bitch in heat. He was thankful when the carriage stopped in front of the inn.

Jeff could hardly contain himself as he leaped down first and helped Betty Jane from her seat. Travis was about to get out when Alicia pulled him back. "Y'all go on, Jeff. We'll catch up."

Jeff took hold of Betty Jane's arm and shut the carriage door, saying, "All right, but don't be too long. I'm starving." Jeff walked into the building with a smile of satisfaction on his face. He hoped this night would bring back the memories of the fair damsel Travis had rescued. He was doing the best he could without letting Travis suspect his motives and from the looks of it, Alicia was doing her part to perfection.

Alicia didn't waste any time. She pulled Travis to her breast which she had somehow produced from the front of her bodice.

Travis smelled the faint perfume she had dabbed on them. He tried to pull away but her strength was amazing.

Breathing heavily, she gasped, "Take me Travis. I've waited so long for you."

The soft flesh of her breast almost suffocated him. He renewed his attempt to break away, this time succeeding. She was in the corner with both breasts heaving as she breathed. She bent down, taking the hem of her dress, and pulled it up.

Travis was shocked to see she wore no undergarments. What had happened to the Alicia who had flirted with him only a few years before?

She spread her legs and Travis had an unrestricted view of her most private parts.

"Travis, I know you want me. Take me! Take me now!" She panted in her passion.

Travis would never have turned down an invitation

like this before, but for some reason this display disgusted him. "Alicia, I think you had better go find yourself another stud," he said with obvious disinterest before opening the door and walking toward the building.

Alicia leaned out the window, with her breasts still exposed and hanging down in front of her, yelling, "You bastard! How dare you!"

Travis turned around and looked at her. "Why Alicia, how dare you." He turned and walked into the building without looking back.

Alicia steamed while she put herself back into her gown. She had waited too long to let this incident deter her from her goal. She got down from the carriage and joined the three as though nothing had happened.

While they ate the cold, boiled shrimp and steaming hot clams, Travis marveled at Alicia's ability to forget her brazen display and act as though nothing had happened. She was carrying on a conversation with Jeff while he watched her unobserved. She really was a beauty. Rich auburn hair, a creamy white complexion, big green eyes and rosy lips. He knew of at least three men who had asked for her hand, only to be denied. She obviously wanted him, but he wasn't interested at the moment. After tonight, he doubted he would ever partake of her.

He wondered about the change in himself. If she had done this a year ago, he would have probably taken her up on her generous offer. A vision of loveliness came to him. A woman with golden hair and big blue eyes. He shook his head to dismiss the vision. He would not think of her again. He had been thinking of her constantly since watching her walk from his ship. What is she doing now?

Alicia invaded his reverie. "Were you thinking of

me?" She smiled at the look of surprise he gave her. "We're ready to leave, if you are?"

Travis stood up and helped her with her chair. They walked out with Travis holding her arm and staying just behind her. As they all got back into the carriage, Travis said, "I hope you don't mind, but I've asked the driver to drop me off at home. I'm terribly sorry but I have developed a terrible headache." He hoped his ruse was not too blatant.

However, Alicia saw her chance and said, "I'll go with you." Looking suggestively, she lowered her eyes. "In some ways a woman is better. I'll get rid of that nasty old headache for you."

Travis abruptly waved his hand. "That won't be necessary, Alicia." He glared at Jeff. "I'm sure Jeff won't mind dropping you at your house, *will* you Jeff?"

Jeff smiled but understood the warning in his brother's voice. "Of course not. Alicia, it would be a pleasure."

Seeing no way to contradict these two men, Alicia sat back with a huff and stared out the window. She was thinking of an alternative plan of action, when she again faced Travis. "Will I be seeing you again?"

Travis did not look at her as he said, "I assume we will bump into each other from time to time. After all, Charleston isn't that big."

Alicia needed a commitment, something to hang onto. She sensed his disgust at her display earlier and was hard put to understand the change in him. She had heard all the stories of this man's prowess. Although he had always been the proper gentlemen with her, Alicia had always assumed it was because he was seriously considering her for marriage. His manner tonight suggested just the opposite. She had to convince him of her virtue. But how? After her brazen display tonight he would assume her to be a whore. She straightened as a thought came to her that was worth a try. "Travis, I wonder if I could come out to Moss Grove this week? I really must get your advice on something." She hung her head as though in abject misery.

Travis noted the ploy and quickly said, "I really won't have much time available, Alicia. I must get into the role of owner, now that Jeff has succeeded so well at being a lawyer. I'll let you know when things settle down for me, then we will talk." He noted, with thanks, that the carriage had stopped before the Tradd Street house.

As Travis said his good-byes, Jeff leaned out the window, saying, "Will I see you before you go to Moss Grove, old boy?"

The slight was not missed on Travis, and he said with obvious authority, "Oh, I expect to see you for breakfast." With a sneer, he added, "At seven *sharp*."

Jeff had the distinct impression he had better be there. "See you for breakfast, then. Good night."

Travis watched the carriage until it rounded a corner and disappeared into the night. He would get Jeff for this. So help him he would.

At seven the next morning, Travis was at the table when he saw a white handkerchief being waved in the doorway. "It's all right, Jeff. No need to surrender so soon."

Jeff walked in and carefully skirted the table to put it between himself and his very disgruntled brother. "How's the headache this morning?" he asked casually.

Travis put down his teacup and raised his eyes to

look into the amused eyes across from him. "My head is not the issue, but yours may be after you tell me what the hell you were thinking of, inviting Alicia Adams as my date!"

Jeff looked down at the plate Darby had put before him. "I thought you would enjoy her. She did seem to be accommodating."

"Accommodating!" Travis repeated. "Hell yes, she was that."

Jeff looked up and almost choked on a spoonful of eggs. "Are you saying you didn't take her up on her obvious invitation? Boy, Travis, you sure have changed. I remember when word would get out—"

"That's enough, Jeff," Travis interrupted. "Let's just say I like my women a little more enticing. Alicia came on too strong. She wants only one thing, and that's my name. If she wants the Gardiner name, it will have to come from you."

"Now don't get me involved with her. But what did she do to you?" Jeff grinned excitedly.

Travis looked up at the eager expression on Jeff's face, but being a gentleman, he changed the subject. "I'm leaving for Moss Grove. I would like you to come out and show me all these changes you've made. When can you come?"

"I could come on Saturday, or do you need me to come earlier to fight off the local women when they find you've returned?"

Travis scowled. "I don't see them lining up for you, dear brother. Seems to me you used to be quite popular when I left. Losing your appeal?"

Jeff's face turned red as he looked at Travis. "Actually there is someone I'm rather serious about."

Travis's expression softened when he saw the look on Jeff's face. "Not that mouse you saw last evening?"

Jeff shook his head. "She was just a friend of Alicia's."

"I don't wonder. Alicia always did try to set herself off. What better way than to be able to compare her to that simp of last night." Travis looked at Jeff thoughtfully. "Well—who's the lucky girl?"

Jeff's face lit up when he told Travis. "Her name is Mary Lou Jenkins. She teaches school and she's as pretty as a picture."

Travis leaned back in his chair. "Seems like you do fancy this one."

"Oh, Travis, I've never felt this way about anyone." Jeff's eyes gleamed.

"How did you meet her?"

Jeff hung his head as he said, "She found me passed out on a curb, in front of the school after Celeste . . ."

"Go on, Jeff," Travis prodded.

Jeff swallowed hard and raised his head. "She helped me through that time and we just got to know each other. You'll like her, Travis."

Travis stirred his tea and looked up. "I'm sure I will, Jeff. Bring her to Moss Grove sometime. Now I must be going." Travis stood and started for the door but turned and pointed a finger at Jeff. "Just don't bring Alicia as a surprise. Surprises like that tend to make me want to *kill* someone."

Jeff laughed and stood up to stand by his brother, slapping him on the back. "Don't worry, I don't think I want to test your temper anymore. Come on, I'll walk you out." He reached over the table, taking a hot scone before following Travis outside.

The brothers shook hands, then Travis swung up in the saddle of the big roan he had purchased yesterday. He waved to Darby who was putting some boxes and baggage into the back of a dray.

184

"See you at the house, Darby," Travis called over his shoulder.

Jeff called after Travis, "See you Saturday."

Travis turned in the saddle and waved.

Darby came up to stand next to Jeff, and they waved in unison at Travis's receding figure. Glancing up at Jeff with mirth changing his wrinkled bewhiskered face, Darby cleared his throat to get Jeff's attention. "What were you thinkin' last night, lad, when you sicced Alicia Adams on the cap'n?"

Jeff's grin suggested that the boy Darby remembered was still lurking behind the respectable personage of the lawyer, Jeffery Gardiner.

"Actually, I thought it a brilliant idea at the time."

Darby scratched his chin. "The cap'n was sure in a state when he come home. She must have really made him squirm."

Laughing, Jeff put his hand on Darby's shoulder while they walked back to the house. "Darby, you should have seen her. I almost died when I picked her up. Her appearance was so obviously created to snare a man, I'm surprised she had the nerve."

Darby looked up at Jeff. "Why'd you pick her of all people? You know the cap'n left on his last voyage early just to get away from her."

"That's precisely why I did. You see, she's been going around town telling anyone who would listen that she and Travis would be wed on his return. I knew she would have to make a display soon because the only way she would ever get my brother to the altar would be to get him to her bed first, then demand he make an honest woman of her." Jeff slapped his knee as he continued through peals of laughter. "Travis was like a cornered boar trying to get out of her clutches. I must admit he did a good job of it."

185

"I still don't understand why you did it, Jeff." Darby looked confused.

"Well, if I must spell it out for you—What better way to bring back memories of his little sea nymph than to put Alicia in his way. If what you tell me about this mysterious woman is true, Travis will probably run to her to save himself from Alicia."

Darby raised his brow with sudden insight. "Why, Jeff, I think you might have somethin' here. Alicia Adams and lady Elaine are 'bout as different as night and day." He turned with a smile to match Jeff's. "Yes, sir, I think with our help, the cap'n might as well be defenseless. We'll get him to the altar all right, but with the little lady."

The two old friends laughed and slapped each other on their backs as they each thought of Travis's finally succumbing to the bite of old lady love.

Chapter Ten

Jenny had spent a restless night lying on a lumpy pallet. At first she was angry at her new position but the anger was replaced by the feeling she had that bugs were crawling over her. She had gotten up twice to strip her bedclothes in search of the hard-shelled water bugs she was sure inhabited every crack and crevice of the cook house. She had killed more than one this, her first day at Salford Manor.

She had cleaned the cook house from top to bottom, but still the place looked dirty and squalid, and the thought of the bugs kept coming back to her.

She had gotten up well after midnight to gaze out beyond the cook house window and saw the moon, large and white above the cypress in the swamp. What had she done during her life to warrant this new torture? All he had ever wished for was a happy life. She had dreamed of a prince who would come on a great white stallion to carry her off to his castle. She had dreamed of gowns and jewels and love, but what she had in reality was one disappointment after the other. Now she was portraying a great and wealthy lady and what was it getting her? Nothing but more torment and distress.

She lay back upon the musty-smelling pallet with her thoughts going back to the one truly happy time of her life: the time she had spent on board the *Sea Breeze* as Travis's lover. If the rest of her life were to remain a misery, she at least had the memories of those days and especially the nights.

She knew in her heart that no one could make her as happy as Travis had. Maybe that was to be her happiness. Memories could be almost as good as the real thing. And so she fell asleep with a smile on her face, remembering the day they swam in Barbados.

Jenny managed to get through the next few days with the hope that once the colonel returned, he would put a stop to this insanity. Jenny had not seen her trunks since she had arrived. The light tan gown was a mess with spills and stains marking each meal she had served. A tear in the hem was caused by the heel of her soft kid shoes catching it as she was down on her knees, scrubbing the floor.

The hopes she had sustained herself with vanished on the day the colonel did, indeed, arrive home. Smiling, he had approached her without the slightest indication he found her attire amiss.

"I trust you have found your duties to your liking, my dear." He patted her cheek then retired to his library, closing the door.

Jenny realized this would be her lot for as long as she stayed here at Salford Manor. With the determination learned from birth, Jenny dusted the piano until it shone with a golden hue.

On the third day of Jenny's stay, while she was polishing the banister, she saw Eudora come down the stairs wearing her blue velvet gown. All the pent-up anger and rage at her situation surfaced in her. She would rather die than see this simp wearing Travis's sister's velvet, which is how Jenny thought of that gown. She rushed at Eudora, startling the woman. Jenny put her hand at the bodice and pulled, ripping the delicate stitches that Darby had so painstakingly sewn. Eudora put her hands on Jenny's chest and shoved her. Jenny caught herself before she fell backward down the stairs and was preparing to attack again, with Eudora screaming at her, when Katherine came out of the library.

"What's going on here?" the slight woman demanded.

Eudora held the bodice of the gown together and rushed down the stairs past Jenny, and screamed, "Mama, this witch just attacked me. See what she's done to my gown."

Jenny's anger boiled over and she yelled, "Your gown! Why you thief, that's my gown!"

Katherine looked up at Jenny with loathing evident on her stark features. "That's enough, Elaine. That gown and all the others you brought to this house are now Eudora's. She needed some new clothes, and as you two are approximately the same size, and only a few alterations were required, I thought this payment for your staying with us." Katherine turned back to her weeping daughter, seemingly dismissing Jenny.

Jenny could not let this happen. "You demand more payment than my working like a slave in this house?"

"The subject is closed, young woman. Now get back to work," Katherine sneered.

Jenny felt all her emotions wage war within her as she said quietly, "Please, since you have all the rest of my gowns— Please, could I at least have that blue velvet one?" She nodded toward the gown Eudora was struggling to hold together.

189

Katherine's steely eyes squinted at Jenny. "Why would you want that rag? It's ripped beyond repair."

Jenny looked down at her stained gown. "The gown was given to me, and I would like to have it for the memories it brings me."

Smiling evilly at her, Katherine walked to the bottom step and placed a wrinkled hand on the banister. "You have no need for memories here, Elaine. We shall dispense with this sentimentality right now. Eudora, go upstairs and change your gown. Then bring me this one when you are finished. I will burn it along with all the happy memories it brings to you, Elaine." She paused until Eudora had passed Jenny on the stairs. "Now get back to work and don't let me see you gazing into space. I will watch you closely now. You should never have attacked Eudora. Maybe a week on bread and water will curb your desire for revenge against my daughter."

Jenny's anger overcame her common sense. "Katherine, I have slaved in this house for the last three days. I was invited to this godforsaken land as a guest. I did not agree to come here to become the inside maid as well as the benefactor of your daughter's wardrobe. You have treated me with contempt since I arrived. It is obvious to me I am not welcome here and I shall have to make other arrangements. I will not stay in this house another minute." She held her head up as she descended the stairs with as much dignity as she could muster.

When she passed Katherine, the woman wrinkled her nose. "Elaine, I would seriously consider what you are about to do. Do you really think anyone would believe you to be a great titled lady by your present appearance?"

Jenny stopped by the door and looked down at her stained, ripped skirt. The bodice sagged, no longer crisp with starch. She looked up at a gilted mirror and saw the image of a street urchin peering back at her. Her hair was snarled and dull looking. A smudge on her cheek stood out against its paleness. Her eyes were larger but with a haunted look of despair. Smoky gray circles were under the faded blue orbs, creating a stark contrast to the appearance she had once presented.

She hated this charade she had chosen to fulfill, but what were her alternatives? If she did somehow manage to get to Charleston, what could she do? Katherine was right about her appearance. No one, not the least of which would be the authorities, would believe her story. After all, she wasn't a great titled lady but an indentured servant. Her mind turned from one idea to another until the only possible source of her freedom was Travis. Travis, who knew her to be here. Travis, who could come any day to see her and thusly take her from this chamber of horrors.

Katherine waited patiently to see the defeat on Jenny's face. She mentally rubbed her hands together. This might not take as long as I thought. She grinned evilly. A couple more weeks and I will have this sniveling guttersnipe ready for the picking. Just a little more pressure. "You see, Elaine, the only thing for you to do is await your funds from London, if they really are to arrive. Somehow you haven't convinced me that you have anything to await. Anyway, you could go take up a profession on the waterfront. The sailors aren't too particular about their pleasures. You could possibly save enough to buy passage back to England. Of course, there is always the pox or some other gruesome disease to think about. I would think you are really better off here. At least you have a roof over your head and kind people who love you," she said with a bitter smile.

Jenny's head snapped to Katherine. "Love! You speak to me of *love*? I doubt you know the meaning of the word." She straightened her shoulders and turned away from the woman's laughter.

"I imagine you don't see me as a loving person, Elaine, but all of this is for your own good. Rich people very seldom get a taste of what servants and underlings go through. Someday," she said leaning forward, "You may even thank me for preparing you for a life you may someday lead."

Jenny could only wonder at this mad woman's ravings. What life could be worse than the one she was living now? Even Sir Reginald's treachery would be a blessing compared to this woman's evil cruelty. "You are right, *Aunt* Katherine." She sneered the name. "I may find I have something to thank you for, but I seriously doubt it will be for treating me like a slave with no shred of dignity. I rather think it will be for showing me what evil is present around us and to be thankful someone like you is not the common practice but should be watched out for, nonetheless." She turned and walked toward the back door.

"I take it you will be staying with us?" Katherine asked anxiously.

Jenny turned with her shoulders squared. "I will be staying with you as you have so thoughtfully pointed out that I have no where else to go. But, I will relish the day my funds arrive and I can take my leave of you and this *charming* house, never to think on you again as something other than a nightmare in my life."

Katherine looked concerned while she watched Jenny's back go through the doorway. Maybe she had been wrong. The girl was showing more spirit than before. Maybe it would take longer than she had thought. She would have to think.

Jenny walked stiffly to the cook house. When she entered and was sure she was alone, she sat down and cried. It wasn't until she placed her hand up to her eyes that she realized she had something clutched in it. Through her tears she looked at the ragged swatch of blue velvet and a strip of lace. She smoothed the remnant over her wet cheek as the tears of frustration and anger spilled. At least she would have this much of the gown to remember her days on board the *Sea Breeze* and the nights with the only man she had ever loved.

Jenny's work had produced miracles in the dark, drab house. No longer were cobwebs evident in the corners, or dust motes freely shifting in the breeze under the piano. Her satisfaction at doing a decent job was always put to the test as Katherine or Eudora would find one fault after another. Jenny had a time holding her tongue as they would find imaginary dust on a sideboard or complained the meal she had prepared was not fit for pigs. However, she always noted that not one scrap was left after they were through eating.

At night, Jenny would pull the little scrap of velvet from under her pallet, and the memories of the wonderful time on the *Sea Breeze* would make, at least, the nights a little less unbearable.

During the day, Jenny was so busy, she seldom had time to think about Travis, not even for a moment. Although, on those rare occasions when she did pause to remember him, Katherine would interrupt her reverie with a smack on her hand. Jenny had contemplated many times why this woman so obviously hated her. Why would they invite Lady Elaine to their home if this was to be the reception? Katherine was a miser.

193

Waste was not tolerated. And Eudora was a mindless simp who primped all day. Jenny had never seen any suitors call but Eudora constantly talked of first one man then another.

One day while Jenny carried in the luncheon tray, Eudora was beaming as she related to Katherine. "Oh, Mama, he waved to me. I just know he will call soon. I must have a new gown to receive him."

Katherine smiled at her daughter. "Why, Eudora, you have so many new gowns. I'm sure you will find something appropriate to receive the captain in."

Jenny knew Katherine was baiting her with the reference to Eudora's new gowns, but what interested her the most was the reference to the captain.

"Oh, Mama, I heard he does not wish to be referred to as the captain any longer. He has given up the sea and plans to remain at Moss Grove."

A stab of pain ran through Jenny when the realization struck her that Eudora was speaking of Travis. Determined to hear as much as possible about him, she slowed her movements to stay as long as possible.

"Mama, he is *so* handsome. I think we will make a very stylish couple, don't you?"

With a glance at Jenny, Katherine leaned across the table and patted her daughter's hand. "Eudora, I think you've made a good choice. We will have to invite the captain— I mean Master Gardiner over for tea real soon."

A lump appeared in Jenny's throat when she thought of seeing him again.

Katherine caught Jenny's look of expectation and turned hardened eyes on her. "Don't get so excited, Elaine. I will find you something to do in the cellar when the captain— Master Gardiner comes to call. You will not spoil Eudora's chances by flaunting yourself before him!"

Jenny was stunned by Katherine's observation of her emotions. She quickly took the tray and almost ran from the room. She had lost her chance to see Travis all because she could not hide her true feelings from Katherine.

As Jenny ran from the dining room, Katherine looked at her daughter with a smug look of satisfaction. "Obviously your father was correct about Elaine's feeings for Gardiner. You handled that very well, Eudora. I almost believed it myself."

Smiling at her mother, Eudora shrugged her shoulders before saying coldly, "I'm just happy I can help, Mother."

"I'm sure once we break her spirit, you will benefit beyond your wildest dreams. Who knows, maybe Travis Gardiner will call, once you are the richest woman around."

Eudora giggled as thoughts of the handsome man holding her took shape in her mind. "Oh, Mama, do you really think so? How long will all this take? With Elaine, I mean?"

"Well," Katherine steepled her fingers in front of her face. "If all goes like your father hopes, it should only be a month or two longer. After that, you may count on a hefty portion going to your crusade to snatch a beau."

Eudora clapped her hands in delight. "You just tell me what to do, Mother, and I promise to make her life miserable."

Eudora steepled her fingers like her mother, and with a squint in her eye, she saw Elaine's future as clear as day. She would bring Elaine to her knees and have her begging for mercy.

When the two stared at each other, the eyes of mother and daughter seemed to take on an almost identical evil leer. Their eyes appeared to have a glow of fiery red vileness like that of a hellhound.

Katherine broke the spell, putting her hands across the table to hold Eudora's. "I think our next step will be to make her alter her gowns to fit you. That should make her feel hopeless. But, just in case, I will have to think of something else before she's through with that task." Katherine thought for a moment. "Your father said we have, at the most, two months to break her. We may have to step up the process so that we don't run out of time. You may even have to think of ways to make the great lady kneel." She smiled.

"All right, Mama. Actually I'm finding this one is fun. To put *miss high and mighty* in her place is going to be a pleasure."

Katherine beamed at Eudora. How proud I will be when you are Lady Eudora Colby, she thought.

Travis had settled into the work of a plantation owner as though he had never been otherwise. He would work from sunup to sundown, going over the fields, asking questions of his workers, taking suggestions on how to improve the yield, and working on the endless amount of paperwork.

He was working on some ledgers late in the afternoon when Mammy came in the room carrying a tray. "You better eats dis heah food, Mis'er Travis. Y'all looks plumb tuckered out from all dis heah work."

Travis gazed up at the woman who had been with his family since before Travis was born, and smiled. He pushed the papers and books aside as she placed the tray before him. "Mammy, this looks good enough to eat." He grinned.

"Why, course it do. Why you think ah brung it? Fer y'all to stare at!" She went about the room straightening things.

Travis loved this big woman who had helped him raise Jeff and Celeste after his parents had died. She, probably more than anyone, knew Travis the best. She could always tell when something was bothering him. She was watching him now as though perplexed. "What's the matter, Mammy? Aren't I eating correctly?"

"You doin' jest fine—" She paused and continued to gaze at him. "What's da matter wid you, Mis'er Travis? You done changed since you come back from dis las' trip."

Travis put down the fork, stood up and walked to the window. "I never could put anything past you, Mammy." He smiled, remembering the past. Turning back to her, he asked, "Do you remember the time I came in and took a whole blackberry cobbler you had put on the porch to cool? I still, to this day, don't know how you knew it was me and not Jeff."

Mammy smiled her toothless grin. "Why you should a know'd how ah done know'd it were you. You come in wid blue tee'f. You washed da stuff off a you face, but you couldn'a got it off'n your tee'f." She chuckled, setting the many rolls of fat under her chin to shaking, when she remembered the little boy's eyes growing wider as she rebuked him.

Travis laughed. "You mean you're not a mind reader? Why, I can't tell you how often Jeff and I were sure you could read our every thought."

Mammy looked at him with concern replacing the grin on her fat, black face. "Mis'er Travis, ah's done have to be a mind reader to knows y'all gots problems. Tell Mammy what's a botherin' ya. Y'all sho' is worried 'bout somethin'."

Travis looked out the window, seeing the face that haunted his every waking moment. How could he tell this woman, who knew him so well, when he didn't know himself. "Mammy, I'm fine. I just have so much to learn. Why, the changes Jeff made alone will take me months to understand." He smiled. "Jeff certainly made the right decisions while I was gone. I'm really proud of him. I only wish he could stay here instead of in Charleston."

Mammy was sure he wasn't telling her all of it but knew better than to press him. "You come on back heah an' finish dis heah meal ah fixed fer y'all."

Travis turned and did as she ordered.

That evening, Travis ordered his horse saddled and rode his fields like he did almost every evening. And, as in the past, he found himself on top of a high knoll, gazing down at the roof of the colonel's house. He could see nothing from this vantage point; he never could. But somehow he felt better just sitting and watching. He had never admitted to anyone how he missed Elaine. If only she would come to him and tell him her secrets. He knew she couldn't have done anything criminal, but he couldn't understand why she persisted in the lie.

It had been several weeks since he had kissed her good-bye on the deck of the *Sea Breeze*. He had checked around, but no one seemed to know anything about her.

The black man, Cicero, had come a couple days after Travis had returned to Moss Grove and handed him an envelope and, thinking it was a message from Elaine, Travis had ripped it open. It contained another bank draft and a note from the colonel, explaining that this money was reimbursement for the clothes Travis had bought for Elaine. No mention of Elaine was suggested beyond that.

Travis wondered if she were still there or whether

she had gone back to England. He hoped she was still down there in the house that he watched every evening.

He turned his horse and rode back the way he had come. For the hundredth time, he questioned his motives where Elaine was concerned. He knew now that is was definitely not a fatherly concern. But, why did it erode away at him like a burning fire? Surely he couldn't be in love with her. Again, he determined it to be physical attraction that made him want her, as he thought of her body molded to his.

He could not understand this desire he felt whenever he thought of her. His power of concentration had become affected. Only yesterday, when Jeff had brought a prospective buyer of Moss Grove cotton out to look over the operation, Travis had ignored the buyer and remained at the gin while they continued on because he had started thinking of her. Jeff had had to call him several times before he had noticed Jeff and the buyer, and he began walking to rejoin them.

He rode to the stable and dismounted, noticing Darby sitting on a hay bale, polishing a brass ring on a bridle. "Say, Darby, I don't see much of you anymore. What have you been up to?"

Darby looked up at the captain and nodded. "You been busy." He didn't want to mention the fact that Travis's disposition lately had not been inviting to friendly chatter.

"Not too busy to see you, old friend." Travis walked up leading his horse. He tied the reins and began taking the saddle off.

"I'll do that for ye, cap'n," Darby offered.

"No. You finish what you're doing. I'll rub him down myself."

Darby watched as Travis swung the saddle off the

big roan's back and started to brush in long strokes the silken flanks of the big beast. Darby had no use for horses. He felt better on the shifting, swaying deck of a ship than on the back of one of those beasts. He decided now would be a good time to ask about the lady.

"Cap'n, you heard anythin' from the lady?"

Travis stopped the brush in midstroke and turned to look at the questioning expression on Darby's face. "I haven't heard a word from her." Starting to brush again, he continued, "I did receive a bank draft from the colonel covering some of the expenses of the clothes I bought her." He looked again at Darby. "Have you heard anything about her?"

Darby looked down at the bridle he was holding. "No. I went by to see her a couple of times, but she was out visitin' or doin' somethin'. Maybe that old crow who answered the door just didn't think me good enough to see the lady."

Travis looked hopeful. "Then she *is* still at the colonel's. I was afraid . . ."

Darby looked up as the captain's words trailed off. "Afraid what? That she done gone back to England?" He watched the guilt on Travis's face. "Ney. She still be here."

Travis was surprised at the relief he felt at learning this, and said, "You will let me know if you hear anything?"

After Darby nodded his assent, Travis finished currying the horse, and with a wave to Darby walked out through the stable doors and into the night, whistling a happy tune.

Darby was sure the captain missed the lady. He was sure the captain was in love with her or Darby had two good legs. He would have to make sure he saw her the next time he called at the colonel's for her.

A month had passed for Jenny at Salford Manor when she finally realized for sure that something was wrong with her. Every morning, as she arose to start the day, before the sun came up, she would become ill. She was constantly tired and would cry at nothing. She tried to convince herself that that had something to do with the way she felt. She kept pushing the logical reason to the back of her mind.

Her days were long and hard. Eudora became demanding as Jenny proved herself useful to her. Almost every gown that had once belonged to Jenny was now altered to fit Eudora.

Eudora was taller and more than a few pounds heavier than Jenny, and Jenny would work for hours letting down the hems of the rich gowns Travis had helped her choose. Each gown represented a memory to Jenny. The peach-colored one was the one she had worn that day Travis had taken her to the secluded beach. The rich blue-green brocade was the one in which he had taken her to the inn in Barbados, where they had watched as a sword dance was being performed by some of the natives.

Jenny would smile as each stitch brought about another remembrance. She was careful not to be observed by Katherine, because Jenny was sure she would be denied this joy if Katherine even suspected that it gave Jenny pleasure.

Eudora made the gowns look somewhat out of place. Her tall stature and sharp, pale features were not embellished by the vivid colors. She somehow became lost in the gowns' radiance.

When Eudora would parade before her mother, showing off the latest gown to have been altered, Katherine would always call Jenny into the room to complain about some trivial matter, such as an uneven hem or loose hook.

Jenny knew the reason for the complaints but never let on that she hated these scenes. Katherine did her best to make sure Jenny felt the wrath of her tongue. If it wasn't an obvious barb, sometimes it would be obscure, like when Jenny had been called in the last time.

Jenny had entered the room when Katherine looked from her to her daughter. "Eudora, that gown was simply made for you. You look absolutely ravishing in that color, don't you think, dear?"

Jenny would seethe inwardly as Katherine's attention was brought back to her. "Elaine, will you ever learn to sew a straight hem? Look at the way it dips in the back. I suggest you rip it out and start over again."

Jenny didn't dare contradict her and tell her that the gown was made with a faint train. She simply nodded and left the room to get her sewing basket. Actually Katherine was doing Jenny a favor by making her do the hems twice. She could sit for hours and work her needle in and out and remember her time with Travis.

Jenny had a reprieve in another way. With her pallet in the cook house, she had privacy. She would end her day by taking the now, nearly threadbare gown from her body and wash it in the tub after her bath. She would carefully hang it over the dying embers of the cook stove to dry and lie down under her sheet to have dreams that not even Katherine could stop.

This morning, when she put the dress on, she noticed it fit more snugly across the bodice, and she was having trouble fastening the hooks around her waist. As the dress had nearly hung on her since the first week of her stay here, Jenny realized, with a start, that what she had been pushing to the back of her mind was now a certainty: She was going to have a baby. Travis's baby.

She sat down at the work table, putting her hands over her face. What would this mean to her? Would Travis be happy if she somehow managed to tell him? Or would he be angry at her and say she just wanted to get that ring through his nose?

Jenny put her head down on the work table. She must think. Her condition would become evident to everyone soon. What would be Katherine's reaction to her having a child out of wedlock? Jenny shivered when the thought came to her, and she quickly turned it aside.

She stood up and lit the cook fire. She would have to come to a decision soon, but right now she would have to hurry to get breakfast ready. If she were late again, today, Katherine said she would be back on bread and water., Jenny hated this punishment more than any other Katherine could do to her, for it meant Jenny would be locked in the cellar at night so she couldn't sneak food. She would lie awake listening to the sounds the rats made while they gnawed through a timber trying to get to the pantry and shivered with fright.

Besides, I have a child to think about now. I must eat to help my baby, Jenny thought as she cut a slab of cured bacon to fry.

A smile came to her still pretty but drawn face. Her baby. Hers and Travis's. "Oh, baby, I will always love you and protect you." She placed her hand over the child within her before picking up the heavy tray and walking to the big house.

On this Wednesday, as with all other Wednesdays

that Jenny could remember here at Salford Manor, she was outside hanging the wash when she saw a movement by the side of the cook house. She gasped and dropped the sheet she was about to hang, when she recognized Darby. She ran to the sheltered side of the cook house and threw her arms around the surprised little man.

Darby tried to calm her and shush the tirade his presence had incurred in her. After he got her calmed down, he looked at her haggered appearance. The dress she wore was one the Captain had bought her in Barbados. It was threadbare and spotted. Her beautiful hair was snarled and dull looking. Her eyes, oh, those beautiful eyes, had faded and looked sunken in her face.

"My lady, what's happened to you?" His concern was evident in his voice.

"Oh, Darby, don't let us talk about me. How have you been and Travis? Is he well?"

"Oh, well— He's not been the most pleasant soul since he sold the *Sea Breeze* and became head of the house, so to speak."

"But, he is well?" she asked anxiously.

"Aye." Darby could not imagine what had happened to her since he last saw her. "My lady, I have come by to see you several times but have been given the information that you were visitin' or havin' a nap and didn't wish to be disturbed. I come here and find you doin' the wash. What's goin' on here?"

"It's a long story, Darby. I have become the inside maid. Since I have no money and could not give the Colbys the funds they obviously expected when they invited La— me, they decided I would have to work for my keep."

Darby was aghast, "But, this is terrible. The cap'n will have somethin' ta say 'bout this."

"Darby, don't say anything to Travis. Promise me. When he wants me because of me and not my circumstances, is when he will come for me." Jenny dropped her hands and hung her head as though she never expected that to happen.

Feeling frustrated and unable to think of how to help her, he took her red, rough hands in his. "But, you shouldn't have to do this kind a work. Look at you! Don't you eat or don't they feed you?" Disgust made him glare at her.

She smiled up at his concerned face. "I'm all right. The work helps me pass the time, and I haven't been hungry lately." She looked pleadingly into his eyes. "Promise me you won't tell Travis."

As he reluctantly nodded his head in agreement, he remembered the way she had eaten on the *Sea Breeze*. She had always had a healthy appetite. "Can I bring you anything, my lady? Anything at all, you just name it."

"No, Darby." She thought and then presented him with a smile that held only a trace of the brilliance he remembered. "But, you could bring yourself back. I do the laundry this time every week. If we are careful, no one will see us."

Darby didn't like the sound of this, but nodded. "I'll be here."

They both turned in unison when they heard the back door slam and a woman's voice calling, "Elaine!"

Jenny turned quickly to Darby and whispered, "I must go. Thanks for coming." She turned and walked to the woman. Darby stayed to hear the exchange of the two.

"Elaine, I have been calling you. Are you deaf? I need a dress pressed. I am going to a ball tonight and want everything perfect."

Jenny looked up at the woman and asked, "Which dress do you want pressed, Eudora?"

Looking at Jenny with a sneer on her thin lips, Eudora state, "Oh, I think the black beaded gown you *so* thoughtfully gave to me."

Jenny could not let this pass. "Eudora, I gave you nothing. You took!"

Shaking her long, thin finger with a smile on her austere-featured face, Eudora smirked. "Now, now, Elaine. I will tell Mama if you start again. Or maybe bread and water are to your liking." She turned with a smug smile of satisfaction. She hated Elaine for her beauty and liked being superior to her in her present position.

Jenny knew the threat was real and lamely hung her head as she followed Eudora into the house, while Darby watched from his hiding place.

Darby didn't know what to think. She was obviously being mistreated, but what could he do? She didn't want the captain to know, but Travis was the only one who could help her.

He thought about the child's predicament all the way back to Moss Grove. As he put his horse in its stall, Darby saw a way to help the little lady without betraying the promise he had made to her.

He marched up the front steps to Moss Grove and walked into the reception hall. He saw Obediah, the butler, and asked him where the captain was.

Obediah liked Darby and reminded him, saying, "Darby, you bes' remember what Mis'er Travis done told us 'bout callin' him da cap'n. It's mis'er now."

Darby could not get used to the captain's being anything other than captain.

Obediah pointed to the study, and Darby went and knocked on the door but did not wait for permission to enter.

Travis didn't even look up from his ledgers but bellowed, "What the devil do you want now!"

"Sorry, cap'n, but may I speak with you?"

Looking up at last, Travis saw Darby walk directly across the room. "Oh, it's you, Darby. Come on in. What can I do for you?"

Darby stood in front of the captain's desk with his hat held in both hands before him. He rocked from his peg leg to his other leg, seemingly ill at ease in the unfamiliar surroundings.

Travis smiled and said, "Well, Darby, you look like you've done something. What's up?"

Darby took a breath and started his speech. "Well, cap'n, I just come from visitin' with the Lady Elaine."

Travis stood up abruptly. "Did you see her? How is she?"

Darby smiled at the captain's obvious interest. "She be lonesome, cap'n. You know that uncle and aunt of hers don't do much socilizin' and she hasn't met many people here abouts. Well, I be thinkin' that since you rescued her, maybe it would be nice to have a party for her, to get her acquainted with some of the fine people around here." Darby looked at the captain for some response.

Travis looked at the top of his desk, not really seeing anything. "I guess I have neglected my duties in regards to the lady. Maybe I will go see her."

Darby smiled. "Oh, cap'n, I think that's a splendid idea."

"Oh, you do, do you? Well, I shall go this afternoon and convey my respects."

Smiling to himself, Darby strolled out to the stable again, saying, "I didn't say a word, my lady."

Travis could have hugged the old coot. He had been battling with himself for weeks, trying to think of a reason to go see her. Darby's plan of a party was just the thing. Travis could invite her and have the protection of a large gathering to shield his emotions.

While he rode down the lane, Travis examined again the feelings the lady brought out in him. Just the thought of seeing her again made his heart beat faster. Again, he decided it was the physical attraction that made him want to see her. There was no denying she was beautiful, breathtaking, and the most pleasant woman he had ever known.

He spurred his horse to a faster gait when he saw the top of the manor, which seemed to be rising out of the swamp, before him. Travis had always wondered about the colonel's choice for the house. The swamp seemed too dark and dank to live near.

Jenny was just finished with the pressing of the black gown and was returning to the cook house when the front door knocker sounded. Opening the door, she saw Travis. Her heart started beating faster and her breath caught in her lungs. All at once the light dimmed and then went out completely.

Travis quickly caught her as she fainted and picked her up, noting the lightness of her. He laid her on a worn, but clean settee in the parlor and sat next to her, staring at her with a concern he had never felt for anyone before. She looked terrible. Her skin was stretched across her face, making hollows under her cheekbones. Her golden hair was snarled and lacked the luster of silvery highlights that he remembered so well. Her gown was a mess, and the shoes she was wearing had a hole in the soft leather soles. He picked up her rough, red hand in his, noting the smallness of it as it lay in contrast to his large brown hand. He felt a longing of protectiveness that made him shake with anger. What had happened to her? Were these people treating her badly? He rubbed her hand to get her awake. She would be the only one to tell him what had happened to her.

When Jenny woke up, she was lying on the settee in the front parlor. Travis was beside her rubbing her hand.

He saw her eyes open and said, "Elaine, what on earth has happened to you? If this swamp trash has mistreated you, I'll . . . I'll . . ."

Blinking, to again make sure this wasn't a dream, Jenny reached out her free hand to touch his arm. "Travis, I'm sorry. It's just—I didn't expect to see you when I opened the door." Jenny continued to rub his arm in an attempt to calm him.

"Obviously!" He looked closely into her eyes. "You look like the devil!"

Laughing to cover her dismay at his observation, Jenny sat up and patted her snarled hair. "Oh, you caught me on a bad day. I was just helping supervise the spring cleaning."

Travis lowered his eyelids and gazed again into the faded blue eyes. "This is June, Elaine. Aren't you a little late?"

Covering up, she couldn't look into his eyes boring in on her. "Well, we are short-handed right now."

"Elaine, tell me the truth. What's been going on here?"

Before Jenny could think, they were interrupted. "Why Captain Gardiner, may I ask what you are doing here?" Katherine asked as she walked in on the scene.

Travis stood up to face Katherine Colby. "I came here to see the Lady Elaine. She fainted and I helped her to the settee."

Jenny stood up and saw the look of hatred on

Katherine's face.

Travis didn't miss the look that passed between the two women: Katherine's hate and Elaine's humiliation. He hastily continued: "My actual reason for coming was to extend an invitation to you and your family and Elaine," he said and turned to Jenny, "to come to a barbecue at my plantation this Saturday."

Katherine looked from Travis to Jenny. Condemnation made her already sharp features a mask of hatred. "I'm afraid we won't be able to go, captain, but thank you for your kind invitation."

Travis was not to be denied. "I am giving the party to introduce Elaine to some of the people around here. I'm sure, since she will be the guest of honor, that you will change your plans and come."

Katherine stood up to her full height, grasping her talonlike hands to her waist. "I am sorry, captain, but our engagement Saturday cannot be changed."

Travis felt this woman's contempt. However, he would get what he wanted in the end and, smiling at her, said, "All right. I realize this was short notice. We will simply make the party on the next Saturday. Surely, you don't have plans for then?"

Caught off guard, Katherine had to accept.

"Very well, I will see you at about two o'clock a week from Saturday." He turned to Jenny and gave her a reassuring look. "I will see you before the barbecue and after you have finished your spring housecleaning and are more presentable." He took Jenny's work-roughened hand in his and kissed it. He looked deeply into her eyes as if to say, *I am here if you need me.*

Jenny looked up into his dark eyes, her expression one of love and longing that Katherine couldn't help but see.

Travis turned and bowed to Katherine, then he

walked through the front door.

Jenny walked to the window and pulled back the heavy drape enough to see him as he rode slowly down the lane.

Katherine came up behind her, watching the same scene. "You think you are pretty clever, don't you? Getting Travis Gardiner to invite you to a party." She sneered the words and turned Jenny roughly to look into her eyes. "Well, missy, you will be ill that day so don't get any ideas about going. Now get back to your chores and see that they are done properly this time." She turned and walked stiffly out of the room, leaving Jenny to her own misery.

Jenny stared after her. Her shoulders slumped as she put her hands over her eyes and cried, "Oh, Travis, save me." It was a plea from the heart. She didn't know how much longer she would survive at Salford Manor.

When Travis mounted his horse, he hesitated. He had the feeling he should stay but continued on to Moss Grove. He hadn't missed the expression on Katherine's Colby's face. She hated Elaine for some reason. Travis remembered the look in Elaine's eyes as he had kissed her rough hand. She was begging him silently to do something. She looked like hell. She had lost a great deal of weight, and the dress she had on, one he remembered buying her, was a mess.

He led his horse to the stable at Moss Grove. Darby was in the tack room, rubbing saddle soap over a fine leather saddle, when Travis walked in and leaned against the door frame.

Darby looked up at the captain's unhappy face and asked, "Did you see her?"

Travis missed the expectation in Darby's voice

while his mind recreated the scene at the manor. "Yes." He thought for a moment before looking up and asked, "Darby, did she seem all right to you when you saw her?"

Darby remembered what the lady had made him promise. "Why you askin', cap'n?"

"She looked like the devil to me and she's lost weight. She gave me some story about supervising the spring cleaning, but I got the impression she was doing more than that. What do you think?"

Darby rubbed harder on the saddle. "Well, I don't know, but sometimes things ain't always the way they seem." He couldn't look Travis in the eye so he continued rubbing in the soap.

Travis stood away from the door. "Maybe you're right. Anyway, we are going to have a barbecue a week from Saturday. I'll need you to deliver invitations."

"Aye, cap'n. I'll do her for ya." Darby was thrilled that the captain had been able to get her to come. He smiled as he realized his plans were starting to bear fruit.

Travis had the feeling Darby knew more than he was telling, but he also knew how much the old man liked Elaine. He would never do anything to hurt her.

Jenny was hanging the laundry the next week when she heard, "Pssssst." She looked to the cook house and spied Darby. She almost ran but didn't in case someone were watching her from the house. She wandered over to the cook house as though looking for something.

Darby thought she looked worse than before but said nothing. "How you been, my lady?"

"I'm much better seeing you again, Darby." She smiled when he took her hands in his.

212

"I guess you are all excited 'bout the party this Saturday, you being the guest of honor an all." He saw the sadness invade her face.

Hanging her head, Jenny confessed, "Darby, I won't be there. Katherine will send a note saying I am ill, and I will have to stay in bed." She almost cried as the injustice hit her again.

Darby was beside himself. "But, the cap'n's got everything planned. He'll be so upset if you don't come."

She looked up at him with pleading eyes. "Darby, I would give anything to come—but—Katherine won't let me."

"Won't let you? Are you sayin' you're a prisoner here?" he asked incredulously.

"No. It's just that I have nowhere else to go." The pain of her lifetime of betrayal, servitude, and lovelessness was reflected in her voice.

Placing his wrinkled hand under her chin, he lifted her face to meet his gaze. "You tellin' me, lass, that if'n you had somewhere to go, you'd leave this place?"

"I would be gone in a minute."

Darby thought a moment at the seemingly obvious answer to her problems, then beamed. "Well, my lady, fret no more. You just come with me to Moss Grove. You can stay there with me and the cap'n. It would be just like the old days on the *Sea Breeze*."

"I can't," she said so fast that she felt an explanation was necessary. "I mean with my not having any funds and not being able to pay my own way, I would feel as if you and Travis were doing this out of pity and charity." Her eyelids slowly closed as she looked down into the dirt at her feet. "I could not stand that." She looked up once again, saying, "When my funds arrive from London, I will leave here."

"But, it could be months before you hear from

London."

"Then I will just have to wait. My uncle made the arrangements shortly after I arrived." Jenny silently knew that if funds did arrive, she would never see any of them.

"What can I do to help you, lass?" he asked quietly.

His concern for her made Jenny feel better. At least she had one friend in this world. "Nothing, Darby, but thank you. This is something I will have to handle myself. But, could you bring me news of the barbecue, so I can think about it sometimes when it gets so lonely here?"

Wanting to take her away with him right now, Darby felt again the frustration and anger of not being able to do anything. "Of course, but you may be there anyways. The cap'n don't usually take no for an answer."

Jenny didn't even want to hope Travis would rescue her again. It would be too much of a disappointment if he didn't come.

"I had better get back to work. Thanks for coming, Darby. I will see you next week, won't I?" At his nod, she continued: "Darby, you are truly the best friend I ever had and I love you. Good-bye." She kissed his whiskered old cheek and turned to walk back to the wash.

Jenny hung the sheet while she thought of how she looked forward to Darby's visits. She somehow felt closer to Travis.

Travis. She wondered again what he would say if he knew she was with child. She would have to tell him sometime. She just wished he would come for her. She knew, or thought she knew, that he loved her. He couldn't have treated her the way he had and made love to her like that if he hadn't.

Her thoughts were interrupted by Katherine when she called from the porch. "Hurry up with that wash. You've been out here long enough," Katherine said, then turned and walked back into the house.

Jenny bent to get a petticoat and hang it next to the sheet. She wiped a tear from her cheek and wished again that one dream would come true for her, but realized her life had so far been just one nightmare after another, and would probably remain that way for the rest of her life.

Chapter Eleven

Darby rode back to Moss Grove in a tither. The further he rode, the madder he became. They were treating her worse than a darkie. He would have to get the captain going on this. He knew the lady meant more to Travis than Travis was willing to admit. The man was just so stubborn. How to do it, though, without betraying the lady's confidence? This was getting to be a lot of trouble. The lady demanded he not say anything, and he had to find ways to tell the captain just the right amount without telling too much.

Darby saw Travis standing by the house, supervising the digging of the pit that would be used to roast the pig. He moved the horse in the direction of the house.

Travis looked up to see him coming closer and called out, "Darby, where have you been? You got a girl in town, all this mysterious travel you're doing of late?" Travis smiled up at the little man.

Darby got off the horse and rubbed his posterior. "I surely don't know why God put these creatures on earth. They're certainly not as smooth as the *Sea Breeze*."

Travis laughed. "But, wouldn't it look a little odd to be moving on land under full sail?"

Darby realized the captain's disposition had improved immensely since planning the barbecue. "You are sure in a good mood," he said.

"And, why not? It's a beautiful day, and I am having a party in three days."

Darby gazed at Travis and, hating to foul the captain's good humor, he said, "Well, the day may be beautiful but I think the party may be shanghaied."

"What are you going on about, Darby?" Travis asked in a concerned voice.

"Well, I promised not to tell you, so don't ask." He looked around avoiding Travis's questioning gaze.

"Promised who?"

Darby looked down at his boot and dug into the ground with his peg leg.

Travis was getting anxious, not liking the sound of this at all. "Darby, answer me!" he shouted.

Darby looked up at Travis with a twinkle in his eye. "Is that an order, Cap'n?"

Looking up in the air, Travis felt exasperated and replied, "Yes, Darby, if it will clear your conscience, it is an order."

Delighted, Darby started to explain. "Well, cap'n, I just come from seeing the Lady Elaine." His voice dropped when he added, "She won't be comin' to the barbecue."

His heart suddenly in his throat, Travis yelled, "Why not?"

"Well, you don't have to bite me head off. I'm gettin' to it." Darby looked again at his boot. "Well, it seems her Aunt Katherine is to be sending you a note tellin' the lady be too ill to come to the party and has to stay in bed."

Concerned, Travis bent down and grabbed the little

man by his shoulders. "Is she ill?"

"She don't look good, cap'n, but it's from all the work she be doin' and not eatin' proper. I tell you she be treated worse than the colonel treats his slaves."

"Are you sure about this, Darby?"

"Aye, cap'n. I heard that daughter, what's her name . . ."

"Eudora."

"Aye, Eudora, hate that name. Anyway, I heard her say to the lady, somethin' 'bout did she like bread and water. Well, cap'n, just lookin' at the wee lass, she might be a livin' on that right now."

Travis turned slightly as though in thought. "She did look terrible the day I stopped by." He mentally kicked himself for not going back to see her before today. But he had told himself not to get involved in family matters.

Seeing a chance, Darby said, "Cap'n, the lady wants to get away from there bad. Can't you do somethin' to get her out of there? Maybe she could come here?

Travis turned to look at the rushing river. "I can't take her away from her family, Darby."

Darby kicked a stone with his peg leg and yelled at Travis's back, "You could marry her!"

Travis spun around to look at Darby as though he had lost his mind. "Did you say marry her?"

"Aye, cap'n. In case it hasn't dawned on you yet, you be in love with the lady."

"Darby, you old fool, you don't know what the hell you're talking about."

Standing up to his full height, indignation on his wrinkled face, Darby talked back to Travis for the first time since they had met. "I know that on the ship you were walkin' two feet off the deck after she come on board. I know since she's been at the colonel's we

218

couldn't say boo to you without you jumpin' down our throats. And I know that since you planned this here party for her, you been back up in the air like on the *Sea Breeze*."

"And, just what makes you think she would even want to marry me?" Travis walked closer to him and added, "Besides, let me tell you something. I am not sure that the Lady Elaine Seaton is who she pretends to be. In fact, I seriously doubt, she's a *lady* at all."

"Aye, cap'n, I be thinkin' the same thing. But that don't make no never mind. The girl be the one you love, not the name, and I also think you be the one she be in love with."

Exasperated, Travis tried again to prove his point. "But, if she isn't Lady Elaine, who is she?"

Darby looked at Travis. "I know she be a frightened lass who is in over her head and needs our help."

"So you want me to marry her?" Travis yelled, then turned again to look at the river. "Really, Darby, you can be insane sometimes," he said under his breath.

Darby stood up, tilting his chin to show his determination. "Aye, I think that be the logical way of things for you to marry her."

"Darby, you have really lost your mind." Travis gave a nervous laugh.

"Maybe, but if'n I was you, I'd think 'bout it or you may lose somethin' a lot more precious." Darby turned and led his horse to the stable, hoping he had said enough to make the stubborn captain see that he really was in love with the lady.

Travis watched the little man, thinking it was cruel to take him away from the sea. He was losing his perception of things.

A little voice nagged at him, saying, He's right, you do love her. Travis walked up the hill and gazed in the direction of Salford Manor. He picked up a stick and began stripping off the bark.

Was Darby right? He did look forward to seeing her, and the barbecue was just another excuse. He had thought to sever all ties once she was off the ship, but this seemed to be more difficult than he had planned. He had made up his mind many years ago that to love someone and marry her would be the means for his own demise. He had determined that to be vulnerable to the ways of love was not to his liking. He had seen the longing and desire between his parents cause his beloved mother's death. But what of Elaine? Could he continue to stand by and watch the light go from her eyes, the passion and love of life leave her? Was it pity for her circumstances that tore at his heart, or was it, indeed, a love so great it threatened to consume him? Would his life be fulfilled with her presence at his side, or would he become a spineless cad like he believed his father to be for so many years? Was his father a cad or truly so much in love that the momentary indiscretion was a punishment of his love? Would he be able to do as well if confronted with the same circumstances? He knew, to the depth of his being, that he would have to have her or die himself in abject despair. He knew to be near her and not touch her would be an impossible task to bear.

He stood up straighter with a start. Why? Why did it hurt him to think of never seeing her again? Because he did love her with all the doubts about her personage and all the questions unanswered. He loved her with all his heart and soul. He had loved her from the moment he had picked her up when she had fainted on deck after he had rescued her. A love that threatened now to make his heart race and his senses reel. He found his mind occupied with thoughts of her in the tub, in the breeches and big shirt with her feet bare, and in his bed making love. He knew she was a virgin when he first took her, but she had proven to be an apt pupil in the ways of love. He remembered all the little things that had suddenly become precious in his mind's eye.

With a groan, he threw the stick and marched down the hill to the stable. He called out to the groom to saddle his horse, then paced the enclosure with fast, sure steps.

Darby was wiping down his mare when he noticed Travis pacing the stable.

Travis looked at him, daring him to say anything, as the groom led his big roan into the yard. He swung up into the saddle and spurred the big beast into a full run.

Jenny was taking down the laundry from the many lines strung across the side yard when she heard a horse gallop up the drive.

Travis saw her standing at the clothesline and wheeled the exhausted horse toward her. He jumped down and came to her, gripping her thin arms. Before she could say anything, he asked, "Will you marry me?"

She was stunned. She could not find her voice but simply stared into his dark eyes.

"Well—Will you?" he asked again.

"Travis—I—"

"Damn it Elaine, or whoever you are, I want an answer!"

Astonished, she whispered, "You know?"

He grasped her by the shoulders and looked deeply into her wide blue eyes. "I knew you weren't a titled lady from the minute I laid eyes on you."

"But how?" She could not believe he hadn't bought

her act.

"You weren't dressed in a lady's bed attire and you had calluses." He took her hands and turned them over to gaze at them. "Much like now, on your hands. Besides, it doesn't matter. I really don't give a damn. The question is will you marry me?"

"You know and you still want to marry me?" She looked closely into his eyes. He had not said he loved her. Had this anything to do with Darby's visit? Oh! God, don't let this be pity.

He lowered his voice and simply said, "Yes."

She looked down and said quietly, "There is something you don't know about."

Travis grabbed her and pulled her close to look in her faded eyes that he longed to see returned to their original brilliance. "Elaine, there are probably a million things about you that I don't know. One comes to mind: What's your name?"

Jenny stood up straighter. She would not lie to him ever again. "Jenny. Jennifer Grayson."

He pulled her toward his horse. "That's all I need to know. Now, come on."

Pulling back, Jenny said softly, "No, Travis."

He turned to look at her, not believing her rejection. "You don't want to marry me?"

She looked up at him. "Travis, I cannot marry you when the reason for your pronouncement is pity for me. I could never be happy without your love." She hung her head in misery when he came up and made her look at him.

"Why would you think it pity I feel for you?"

A tear came to her eye unbidden as she squeezed them shut. "You have never spoken to me of love, Travis. I could not live without that."

Travis placed a finger to her cheek, tracing the path of her tears. "But, I do love you," he said quietly. "I love you more than life itself. I have been so stupid and stubborn. I never thought to have that emotion within my hard heart. But you, my beautiful sea nymph, have made my hard heart melt into a puddle of love and longing. My mind has not been my own since the day you walked away from me. I have thought of nothing but you and our time spent together. If not for my stubbornness, I would have taken you posthaste to become my wife the day we arrived in Charleston. But all I can say is my lack of good sense was responsible for that failing." He pulled her to him and wrapped his arms around her thin, shaking body. "I love you, and I would be honored if you would consent to becoming my wife and the mistress of Moss Grove."

Tears of happiness replaced the ones of misery on Jenny's face. "Oh, Travis, I love you, too!" She hugged him to her as all the dreams she had ever had seemed to be coming true. But she had to tell him of the child. What would he say after she told him that he was to be a father? A little afraid, but determined to tell him, she stepped away from his arms and looked into his dark eyes. "I am going to have a child, Travis."

He was stunned and asked, "Are you sure?"

Still looking at him, she answered, "Yes. I guess this might change your mind about marrying me."

"You're damned right it does! We will be married this very afternoon. Why you're about two or three months along. We had better hurry."

Still not able to believe this was happening, Jenny looked at him with a strange look of instensity in her expression. "Travis, are you sure?"

He came to her and kissed her on the eyes, nose, and finally he captured her lips to his before pulling away to look at her with eyes full of boundless love.

"Jenny," he said laughing, "that sounds funny—I have never been more sure of anything in my life."

"But, what about the baby? People—"

"What about it? he interrupted. "Babies come early and he will be a godsend to Moss Grove."

"Travis, the baby is yours."

"I know. I'm the only one that could be the father." He smiled, looking at her with love for her reflected in his smile. "I know you had no one before me."

"I love you, Travis," she whispered.

"And, I love you, Jennifer Grayson."

Jenny's heart soared at his statement, and she threw her arms around him in happy abandon.

The scene that greeted Katherine Colby, when she walked outside to check on Jenny, made a scream come from deep within her throat.

Travis and Jenny separated but held hands as they looked at Katherine, advancing on them like a wild boar.

"What's the meaning of this? Get in the house, Elaine, and I think you had better leave, Captain Gardiner and don't come back." Katherine walked up and grabbed Jenny's arm and started to pull her toward the house.

Travis leaned over and forcefully took her hand away from Jenny's arm. "It's all right with me, Mistress Colby, but I will be taking Elaine with me."

Katherine turned red with rage and yelled, "Just what makes you think I will allow her to leave here with you?"

Travis pulled Jenny behind him and leaned closer to Katherine. Glaring at the woman, Travis started, "I don't know what's been going on here but I'm taking Elaine with me and away from you and your obvious cruelty and mistreatment of her."

Katherine was frightened of this man, but the

wrath of her husband who would learn of Elaine's leaving was a more powerful force. "My husband will have something to say about this. Elaine is his responsibility and *he* will decide where she will stay." She took a step to the side and reached again to grab at Jenny.

Travis sidestepped to come between the two. "Elaine has agreed to come with me, Katherine, and I would suggest you leave your hands off her. If your husband does not like this arrangement, he may call on me. Now we are leaving and I would advise you to step aside. I have never hit a woman before but you are sorely tempting me, Katherine."

Katherine stepped back at his threat, then stood by and watched while Travis helped Elaine up on his horse and climbed up behind her. As he spurred his horse down the lane, Katherine ran after them yelling, "You haven't heard the end of this, Captain Gardiner. I will get you for this!" She shook a fist at them. "You will pay for this!"

Travis stopped the horse and turned in the saddle. He saw Eudora behind her mother, wearing one of the gowns he remembered he had especially liked on Jenny. "I think your daughter's wardrobe is payment enough. You can tell your husband that his payment did not even buy the stays." He looked menacingly at Katherine and added, "And, I wouldn't be threatening me, Katherine. I should send the constable out here to investigate what has been going on here. I trust I will never see or hear from you again." He turned the horse and rode away from the still fuming woman.

Jenny thought she would wake up any minute from this dream. She had her arms around Travis's neck

225

while he slowed the horse to an easier gait. She smiled at the handsome profile he offered her. Reaching up, she touched his temple, bringing his attention to her.

"Are you comfortable?" he asked.

"I don't know. Right this minute, I feel I am floating." She closed her eyes to keep the dream alive.

Travis steered the horse off the road and pulled at the reins. He got down, pulling Jenny into his arms.

"I have been so stupid, Elaine—I mean Jenny." He laughed and stepped back to look at her, becoming serious again. "Tell me about it. Did they hurt you?"

She looked up into his pain-filled eyes and wished the look away. "No, they never physically abused me. They expected me to work to pay for my room and board. But let's forget about that now. Just tell me about you. How have you been?"

He smiled and touched her cheek. "Jenny, I have been miserable but didn't know why until Darby set me straight. He kicked me in the jaw this afternoon and I finally realized I wanted you. I want you forever." He hugged her gently to him. "Now, Jenny Grayson, I think we had better discuss your charade." He watched her eyes that expressed her soul.

"I decided to be Elaine that day you rescued me. I didn't know how you would treat me if you knew me as a commoner and not a titled lady. I was so afraid. I was all alone and nowhere to go. I knew Elaine had relatives here in the Carolinas and that they had never met her. For some reason, which seems ridiculous now, I thought I would be better off as Lady Elaine." She looked up at him and gave a nervous laugh. "After I got to know you, I was going to tell you the truth but you treated me so horribly when thinking me a lady that I was sure you would have put me to scrubbing and bowing before you if you knew I wasn't titled." She didn't want to tell him of her indenture just yet. The humiliation would be too great after what he had witnessed at the Colby's. She didn't want to tell him, but she would not lie to him, either.

Travis knew she was holding something back but didn't press the matter. She would tell him in her own way, and so he said, "I'm sorry about the way I treated you in the beginning, Jenny. I guess even then I was trying to deny the effect you were having on me."

Jenny looked around to the river and said softly, "What about my name? If you continue to call me Jenny, people will know I'm not who I said I was."

"Well, we will just go by your new name so as not to arouse anyone's curiosity. Elaine Jennifer Gardiner. I will simply tell people who matter that I liked your middle name better." He smiled. "Will that suit you?"

Jenny thought him the most forgiving, the most exciting man she had ever known and kissed him passionately.

Travis slapped playfully at her bottom, saying, "We had better get going. I have a wedding to plan. Come on."

Travis and Jenny rode up the winding, oak-lined drive to Moss Grove. Jenny was in awe of the beauty around her. Green fields with white fences and beautiful horses romping in the summer sunshine to her right. To the left she saw row upon row of dark green plants. She asked Travis what they were and he told her cotton.

Bending to her ear, he extended a finger pointing to the fields. "Later they will be filled with white cotton balls and that sight will be glorious. I can't wait until I can show you."

Jenny snuggled up to him and smiled at the pride in his voice. Later she would learn that Moss Grove was one of the biggest cotton producers in the Carolinas.

The sun that had blinded them was obscured as Jenny turned to look in the direction they were heading. Huge oak trees lined the lane they were traveling. Jenny remembered the description Darby had given her of the moss hanging from the trees and knew she was approaching her new home. Then it was before her. An immense house was seen through the trees. Three stories high, the house was fronted by six columns that spanned the front. Green shutters adorned the many windows, and a delicate rose brick embellished the portico. Jenny was entranced by the graceful elegance of the stately mansion.

"Travis, it's beautiful," Jenny stated in awed excitement.

Looking at the expression in her face and voice, Travis smiled tenderly. "Moss Grove is now your home. I hope you will be happy here."

She tightened her arms around his neck and said, "I know I will be happy here as long as I am with you."

Travis stopped the horse in front of the house and helped Jenny down, calling for a groom to take the horse. As they were walking up the rose brick steps, a big black woman with a red kerchief tied around her hair and a big white apron tied over her full black skirt came out to meet them.

"What's you done been up to, Mis'er Travis? You done hit dis chile wid dat big ole 'orse of yore'n?"

"No, no Mammy. This is Jenny. She is going to be staying with us and I believe she needs some rest and a bath."

"Look more lak she need some food in her," the big woman stated flatly.

Jenny turned to Travis. "I am hungry."

"First, Mammy, you bring a bath to Miss Celeste's

room, then you can bring a tray." He turned to look at Jenny. "You will feel better after a bath, and I want you to eat your fill. Dinner will be late tonight."

Mammy came down the stairs, put her arm across Jenny's back and walked her up the steps of Moss Grove and Jenny's new home.

Travis called after her, "I'm going into town to get some things. Plan on guests for dinner and be ready at seven tonight, Mammy." He winked at Jenny. "Mammy will take good care of you. Just rest until I get back."

Jenny felt safe and secure for the first time in months with this big woman beside her. Mammy ordered the tub and water brought up while she led the way up the polished staircase.

Jenny did not have a chance to look around her at the splendor of this house, but her nose gave evidence of beeswax, fresh air, and aromas of beef and bread wafting from the cook house.

She was amazed at the efficiency of the house servants. They brought water, soap, and towels within moments. Mammy shooed them out and came over to Jenny, giving her a hand at taking off the offensive gown. Jenny was embarrassed by the odor and condition of the gown, but she hadn't been able to wash it for several days, as Katherine had used Travis's last visit as an excuse to put her back in the cellar. She wanted to say something to this kind woman about the gown but knew nothing could explain it but the truth, and she couldn't bring herself to tell this stranger of her past predicament just now.

She took off her chamise and pantalets, and Mammy came over with a cry of delight, saying to her, "Why, chile, you goin' to have a babe and you no bigger than a minute. Heah, y'all set yoresef down in dis heah tub and old Mammy will take care a you."

Jenny was grateful to the old woman for taking care of her. She eased down into the hot water and felt the tension and fatigue leave her body. The water was so warm and relaxing it made her want to go to sleep. But Mammy knelt down, picked up the cloth and started applying the lovely scented soap to the cloth, making Jenny aware of her state.

"Set up heah, chile, and let Mammy scrub some a dat ole grime off'n you."

Mammy hummed along while she scrubbed Jenny from top to bottom. As Jenny was beginning to feel that Mammy was taking skin along with the dirt, Mammy sat back and told Jenny to lie her head back.

Jenny did as she was told, and a warm bucket of water was applied to her hair. Mammy used an egg shampoo that she told Jenny was guaranteed to make her hair beautiful. She then rinsed it clean in heated rainwater. Mammy helped Jenny stand up and then wrapped her in a big, fluffy towel. Jenny marveled that the woman never asked questions. In a way, Jenny was glad she didn't. She just wanted to relax and think about her wedding.

While Jenny dried herself, Mammy stepped to the clothes press and pulled out a delicate pink dressing gown. "Dis heah will do right nice 'til y'all caine get you own clothes." She helped Jenny into it, then said, "Why don't you lie down heah on dis heah bed whiles ah goes an gets you somethin' ta eats." She pulled down the white organdy counterpane and made sure Jenny was snug before silently walking to the door.

Jenny lay down on the soft feather bed and in no time was fast asleep.

Mammy looked back at the child on the bed. She had fallen asleep, which Mammy thought was best for now.

Shaking her massive head, Mammy wondered what

Travis was up to now. What was this child doing here? She crept silently over and picked up the gown the girl had worn. Holding it at arms' length, she walked out of the room, closing the door quietly behind her. She stood in the hall for a moment then slowly began the long walk to the cook house.

"What had Mis'er Travis done gone and done dis time and what he 'spect me ta do wid dis chile?" She shook her head in wonderment. She knew she would find out in time. The master never did anything without telling her.

Chapter Twelve

Travis had galloped at full speed into Charleston. When he pulled in front of Judge Oscar Shealy's chambers, he jumped down and led the horse to a water trough and patted his perspiring neck.

He ran up the steps to the courthouse, then went directly to the office occupied by his longtime friend. When he entered the judge's outer office, he spotted the immaculate and somewhat effeminate secretary that Oscar could not function without.

"George, is the judge in or is he in court?"

George looked up from the transcripts he had been copying. "Oh! Captain Gardiner. It is such a pleasure to see you again. I do trust you had a marvelous voyage?"

Not really wanting to take the time to exchange pleasantries, Travis was a little short with the man. "Yes, George, a very nice trip. Now, where is the judge?"

"Oh, my, well, he is in his office, but I'm afraid he has someone with him at the moment." He giggled, which set Travis's nerves on edge. "In fact, he's with your brother."

Travis walked to the door, saying, "I'm sure they

won't mind my interruption."

"Wait!" George jumped up and run to the door, trying to block the way. "At least allow me to announce you."

"That's all right. I'll announce myself." Travis opened the door on the two men inside. "Sorry to interrupt, but—" He stopped in mid-stride. "What's the matter with you two? You look like you just heard the world is coming to an end in an hour."

Oscar motioned Travis inside the office. "Close the door, Travis."

Travis turned and gently closed the door on a very disgruntled George. Turning and walking to the chair next to Jeff, Travis sat down with a foreboding that he needed explained. "What's the problem?"

Oscar sat back, removing the spectacles that Travis knew he wore only to add an air of distinction to his boyish face. "Travis, something has been going on here for sometime. Today we were advised it has affected one of our own."

Travis became worried at the continued expressions of unrest that his brother and his friend were wearing. "Oscar, would you please explain what *it* is? I'm at a loss."

Oscar continued, "Maybe I should start at the beginning since you've been gone so much." He stood up and walked to the window, looking out at Charleston Harbor. "Remember when that mulatto of yours showed up missing six years ago?"

Travis looked to Jeff then back to Oscar. "Yes. But I always thought she had run away with a slave from Salford Manor. They lost a slave during that same week."

"That's what we all *assumed*," Jeff added.

"All right, assumed. Would you get on with this?" Travis was becoming concerned by the two men's continued unrest. Oscar looked directly at his friend. "We have had a number of other disappearances in recent years. Most have been young, light-skinned, beautiful Negro women and girls." He turned again to the window. "Nothing was put together until today." Oscar turned back to look again at the harbor. "Jessy Harmon's daughter has turned up missing. No one knows where she is."

"Couldn't there be a number of reasons for her disappearance?" Travis still could not understand the reasons behind the two men's expressions.

Jeff leaned over and said, "Jessy's daughter is beautiful, Travis. She was to be married next week and, according to her father, she was very happy and excited. He's beside himself with grief." Jeff stood up and walked behind his chair, putting his hands on the backrest. "Why would she run away?" He looked at Oscar before continuing. "What we fear, Travis, is that someone is taking these girls. For what purposes, we don't know, but the Harmon girl is the first white woman to turn up missing like the others. Just vanished without a trace."

Travis looked at his brother's worried face. "But Jeff, couldn't you be wrong? I mean, maybe the girl got cold feet about getting married or maybe she had a disagreement with her intended and decided to run away to make him worry. There are probably a number of reasons she may be missing."

Oscar returned to his chair and sat down. He put his elbows on his desk, folding his hands in front of his chin and looking directly into Travis's eyes, he said, "Travis, we have been making excuses all along for the disappearances of the blacks. They weren't that important being women slaves, but now we are confronted with the missing white girl. We must get to the bottom of this before any more of the ladies of

Charleston turn up missing."

The three men sat contemplating their own thoughts until Travis was brought out of his reverie when the chimes struck the hour of five. Jumping up, he looked at Oscar and Jeff with a grin on his handsome face. "If you two can put your thoughts of kidnappers aside for a moment, I have something to tell you." He smiled a nervous smile as the two men looked at him. "I am getting married."

Jeff jumped forward and grabbed Travis's hand. "Travis, I am pleased as can be. Who's the lucky girl?" he said with a grin that told Travis he thought he knew.

Travis groaned. "No, it's not Alicia."

A look of genuine happiness came over Jeff. "Well, who is it then?" Jeff asked, hoping it would be the damsel Travis had rescued.

Smiling, Travis walked back to his chair and sat down. "You don't know her. She's the woman I rescued from the *Himes*." He looked up at Jeff. "I think you will agree with me that she is lovely when you meet her."

Jeff came up beside the chair Travis was sitting in, pleased that his plan had worked to perfection. "I can't wait to meet her. When's the big day?"

Travis looked at Oscar. "Today," he quickly added, "that is if I can persuade Oscar to come out to Moss Grove and perform the ceremony."

Oscar had been sure Travis would never travel down the aisle, and he had never seen Travis happier. Pansy would have a fit if she knew this was going on behind her back. He stood up and walked around his desk extending his hand to the bridegroom. "Travis, I couldn't be more pleased. Of course, you know Pansy will probably never get over the fact that you picked someone she hadn't thoroughly screened for you

235

first."

Travis laughed. "It wasn't for her lack of effort. That wife of yours led me around like a prize bull before all her friends and some she didn't know."

Oscar shook Travis's hand, saying, "Of course I'll be there. What time?"

"Could you be at the plantation at seven?" Travis knew it didn't give Oscar much time.

"I'll be there, but I'm afraid Pansy will not be able to come. She is at her parents' plantation in Savannah." He looked at Travis with a grin. "She'll be mad as hell you're doing this behind her back. Especially since she didn't get a chance to get one more of her friends into your arms. She has always felt your bachelorhood's coming to an end to be her direct responsibility."

"I think when she meets Jenny, she'll understand." Travis looked at Jeff. "I trust I can count on you to be there."

Jeff turned a confused look to Travis. "Jenny? Travis, I was under the impression that the lady you rescued was named Elaine." He put his hand to his chin, adding, "You didn't by chance rescue two, did you?"

Travis looked on his brother with his own confusion evident. "I don't remember mentioning the lady by name to you, Jeff. How would you know her name?"

The grin on Jeff's face spoke multitudes as he tried to stifle his glee. "Someone must have mentioned it."

All at once the scene with Alicia came back to him. "Why, you! You planned that evening, didn't you? When I get hold of Darby, I'll wring his neck."

Jeff put both hands up and came to stand in front of his brother who looked so much like himself. "Don't go blamin' Darby, Travis. He just mentioned you had taken a liking to the Lady Elaine. I just

236

thought I would do my best to show you your alternatives."

Travis smiled at the idea his brother exhibited. "Well, I must say it worked." A softness came to his eyes when he thought of Jenny, his sweet Jenny.

Jeff looked at Oscar and winked, saying, "I can see that, Travis."

Travis looked chagrinned and in explanation of Jenny's name said, "I never liked the name Elaine so with Jenny's permission, I call her Jenny, which is her middle name." Travis hated the ruse between his brother and friend but for now it would have to do.

"I like that name better, too. Jenny." Jeff had a far-off look as though wondering what an Elaine Jennifer would be like.

Travis came back to the two men before him. "Well, Jeff, can I count on you to be there?"

Jeff smiled. "You couldn't beat me away with a stick. Can I help with anything?"

Travis thought a moment then asked, "Do you remember where Mother's wedding gown is?"

"Sure do. Sally Bradshaw has it."

Travis turned to the door. "Thanks, I'll go get it." He paused and turned again to his brother. "By the way, Jeff. Can I count on you to be my best man?"

Jeff beamed. "I thought you had forgotten that formality. I would be honored."

"Good. I will see you back at Moss Grove, and thank you both. Oh! Do me a favor and don't mention this to anyone, all right?" He smiled and walked out the door almost bumping into George, who was standing just on the other side.

George looked embarrassed and said, "I couldn't help but overhear your news. Congratulations, captain."

Travis accepted the proffered hand, noting the

clammy weakness of George's handshake. "Thank you. See you later." Travis left the office to the strange secretary, never wondering why he felt compelled to wipe his hand on his breeches.

George stared after him. "What a disappointment," he said aloud. He had longed to get to know Mr. Travis Gardiner better. He was such a tall, good-looking man. And George did like men.

Travis pulled on the reins as he came up to the two-story townhouse of Sally Bradshaw. He tied the reins to the brass hitching ring and ran up the steps to knock on the door.

A small, black woman of indiscriminate age, opened the door and when she recognized Travis, a broad grin transformed her face. "Why, Mr. Travis. I heard you was back in town. Miss Bradshaw sure been a wonderin' when you was goin' ta come by an see her." She stepped back letting Travis in the entrance hall.

Travis heard the sounds of female voices coming from the parlor and asked, "Is Miss Bradshaw entertaining?"

"She's got a sewing bee goin' on in the parlor. Let me sneak in an tell her you heah." She slid the door back and walked into the bedlam of six elderly ladies all talking at once.

Travis saw Lucy bend and whisper in Sally's ear.

Sally looked up at him and gave a brilliant smile. She excused herself and hobbled with the aid of a cane to Travis. Lucy closed the doors after Sally emerged.

"Why you young scamp, here I've waited weeks for you to show up. I wouldn't even have known you were back except for the invitation Darby brought for the barbecue. I really should box your ears, you know." Her smile laid the lie to her words.

Travis returned the smile of the woman who had been his mother's best friend. "Actually, I can't stay to visit now. I just came by to get something you've been keeping for us."

Sally looked up at him questioningly. "Well, Travis, I really don't know what you're talking about. The only thing I'm keeping for you is your mother's—" She stopped and looked closely at him. "Just what is it you want?"

Travis looked at her with a grin. "I need the wedding gown you are keeping."

Sally caught his sleeve and leaned closer to him. "Is this for you or Jeff?"

"It's for my wedding, Sally. I'm getting married this evening."

A tear appeared in the old woman's eyes. "Travis, I don't know what to say." She smiled in genuine happiness. "I was beginning to despair of ever seeing that beautiful gown used again. Your mother would be so pleased." She raised her head and pulled Travis down to kiss his cheek. "My only regret is that I shan't be able to come. I have all those old busy bodies staying for supper."

Travis thought for a moment before saying, "Sally, I can't go into it just now, but I would appreciate it if you didn't say anything to anyone about this."

Sally looked at the concern Travis displayed, and said, "All right, Travis, I won't say a word." She remembered something and added, "But, what about the barbecue? Will you announce your marriage then?"

"Yes, but I won't be specific on the date." He stopped and looked at the confusion on Sally's face. He hugged her frail shoulders to him. "Sally, I know

239

this all seems mysterious and confusing." He stepped back to look at her. "But, I'm sure, once you meet Jenny and understand, you will be happy for us."

Surprise now replaced the confusion on Sally's wrinkled brow. "Jenny? Jenny who? I thought you were marrying Alicia?"

Travis was now the one confused. "Why would you think that?"

Sally walked over to a chair in the hall and sat down. Putting her hands on the head of her ornately crafted cane, she looked up at him. "I had supper with Alicia and her parents last week. All the girl could talk about was you and the plans she was making for her wedding." She looked at the door to the parlor to make sure of their privacy, then back to Travis. "She was so sure. This will crush her."

Travis was fuming. "That's really not my concern, Sally. I never gave her the slightest idea I would marry her. In fact, if she were the last woman in Charleston, I would remain a bachelor!"

Sally saw the wrath her admission brought out in him and quickly turned his mind to more pleasant thoughts. "Tell me about this Jenny. Do I know her?"

Thinking of Jenny brought a smile to his lips. Sally, feeling more comfortable about the mysterious wedding, smiled too.

"I haven't time to tell you now, but you will meet her Saturday and will know I am a lucky man." He paused, changing the subject when he said, "I really need to get back. Could you get me the gown?"

"Of course." She turned in her chair and called, "Lucy!"

Lucy came from the back rubbing her hands on her apron. "Yes, ma'am."

"Lucy, would you go up to my room, to the cedar

240

chest, and bring me the box on the bottom?"

"Yea, ma'am," Lucy said then ran up the stairs, surprising Travis with her agility.

"That Lucy is amazing. She must be close to sixty, yet she'a as spry as a young girl." He looked after the retreating woman.

"It's all in the way she thinks. She tells me I need to get up and get going. She's in love with life and will probably outlive us both."

"Not me!" Travis turned and gave her a gay smile. "I have something to live for now."

Sally watched him pace the foyer. He certainly was anxious to return to his bride.

Lucy came down the stairs, carrying a big yellowed box. She handed it to Sally then turned and left them alone again.

"Here you are, Travis. I hope your lady is slight of stature. Your mother was a small woman. I always wondered how she managed to have two such big sons."

"It will do fine." He bent and kissed Sally's cheek. "Thank you and I'll see you on Saturday." He left, closing the door behind him.

At six o'clock Travis was racing back to Moss Grove.

Jenny awoke to the smell of broth and fresh baked bread and creamy butter. Mammy was standing by the side of the bed holding a tray. "Dis be somethin' ta tide you over 'til supper." She placed the tray on Jenny's lap and went to open the curtains. "You sho' done take a nap, missy. Ah figgered you done sleep 'nough. Dats why ah come up jes' now."

Jenny spooned the rich beef broth into her mouth. "What time is it?" she asked between bites of the

241

warm bread.

"It be close to seben, missy."

Jenny buttered another slice of the warm bread and munched on it contentedly. Mammy came over and poured her a cup of strong tea from a delicate china teapot. While Jenny sipped the tea, Mammy stood over her like a guard watching her charge.

Sitting back, Jenny indicated she was finished, but Mammy would have none of that. "You be goin' ta finish dat dare soup, missy. You's gots ta keep up your strength. After all, you's goin ta be a mama."

Jenny smiled at the woman and finished the soup. Mammy picked up the tray and told Jenny, "Ahs be right back ta hep y'all get dressed. Y'all jes' stay put in dat dare bed." She started to leave but heard a commotion and turned to the window. "Dat must be dat Darby back from gettin' yore trunks, chile. Ah wonder what took him so long. Ah done sent him hours ago." Mammy shook her head and walked from the room.

Jenny knew it couldn't be Darby with her trunks. She had no trunks and she was sure Katherine would never relent and give her her due. She wondered what Darby had said when Mammy sent him on this wild goose chase.

As the woman walked out, closing the door behind her, Jenny looked about the room she was occupying. The walls were white with little pictures of ballerinas and kittens here and there on the walls. A white dresser, with full mirror, held fancy bottles of perfume, oils, and powders. The bed she was lying on had a white organdy counterpane with a matching canopy top. The curtains, blowing in the evening breeze, were also made of white organdy. The floor was polished hardwood with a thick persian carpet lying on it with hues of pinks and roses. All in all

Jenny liked this room. It was a young girl's room, and Jenny felt comfortable here.

She heard another commotion coming from outside the windows. Not recognizing the sounds or the voices, she got up from the bed and walked to the window. The room faced the drive with the Ashley River in the distance. While she was looking at the scenery, she noticed Travis galloping up the drive. Her heart started beating faster as she followed him with her eyes until he was lost to her sight. Looking back to the drive she saw a carriage coming up with another following.

Jenny watched intently as strangers started getting out of the carriages. She didn't hear the door open behind her, her mind on the scene below, until she heard the rustle of crisp crinolines behind her. She turned to see Mammy approaching her with a huge smile on her fat face and tears rolling down her cheeks.

"Chile, y'alls made ole Mammy da happiest person alive." She put the box on the bed and came to Jenny. "Ta think that the cap'n goin' ta be marryin' you tonight." The woman raised her hands and tilted her head back as she yelled, "Praise da Lord!" Putting her hands down, she rushed to enfold Jenny in her arms. "Come on now, chile. We'uns gots ta get y'all ready for da weddin'!"

Mammy opened the box she had brought in with her, and inside was the most beautiful ivory lace gown Jenny had ever seen. Reverently, Mammy picked the gown up from its tissue encasement. She gently unfolded it and laid it out on the bed. Smoothing it, she explained to Jenny, "Dis heah be Miss Ellen's weddin' gown. She done looked lak an angel in dis heah dress. 'Course, it be white back den. But time ain't ruined its beauty none."

243

Jenny saw the remembrance in Mammy's face and asked, "Was it a big wedding, Mammy?"

Mammy looked up at her with misty eyes and said, "It be lak a fairy tale. Miss Ellen come over heah from France ta be marryin' Mis'er Jack. Dat be Mis'er Travis's daddy. He done come from France as a young'un. He done bought me in Charleston when ah was a young'un, too."

"You mean you are a slave?" Jenny asked in surprise.

Mammy stood up straight and turned to look directly at her. "Ah done be a slave *no more*. Mis'er Travis done free me long time ago."

Jenny felt she had somehow upset the woman and quickly tried to apologize. "I'm sorry, Mammy. Please continue with your story."

Mammy smiled at her and continued as though nothing had happened. "Well, ah be heah only a few months when dis lady come heah. Ah mean she were a lady. So small and delicate. Mis'er Jack was in heaben. Had us a workin' from sunup ta sundown ta get da house in Charleston ready fer her. Dey was married downstairs in da parlor. When she come down dose stairs, ever eye was wet. She was beautiful." Mammy closed her eyes as though bringing back the memory of that day, then turned to look at Jenny. "Jes' lak you, chile," she added softly.

Jenny turned red with embarrassment at the reverence in the woman's voice and lowered her head with a slight smile on her face. "Mammy, I hope to be a good wife to Travis."

Mammy came over and patted Jenny's hand. "Y'all will, chile." When she heard voices from downstairs, she rushed to add, "Come on now. We'uns gots ta get y'all ready for da weddin'." She picked up a brush, applying it to Jenny's hair in long vigorous strokes.

"Let Mammy do somethin' wid you hair." She held the soft, golden tresses and was pleased at the difference a bath and a nap made in the girl's appearance. Jenny looked refreshed and the hot soup had put some color in her cheeks. But, as Mammy studied Jenny's reflection in the mirror, she noticed something else. An inner glow radiated from within her spirit. Mammy had seen this look before only once, and that had been on Miss Ellen's face on her wedding day. Mammy silently said a prayer to her Lord to bless this child and the man she was to marry in a few moments. To bless the child who would be brought into this world and to help bring about a safe and healthy birth to mother and child.

Noticing again the thinness of the girl before her, she leaned down to whisper in her ear, "Give me a month an ah'll have y'all in da pink, chile."

Mammy arranged Jenny's hair back from her face with curls running down from a chignon on top. Little wisps were arranged to fall from above her ears. It was a masterful arrangement, and Jenny thought she looked like a princess in one of the fairy tales she had heard as a child.

Mammy stood back and said, "That's 'bout perfect, chile. We'un better hurry an' get y'all dressed now. Done wont Mis'er Travis mad on his weddin' day, and if'n ah keeps y'all from him longer den a few mo' minutes, dat boy will be chompin' at da bit." She giggled, then went to the wardrobe and withdrew a camisole, chamise, pantalets, stockings, and then into the clothes press for petticoats.

Jenny asked her about the clothes, wondering why so many were in this room. "Whose clothes are these, Mammy?"

Mammy turned to her with a sadness evident on her features. "Dey be my baby Celeste's, but she'd

245

been pleased for y'all ta use dem. She was one a da most generous peoples you'd ever met." She went on as if she thought an explanation was needed. "Ahs knows you be wonderin' why dese heah clothes be still heah. Mis'er Jeff done told me to pack dem up, but ahs just could'na bring myself ta. Now ah knows dat da good Lord done been try'n ta 'splain dat dey would be needed again."

Jenny wondered at this woman's serene faith in her Lord but was quickly rushed into the many undergarments presented her. When Mammy pulled the gown down and smoothed the folds, Jenny turned to see herself in the mirror. Why the gown was breathtaking. The ivory color set her complexion and hair off to a high luster, bringing added color to her eyes. The dress was closely fitted across the bodice with a high neck, clustered in pearl buttons which matched the buttons on the closely fitted sleeves that ended in points on the backs of her hands. The skirt flowed about her like a cloud. Jenny never had a gown as beautiful as this one.

While Jenny basked in the glow of her reflection, Mammy placed an ivory lace veil over her head. Jenny remembered the dreams she had on her way to London, that day so long ago with her father. All her dreams were about to come true. Poor father. If only you could see me now, she thought.

A knock on the door brought Jenny back to the present. A young man came in with a bouquet of pink and white roses. He smiled at her and came up and gave her a brotherly kiss on the cheek, saying, "My dear, you are lovely. Trust that brother of mine to come up with a beauty. Welcome to our family."

Jenny was amazed at the resemblance between Travis and his brother. "You must be Jeff. I am so pleased to finally meet you."

"It's pleased we all are to meet you, Elaine Jennifer."

Jenny looked at him closely with a slightly puzzled expression in her eyes. Then she remembered Travis's idea of the name. She said, "Please call me Jenny."

A knock on the door interrupted them and Jeff said, "That will be Darby. I will say good-bye until later." Jeff gave her another kiss on the cheek, then turned to open the door to Darby

Darby looked like a new man. He had trimmed his hair and beard, had a new black satin eye patch on and had polished his peg leg to a shiny luster. But the best was his dark blue waistcoat over a ruffled white shirt and black satin knee breeches.

Jenny smiled as Darby walked up to her and bowed. Then in a most dignified voice, he said, "My lady, it be me pleasure to escort you to the cap'n."

Jenny curtsied and with a large grin, replied. "Why thank you, kind sir. It would be my honor and great pleasure to go with you."

Mammy intruded, looking at the little man and shaking her fat finger in his face. "Ahs been waitin' fer de trunks dat you was 'spose ta bring. What y'all been doin' 'cept primpin'?" She looked him up and down, making her point.

Darby looked to Jenny with a helpless expression.

Jenny knew the little man didn't know what to say so she turned to Mammy with an apology. "I'm sorry, Mammy. I should have told you that my trunks were lost.

Mammy scowled at Darby. "Did you know dey was lost?"

Darby gulped visibly before answering this formidable woman before him. "No, ma'am. I just found that out myself."

After giving Darby another thorough glance,

Mammy turned to Jenny. "Well, chile, looks lak we'll jes' have ta make do wid Miss Celeste's clothes 'till you gets some a yo' own."

Jenny smiled at the helpful old woman. "Thank you, Mammy." Then she turned to Darby and put her hand through the crook of his arm. They walked down the hall to the stairs with Mammy fussing over the train in the back of Jenny's gown. Jenny knew this little man, whom she had learned to love, was partly responsible for this day's happening and was determined to thank him when she got a chance.

They descended the stairs, and Jenny noted the small group of people watching her. She saw Jeff and smiled, then she saw Travis standing by the fireplace, looking quite handsome in his gray waistcoat with a darker gray cummerbund over a white shirt with ruffled sleeves. His white knee hose and breeches were set off by black shoes with gold buckles.

Travis watched the vision come down the stairs toward him. The ivory veil obscured her features, but he knew she was lovely under the concealing web. She was holding herself straight as though this were a proud moment. A thousand thoughts raced through his mind while he watched her. For some reason he relived a moment when Jeff, Celeste, and he had been children. Mammy would tell them of their parents' wedding day. She would inevitably weep while she told them how beautiful their mother had looked as she had walked down the staircase in the same gown Jenny was now wearing. How had his father felt when he had stood, much like Travis was now, waiting for his bride to join him? Had his father felt the racing pulse, the uncertainty of their future together or the overwhelming feeling of love for the woman? Had his father asked himself what he was doing like Travis had only moments before, only to realize that this was a moment that would change him for better or worse forever? So many questions still left unanswered. So many years ahead to explore each other's minds. Darby had been right. What did it matter? She was beautiful, kind, and loving. What more could a man ask for?

As she drew abreast of him, he held out his big, bronzed hand to her, and she placed her small, delicate white-laced gloved one in his. They looked at each other then turned to Oscar as the ceremony began.

Jenny only heard bits and pieces of the words Oscar spoke. Her mind was filled with such joy and happiness she could not concentrate on the words until Oscar smiled at her as though waiting for her attention. She looked up and he continued.

"Travis and Elaine Jennifer, you have come here today to seek the blessing of God and his church upon your marriage. I require, therefore, that you promise, with the help of God, to fulfill the obligations which Christian marriage demands."

Oscar turned to Travis. "Travis, you have taken Elaine Jennifer to be your wife. Do you promise to love her, comfort her, honor and keep her, in sickness and in health; and, forsaking all others, to be faithful to her as long as you both shall live?"

Travis turned to look into Jenny's eyes and in a commanding voice, responded, "I do."

After Jenny had promised to love Travis in sickness and health, she responded in an awed voice, "I do."

Oscar then looked up at the assembly and said with a smile on his boyish face, "I now pronounce these two as man and wife. You may kiss your bride."

Travis turned to Jenny and gently raised the veil,

kissing her tenderly before the group of well wishers.

Jenny couldn't believe she had actually become Travis's wife. She was so happy she didn't think anything could spoil this moment. She could not know that her happiness was only to be temporary.

Jeff came up to her taking her hands in his, saying, "May I kiss my new sister?"

Travis stepped back and Jeff placed a brotherly kiss on Jenny's lips.

Oscar tapped Travis on the shoulder. "She's beautiful, Travis. I hope you will be very happy."

Travis turned to his friend, taking the proffered hand. "If my marriage is half as good as yours, Oscar, I will be a lucky man."

Oscar smiled, then turned to the bride. "My dear, I wish you all the happiness in the world. You have a fine husband here." He smiled at Travis, then turned back to Jenny. "I hope you won't let the local ladies get to you. Needless to say, several of them had designs on him. But I think he picked the best. Now may I kiss the bride?"

Jenny smiled up at this man who had just married her to the man of her dreams. "Of course you may."

Oscar leaned down and kissed Jenny's cheek, whispering in her ear, "Don't want Travis to get the wrong impression."

Jenny smiled then turned her attention to Travis who was being thoroughly hugged in the immense arms of Mammy.

"You's made ole Mammy so happy." Tears were streaming down her cheeks when she turned to Jenny and hugged her until Jenny thought she would surely break. Mammy stepped back and, taking a kerchief from her apron pocket, dabbed at her eyes, saying, "Ah's got ta go an get the dinner goin'." She smiled again at Travis and Jenny, then added, "Yes sir, y'all done made me happy dis day." She turned and waddled toward the dining hall.

Jeff called Obediah standing in the corner. "Obediah, bring the champagne."

The butler opened the bottles Jeff had brought. He poured the sparkling beverage into delicate crystal goblets marked with the initial G. While he passed the tray around, Jeff called Mammy and all the other house servants to come join in the toast to the bride and groom. He turned to Jenny and held his glass up. "To the bride. May you be happy here at Moss Grove and may you produce many heirs to follow you."

Travis almost choked while Jenny turned beet red. Everyone present, except Mammy, thought the couple embarrassed at the reference to what would happen tonight.

After much toasting and the clinking of glasses, Mammy announced, "Dinner be ready. Come on, ever'body."

Travis led Jenny into the dining hall and held her chair for her at the end of the table. The candlelight coming from a huge crystal chandelier added to the fairy tale Jenny thought she was living.

Mammy supervised the serving girls as they brought in a soup that Jenny found had small bits of crab and tasted of cream and a sweet liqueur.

Travis, seeing her wonder, explained, "This is she-crab soup, Jenny. Do you like it?"

"It's delicious," Jenny remarked before taking another spoonful.

They were next served little game hens, stuffed with wild rice and spinach. Jenny looked up when Travis laughed.

"This *is* spinach, Jenny."

Of the three other men at the table, two were lost as Travis, Jenny, and Darby exchanged smiles.

Mammy cleared off the table and proceeded to call for dessert. The two girls brought in dishes of what Jenny was to learn was raspberry ice. It was delicious and a thoroughly foreign dish to Jenny.

Feeling full and content, they arose to have brandy and coffee in the sitting room. After plenty of good conversation and a lot of fun, Jeff turned to Travis. "Travis, Jenny, I must get back to Charleston, but I'm so pleased you two invited me to your wedding. If I can be of any further assistance, just whistle. I'll see you Friday to help with the barbecue. Good night."

"I'll go with you," Oscar called after Jeff, then turned to Travis and Jenny. "I will say my good-byes until Saturday. It was a pleasure presiding at your wedding." Oscar shook hands with Travis and smiled and nodded to Jenny before turning to follow Jeff.

The house servants came up one by one to offer their congratulations. Soon Darby was the only one left and he walked up before the couple with a tear in his eye. "I just want you two to know that you've made an old man very happy." He withdraw a kerchief and noisily blew his nose as he walked out of the room leaving the two newlyweds to themselves.

Travis turned to Jenny and swept her into his arms, feeling suddenly shy. "Jenny, I hope to make you a good husband. At times I can be a tyrant, I know, but I will always try to be good to you."

Jenny gazed at him with all the trust and love any man could expect.

A wave of longing came over him as he asked, "Shall we go up?"

Jenny nodded and hand in hand they ascended the stairs as husband and wife, each feeling the longing that the weeks of separation had enhanced.

They were at the top of the stairs when they heard the front door knocker bang against the oak door.

Travis called down to Obediah, who was just coming to answer the summons, to tell whoever it was that he was not in. Travis and Jenny walked around the landing but were halted in their tracks by the loud voices coming from the entrance hall.

"I know she's here. My wife told me what happened. I want to see her now!"

Travis went back to the head of the stairs and looked down. Jules Colby and a stranger were standing in the hall. Both gentlemen wore scowls on their faces, and Travis decided he had better go see what the problem was and get it over with as quickly as possible. He turned to Jenny and said, "You go on. I will see what this is all about and I'll be right back." He kissed her cheek and started down the stairs.

Jenny crept to the banister to listen to what the colonel would say and she almost fainted when she saw the man standing beside the colonel. He stood in the hall resplendent in brocade, gold braiding, and silk. He wore a pure white periwig with a gold ribbon tying back the curls. In one long-fingered hand he held a lace-trimmed handkerchief to his nose as thought the magnificent home of her new husband was so far beneath his social being. It was Sir Reginald Wenthrop. My God! What was he doing here? She listened carefully to what was being said as all the hopes for a happy future were being dashed before her eyes.

Travis walked casually down the stairs. When he reached the bottom, he asked, "Jules, and to what do I owe the honor of this visit?"

A look of pure rage contorted the colonel's normally comical face into a mask of vengeance. "Come off it, Gardiner. You took Elaine this morning from my home. My wife is most distressed over what's happened. I want to see Elaine now!"

Travis leaned against the banister and casually perused the two gentlemen before him. "I am afraid that is not possible. Elaine has had a trying day and has retired for the night."

The stranger spoke up, giving evidence of a thoroughly British heritage. "I demand to see the Lady Elaine this instant!"

Travis looked at the stranger, wondering what his presence would create in his life. "I don't believe we have been introduced," he stated casually.

With a haughty air of disdain toward Travis, the gentleman looked down his aristocratic nose and replied, "My name is *Sir* Reginald Wenthrop of the British Empire, the Lady Elaine's betrothed."

Travis's expression never waivered while he casually lit a cigar and gazed at the man opposite him through drifts of blue smoke. Travis's calculations were correct when he thought the man to be a pompous fop. After giving the man another cursory inspection, Travis said, "As I have said, the lady has retired."

Clearly agitated by this man's boldness, Reginald puffed out his cheeks and turned to Jules Colby. "Do something, man!"

The colonel turned to Travis, knowing he was in a very difficult situation, and used a calmer tactic. "See here, Gardiner, I am the child's uncle and this is her fiance. Surely you won't keep the two apart. I'm sure Elaine would want to see Sir Reginald. He's just arrived from England."

Travis spoke softly but with no doubt as to his meaning. "Gentlemen, if you will excuse me, I am rather tired myself."

Jules Colby was completely at his wits' end. A confrontation with Gardiner was not what he wanted. The man was powerful and usually got what he wanted. But Sir Reginald could make his life a living hell if he botched this. "Fine, fine, but send Elaine down here at once?" His voice squeaked in his agitation.

Travis looked at the two men for just the right amount of suspense to build before saying, "I am afraid I don't want to disturb my wife." At their looks of confusion, he added, "Of course, Elaine is my wife."

Both men stood rigid. Disappointment crossed Jules's features, and rage distorted the austere features of Sir Reginald who was the first to speak.

"My God, sir. Do you mean Elaine has married a common country bumpkin? Did you drug her?"

Wanting to conclude this meeting the fastest way he could, Travis stood up straight and turned to go back up the stairs. "I think you gentlemen had better leave. My patience is about at an end." Travis looked at Obediah and said, "Please show these—*gentlemen* out, Obediah, and make sure they find their way."

Obediah opened the door, his overbearing presence intimidating the men to go.

Colonel Colby looked back and shook his fist at Travis. "You haven't heard the last of this. I will get answers, by God!" He turned and walked out the door Obediah held open for them.

Travis heard the carriage go down the drive and said, "Thank you, Obediah. You may lock up for the night and go to bed yourself." He walked up the stairs slowly, wondering what this new development would mean. This Sir Reginald surely would know Jenny wasn't Elaine if he was supposed to marry the lady. He rounded the head of the stairs and saw Jenny sitting on the floor with her head on the spindles. He rushed to her and bent down, taking her deadly white face in his hands. Her eyes were full of tears as he put his arms under her, picked her up and took her to his

255

bed.

Jenny couldn't believe Sir Reginald was here in America. Fear overcame her and she asked, "Oh, Travis, what will I do? That man—he—he knows—I'm not—Elaine. You—will be—disgraced."

"Sssh," Travis crooned to her. "You haven't done anything criminal. You simply borrowed a name. They can't do anything to you for that." He smoothed her hair and pulled the pins Mammy had so skillfully used to create her masterpiece.

Jenny looked up at the man whom she loved with all her heart and soul. "Travis, Sir Reginald can take me away from you."

"Now, now, Jenny. No one is going to take you anywhere. This Sir Reginald can't hurt you."

Jenny didn't know what to tell him. He had not pressed her about why she had taken Elaine's identity. What would he say if she told him she was an indentured servant now, on her wedding day? He would hate me, she told herself. What was she going to do? If she ran into Sir Reginald, or if he just saw her, she knew he would take her back to England and Eden Hall. She still had five years to serve on her indenture.

She threw her arms around Travis and held him tightly, wanting the security of his arms to quell her anxiety and fear. Thinking it was a show of her passion, he took her clothes and laid them on the chair, then he undressed. When he came to her, all the longing and love he had tried to repress for these past weeks came out in him. He marveled at the silken texture of her skin as his hands gently caressed her. He kissed her lips, her cheeks, still wet with tears, her neck that was as soft as cotton. He felt the rapid pulse in the hollow of her throat. His lips moved to her breast to trace around one peak, and he let his tongue flick the nipple into a hardened crest.

Jenny's mind was now only on this moment, this man, her love. Her hands sought the rippling muscles that ran across his back, feeling the warmth and power of him beneath her fingers. Her mouth gently traced his shoulder to where the cords of his neck were pulsing. Her hands moved to his hair as she moved his lips to hers in urgent need of him. When his tongue traced the inside of her mouth, her will was won. She wanted to be possessed by him in an urgency that was overpowering. So long she had dreamed of this moment. So long she had had to cry herself to sleep with the need of him. This was her destiny. She knew in her heart that he would protect her. Her fears were gone as she relished this moment in time.

Travis emitted a low, deep groan when they came together. All the days and nights of the past, when he would feel unfulfilled and empty, were gone. He loved her like never before as she moaned beneath him until at last they reached that pinnacle of release together.

He lay beside her, holding her small form next to him. She was so small, so frightened. What could he do or say that would make her trust him. "Jenny, I am going to take care of you and our baby. You will never have to go through anything like you have with the colonel again. You are the mistress of Moss Grove now, with all the respect and admiration that that position entitles you to. I wish you would tell me why you are so afraid. Why would you think that man, Reginald, would take you from me? I have just found you again, and no one will take you from me." He rubbed his thumb over her temple waiting her response but felt her even breathing and knew she had fallen asleep. "Oh, Jenny." He kissed her forehead and cradled her in his arms.

But he could not fall asleep himself. He was

concerned for her. Why is she so afraid? Where was the spunky little waif he had plucked out of the ocean? She used to be so full of life on board the *Sea Breeze*. He wondered what she had had to endure while staying at the Colby's. Even though she assured him she had never been physically abused, he wondered. She was so thin, so exhausted that his mind could not fathom her treatment. He vowed she would never be treated like that again as long as there was breath in his body. And he vowed to find out why she was treated so brutally by a man who was supposed to be her uncle.

As the stars faded and the first light of a new day began, Travis finally fell asleep, still holding Jenny gently to him.

Chapter Thirteen

Jules Colby was furious with his wife and with Travis Gardiner. How could his stupid wife allow Gardiner to simply take Elaine away? He had only needed two more days to see his plans come to maturity. He would have to think of something to recoup his investment.

Reginald was livid about this situation. So much time had been wasted. He had sat cooling his heels at Elaine's solicitors for her to show up the day she had sailed from England, only to be given the information that she had been detained in leaving Eden Hall and hadn't had the time to stop for their appointment. It had taken him two and half weeks to make the arrangements to sail here to see the papers signed. The only ship available had been a frigate out of the Colonies that stopped at every port of call and was plagued with one disaster after another. Now this imbecile, Colby, had botched his part in this. It had taken Reginald a year to find this jackass, and now all his carefully laid plans were going awry.

He had to think. He stared out of the carriage window into the dark moonlit night and then an idea formed in his mind. If Elaine had married this colonial, then she wouldn't want to leave him to administer to her English estates. She would be more willing to have a fellow Englishman take over the estates by giving him the powers he needed. Of course, the chap she married might have something to say about it. Reginald didn't think he would like to tangle with Travis Gardiner. He looked quite capable of taking over Elaine completely. Reginald surmised that he would have to see Elaine alone. He would have to convince her and possibly her husband of the advantages of his running her vast estates in her absence.

A smile played on his lips while he mentally went over the scene that would take place. Elaine and her colonial would be so grateful for his help, they would fall over each other in their haste to sign the papers. After all, the colonial didn't look stupid and would welcome the advice and guidance of a titled lord to oversee his wife's affairs. But he had to see them to accomplish that. He turned to Colby. "Colby, I have to see Elaine. There must be someway to get to her. Think damn it!"

Jules sat across from the man who had made him a party to this charade. "Don't yell at me, Wenthrop. It's not my fault that damn ship sank leaving Gardiner to come into the picture."

Sir Reginald looked across at the little man. "Colby, I have to get her name on these papers. If I don't, you don't get your forty pieces of silver, so to speak," he said with a sneer.

Jules was not the sort to jump into things. When Reginald had approached him last year about taking on this project, he had checked things out for himself. From the reports he had received, Elaine was different from how she had been described. As this in no way effected Jules's purpose for her, he did not tell Reginald. He wondered now what Reginald's reaction to the girl would be.

"Gardiner is having a barbecue Saturday. I received an invitation last week before all this came up." He damned his wife again for the way she had treated the girl. It was bad enough that the girl was losing her looks, but because of this, Gardiner had felt it necessary to spirit her off. He said, "If we time our arrival just right, we could come in with a crowd. He would never make a scene before his good friends."

"Fine. As your houseguest I am sure he will also be obligated to accept me." Sir Reginald couldn't wait. He licked his lips, thinking of the fortune that awaited him.

When the coach pulled in front of Salford Manor, Jules reached to open the door of the carriage when Sir Reginald placed his hand over the colonel's to stay him.

"I don't think I would be very civil to your wife at this point, Colby. I believe I will go into Charleston for a couple of days. You won't mind, will you?"

The colonel didn't miss the thread of contempt in the other man's voice. It would suit his purposes to get rid of this fop. "By all means. I can certainly understand your apprehension. You may use my home there if you so desire."

"That won't be necessary. Actually, your house there depresses me more than this one does." He looked toward the house with obvious revulsion. "I think I will take a room at one of the inns. I do, however, plan on returning in time for the barbecue on Saturday."

"I'll see you then." Colby stepped from the coach and gave Cicero his orders. "Take Sir Reginald into Charleston and deliver him to the Colony House. Return here at once." The big black man nodded, then the colonel turned back to the man seated within the dark interior of the coach. "Have a pleasant stay, *Reggie*." He laughed inside at the look of scorn the English fop gave him for not using the title.

Jules watched the coach disappear into the swamp then turned toward the door, surprised to see two silhouettes defined in the open doorway. He climbed the steps and brushed past his wife and daughter without a word.

Katherine was horrified at not finding Elaine present and said angrily to her husband, "What happened, Jules?"

Jules Colby went to a cabinet and withdrew a bottle of whiskey. After pouring a generous portion into a glass, he drank it down in one swallow.

"Jules, answer me! Where is Elaine? Why didn't she come back with you?" Katherine's hands knotted in front of her while she tapped her foot in impatience.

Jules turned to glare at his wife. "Really, Katherine, you are amazing." He laughed, sending a chill down Katherine's neck. "You botch a simple job of watching her and then turn your anger on me." He laughed again, but the sound held no humor. He turned and again poured another generous amount of whiskey into his empty glass.

He walked over to Eudora and asked, "Well, Eudora, what do you have to say for yourself? I had imagined that you would have been more careful, considering you had a trip to Europe riding on this one."

Eudora was shaking but not from fear of her father's wrath. She had waited too long to see that titled bitch get her just desserts. So close.

Eudora Colby had been shunned by the most righteous and pompous people in Charleston because

262

she had not been prosperous or influential enough to suit their ideas of the southern aristocracy. Why only today, that simple bitch Alicia Adams had inferred, in Euroda's presence, that only real Ladies had had a tour of Europe. That common seamstress Madame LaFarrier had agreed only too readily. Eudora knew these Charlestonians felt the same way. Her one chance to become one of them had flown out the window with Elaine's escape. But the most outrageous part of this whole mess was that she had been rescued by none other than Travis Gardiner. A man Eudora would have sold her soul to have.

She turned to her father, desperation in her voice. "Surely there is something we can do to get her back? The constable maybe?" she asked hopefully.

Jules shook his head in exasperation. "That's just what we want, isn't it? The constable involved. Really, Eudora, you become more like your addle-brained mother everyday."

Katherine stood up and leered at her husband, saying, "Jules, you have no right abusing me in front of Eudora."

"No right! How could you have been so neglectful of your duties? That stupid girl married Travis Gardiner and is completely lost to us."

"Married!" the two women repeated in unison.

Katherine found her voice first and asked, "But how—When?"

"I don't know. He says they are married, and I'm sure Travis Gardiner wouldn't lie about something like that. Boy, did you botch this. I have a ship ready to sail and no one to put on it."

Eudora's smile was lost on the two as the colonel continued. "Why couldn't you have treated her better, Katherine, and why couldn't you have kept her here?"

Katherine had had enough of this abuse. "Listen to me, Jules Colby. This is the first time I have been unable to deliver for you. Don't you remember the Gardiner girl? You certainly didn't go on like this about her, and you certainly *botched* that job all by yourself."

Jules knew only too well that particular incident was his fault. He had acted too quickly. He remembered his surprise at seeing her gallop over the hill with her hair flying behind her. He had already decided she would be next, but he should have waited. He remembered thinking how convenient for her to ride into his waiting grasp. That damn horse had foiled his plans when it had bolted, sending the girl crashing to the ground. He had thought her dead and actually she was dead for his purposes. Her legs had been as useless to him as they had been to her.

"Shut up, Katherine, or so help me I will let you feel the bottom of my boot. The last thing I need from you is sarcastic remarks. I have more pressing things to think about than your snibbling barbs. I have a ship ready to sail and no cargo for it!" he repeated, yelling.

"None, Jules? Or do you mean no whites." Katherine smirked again.

"You know as well as I do that one white is worth ten mulattoes." Jules hit his hand against the mantle. "I was so hoping to make enough on this voyage to leave this godforsaken country and go back to England."

Eudora turned to her father with a smile. "Father, I may be able to help you find a replacement for Elaine."

Chapter Fourteen

Travis was awakened by a light tapping on the door. He awoke immediately and eased out of bed so as not to disturb Jenny. He put on his breeches and gently covered his sleeping wife.

He eased the door open to see Mammy standing in the hall.

"Y'all goin' ta sleep all day?" Mammy yelled while bustling into the room with a girl behind her, carrying a tray and giggling at being present in the bridal chamber. As Mammy pulled back the curtains, the girl placed the tray on a low table in front of a small settee.

Jenny had come awake at the commotion and was crouching under the covers so as not to reveal her nakedness. Travis was amused at all the fussing going on and held the door for the girl to go out but Mammy acted liked she had no intention of leaving as she started hanging up the wedding gown and folding all the lacy undergarments.

Travis tapped his foot and finally, to get her attention, cleared his throat.

Mammy saw his expression and started toward the door. "Done y'all harrumph me, Travis Gardiner. Jes' 'cause y'all done jes' get married ain't no reason ta sleep all da day long." She shook her finger at a thoroughly amused Travis, then turned to Jenny with a sweet smile transforming her face. "Missy, y'all jes' shoo him out a heah, an' then y'all call Mammy when you ready ta get dressed." She sniffed at Travis then pranced from the room.

Travis closed the door and walked over to the bed, saying, "Good morning, Mistress Gardiner. Breakfast is served."

Jenny looked up at Travis and calmly said, "I need a wrap."

"No you don't." He bent down and gave her a kiss, pulling the cover off her as he did so.

Jenny gasped and tried to pull it over her again, but Travis playfully slapped her bottom. She tried to roll up in the cover, and Travis gave a laugh at her embarrassment.

"Madam, if you insist on being decent to eat, I will get you something to wear."

"I do insist," she said, pouting playfully.

Travis went to his wardrobe and pulled out a red silk smoking jacket with a black sash and matching lapels. He came back to the bed and handed it to her.

She jumped up and put the jacket on, noticing that the sleeves were the only thing that was too long. The hem of the jacket came just below her buttocks.

"Travis, this is positively indecent!" She giggled.

Travis smiled and backed up, putting his hand to his chin. "Well, if you really want my opinion, I think I will keep you in smoking jackets from now on. I could get you all different colors. Let's see: pink for morning, light blue for afternoon and—" He came up and nuzzled her neck, adding, "And this red one for at night."

Jenny laughed and said, "Oh, you."

They joined hands, and he led her to the settee where they ate in companionable silence. Travis finally sat back, saying, "What would you like to do today?"

Thinking, Jenny suddenly sat back and said, "Why I believe I will have to find something to wear. I am afraid the gown I arrived in is beyond hope. And, I really don't wish to see it again anyway." She hung her head, remembering the humiliation she had felt wearing the smelly, torn gown.

Travis felt his heart go limp watching her face. He got up and held out his hand to her. "Come with me, little one. I think I know where we can find something for you."

When he approached the door, Jenny pulled back. "Travis, I can't go out in the hall dressed like this." She looked down, seeing her legs from under the jacket.

Travis smiled and looked at her shapely legs revealed by his jacket. "Just a minute." He stuck his head out of the door and looked first one way then the other. "The coast is clear. Come on."

He grabbed her hand and ran to the room Jenny had used yesterday, opening the door and pulling her in behind him.

Jenny put her hand to her heart and sat down laughing on the side of the bed. "People are going to think we are mad, running around like this."

"I don't care what people think, Jenny," he said seriously, then went to the wardrobe and opened the doors. A flood of memories overcame him when he looked at all the familiar gowns hanging neatly before him.

Jenny came up behind him, putting her arms around his waist. "It still hurts you doesn't it?"

He turned to look in her eyes. "Celeste was the only

267

person I have ever known who was truly at peace with herself. She never complained and she always had a smile on her face."

"You miss her terribly, don't you?"

He looked around the room before saying, "It doesn't seem like the same house somehow, without her presence. I will always miss her, Jenny. She was my sunshine and my reason for living for so long." He kissed Jenny tenderly, then added, "But, now I have you." He hugged her tightly then stepped back and indicated the wardrobe. "I'm sure Celeste would have been the first to suggest you avail yourself of her gowns. I'll take you into Charleston this afternoon to buy you some of your own."

Jenny felt panic rising at the thought of leaving the protection of this house. Outside was Sir Reginald and his possibly taking her away. "Travis, couldn't the seamstress come here to Moss Grove?" She wrung her hands in agitation.

Travis watched her, noticing the panic and fear. God, how he wished she would tell him why she was so frightened so that he could help her. He surmised she must be given every opportunity to learn to trust him and his love for her.

"There is nothing to be frightened of, Jenny. I'll be with you constantly. Charleston is a wonderful city, and I'm sure you will enjoy the outing." He came to stand before her. "I will show you things that not every visitor would see. Our home there is quite a museum of sorts. I think you will like it." He held her hands, feeling them shake while he continued. "There is a row of some fourteen homes on East Bay Street known as Rainbow Row. You've never seen anything like it. All the colors of the rainbow are mirrored in those homes. We have a signer of the Declaration of Independence living right in Charleston. The first president of the United States, George Washington, lived in his home for a while. Jenny, I will take you to Saint Philip's Church where we attend services when we are in Charleston. It's very old and beautiful." He saw that his words had made the tension ease somewhat but knew she was still unconvinced. "Jenny, come with me and let me help you over this. No one will hurt you. My name commands respect in this town. The colonel can bring no harm to you and as for that Reginald character—well, let's just say that feelings still run high against the British. You will not see much of this as my wife, and that man would find his hands full if he tried anything with my wife. I won't let him near you if that is your wish?"

"Oh, Travis, you're so good to me." She hugged him hard, and Travis laughed and pushed her away a little.

"If you want to get going, you had better not distract me in that getup." He let his gaze travel the length of her.

Jenny giggled and he was delighted to see some of the old Jenny coming out at last.

"I think you'll find everything you need in here. I'll go make arrangements for the trip. Better pack enough for overnight. We'll stay at the Tradd Street house tonight." He walked to the door but turned back to her saying, "I can't wait to get you all alone where no servants can disturb us." He winked as a blush stained Jenny's cheeks. "Come downstairs when you're ready."

Jenny started her toilette thinking about what Travis had said. He would protect her and he did love her. Sir Reginald would not be able to get to her as long as Travis was by her side. Should she tell Travis the truth? She was so afraid that his feelings for her would change if he knew the truth. She would just have to have faith that Sir Reginald would just go back to England now that he knew Elaine was married and out of his reach.

She was standing by the wardrobe in her chemise and pantalets when there was a knock on the door. "Who is it?" she called.

"Mammy, honey. Ah's come to hep you."

"Come in, Mammy. I am having a problem."

As Mammy stepped in and closed the door, Jenny spread her arms in a helpless gesture. "What would be appropriate attire for Charleston, Mammy?" There were so many gowns to choose from, Jenny was overwhelmed.

"Chile, you jes' go over dare and let Mammy pick you out somethin'." She started going through the gowns, pulling one out, shaking her bandana-covered head, then pulled out another. She finally picked a peach-colored, watered silk with short sleeves and a low-scooped neckline. "Dis be perfect for today, missy."

Jenny stood up taking the gown in her hands. It looked so much like the gown she had worn to the beach that day with Travis. She let Mammy pull the dress over her head and start hooking the back.

As Mammy got to the hooks at Jenny's waist, the old woman pulled and tugged to get them fastened, then said, "Chile, y'all best get some more gowns dat cain be let out. You sho' startin' ta show, and I cain't pull dat corset no mo' tighter than ah's already done. How far 'long you be, missy?"

Jenny turned red and looked away from the old woman's searching eyes. "I'm not sure, Mammy. Maybe two or three months."

Mammy smiled at the embarrassment shown by her new mistress. "Honey, it's been 'long time since Mammy done hold a babe in dese heah arms. Ah be lookin' forward ta talkin' care a yore babe."

Jenny hugged the old woman and kissed her cheek. "Mammy, I'm very happy."

"Chile, ah knows dat. Y'all look happy an' y'all startin' ta get some color back in dose pretty cheeks." The old woman backed up and started going through the wardrobe again.

"Don't you like this gown, Mammy?"

"Oh, chile, y'all goin' ta stay in town tonight, so's ah jes' gettin' you something' else ta wear in case y'all don't gets anythin' from da dressmaker. Mis'er Travis maybe goin' ta take y'all out ta supper tonight, too. We'uns jes' gots ta be ready in case of anythin'."

Jenny suddenly realized that she really didn't know anything about how a plantation functioned or what Travis did. "Mammy, what do you all do here on the plantation?" Seeing the look of confusion on Mammy's face, Jenny asked, "I mean what does Travis do?"

Mammy understood. "Why chile, y'all been goin' 'round in circles, haven't you? Well, let's see. Ah guess Moss Grove be one a da bess places 'round dese parts. Mis'er Travis, he be a smart one." She tapped her forefinger to her head. "When cotton come ta be da king in dese heah parts, Mis'er Travis say'd we'd still be rice planters. An' den we started on 'baccy. Mis'er Travis been tellin' dose other planters dat cotton be ruin'n they land."

"How does cotton ruin land, Mammy?"

"Well, ah don' rightly know, but Mis'er Travis he done 'splain dat da cotton takes ever'thin' from da soil an' don' put nothin' back. Da other planters has been gettin' smaller crops ever' year, but not Mis'er Travis. He plants one field in cotton and one in 'baccy and then he switches dem da next year. He got a name fer dis but ah forgets what it be."

"It's called field rotation, Mammy." Both women looked up at Travis standing in the doorway. "Are you ready?" he asked Jenny.

"She be ready but y'all better take da time ta 'splain things ta da chile. She be lost in all dis hubbub."

Jenny stood up, and Mammy placed a wide-brimmed straw hat over her hair. "Honey, y'all don' want to go outside widout a hat on you head or you'll get all dark lak Mammy."

Jenny smiled and took Travis's arm while they walked together down the winding staircase. Mammy followed with a valise clutched in her hand.

"Mis'er Travis, you wants me ta send some house servants wid you ta open up dat house?"

Envisioning the coming night, alone with Jenny and no servants to interrupt them, Travis quickly said, "No, we'll muddle through without them. Besides, I'm leaving the barbecue for you to get ready for. You'll need all the girls here to help you."

"Why, we gots most ever'thin' ready. Only thin's dat cain't be done 'til tamorrow is left."

"Well, you'd better get the house in shape. I'm sure some of our guests will spend the night."

"You jes' worry 'bout Miss Jenny, an' ah'll worry 'bout dis heah house." Mammy stood with both hands on her wide hips and a scowl on her face.

Travis laughed and went over to give her a hug. "I'll take mighty fine care of Miss Jenny, Mammy, and I'm sorry I tried to interfere with your house."

Mammy smiled and winked at Jenny, saying, "Chile, you gots ta larn how ta handle dese heah menfolk. You take care now."

Travis climbed up on the buggy next to Jenny and started for Charleston as the sun came up over the top of the oak trees lining the drive of Moss Grove. He drove along, making note to Jenny about this field and that.

Jenny was amazed at the intricacies of the rice fields with all their levies that, as Travis explained, flooded the fields during the first stages of growth. She stared in awe at the many acres of cotton showing dark green leaves in long rows.

Travis grinned down at her, saying, "You saw all this yesterday. Why are you going on like this is the first time you've seen it?"

Jenny hugged his arm to her, hiding her reddening face from his view. "I guess I wasn't paying much attention to anything but you yesterday."

Travis told her about how Moss Grove used to grow only rice as its cash crop, but since the invention in 1793 of the cotton gin by Eli Whitney, cotton had become the biggest cash crop in the South. "The only draw back," he told her, "is that slavery has been reinstated." He shook his head as he looked at the rows of cabins that looked like they would fall down if you leaned on them. Several small black children looked up at the passing carriage with wide vacant eyes.

Jenny hadn't seen the children when she asked, "But don't you own slaves?"

A muscle twitched in his cheek and he said, "I do *not* own people, Jenny. The blacks who live at Moss Grove are freemen." He indicated the cabins and children they were passing. "The blacks you see here are slaves of your uncle—I mean the colonel."

Jenny felt a sadness invade her being while she watched the children. "But those children look like little old men—almost hopeless."

"The colonel never has been known for treating his slaves well. Those cabins could be fixed up, but he doesn't care. The funny thing is no one knows why he even owns them. He hasn't planted a crop in fifteen years, and they just stand around with nothing to do."

"How awful for them. In England we don't allow black slavery." But they allow another form of the disease to thrive, she thought to herself.

Travis sat up straighter and said softly, "Jenny, England may not allow herself to hold slaves, but the majority of the slaves brought to South Carolina are brought on English ships."

Jenny gasped. "But that's terrible to make one's living selling these poor people into slavery. It makes me ashamed of my own country." She put her arm through Travis's and hugged it to her breast. "I'm glad you hold no man as a slave, Travis."

Travis gazed down into his wife's eyes and felt a longing in him. "Little one, you had better stop looking at me that way or I will take you here on the road."

Jenny laughed and let go of his arm, saying, "You, sir, are a rogue."

"Just so you know now that I plan to bed you often. You may be with child most of the time."

"Oh, that's just fine with me. I was an only child and I want at least six children."

Travis looked thoughtfully at her and thought of his mother. If Jenny died giving birth to his child, he would never forgive himself.

Jenny felt a compunction to turn back to stare at the little boys who still stood watching the carriage. The eyes were what Jenny found the most haunting. With no expression evident of their small, thin faces, they appeared to Jenny to be the most lost, hopeless children she had ever seen. She remembered the little street children in London. Even those children would smile.

She was glad Travis owned none of these pitiful

creatures. She turned back to look ahead of them with a feeling of relief and one of sadness. She wondered again if this might not be the time to tell Travis the truth. Surely he would understand her predicament, but would it somehow alter their happiness? Jenny didn't want anything to come between them now. Then she remembered Sir Reginald was here. She knew he would never let her get away with the deception. He would take her back or worse: He would tell Travis. She had to think.

Travis watched Jenny out of the corner of his eyes. He saw the sadness she exhibited when she looked back from watching the children. Then some new expression took over her face. Was it fear? How he wished she would confide her problems to him. Whatever she was hiding was eating away at her, and he felt a powerlessness invade him. Thinking he could possibly glean an understanding if he got her to talk about herself, he asked, "Jenny, I really don't know much about you before we met."

Jenny looked up into his eyes.

"Tell me about your childhood," he persisted.

Jenny's face transformed as she thought about Connie and the little cottage they had shared. "I was born in London just before the new century began. My mother died giving me birth."

A pang of understanding and fear went through Travis like a knife. Could the fact that his mother and hers both died in childbirth be an omen for them? He pushed the thought aside as she continued.

"My father. He was at a loss as to how to care for a new baby, and so I lived with Connie Darrow in Salford, while my father went back to London to seek his fortune. She had a pleasant little cottage on the outskirts of Salford, and I lived with her for four and ten years. I didn't see my father in all that time."

Travis sensed her pain and begged her to continue. "Come on, Jenny, tell me more."

Jenny looked up into his kind, understanding eyes and did indeed feel like telling him. "I don't remember much before my fourth year. After that I remember helping Connie with chores around the cottage. She did laundry for the village and after a time, I would help her. I never remember being hungry or lonely during those first years. Connie was not an affectionate person, but she would read to me and helped me learn things that other girls did not. She had been the daughter of the vicar of the village who thought reading and writing a valuable tool for anyone. As most girls in the village were only taught to play the pianoforte and do needlework, I was thought to be different because I enjoyed reading and writing. I never had a close friend except for Connie. She understood the way I felt, as she had experienced the same shunning as I." Jenny laughed when she remarked, "I really don't think Connie liked men much. She would always tell me that if I had a mind of my own, with some sense and learning, I would never need a man to take care of me."

Travis cocked his head. "Is that how you feel? That you don't need a man to take care of you?"

"I don't know about being taken care of other than a partnership where you take care of me and I take care of you." She snuggled closer to him and laughed, saying, "I think Connie should have had a husband after her first one died. Maybe she would have understood how I feel now." She touched his hand and gazed up at him with love filling her eyes, making them turn a deep purple.

Travis wanted her to continue her story and asked, "You say you only lived with this Connie Darrow until you were fourteen. What happened after that?"

Afraid to say too much, Jenny simply said, "My father came for me and took me to London to live with him. After a while, I went to work for Lady Elaine and I haven't heard from him since."

Travis knew she wasn't telling him everything. Something happened during this time of her life. She had brushed over the time with her father too rapidly. He was about to ask for more information when Jenny looked up and asked him, "Tell me about you. What was your childhood like?"

Travis knew he would have to wait for the rest of her story, and he started to relate his past. "I was born in Charleston at the Tradd Street house. My father was a captain of a merchant ship. He loved this country as his own and brought my mother over from France to become his wife."

"Your father was French also?"

"Oh, yes. I think that's where I got such a romantic nature." He smiled down at her.

"But your name doesn't sound French," Jenny stated.

"That's my father's doing. He went by the name of Jack instead of Jacques and changed Gardinere to Gardiner. He wanted only American names for his children and named Jeff and I after some people who had believed in him when he first started his own shipping line. Celeste was named by me after my mother's death," he added in a softer tone.

"How did your father and mother come to this country?" Jenny asked, becoming caught up in the romance of his tale.

"My father had left France as a young man to sail the sea. He arrived in Charleston and fell in love with it. He saved his money and finally bought his own ship, but as he would tell Jeff and me later, he never forgot the little girl he had left behind, and after

277

making his fortune in trade, he sent for her. She arrived to find my father had done quite well for himself when he drove her and her chaperone to the Tradd Street house. At the time, there weren't many houses to equal ours, and she was captivated by the beauty of the house. My father had brought back items for it from all over the world. You'll see it tonight, and I think you will know why she loved it."

Jenny felt an excitement as the adventure filled her being. "Go on Travis. What happened next?"

Looking into her beautiful, excited blue eyes, Travis continued: "Nine months and four days later a bundle of absolute joy arrived. Me! My father was said to have shouted from the rooftops that he had a son." A look of pride came over him in thinking of his father's deed. "My mother was a small woman, like you, but she breezed through my birth as I was a *small* baby."

Jenny looked up sharply, saying, "*You* were a small baby? My, they must have fed you well."

"That they did. Mammy was always making up things to tempt our appetites. She would make blueberry cobbler but make us eat all our greens before we would get any. I thought I would fool her once and took a cobbler she had on the sill to cool. She knew it was me who had taken it though, and made me eat twice as many greens that night." At the memory, he smiled, then chuckled. "Jeff and I were sure she knew everything in our minds and never tried to sneak anything by her again."

"Did your father sail often after you were born?" Jenny thought back to the feelings of desertion she had experienced when she was old enough to realize her own father didn't have time for her.

"He would only take on a voyage he particularly wanted to go on, which wasn't very often until after Jeff was born." He hesitated before going on. "After

278

Jeff's birth, the doctors told my father that mother shouldn't have any more children. Her confinement with Jeff had not been easy for her, and the doctors feared another child would do her a lot of harm. As my father found it difficult to stay away from her and sleep in another room, he took to the sea again with a vengeance. He would only come home long enough to schedule another trip, then he would be gone again. My mother would stand for hours up on the second floor veranda of the Tradd Street house and wait for him to come home. On the last day I ever saw him, the longing obviously became too much for them, as mother became with child again. He set sail without knowing of the deed. I was fourteen and Jeff was nine. I don't think I realized at the time what was happening. Mammy would hover over mother and make sure she didn't get out of bed. We would be allowed to see her only a few minutes a day. She would implore me to watch for my father's ship for her. He had been gone a long time, and she wanted to see him before the baby came. I didn't understand that either."

He paused and Jenny was conscious of his hands stiffening on the reins as they proceeded along the road. "If it's too painful for you, Travis, you needn't continue."

"No. I've made my peace with my memories, Jenny. I did hate my father for what his lust had done to my mother and not being around to comfort her. I remember the night Celeste was born. I heard a scream from my mother's room and ran to see what had happened. Mammy wouldn't let me in to see her. I paced for what seemed like hours outside her room, hearing sounds that only added to my unrest. Finally, Mammy let me in but said I must be very quiet and let my mother rest. She was lying in the bed with the baby next to her. She was staring at Celeste with all the love I had felt from her. I bent down and took her cold, dry hand in mine. She turned to me and with pain in her pretty dark eyes, told me to take care of Jeff and the new baby. After I agreed, she closed her eyes and died."

Jenny felt tears well up in her eyes as Travis's pain found her. "That must have been a terrible time for you."

"Oh, I did a lot of the pain to myself. I blamed by father and Celeste for my mother's death. I would wait everyday up on the veranda for my father to return. I paid no attention to Jeff or expecially Celeste. My hatred consumed me, and I would pray for my father to suffer like he had made my mother suffer. The day I was notified that my father's ship had sunk, leaving no survivors, I felt a loss so profound I cried for weeks and prayed to God to tell my father I never meant my hatred. You see, no one could help me out of my self-pity. Then one day Mammy came to me holding Celeste and put her in my arms, saying I was now the man of the house and I had better start acting like it. It was like someone had thrown cold water in my face. I gazed at the little pink and white bundle in my arms, and I was consumed with a love I never thought to feel again. I determined that Celeste would indeed be loved and cared for just the way my mother would have wanted. I moved us all out of Moss Grove and proceeded to be both mother and father to Jeff and little Celeste. I don't think I could have done it by myself. Mammy helped me more than I will ever be able to repay her."

"She told me you freed her," Jenny said with pride for her new husband's deed.

Travis laughed. "She framed the papers and hung them in the nursery so she could rock Celeste and look up at them. I freed the rest of the slaves that same year. I got a lot of flack from the other planters around when I did. There's still some who resent what I did, but they couldn't very well hang a fifteen-year-old. Besides, I took my responsibilities very seriously, and I'm sure I was cocky back then."

"Why do the people have to have slaves, Travis? If you can run a plantation as big as Moss Grove without them, why can't they?"

"I'm really of the opinion that some of them consider it a sign of prosperity to own slaves. The more they can own the more socially accepted they are. But, then most are used for the planting and harvesting of the cotton, and they do multiply with little investment required by their owners. That's why the colonel is so mysterious. He owns many slaves with nothing for them to do. His wife won't have them in her house, as I'm sure you noticed. But the Colbys do not socialize either. Sometimes, I think he does it just to feel the power it gives him over them."

"He has some slaves at his Charleston house, but I only saw two. How many does he own?"

"I don't know. With births and deaths the figures are always changing. He sells some too, so your guess is as good as mine." He leaned closer to her. "Don't worry about the colonel. You're going to have your hands full with me." He was delighted to see a smile, although tentatively expressed, light up her face.

Jenny contented herself with the nearness of him and security he meant to her. Thoughts of Sir Reginald and the complications of his presence were far from her mind in the lazy summer sunshine.

Chapter Fifteen

As their coach approached the outskirts of Charleston, the traffic became more congested with wagons bringing vegetables to market and buggies bringing people into the fast-paced city. Travis would nod or tip his hat to most of the people they passed, while Jenny would get a thorough going over by some of the women. She held her head high and smiled sweetly at them, knowing what must be going through their minds, and upon hearing scattered bits and pieces of their conversation, she knew she would be in for an interrogation if she ever was introduced to these women.

"Who's that with Travis Gardiner?" one would ask.

"Skinny little thing. I wonder where he picked her up from?" another would inquire.

"Must be a relative," another said, nodding knowingly.

Finally, they pulled up in front of a shop on Meeting Street, and Travis helped Jenny down from the carriage, winking at her to let her know he had heard the comments. They were just about to go into the shop when Travis was hailed from down the street. They turned to see a woman approach them wearing a purple gown, cut extremely low, and a saucy purple hat with a purple plume sat at an angle atop her auburn hair.

Jenny thought the woman's attire completely inappropriate for the morning hour and took an immediate dislike to the woman.

Travis tipped his hat as the woman drew near, saying, "Good morning, Alicia."

"Good morning to you, and where, may I ask have you been keeping yourself? I haven't seen you in over a month. I have been put out with you." She tapped his lapel with her parasol familiarly, then continued: "But, I did receive your invitation to the barbecue on Saturday." She lowered her eyes and put on a coy expression as she moved closer to stand beside him and brush his arm with her breast. "I plan on keeping you all to myself all day, so don't get too involved with your other guests." She glanced over at Jenny as if she were of no importance and rubbed her breast up and down Travis's arm.

Jenny could only stare at this brazen display with her mouth open but with a gleam in her eye of a woman ready to fight for her man.

Travis, noticing her wrath, tried to extricate himself from Alicia's clutches, saying, "Alicia, I don't believe you two have met."

Alicia glanced back at Jenny and as if dismissing her as an annoyance, turned her attention back to Travis, inquiring, "Is this a long lost cousin, darlin'?"

"No, Alicia. This is my wife, Jennifer Gardiner." He held his breath for the tirade he was sure would follow.

Alicia stepped back as though he had slapped her. She couldn't have heard him correctly. "Did—Did you say *wife*!"

Travis smiled at Jenny with tenderness and love in his eyes, making Alicia feel as though she would like

283

to scratch this stranger's eyes out.

"Yes, Alicia, Jenny is my wife."

"But, how—When did this happen?" Alicia stammered.

"Some time ago, Alicia. You see she's been staying with family and has only recently come to Moss Grove."

Alicia couldn't believe this was happening. She saw her plans for Moss Grove and all the money she could ever spend evaporate before her eyes. A viciousness possessed her and she asked, "Where did you meet—Jenny? In a nursery somewhere?" She had sneered the name while she looked Jenny up and down as though finding her entirely unsuitable.

Travis saw the look of anger enter Jenny's eyes and quickly said. "I met her quite by accident actually. She was the sole survivor of a shipwreck, and I was fortunate enough to be the one to rescue her." He gazed lovingly into his wife's eyes.

Alicia was ready to scream in her frustration. She had waited too long to let this bitch come between her and Moss Grove. She looked up at Travis with a wicked gleam in her eyes. "Why, Travis, you naughty boy, you. You should have told me you were married *that night* we were together." She made a reference no one could have missed. She was delighted at the look that wench gave him, but she wanted to add more fuel to the fire. Tapping her parasol lightly on his lapel, to regain his attention, she continued, "After all, we could have stopped."

Travis knew what she was up to and would have none of it. "Alicia, I believe I was the one who remained cool in the heat of your—passionate display."

Furious at him, she sought another method. Turning to Jenny, she smiled sweetly, but the smile did not reach her eyes. "How on earth did you entice Travis out of bachelorhood, my dear? Did you *flaunt* yourself and demand he make an honest woman of you?"

Jenny turned scarlet as the woman glared at her.

Travis saw Jenny's reaction to this slur and quickly pulled her behind him. He stepped menacingly toward Alicia, the muscle in his cheek twitching as he hissed, "My wife needed no such ploys to get me to marry her. I asked her because I love her. I am sure you do not know of this emotion, Alicia. You were not beneath anything short of vulgarity to entrap me. Fortunately, Jenny is not a brazen hussy like you."

He then turned to Jenny and led her into the shop, leaving Alicia staring after them.

"Oh!" She stamped her foot. She would get rid of this obstacle if it were the last thing she ever did. She walked off in a huff to bend someone's ear about this.

Jenny's heart was pounding and her breathing was coming in gasps. The nerve of that woman! She was obviously upset at the news but to lash out at her with so much vengeance. Jenny could not understand the motive of the woman but was determined to find out just what Alicia Adams wanted from her husband.

When Travis closed the door of the shop behind him, Jenny looked around the small interior hung with samples of lace, ribbon, and fabric, and upon seeing no one about, spun round to face Travis.

On seeing Jenny's expression, he knew he had a lot of explaining to do.

Jenny hissed her tirade at him. "And, just *who* was that woman, and what did she mean by *that night*?" Jenny watched him for any sign of guilt on his face. Seeing nothing, she continued: "Travis, does this woman have a claim on you, and will I be forced to go through a similar scene everytime we chance to meet?"

He put his hands on her shoulders and looked deeply into the fiery blue eyes. "Jenny, she means nothing to me. *That night* she referred to was the night after I returned to Charleston. Jeff set up the match, and I could have killed him when I found out it was she whom I was to be escorting that night. Alicia has made no bones about wanting to be mistress of Moss Grove, but—" Seeing the sparks ignite once more, he hurriedly continued, "but, Jenny, believe me, she means nothing to me and never will. She's one of the reasons I sailed so often from here." He watched as the softness came back to her beautiful face. "Believe me, Jenny, until I asked you to become my wife, I was sure I would remain a bachelor forever."

Suddenly very happy, Jenny smiled up at him. "She really is a witch, Travis. I can certainly understand why you would prefer bachelorhood over being married to her."

Travis felt relief flood through him when he realized the crisis was at an end. He also realized he would have to do something about Alicia. He saw a subtle change come over Jenny as she almost pouted. "What's the matter now, little one?"

Jenny was damned if she would let that woman ruin her marriage, and with a coquettish look she gazed up at Travis and asked, "Do we have to socialize with her. I really think she will do anything to throw obstacles in our way. She's so mean, Travis."

God! What a predicament Travis felt himself in. Alicia, he knew, would make his life miserable but she was invited to the barbecue on Saturday, and he knew she would come and make a scene. He knew she had worked too long to become mistress of Moss Grove to stop without a fight. He would just have to protect Jenny as best he could and that included warning her.

"Jenny, I am afraid Alicia has been invited to the barbecue, and I'm afraid she will undoubtedly come." At Jenny's look of anguish, he quickly rushed to reassure her, saying "I will be with you at all times, and if she so much as looks like she will cause a scene, I will ask her to leave."

"But, Travis, you heard her just now. What if she insinuates her dirty thoughts to the other women?" A tear appeared as Jenny realized that Alicia's implied references were not too far from the truth. Whispering to him, she leaned closer. "When they find out I am with child, they will all have enough gossip to throw about without her putting additional thoughts in their heads."

Travis was about to try and reason with her when they heard voices coming from the rear of the shop. They quickly started looking at swatches of material as a slim, attractive woman came out from the back of the shop.

Upon seeing the man standing in her shop, the woman became most gracious and condescending. "Ah! Monsieur Gardiner, welcome to my establishment. And, what can I do for you today? Some bangles or beads?" she asked in a heavy French accent.

"I would like to order some gowns made for my wife." He indicated Jenny.

"Your wife! But, how wonderful, Monsieur." Madam LaFarrier wondered what that big-mouthed Alicia Adams would say when she found out about this *wife*. Always talking about Monsieur Gardiner as though they were betrothed. She would love to be present when the young chit heard this most interesting news.

"Madam LaFarrier, let me introduce my wife, Jennifer." Travis beamed as the woman was obviously

287

impressed with Jenny.

"Ah, you have picked a most attractive wife, monsieur."

"I agree." He turned to the woman with an all business expression. "Now, I would like some day gowns, a couple of evening gowns and several at-home evening gowns. Of course, all other items as would be necessary also."

Thinking of the big order and the money she would make made the madam's mouth water. "Of course. If you will follow me, Madam Gardiner, I will make the measurements. You can sit and wait here, monsieur."

Jenny went into a small fitting room, and the madam helped her unhook the gown in the back.

Madam LaFarrier was very impressed with Jenny and was making mental notes about which fabrics would look the most becoming to the young wife when she noticed the tightness around the madam's waist, and casually asked, "When did you and Monsieur Gardiner get married, madam?"

Jenny didn't know what to tell the woman. She couldn't say *yesterday*, so she said, noncommittally, "Oh, recently." Then, trying to change the subject, Jenny looked at some swatches and said, "This is a pretty color. Maybe a day dress out of this one."

"But of course, madam. You definitely are made to wear blue."

Jenny was dressed again, and Travis had joined them as they bent over swatches that filled the floor of the little room.

Madam LaFarrier showed them several sketches for day gowns, and Jenny picked the fabrics for each. The madam put a swatch on each design and then left to bring back a book that she held reverently to her bosom. "Madam Gardiner, I have the latest designs from Paris here in this book. I have not had the pleasure of dressing anyone here in this town that I feel can wear the designs like you." She put the book in Jenny's lap and stepped away to bring swatches of silks, satins, and transparent gauze to be selected for the evening gowns.

Jenny opened the book and blushed vividly at the risqué designs.

Leaning over her, Travis saw the reason for her discomfort and said, "Really, madam. I don't believe my wife would be suitably dressed in something like this." He pointed to the drawings.

The drawing clearly showed the model's body revealed beneath the material. The madam came up and with shocked apologies explained, "But monsieur, these gowns are the rage in Paris. Women even have been known to dampen the material to cling against their bodies. Really monsieur, your wife is exceptionally beautiful. She would show these women of Charleston what true fashion is all about."

"I'm afraid I wouldn't want other men to see what I alone will see. No, madam. Please bring us something else to look at."

The madam left in a hurry to search out other, less scandalous designs. This man was most protective of his young wife. She laughed to herself when she remembered the gown Alicia Adams had picked up yesterday, saying it was to make sure Monsieur Gardiner had a happy homecoming. Wait 'til he sees her in that gown with all of her showing. She laughed again before stopping to fantasize. Oh! But that he would have picked me. She quickly picked up a book from her desk and rushed back to the fitting room.

Travis and Jenny picked the fabrics to go with the more modest designs. Jenny showed Travis a design for a formal ball gown that had long, closely fitted sleeves with a snug bodice and flowing skirt. He studied it and then picked a black silk that shimmered with sparkles. The madam suggested she could put tiny jet beads over the bodice, and after seeking Jenny's approval, agreed. They were about through when Madam LaFarrier came back into the room carrying a box filled with silks and satins, ribbons and lace.

"You will, of course, wish to select something for a nightgown, no?"

Jenny remembered the feel of the silk nightgown Travis had bought her in Barbados. She lightly touched the silk lying in the box.

Travis watched her and knew she had loved that nightgown he had bought her. "We'll take seven nightgowns in different colors." He winked at Jenny. "All in silk."

Jenny looked at him with all the love she felt for him there in her eyes. He had remembered.

Madam LaFarrier noted this look and knew this was a love match. "I will have everything ready within the month. I will bring everything to Moss Grove myself."

"Very well, madam, but you had better leave room in the seams for expansion. My wife is with child and in a month the child will be noticeable."

A smile played on the woman's lips. "You must be very happy, monsieur and madam."

Pulling Jenny to him, Travis said, "We are."

As they rode through the streets of Charleston, Travis would point to this building and that person, telling Jenny some of the history of the great city he loved.

Jenny listened to him with eyes darting from left to right. The city was alive with activity. Jenny's eyes lit on a group of men standing under what appeared to be a roof with no walls. She could see a man standing on a platform gesturing to first one in the crowd then another. Wanting to know everything, Jenny picked at Travis's sleeve to get his attention. "What's this going on here?" She pointed.

Travis's smile faded and a look of contempt replaced it. "This is the slave market, Jenny."

"Market? What do you mean? What are all those men doing?"

Travis pulled on the reins and stopped the buggy. "They are bidding on that man up there on the platform."

Jenny followed the direction he was indicating. She gasped when she saw the terrified man leave to be replaced up on the platform by a little girl, no more than ten or twelve. The child was frightened and alone up there all by herself. Jenny's heart went out to the child as the man standing next to her opened her mouth, as one would a horse, to inspect her teeth.

All the happiness she had felt earlier was suddenly gone, replaced by a heart-wrenching hurt that Jenny knew would never go away. She could almost see herself being inspected by Sir Miles again.

Travis was watching the agony on her face, and he placed his hand on her suddenly cold one.

Jenny looked up at him with eyes that begged him. "Oh, Travis, can't you do something."

His Jenny was gone again. The look she bestowed on him tore at his heart. "What would you have me do, little one?"

Jenny thought about the life the child would have being owned. She looked at the men who stood around, waiting for their turn to inspect her. She saw another man take the platform and put his hand on the child's chest, as though she would be of an age to

291

show the breasts he was hunting for. She tore her eyes away from the child's shame. She had seen the looks before. Sir Miles had looked at her with just such thoughts on his mind.

Travis worried about the effect this child was having on his new bride. Making a decision, he patted her hand, saying, "You stay here. I'll go see what I can do."

Smiling her gratitude, she watched him walk up to a man who seemed to be in charge. The man listened to Travis and then shook his head, as though denying his part in this. Travis walked into the crowd in front of the platform and became lost to Jenny's sight.

The time came when the auction started. Jenny noted the man talking fast would indicate with his hand as each man placed his bid. Jenny saw the girl's eyes, eyes that did not understand what was happening to her. She noted the child was beautiful. Light coffee-colored skin with huge brown eyes. She was tall for her age but thin to the point of looking starved. As Jenny watched the girl, the bidding was halted. Her heart almost stopped when the man roughly handed the child down to an unseen winner. A tear escaped from Jenny's tightly closed eyes. She hung her head and placed her work-roughened hands over her face. How could she be happy knowing that that child was going to a life of slavery.

Jenny felt a hand covering her own and looked up into the black eyes of her husband. Travis was smiling at her and when he stepped back, Jenny saw the child. "Oh! Travis, you did it." She jumped down from the wagon seat and eveloped the child in her arms. Bending down, Jenny looked at the child closely.

"What's your name, child?" she asked.

The little girl looked up at her new master with

confusion marking her features. Travis smiled down at her, and she looked again at the pretty lady who was before her. Quietly, she said, "Rosalie."

Jenny loved the name and inquired further, "Rosalie what, dear?"

Rosalie looked confused again as Travis placed his hand on Jenny's shoulder and she stood up.

"Jenny, she probably only has the one name. Most of these people are not given surnames." He looked around the slave market and decided it was time to go. "Come on. Let's get Rosalie home." He helped Jenny, then Rosalie, up on the buggy seat. He walked around the back of the carriage, climbed up beside Jenny and started the carriage on the way to Tradd Street.

Jenny sat beside the child with an arm around her, murmuring comforting words as they moved on out of the slave market.

Jeff had had a busy morning. He was just about to leave his office when he heard a commotion coming from the outer office. He stood up to investigate the ruckus when Alicia swept into his office in a fury. She almost flailed her parasol at him when she saw him.

Chest heaving and fire spitting from her eyes, she stalked him, gritting out between her teeth, "You knew about this *wife* of Travis's all along, didn't you? How could you have come to me and forced me, begged me to go out with him, and he married to that guttersnipe!"

Jeff leaned back in his chair and grinned. "Why Alicia, I do believe you almost did a flip when I suggested you go with Travis that night. I'm afraid, my dear, that his matrimonial state never came up once I told you he was back."

Alicia glared at him and leaned over his desk,

putting both hands on the edge and effectively displaying her bosom to his eyes. "What do you know about this whore he has saddled himself with? What gutter did he pick her out of?"

"Now, now, Alicia. I do believe my new sister is far more cultured and well bred to be called a guttersnipe." He found he was enjoying this immensely while he watched her walk back and forth before his desk, slapping her parasol into the palm of her hand like she was hoping it to be Jenny's head.

"He won't get away with this. I'll show him how much of a mistake he's made. We were practically betrothed," she screamed, which made Jeff raise his eyebrows.

"Really, Alicia. I don't believe Travis was aware of that."

She turned on him with all the venom she could. "This is quite a treat for you, isn't it? To see me play second fiddle to a little snip barely out of the classroom. Well, let me tell you something, Jeffrey. I haven't lost yet. By the time I'm through with little miss high and mighty, she'll go back to her gutter so fast she won't know what hit her."

"Really." he grinned. "I would certainly think twice about causing any problems where Travis is concerned, Alicia. He has such a mean temper, you know."

"I'll just show him what a real woman is like, and compared to the little tramp he's bestowed his name on, she won't stand a chance." An evil leer played across her face as she saw the image of the girl crumble like dust.

Leaving Jeff to shake his head, she turned and stormed out of his office just as dramatically as she had stormed in.

Jeff wondered if he should warn Travis and Jenny

about Alicia but decided not to spoil their first days of wedded bliss. He would talk to them at the barbecue, or maybe it would be better to talk to Travis alone and let him straighten out the storm of Alicia Adams. He was sure glad that he didn't have Travis's problem.

He put his papers away and left to have a quiet lunch with Mary Lou.

Travis guided the carriage to Tradd Street and pulled up to a large three-story rose brick home that was sheltered with trees around the side. An iron fence connected with brick pillars that matched the house ran around the yard from front to back. Travis unlocked the gate and led Jenny and Rosalie up to the front door where he inserted a key and opened it upon the dark interior of the house.

With a feeling of suffocation suddenly filling her senses, Jenny went to open all the drapes she could see in both the parlor and library downstairs.

Travis watched her as she ran from window to window throwing the drapes aside. He finally said to her, "I didn't know you had this fetish about light, Jenny."

Jenny turned to him and found she was breathing heavily, and her heart was hammering inside her chest. She sank down into a chair and put her hands over her eyes as all the memories of that other house in Charleston came back to her.

Travis knelt down beside the chair, taking her hands away from her face. "Jenny, what's the matter?"

Jenny's face was white as chalk as she tried to laugh. "I don't know what came over me. I felt I had to let the light in. I'm sorry but I can't stand the darkness."

Sure that Jenny was holding back again, Travis persisted. "You were never afraid of the dark before, Jenny."

She looked away from him and softly told him of the night she had spent at the colonel's townhouse.

"What does the colonel have to hide? Surely he gave you reason for keeping the house closed up?"

"Yes. The servant, Cicero, said they were to remain closed by order of the colonel. Then the colonel gave me a lame excuse about the sunlight's ruining his furniture, but the furniture I saw wasn't worth saving."

Taking Jenny's hand in his, Travis leaned closer and told her, "You may open every drape in this house, Jenny. It belongs to you, too, now."

Jenny touched his face, saying, "You are a very understanding man, Travis Gardiner."

"About most things." He left the meaning of his statement hang between them and then kissed Jenny lightly on the cheek.

They had almost forgotten Rosalie who was standing in the entrance hall looking about her in wonder. She had never been in such a fine house before.

Jenny called the child over to her.

Rosalie looked at her and walked timidly toward the two people who now owned her. Her mother had told her that she would be on her own now and must be obedient or she would be whipped. She hadn't expected to be treated like these two were treating her, and she was confused.

Speaking quietly, Jenny asked, "Where did you live before today?"

Rosalie looked about the room, seemingly not able to tear her eyes away from all the beautiful things in the room.

Lightly touching the girl's arm, Jenny repeated

herself. "Rosalie, where did you come from?"

Rosalie looked down at the gentle hand that touched her. Looking up, she determined this lady could be kind, and said, "I lived at the manor, ma'am."

"The manor? Not Salford Manor?" Jenny asked incredulously.

The child nodded her head. "Yes, ma'am."

Remembering the children they had seen this morning on the way to Charleston, the vacant stares, the old men's faces on the small boys, the cabins that were in such disrepair, Jenny pulled the child closer, saying, "You are going to stay with us now, Rosalie. Would you like that?"

The woman's smile was so kind, the child wrapped her arms around Jenny's neck, saying, "I be happy to be your slave."

Jenny looked up at Travis, in a pleading way.

Travis patted the dark blond curly head beside Jenny's golden one. "Rosalie." He waited until she stood up and looked at him. He had the feeling he had scared her when she seemed to shrink before his eyes.

Before he could continue, the child backed away from him and cried. "I sorry I touched the lady. I be good. Don't whip me. I sorry."

Travis felt all the wrongs of slavery rest on his shoulders when this child cringed before him. He went down on one knee and held out his hand to her.

Rosalie saw the gesture and didn't understand. White men had only poked and prodded her. She couldn't understand this big man who seemed to be so kind. She looked at the woman who was nodding encouragement to her while indicating she should go to the man. Rosalie came to him slowly, ready to run should he try to whip her as the woman at the manor had done almost as long as Rosalie could remember.

Travis wiped a tear from her cheek and brushed the hair from her forehead. The gesture was kind and done slowly to calm her. He started talking to her in a low, even voice that visibly relaxed the child. "Rosalie, you are not our slave. You are free. For the time being I would like you to stay with us, but only until you can decide for yourself where and how you want to live." Seeing the confusion again on the child's face, he continued in the same low, even voice: "My wife and I will take care of you. You will never go hungry, and you will always have a home with us for as long as you wish. How does that sound to you?"

Rosalie looked from the man to the pretty lady. The pretty lady was looking at the man with tears in her eyes. The lady was smiling the sweetest smile Rosalie had ever seen. Her life had not been filled with smiles or love. Her mother had smiled only once that Rosalie could remember and that had been when the baby had died. Rosalie never understood happiness or security. Her life had been filled with endless days of hunger and illness all around her. She didn't understand all of what the man had said to her, but she knew she would like to live with them.

"I be good and I work for you and the lady."

Jenny's smile was brilliant as she stood up, taking the small hand of the child in hers. "I bet you're hungry, aren't you?"

The child's eyes grew bigger. She had been hungry all her life. "Yes ma'am, I be really hungry."

Jenny looked up into the smiling eyes of her husband. "Is there anything here for her to eat?"

Travis smiled and remembered all the preserved food in the pantry that Mammy had put up only a short while ago. "Let's go check the pantry." He led the procession as they went to the room off the cook house and opened the doors to an array of foods.

Rosalie selected a jar of peaches from the shelf, and Jenny spooned out the golden spheres for her. They watched as the child gobbled them up and then picked up the bowl and drank the juice, dribbling some down her chin in her haste.

Jenny's heart went out to the child when Rosalie rubbed her eyes and seemed to slump in her chair. "Travis, I believe Rosalie is tired. Where can she take a nap?"

Travis picked up the sleepy child in his arms. Rosalie was asleep before he got up the stairs. He indicated a door, and Jenny opened it on a beautiful room, definitely feminine, and Jenny assumed correctly that this was Celeste's room.

Travis gently laid the child in the middle of the canopied bed, and Jenny pulled a comforter over her thin body, then they quietly tiptoed from the room.

In the hall, Jenny stood up on tiptoes and kissed his cheek. "Thank you for saving her, Travis. I think you are the best person in the whole world."

Travis touched her cheek, and a look of sadness came over him when he said, "Jenny, you must realize that I cannot save them all. The system wouldn't allow it. I'm a threat to most of the men around here as it is. They see me as a 'nigger lover,' as they put it. It could prove that I have created today a means for our own destruction. Slavery can not be tolerated by most people, and I'm afraid one day the system that feeds us may be ignited in a confrontation that will be disastrous for the South, and our way of life will be changed forever."

Jenny knew he was saying these things to warn her of future problems the slave system could inflict on them. She put her arms around him and with her cheek against his chest, said, "Travis, you have saved one child today. I know you can't save them all, but this one child is worth all the problems that could come up. I know it won't be easy, but I thank you again for her future."

He hugged her tighter for just a moment then said, "Come on. I'll show you the rest of the house."

They walked together, hand in hand, exploring the house from top to bottom. Jenny was amazed at the size of the house and asked, "Where did all this room come from? The house looked smaller from the street."

Travis laughed. "It's the way they face the houses in Charleston, Jenny. The front is actually the side. Come with me."

Travis opened french doors and they stepped out onto a piazza that ran the length of the house. It was immense. The wind, coming off the ocean, felt good on Jenny's face when she walked to the front side and looked over the top of buildings to the bay they had arrived in.

Travis stood behind her with his arms around her waist.

Leaning her head back, Jenny felt security that she had never felt before. How lucky I am, she thought as Travis kissed the top of her head.

Realizing this must be the spot that Ellen Gardiner had stood, watching for her husband to return, Jenny turned, looking up into the face that she loved. "I'm glad you are not going to sea again, Travis. Standing here I can almost feel the loneliness your mother felt as she waited for your father to return." She saw a flicker of pain come into his eyes and quickly added, "I'm sorry if my mentioning the past again brought painful memories to you."

He pulled her to him, and with her cheek next to his chest, she couldn't see him look out over the bay and remember the hours he had spent here hating and condemning his father. He finally understood how his father had felt in being denied the woman he loved. He could understand because Jenny had become the most important part of his world. If she were here and he not able to love her, he knew the sea would also beckon his return.

Jenny pulled back just as he carefully hid the pain in a mask of a smile. "Let's go sit over there." She pulled him behind her as she led the way to a wicker settee. When she sat down, she patted the spot beside her and looked up invitingly.

"Jenny, there are some cushions somewhere that will make it more comfortable for you."

Looking up at him with half-lowered lids and a wanton smile on her lips, she said in a low, husky voice, "I will be very comfortable if you are beside me."

Travis laughed and plopped down beside her, putting his arm around her and pulling her to him.

Leaning her head again to his chest, she put a hand on his knew. "Travis, something is bothering me about Rosalie."

"Oh! What?"

"Well, she doesn't look like the other Negroes I have seen. Her hair isn't coarse or black, and her features are more delicate than say—Mammy."

Travis laughed at the comparison, then said, "Jenny, Mammy came from Africa. She's full blooded, but Rosalie appears to have a lot of white blood in her. Probably her mother was a mulatto and her father could have been white."

Jenny didn't understand. "But, are you telling me there are white slaves, too?"

"Not in this country that I know of. Of course, other countries do have such practices but usually it's just women who are taken as slaves. Rosalie's mother was probably accosted by a white man much against her will. I've found that the Negroes usually only mate within their own kind, but some owners or overseers are not beyond bedding the slave women."

Jenny was aghast at the casualness with which rape was condoned among the supposed gentry. "Surely it is not practiced on a wide scale, and this is just an unfortunate exception?"

Travis rubbed his finger up and down her arm while he explained, "I only wish that were true, Jenny. There seems to be a lot of mixed blood Negroes around."

She sat up and looked into his eyes, and asked, "But, why is it permitted? Surely there must be laws to protect these people?"

"I'm afraid the old adage, that a man controls his own property, holds true here, Jenny. It's just like this house. I own it and can knock every window out if that's what I wanted to do. The same holds true for the slaves. Their owners can virtually do what they want with them. In some circles a man is considered rich if he has a Negress mistress. Of course, in that case the woman is usually a willing participant in the matter."

"Well, I hope that is not the custom here." She glowered at him. "I plan on keeping you too busy to need a mistress."

Travis hugged her to him, saying, "Madam, I am counting on that." He slapped her bottom and exclaimed, "Come on. I'm hungry. Let's go back and see what else is in the pantry." He took her hand as they walked downstairs and to the back to the huge cook house that had bright copper kettles and skillets hanging from the beams running over the ceiling.

Travis walked to the pantry, and they gazed on row upon row of preserved fruits and vegetables. The smell of apples and onions came from somewhere but Jenny couldn't see evidence of them. Travis opened a door to the right of the pantry, and Jenny saw steps going down into a dark cavern under the house.

"That's the root cellar," Travis explained. "Mammy puts apples and onions down there, and they'll keep for months. We're coming to stay here in a few weeks and by some of the smells I detect, Mammy lost some of her apples."

Jenny smelled the strong, pungent odor of vinegar and wrinkled her nose.

Selecting a jar of figs from the pantry, Travis proceeded to open them and spoon the brown mass into two bowls. "This should tide us over until supper. I think I will take you to the Colony House for supper. You'll like it there."

Jenny was thinking about her conversation with Madam LaFarrier this afternoon and decided to broach the subject with Travis. "Travis, today Madam LaFarrier asked me when we had gotten married. I didn't know what to say since it will be obvious to everyone that I am with child. I told her recently and then changed the subject."

Travis thought a moment then put down his spoon, looking at her with tenderness. "I am simply telling people we were married in Barbados. No one from Moss Grove will talk, and I'm sure Jeff and Oscar won't. Don't worry, Jenny. It really doesn't bother me what people think, but I know you feel it somehow detracts from you. Don't. Once people get to know you they won't care either—at least the people who matter."

Jenny lowered her eyes, unable to meet his gaze. "It's just that I don't want people to think I am a harlot." She looked up at him and said sincerely, "I want to be a good wife to you and make you proud of me. I'm afraid you would be a laughing stock if it were known we married after the conception of our child."

Travis tilted her head up to meet his eyes, and said, "All right, Jenny. I'll spread the word. Don't worry about it. Saturday at the barbecue, we will simply say we have been married for three months and are expecting our first child. No one will dispute it." He picked up his spoon and began again on his pickled figs. He thought of Alicia. She could certainly put a wedge in his story. He would have to do something about her.

He never wondered why he felt compelled to wipe his right hand on his breeches. Some nagging memory but it was lost.

Jenny was amazed at how easily he handled all her problems. Her love for him overcame all the doubts about her future. Even the presence of Sir Reginald became a mere inconvenience.

She picked up the empty bowls and took them to the sink. She was about to pump water into a kettle for boiling, when Travis came to her and picked her up.

He nuzzled her neck and started walking from the cook house, saying, "The dishes can wait, wench. I have other plans for you right now."

Jenny held on around his neck and let the sensations wash over her. He walked up the stairs and opened a bedroom door, putting Jenny down and, while kissing her, unhooked the gown, the corset, untied the pantalets and muttered something about the amount of clothing women wore.

When Jenny stood naked before him, she felt her breath coming in fast, jerky timing. She walked up to him and brushed his hands aside from the unbuttoning of his shirt. Looking into his half-lidded eyes, she

304

took the shirt off his shoulders, letting it fall to the floor. Then she opened the buttons of his breeches and they too joined the shirt.

He became impatient with the slowness and quickly divested himself of his underdrawers and stockings.

They stood apart, staring at each other with passion-filled eyes. Then Jenny stepped into his waiting arms, feeling the smooth swell of tendon and flesh under her exploring hands. His lips captured hers, placing little bites on her lower lip, then he sucked gently, pulling her into him making faintness seem a definite possibility. Her knees became mush when she felt him grow rigid against her.

He picked her up and carried her to the bed and then lay beside her, stroking her, loving her until her frenzy made her beg him to take her.

As they lay together, some minutes later, each experiencing the afterglow of their love play, Travis gazed at her beautiful face for a long moment. When she opened her eyes to look upon him, he gently told her, "Jenny, I never knew I could feel this way about any woman. You have come to be my most treasured possession." He rubbed his thumb over her jawline, while his eyes spoke volumns of love and longing. "I will protect you, Jenny, from whatever is frightening you. No one will hurt you as my wife. Please come to me if you ever need my help." He saw the strange, almost haunting expression in her eyes. "Is there something I can help with, Jenny?"

She wanted to tell him everything but was so afraid. How could she tell him that she did not really belong to him but to an aged estate in Northern England. The moments ticked by as she debated the wisdom of telling him the truth. If she lost him now she might as well die. To be loved by him meant more to her than anything she could possibly dream of. What if he did understand and helped her? But a little voice inside told her that she once trusted her father, too. She closed her eyes against the pleading black eyes before her.

"Travis, I love you."

Still convinced she was hiding something, Travis debated whether he should make her tell him but decided not to push it. She just needed time. After all, he had left her to the life of a servant at Salford Manor. He went about trying to convince her that she was truly safe as his wife. He smiled. "If someone had told me a year ago that I would have found my own true love, I'd have laughed and told them they were crazy." He brushed a strand of golden hair from her brow.

Jenny opened her eyes and smiled. "Darby told me you would never wed as you felt women just wanted to put rings through their husband's noses. What makes you think I won't try to put one through yours?"

Travis's embarrassment was acute when he thought back to all the disparaging remarks about marriage he had uttered in his ignorance. "Had I but known of you, I would have been the first to marry."

"But, why would you think such a thing?" she wondered aloud.

His face took on a sadness when he related, "It started with my mother and father. He loved her so much that the pain of not being able to come to her nearly tore them apart. As you know, when the pain became so acute, they relinquished their better judgement to their passion and as a result, my mother died. As a boy, I interpreted it to be the marriage that had done it and determined in my young mind that I would never be thus." He smiled at her. "Jenny, there is something you had better understand. I am a stubborn man and when I want something I'll get it one way or another, and if I'm wrong in my headstrong stubbornness, it will usually take a miracle—" He grinned. "Or Darby to bring me around."

At the mention of Darby's name, Jenny remembered his last visit to her at Salford Manor. "Travis, what did Darby tell you that made you change your mind?"

"Why only that I loved you and that I would lose you if I didn't go marry you." He kissed her tenderly. "Remind me to give him a bonus."

They only knew each other as their passion once again consumed them.

Jenny was nestled in Travis's arms when she suddenly remembered Rosalie. She got up swiftly, donning her gown that had once belonged to Celeste.

Travis watched her with an amused expression. "Where are you going in such a hurry?"

"I'm going to check on Rosalie. She'll be frightened if she wakes up and we are not there." She was having trouble with the hooks and walked over to the bed, presenting her back to Travis, saying, "Hook me, please."

Smiling, his fingers fumbled with the tiny hooks and he said, "Jenny, I'm beginning to think my life with you will be just *hook me, please.*" He mimicked her accent, then laughed when she turned to look at him with a scowl. "Just kidding." He shrugged.

She was about to go into the hall when a knocking came from the front door. Travis grumbled and began to dress. "You go check on Rosalie and I'll get rid of our unwelcomed visitor."

He marched down the stairs and pulled the door open. Darby stood on the steps with a sheepish grin on his bewhiskered face. "Darby, what are you doing here?"

"Well, cap'n, I had to come to town to pick up a

few things for the barbecue and I just thought—since I was here— I'd just pop over here and see if you were gettin' along all right and drop off some food Mammy sent for ye."

Travis didn't know what to say to the little man who was just looking out for his comfort. "Well, come on in." He shut the door, turned and watched as the old man's attention was drawn to the stairs.

Jenny was coming down holding the hand of Rosalie. Rosalie spotted Darby and froze. Jenny looked at the little girl and understood immediately what the child was thinking. She had felt the same fear and trepidation that night she was rescued. But how to convince Rosalie that Darby was a friend escaped her.

Darby knew what the little girl was thinking, too. It wasn't the first time a child had stared at him with that look.

He walked to the bottom of the stairs and smiled up at the child. "Well, well. If you aren't the pretty little thing." He noticed the relaxing of muscles in her face. "I bet you wonder who I be, don't you?" Putting his hand on the knee that stopped with the peg leg, he continued to smile at her. "Me name's Darby. Darby Combs." He paused, then added, "And what be your name?"

Rosalie looked at the man then stepped closer to Jenny, and whispered, "Rosalie."

"Rosalie," Darby repeated. "Why that's the nicest name I ever heard." He reached in his pocket and pulled out a piece of hard candy. Holding it up to Rosalie, he said, "I bet you like candy 'bout as much as me."

Rosalie smiled and hid her face in Jenny's skirt.

Jenny smiled at Darby and, placing her hand on the little girl's head, said, "Rosalie, wouldn't you like the candy Darby has for you?"

Rosalie peeked around to see the funny-looking man still smiling at her. She stepped down the steps and took the candy, popping it in her mouth, smacking noisily, and smiled at Darby.

Darby patted her curly light brown hair and then turned to Travis with a questioning gaze.

Travis stepped up to the little girl and smiled. "Darby, Rosalie has agreed to come live with us at Moss Grove. What do you think of that?"

"Why, cap'n, I couldn't think of nothin' better." He looked at the little girl. "Rosalie, how 'bout you come help me bring in the food from the wagon. Would you help me?"

Rosalie walked over to Darby and placed her now sticky hand in his. Darby smiled at her and opened the door as they walked out hand in hand.

Coming down the rest of the stairs, Jenny said, "Travis, we can't go out tonight and leave her here alone. She would be too frightened."

Travis laughed and hugged her to him. "You are going to be a fantastic mother." He kissed her lightly. "But, I have a feeling we won't have to worry about Rosalie. Darby will stay with her. He can go back with us tomorrow."

They turned when the door opened and watched as Rosalie told Darby all about a puppy she had seen that morning. She didn't stop talking all the way to the back of the house while she led the way for Darby.

Jenny and Travis decided Darby was a godsend, and they walked up the stairs to get ready for their first evening out as man and wife.

Chapter Sixteen

That evening Travis took Jenny to the Colony House where they had fresh oysters on the half shell, shrimp creole, and baked potatoes oozing with fresh churned butter. They had wine with dinner and strong black coffee with cream after. They were having a quiet, subdued conversation when Jeff appeared at their side.

"Well, well, if it's not Mr. and Mrs. Gardiner. What are you two doing in town?"

"Hello, Jeff. We came in to do some shopping and have an evening out." Travis shook his brother's hand.

Jeff hid a grin as he related, "Actually, I assumed you were in town. I was visited by a very dispirited young lady this afternoon, and she filled me in on you two."

Travis scowled. "Who was that, as if I have to ask?"

"Why Alicia, who else? I must say, old man, she took the news of your marriage rather poorly. I think she had designs on your herself." Jeff winked at

Jenny.

"Well, I can tell you, it was only my good fortune that I escaped her clutches. She's a conniving wench, and I pity the poor man she finally does land."

Jeff looked at Jenny. "You certainly look ravishing tonight, Jenny. Marriage seems to agree with both of you."

Jenny and Travis exchanged loving glances.

Jeff, noting their expressions, asked, "I see you have finished with dinner. Why don't we go over to the Dock Street Theatre. I hear there is a new play opening that all of Charleston is dying to see, and I happen to have four tickets. Well, what do you say?"

Travis looked at Jenny. "Would you like to see a play, Jenny?"

Nodding eagerly, Jenny's eyes shown brightly.

Turning back to Jeff, Travis nodded his head. "All right, but where is your young lady?"

"She's in the powder room. Come on, she should be ready by now. I hope you like her."

"I'm sure we will, Jeff. Let me pay the bill." He turned to Jenny. "You go with Jeff, Jenny, and I'll meet you in the foyer."

Jeff wondered if he should warn Jenny about Alicia and her threats but decided not to spoil her evening as they walked in the direction of the foyer.

A pretty young woman came out of the powder room just as they reached the marble foyer. Jeff smiled at her and led Jenny in her direction.

"Mary Lou, I would like to introduce my new sister, Jennifer."

The young woman smiled and Jeff continued the introductions, saying "And, Jenny, may I introduce the light of my life, Miss Mary Lou Jenkins."

Jenny extended her gloved hand to the other woman, saying, "I'm pleased to meet you, Mary Lou,

311

and please call me Jenny."

The young woman had soft brown hair with large aquamarine eyes that were looking at Jenny with a puzzled expression. She shook Jenny's hand with a firm grasp but the puzzled expression remained.

Jenny asked her, "Is something the matter?"

Mary Lou gave a nervous laugh, then looked at Jeff before turning back to Jenny. "No, no, it's just I thought your name was Elaine. Lady Elaine."

Travis had come up to them and had heard this last exchange. He came to Jenny's rescue, saying, "I prefer her middle name which is Jennifer."

Jenny smiled up at him, and Travis returned his attention to Mary Lou. "I'm Jeff's brother Travis, and you must be Mary Lou."

"Yes. I'm pleased to finally meet you, Travis. Jeff has told me so much about you I feel I already know you."

"Obviously," said Travis as he looked to his brother.

Jeff took both ladies by the arm and said, "Shall we go?"

Travis raised an eyebrow then took Jenny's hand and extricated her from Jeff's clutches. "This one is mine, little brother."

Jeff grinned. "Possessive, aren't you?"

"You're absolutely right." He gazed into the blue eyes that held so much promise of things to come and smiled.

They arrived at the Dock Street Theatre and joined in the bustle of the crowd. Travis introduced Jenny to first one surprised friend then another, and another. The reactions were the same as Travis would explain they had been married in March in a little chapel in Barbados.

312

Jenny's head was spinning at all the new names and faces, and they rushed to their seats as the curtain rose on the first act.

Jenny thoroughly enjoyed the play which was a British farce. She laughed along with the rest of the audience at the puns that were directed at England.

At the intermission, Travis asked if she would like a glass of champagne. She and Mary Lou stayed in their seats while Travis and Jeff walked out to the reception area leaving the women to talk of general topics, thoroughly enjoying each other's company, completely unaware of the commotion their presence was about to cause.

Reginald was not enjoying the play. He was insulted by the insinuations of the actors and equally insulted by the woman who had trapped him into coming here. How had she talked him into coming here with *her?* He glanced at her, noticing again how she looked like a dried prune in the mauve gown. Eudora Colby need never fear rape, Reginald thought to himself and he started to chuckle as he leaned forward to peruse the crowd below. There isn't a decent-looking woman in the bunch, he thought until his eyes rested on Jenny. "What's this?" Jenny! But, she's dead!

Eudora had been saying something she thought witty, when Reginald abruptly leaned forward. Following his gaze, she spotted Elaine. A red haze seemed to mist before her eyes. Elaine! All the loathing she felt for the girl and her beauty returned when she saw the handsome Travis Gardiner return with a glass of champagne for her and take the seat next to her. Of all the luck.

She turned to bring Reginald's attention back to her but stopped when she saw his expression. "Reggie, is something wrong? You look like you've seen a ghost."

He continued to stare, thinking he had.

"Reggie." she tapped his shoulder. "Reggie, are you listening?"

Reginald turned to her, making her heart almost stop. The look on his face made her skin crawl. She had never seen such evil.

"Why, Reggie, what is the matter? You look positively morose."

Reginald was thinking that if Jenny were alive then Elaine must be dead! The more he thought, the clearer everything started to become and the more amusing this whole mess became. He started to laugh.

Eudora saw the faces turn to stare at her escort from the adjoining boxes. "Reggie, people are staring. Please control yourself." She sat back smoothing the folds of the gown that had once belonged to Elaine. The second act started, and a slight blush rose in Eudora's pallid cheeks when a man in the next box cleared his throat loudly. All her thought of impressing these people who had scorned her with this titled gentleman were evaporating as Reginald kept making such a scene. "Reggie, please. People are staring," she implored him again.

Reginald dabbed at his eyes with a lace-edged handkerchief as he finally brought himself under control. He would have to see how he could turn this to his advantage. If Jenny were taking the identity of Elaine, then no one knew Elaine obviously had perished in the shipwreck. He soon realized that Elaine's fortune had not eluded him. In fact, it now seemed that Elaine's fortune was sure to be his.

He stood up abruptly and walked quickly from the box leaving Eudora to stare at his back.

Noticing the people in the next box observing her,

314

she quickly jumped up and ran after him. "Reggie, where are you going?" she yelled at his retreating figure.

Reginald continued to walk out of the main lobby and stood on the curb, waiting for the doorman to inform the Colby's coachman that they were ready to leave.

Eudora, breathless after her chase and gasping for breath, asked, "Reggie, what is the meaning of this? I wanted to stay and see the rest of the play."

Reginald turned to glare at her. "Shut your mouth. If you want to see the rest of the play, then stay, otherwise, we are returning to the townhouse. Now be quiet. I must think." He paced in front of the theatre while his mind whirled with plans and ideas.

Shocked at his tone, Eudora clamped her mouth shut. *How dare he speak to me like that!* She would have to reconsider her plans. After all, a title wasn't everything, and the real thing was all but a few months away, anyway. A smile that resembled a leer came to her thin mouth. *A lot of good a title did for Elaine. She slaved for me. A common plantation owner's daughter.*

When the twosome emerged from the coach outside the townhouse, Reginald knew the course to take. He smiled while he helped Eudora from the coach. *Yes, it would work.*

Travis and Jenny had a marvelous time watching the play and reluctantly said good-bye to Jeff and Mary Lou. "See you tomorrow, Jeff and Mary Lou. We'll see you on Saturday for the barbecue."

"I wouldn't miss it for anything. Jeff's told me all about the Gardiner's barbecues. It was so nice meeting you both."

"It was nice meeting you and come out to the plantation anytime you can."

Travis and Jenny waved good-bye and walked hand in hand into the house, not knowing of the impending problems that were being laid out for them.

Chapter Seventeen

Travis was awakened early the next morning by the sounds of giggling coming from the hall. He stretched his big frame then pulled Jenny into his arms for a light kiss.

Smiling, Jenny snuggled closer into his chest, smelling the fresh male scent of him. This was the way she hoped to wake up every morning.

Brushing her hair from her face, Travis whispered into her ear, "We'd better get up and check on our ward. Darby might be playing tag with her from the sounds I'm hearing."

They heard running feet and a hearty laugh, then the giggles of Rosalie again.

When they were dressed, Travis put a finger to his lips, then slowly opened the door. There in the hall were Darby and Rosalie playing a game of jacks.

The little girl looked up and saw them standing there, and she favored them with a brilliant smile, jumping up to run to Jenny.

Jenny noticed again the tattered dress and the

soiled stockings which had big holes in the heels from her shoes that were too tight. She looked to Travis as the little girl grasped her around the waist, resting her head on Jenny's breast.

"Do we have time to get her some clothes before we go back to Moss Grove?" she asked Travis.

Ruffling the child's head, Travis smiled and said, "If I know Mammy like I think I do, I think I know where we'll find ample supplies of clothing for her. Come with me."

Darby excused himself to prepare breakfast and hobbled down the hall, tossing the horsehair ball in his hands.

Travis led the way up to the attic which was filled with trunks and boxes, each labeled by a big, T, J or C. He stood watching his wife and the little girl while they held up first one frilly dress then another. He noticed the little girl's eyes as she would first touch one then another as though she were afraid they would disappear before her eyes. It dawned on Travis that Jenny's expression had been the same as when he had led her through the many fabrics in the shop in Barbados. He could certainly understand Rosalie's disbelief since he was sure she had never owned any dress to compare with what she was seeing now, but Jenny should have been used to fine clothing as a companion to Lady Elaine. She was an enigma to him. He hoped one day she would tell him of her life more fully.

Feeling his talents not required, he backed out, leaving them to their task. As he walked down the hall toward his bedchamber, he met Darby coming toward him with a worried look on his bewhiskered face. "What's the trouble, Darby? Forget something?"

The old man stopped and looked back to the direction from which he had just come, and said,

"You got a visitor, cap'n."

"Who would call at this hour?" Suddenly he wished for the island beach and the privacy it afforded him.

"It's Miss Adams, cap'n, an' she looks ready to do battle."

Travis did not want a repeat of yesterday's scene in front of Jenny and decided he had better get Alicia straightened out once and for all. "You go up and keep Jenny and Rosalie busy. I'll go get rid of Miss Adams."

"Aye, aye, cap'n," Darby replied, then watched as Travis threw back his shoulders and descended the stairs. "Wait 'til you sees her," he said chuckling while he made his way up the attic stairs.

Travis walked into the parlor to see Alicia standing in the center of the room in all her glory. For this morning's visit she had chosen a transparent beige gown that left nothing to the imagination. Travis remembered the sketches Madam LaFarrier had suggested for Jenny and figured correctly that Alicia would have all the nerve it took to wear the latest fashions from France. While his eyes raked her statuesque form, she gave him a brilliant smile.

"Good mornin', darlin'," she drawled.

Nodding, Travis found his voice suddenly gone and went to pour a cup of coffee from a silver pot on the sidebaord. He didn't ask Alicia if she wanted a cup, which Alicia found to be a snub and would have none of that.

"Would y'all mind pourin' me a cup? I'm afraid I haven't had breakfast as yet."

Giving her a sidelong glance, Travis poured another cup of the strong brew, then asked, "What do you want, Alicia?"

"Why, Travis, why are you so stern this beautiful

mornin'? Are the bonds of marriage startin' ta choke?" She grinned at him as she put down her cup and started to remove her gloves.

He decided to ignore her statement and repeated his question while he went to stand in front of her. "What are you doing here and why did you come dressed like that?" He pointed with his cup.

She preened under his gaze, asking, "Do y'all like my gown? I bought it in New Orleans last winter. It's the latest design from France." Lowering her lashes, she looked at him with an invitation in her emerald eyes. "I bought it for you, darlin'. I just know how you loved to see me at my finest."

Privately thinking she had gotten the gown from a prostitute in the French Quarter in New Orleans, Travis turned away from her and said, "Alicia, we are getting ready to go back to Moss Grove, so if you will please tell me why you are here, I would appreciate it."

This meeting was not going as Alicia had expected. She had thought he would take one look at her in this gown and lose his senses. She decided a bolder approach was necessary. "Well, darlin', I want to apologize for my ouburst yesterday. I realize now that you probably were regrettin' your marriage, but you, being a gentleman, would never let the world know of your mistake. I'm here to tell you that I don't blame you for takin' that little street urchin as your wife. Let's just continue as before and when the time is right, you can get an annulment and we'll be able to marry."

He stared at her as though she had lost her mind. He had known that she had wanted to marry him, but he had never given her any encouragement as to his wanting to marry her.

When she noted his surprise, she became bolder.

320

"In the mean time, darlin', we could pretend it's you and I that are wed, and you can have all husbandly rights." She stood up and placed her delicate white hand on his shoulder.

He stepped back as though her touch stung him. "Alicia, your obnoxiousness bores me. There has never been any hope for the two of us, and I have never suggested there would be anything between us." He walked to the window and rubbed his hand through his hair. Turning back to her, he continued: "Besides, I love Jenny very much and she is to have my child."

Alicia was struck with a pain so severe it threatened to knock the breath from her. To fight a woman was one thing but to fight his child was too much. "Your child!" she screamed. Suddenly she thought she understood and determined to tear down his little ivory tower. "Are you sure it is *your* child, darlin'?"

A look of intense vengeance overtook Travis's expression, and he said through gritted teeth, "I think you have overstayed your welcome, Alicia."

Fearing she had gone too far, Alicia quickly replied, "Travis, darlin', this doesn't change how I feel for you. We could still have our moments. After all, she will start to get big and clumsy and I'll still be me." She put her hands up to her bosom, that she had obviously rouged, and looked enticingly at him. "Travis," she continued in a husky voice, "I'm all yours."

Afraid of his emotions while he contemplated squeezing the life from her, Travis spun toward the window and hissed, "Alicia, I think it best if you leave now."

Alicia mistook his quietness and his turning away from her as a sign of regret. Determined not to be shunned aside, she walked up and placed her hand on his shoulder. "I'll be waitin' for you, my darlin'. You need only to call me."

He pushed her away from him as he stated, "Alicia, I'm going to tell you this for the last time. My wife is the most important person in my life. You sully yourself with this brazen display." When he turned away from her, he noticed Jenny standing in the doorway.

Following Travis's eyes, Alicia turned to see her rival. Jenny had a smudge on her cheek, and dust clung to her skirt front. Her eyes looked from Travis to Alicia.

Alicia sensed her advantage and walked slowly toward this child she so despised. "Travis, I must say you know how to treat a wife. Were you dusting, dear?"

Jenny looked at Alicia's beautifully coiffed hair and her daring gown. The two stood leering at each other like two cats, bristling the hair on their backs.

Travis quickly came to stand beside Jenny, placing a restraining arm across her shoulders, and quickly said, "My *wife* was doing a chore of love, Alicia. I'm sure you wouldn't understand." He looked down at Jenny, and his eyes expressed more than his words could ever declare.

Sensing she had lost this confrontation, Alicia decided to leave and let Travis think about his choice. She hadn't lost this war yet. She started to walk past them when she paused next to Jenny. She looked down her nose at this chit who would take her man, then flung her head back and continued toward the door to let herself out. There was more than one way to become mistress of Moss Grove.

Travis turned Jenny to him and said, "I'm sorry you had to witness her display. Hopefully today has put an end to her conniving."

Jenny looked back at Travis with a sad expression.

"I think I almost feel sorry for her, Travis. She obviously wanted you very much. It must have been a shock for her to find you had married."

He smiled at her concern for a woman who would try to take away her husband. "Jenny, Alicia only wanted one thing from me. She wanted my name that would give her the money to buy her every whim. I don't think she's capable of the kind of love you have given to me."

Jenny looked down at her dust-covered gown and her work-roughened hands and said quietly, "She is very beautiful, Travis."

He put his fingers under her chin and tilted her head up to meet his gaze. "I think you are the most beautiful woman in the world just as you are."

She smiled as her confidence and happiness rose. Throwing her arms around him, she whispered, "Oh, Travis, I love you so."

He could not explain the feeling of tenderness and love this girl, his wife, brought out in him, but he made a vow to always keep her safe and to cherish her for the rest of his days.

When they walked into the hall of Moss Grove that afternoon, they felt the excitement in the air. Servants were busy polishing wood and cleaning floors. The aromas coming from the cook house were making both Travis and Jenny hungry.

Mammy came down the stairs with two girls in tow, each carrying a bundle of sheets. "Well, ah's 'bout ta give up on you two." Turning to the girls, she told them to take the sheets to the laundry room, then turned back to Travis and Jenny. She walked up to Jenny and placed a big arm around her shoulder. "Come on in heah and set yoursef down.' Y'all should not be out gallivantin' all over da country like you done." She cast a long look at Travis. "You's got ta be careful wid dis chile, Mis'er Travis."

Suddenly he felt like the young boy again and shrugged his shoulders helplessly. "I have been careful, Mammy. You'll see she's in the pink."

"An ah plans on keepin' her in da pink." She huffed at him. "Now honey, ah'll go and get you some nice hot tea."

"That would be nice, Mammy," Jenny replied.

They both watched as the big woman sashayed out of the room, then Travis said, while slowly shaking his head back and forth, "You sure have made an impression on Mammy."

"The only one I want to impress is you, Master Gardiner." She took his hands in hers.

"My dear, you have done an excellent job of that." He bent down and kissed her nose. "Now, I must act the part of a plantation owner and go check on how everything is progressing. I won't be long."

Jenny removed her hat and gloves while she walked around the beautiful room. She noticed a portrait of a woman over the mantle. The woman's eyes stared into the room. She was lovely, the expression on her face serene.

Mammy came bustling in with the tea tray and Jenny asked, Mammy, is this Travis's mother?"

Mammy stared at the portrait and walked over to dust an imaginary speck of dust from the frame. "Yes. Dat's Miss Ellen. She was one a da sweetest woman. Celeste was a lot lak her. Looked lak her, too!"

"She was very pretty," Jenny said while gazing up at the picture of the mother she would never know.

"Y'all will be a perfect mistress ta Moss Grove, jes' lak Miss Ellen was." She beamed at Jenny.

Jenny hugged the old woman and with a tear in her eye, said, "Thank you, Mammy. With your help, I hope to make Travis proud of me."

"Honey, y'all gots nothin' ta worry 'bout. Dat man be in heaben over you. Ah was thinkin' dat boy never bring a wife heah, but he shore done picked a good'un."

Jenny smiled at the woman and could only pray she would make the best wife possible. "Mammy, I'll need a lot of advice. I have never had to run a big house like this before." She thought of Eden Hall but that seemed to be in another lifetime.

"Y'all will do jes' fine, honey. You jes' worry 'bout dat babe you be carryin', and ah'll do what ah caine ta hep you. Now you jes' set heah and drink dis heah tea. Ah's got to check on dose girls ta make shore they's not loafin' on da job. Ta'mary be heah fore we knows it," she was saying as she walked out of the room.

Jenny heard Mammy exclaim from the foyer, "An who might you be, little one?" Jenny remembered Rosalie had gone off with Darby when they had arrived. Darby had promised to show her some puppies they had in the barn.

"Rosalie, I'm in here," Jenny called as the little girl ran to her.

Mammy came in on Rosalie's heels, asking, "Miss Jenny, what be goin' on heah? Who dat chile?" She put her plump hands on her even plumper hips.

Jenny smiled at the child and brushed the hair off her forehead. The child was staring at the big woman who stood before her. Jenny turned to look up at Mammy, saying, "Mammy, I would like you to meet Rosalie. Rosalie, this is Mammy."

Mammy's fat face softened when she saw the way Jenny treated the child.

Jenny was especially concerned for Rosalie. As they had driven to Moss Grove, Rosalie started crying and screaming. She had clung to Jenny as she sobbed making Jenny wonder what had set her off until Travis had nodded to his left. Jenny had turned her head and had seen the cabins with the little boys, who had the old men's faces, staring at them.

Rosalie had obviously thought they were taking her back to the manor. Jenny tried to hush the child, but with little success, until they were far away from the staring eyes that would haunt her for many years to come.

Mammy leaned down to the little girl, saying, "Rosalie, would y'all lak somethin' ta eat?"

The little girl put her small hand into the big hand of Mammy, who winked at Jenny, then led the child to the cook house.

Jenny took her teacup and walked around the bright, cheery room. The room had high ceilings and the walls were white. White curtains billowed at the windows with the breeze that came off the river. The furniture was done in yellows and greens. There was a persian rug that had a hint of yellow in its intricate pattern. The room was very restful, and Jenny thought the person who had decorated it was very happy. Only a happy person could have used these colors so expertly.

She put her teacup down when she saw the baby grand piano in the corner. She walked over and raised the lid, fingering the familiar keys. Sitting down, she played her favorite song, "Greensleeves." She was playing as if in another world and when she finished, applause broke out behind her. She turned and found Mammy and all the house servants standing in the doorway with Rosalie munching a tart between them. Travis came in and stood beside her.

"No one has played this piano since Celeste's accident," he said softly.

"Did I do something wrong?" Jenny asked hurriedly.

"No, no. It's about time someone used this old thing." He ran his fingers across the keyboard. "Play something else."

"All right." She played a soft English love song, and when she finished Travis kissed her lightly and the house servants applauded again.

Mammy shooed everyone back to work and closed the parlor doors behind her. "Shore do look lak Mis'er Travis done gone and fall in love wid dat girl." She chuckled to herself while she walked back to the cook house with Rosalie in tow.

Jenny looked up at Travis. "Travis, this is such a beautiful room. Did your mother decorate it?"

Travis smiled at the memory, saying, "Oh, yes. She had carpenters and painters running around here like mad. I was only a boy, but I remember her being stubborn about the bright colors she wanted. Everyone said she would be sorry with two lively sons to track up the carpets and soil the cushions, but she was adamant in her desire for *freshness*, as she called it."

Jenny looked again at the beautiful carpet that looked like new. "How did she keep them from becoming soiled?"

Travis laughed and tweaked her nose before saying, "My mother was a small woman, but she wielded authority like she had invented it. Jeff and I were taught never to come within the confines of this house unless we were clean. Many a time Mammy would bring us clean clothes to the back, and we'd go wash off the dust and mud in the river." He chuckled at the memory of the fall and winter days when the river was ice cold, but they knew if they weren't clean they

327

would stay outside.

Jenny leaned into his arms and shyly said, "I guess I will have to remember that for your son."

He hugged her to him. "Would you like to see the rest of the house now? You've really not seen most of it."

"Oh, yes. Let's go." She jumped up, dragging Travis with her.

He led her to his library, where the business of Moss Grove was conducted. She felt the masculine room fitting for her husband. The tall book shelves that reached from floor to ceiling were filled with leather-bound classics and novels. Her eyes scanned the titles for future reference, then she walked over to the massive oak desk that contained neat piles of correspondence and papers. The big red leather chair behind the desk looked appropriate to fit her husband's big frame. She noticed a small miniature portrait of a girl who looked similar to the woman in the portrait in the parlor. Picking it up, she studied the kind, dark eyes then stated, "This is Celeste."

Travis walked up behind her and gazed lovingly at his sister's likeness. "That was done just before the accident. She was fourteen."

Jenny turned to her husband and stated, "She was very beautiful, Travis."

Not wanting sadness this day, Travis took the portrait and gently returned it to his desktop, saying, "Come on, you have a lot more to see."

He led her up the winding staircase and past the room she had occupied upon her arrival to a room next to his. Opening the door, he stood back to display a beautiful upstairs sitting room.

Jenny went to the window, which overlooked a massive garden full of blooming wisteria, azalea, roses, and black-eyed susans. Little stone benches were intricately placed in secluded little groups. Turning back to the room, she found herself enchanted. Again, the brightness and freshness of colors pleased her. The walls were hung with a pale green damask, and various shades of green were in the patterns of the settees and winged-back chairs. A tall secretary stood by the window, and a Louis XV commode held an array of spring blooms from the garden below. The carpet was of a pale green and white design that begged to be walked on with bare feet. "This is a wonderful room, Travis."

He smiled at her delight. "This was mother's favorite room. She used it as her office. She would go over the menus and make her shopping lists at that secretary there. Now, it's your office and sitting room, my love."

Jenny noticed doorways on either side of the room. Noticing her attention, Travis walked over and opened the door to the right. "This connects to our bedchamber, Jenny."

"How—convenient." She blushed.

He walked to the door opposite, saying, "And, this goes to the nursery."

She ran to follow him but stopped when she took in the room. It was completely bare of furnishings. At her look of disappointment, Travis hastened to explain, "This was Mammy's way of telling Jeff and I that she had given up hope of having a baby to use this room. Subtle isn't she?"

"Do you still have the furniture she removed?"

"Don't worry. Mammy has carefully protected each and every piece. I'll have one of the boys bring it back, and you can decide what items you wish to keep and what items you wish to add."

"I can't wait. Let's go see now." She started to lead him back out into the hall but he stopped her.

"That can wait, Jenny. I think you've had enough excitement for one day. We'll continue the tour some other time. But for now, let's go back to the parlor, and you can play some music for me."

Wanting only to please him, she acquiesced to his wishes.

Chapter Eighteen

The day of the barbecue, the sun shone in all its glory into a clear deep blue sky. The field hands had been given the day off so that they, too, could enjoy the festivities. Everyone was scurrying around with last minute preparations. The pig had been roasting in a huge pit filled with hot coals all night. Mammy was supervising getting all the food ready to take out to the many tables that had been erected under the oak trees.

Jenny was feeling useless and was looking for something to do when Mammy gave her a sidelong glance and suggested she arrange the flowers in the front parlor and entrance hall. Jenny knew it was a small task but was glad to have something with which to occupy her hands. She was nervous but couldn't quite stop her hands from shaking or her heart from racing. She was to be the hostess at this party and would be meeting people who would affect the rest of her life.

She was finally satisfied with the arrangement of roses in the entrance hall when the first carriage pulled up in front of the house. She saw Jeff and Mary Lou get out and the driver pull the carriage around back. Travis had come up to them and was shaking hands with his brother as yet another carriage and another pulled to a stop in front.

331

Jenny came down the steps to stand beside Travis as he began the introductions to his friends and neighbors. She was introduced to so many people that she knew she would never remember all their names. She smiled sweetly at the shocked expressions that met her as Travis introduced her as his wife. Several matronly women had young daughters with them, and she could tell that more than one seemed quite disappointed at the introduction.

"I must say, my dear," Travis said grinning, "you have received some rather discouraging looks from some of these women. I hope you're not unnerved by the experience."

Jenny looked up at him with a saucy grin as she replied, "Why Travis, you do go on. These women are just upset that you are no longer the eligible bachelor and from what I've seen today, you should be happy I'm here. Some of these young women look like they could eat you alive."

"I am happy you're here, Jenny, but not to protect me." He pinched her nose as another carriage rolled to a stop before them.

Jenny found herself relaxing and actually enjoying herself with these kind, friendly people. She had received some scattered sneers and contemptuous leers from some of the young maids and their mothers, but all in all she was being welcomed into their community and into their lives. She felt a part of them, and all the trepidation she had felt was gone. This was to be her home, her friends and neighbors. Jenny felt her spirits rise and her confidence soar, standing beside the man she loved while the next carriage pulled to a stop before them.

She turned with a confident smile of welcome on her face that suddenly seemed pasted on her bloodless lips. It was over. The charade, the deception, and her happiness. All her dreams of love evaporated before her eyes as out stepped the colonel, Katherine, Eudora, and then Sir Reginald Wenthorp. Waiting for him to turn to her seemed to last forever. He busily tugged at his waistcoat and patted his periwig before turning his pale eyes to hers. She didn't know what she had expected. A gasp, a bold denial of her ruse. Whatever she expected never came, because he stepped away from the carriage, taking Eudora's hand to the crook of his arm, and smiled at Jenny's startled expression.

The colonel was speaking in his usual jovial way, making it seem they were all the best of friends. Anyone seeing the meeting would think nothing amiss except that maybe the new mistress of Moss Grove looked a little pale.

Travis had felt her stiffen beside his, and without taking his eyes from Reginald's foppish countenance, placed his hand over Jenny's suddenly cold hand that rested in the crook of his arm. He could not raise a scene with all his other guests so near, but he would be damned if this pompous ass would ruin Jenny's first meeting with his friends.

Speaking to Jules Colby but watching Reginald, Travis said, "I hadn't expected you today, colonel. It was my understanding *something* had happened to keep you from attending."

Jules laughed, bringing more eyes to the scene. "When my house guest found out that my niece was now residing here as your beautiful bride, he insisted that we attend to pay our respects." Jules turned to Reginald and loudly said, "May I present Sir Reginald Wenthrop from London. Of course, Elaine already knows the gentleman."

To Jenny, it seemed as though time stood still waiting for him to expose her; waiting for his hand to arch up into her face telling all around of her deceit. But what she waited for never came.

Reginald stepped forward, bowing elegantly before her. "My lady, it is so pleasing to see you looking so well after your unfortunate shipwreck. I was absolutely appalled when I found out of your misfortune." He kissed her hand, noting the coldness and the tremor it held.

Turning to Travis, Reginald smiled and said, "And, to you sir, I understand congratulations are in order. I must say, I was surprised to hear of Elaine's marriage, but now that I see you and your magnificent home, I can rest easy that she will be protected and taken care of."

Travis seemed to smile then said very distinctly, "Yes, she will," leaving no doubt to his meaning.

Jenny watched all of this with a growing sense of watching a play unfold before her. They were all playing parts in a story whose ending wasn't even written yet. But Jenny knew a happy ending was only part of her dreams. The nightmare was different. The nightmare was the reality that Sir Reginald held her future in his hands.

Another carriage pulled up, and the Colby's party moved on, leaving Jenny confused and shaken but somehow able to play her part and greet the next guests with grace and dignity.

Travis turned to her during the next lull between guests and noted the color had come back to her cheeks. She had loosened the grip she had on his arm, but he was still concerned for her. "Would you like to sit down? You've had a shock."

"I'm all right, just confused. What's he up to?" she said, wondering out loud.

"I don't know but I'll find out if you wish."

"No," she said quickly. "Let's just forget it."

"For now, I will. Let's go join the party. I think that's the end of the guests."

Jenny walked with him into the midst of the party. Her emotions were pulled taut, stretching to a limit she only hoped she could handle. She must be the perfect hostess in a nightmare that seemingly never ended. She had so hoped that her marriage to Travis would put an end to her life of fright, insecurity, and humiliation. What would Reginald do? Why had he gone along with this farce? She knew in her mind that he would let her in on his plans sooner or later. He held all the cards in this game of chance. He could destroy her or he could let her bluff to the end. What would he do? Travis was speaking. Was it to her? She must get hold of herself. She couldn't fall apart today. Today she must meet the people who would be her future. Or would they?

Jenny took a deep breath and smiled to one or another of the people she would not recognize a moment later. Anyone looking at her would be able to tell that her smile did not reach her eyes. Eyes that were constantly searching the sea of faces for the one who could spell her doom. With a concentrated effort she became aware of the party and pushed to the back of her mind the problems that lay ahead.

Travis nodded and spoke to many people. There were games for the children and good American gossip for the women. The men stood around in groups talking politics and smoking cigars.

When they passed one such group, Travis was hailed by one of the men to elaborate a point. He turned to Jenny, saying, "I must be a good host. I will take you to sit by Sally Bradshaw. She'll keep you entertained with all the sordid details of our family and *my* past." He looked deeply into her eyes that reflected her fear. He only wished he could help her.

Jenny smiled at the woman Travis had indicated and remembered meeting her in Charleston. She seemed nice and had winked at her just before the play, whispering in her ear, "You must come talk to me. You've set every tongue in town wagging." She had squeezed Jenny's hand and walked with the aid of a cane. Jenny had liked the woman immediately as Sally had reminded Jenny of Connie.

Travis sat Jenny in a chair and excused himself. Sally beamed at Jenny and took her hand. "Well, young lady, I must say I was surprised to hear Travis had finally married, but I can tell you, now that I've met you, that I'm also very pleased." She squeezed Jenny's hand and asked, "Where are you from, child?"

"England, ma'am." Jenny smiled back at the pleasant woman and failed to notice the hushed silence her comment had made on the group of women seated around them.

A woman with a plumed hat and ample girth leaned over to a similarly dressed woman and said loud enough for the whole group to hear, "She's a bloomin' redcoat."

Jenny heard the comment but did not react to the slur. Travis had warned her that her heritage might be met with some forms of hostility but to give them time.

Sally looked at her, ignoring the other woman's rude remark and said, "Child, I'm happy you've come to America. After all, all of us have come from somewhere else." She patted Jenny's hand, then continued, "Now, tell me all about how you met Travis and got him to propose. I know of many women who have tried to pin the jackanapes down."

Jenny took a deep breath and started to recite the explanation she had rehearsed. "Actually, we met

336

quite by chance. I was sailing to the Carolinas on the H.M.S. *Himes* when it encountered a storm and sank. I was spared by the grace of God. Travis spotted me and rescued me. We fell in love on board the *Sea Breeze* and were married in Barbados." The lie was not so hard when she thought of the unborn child.

The daughter of one of the women, seated by Jenny, sniffed and said to no one in particular, "Bet he had to marry her. Travis Gardiner would never marry unless he *had* to." She pursed her lips and nodded to the girl on her left.

Jenny turned white at the homely girl's scathing remark that was far too close to the truth, but Sally turned on the girl, saving Jenny again.

"Young woman, you happen to be at the home of this lady and her husband. Just because Travis Gardiner has higher standards than the likes of you gives you no reason to try to associate this woman with schemes you yourself have tried but failed."

The young woman gasped and shook before her embarrassed mother took her away, apologizing profusely for her daughter's rude behavior.

Sally glared at the other women gathered around, daring anyone to say something. Most of the women knew of Sally's fierce loyalty to the Gardiner family and quickly turned to each other to discuss recipes and families.

Sally turned to Jenny once again and noticed some of her color had returned to her cheeks. But Jenny was staring at her hands in her lap, trying desperately to fight the tears that threatened to spill. Sally's heart went out to this girl. She was so frail and completely unlike the girl Sally had always pictured for Travis. She had supposed someone like Alicia would eventually snare Travis. The comparison between the two was significant. Alicia would have told that young busybody a thing or two if she had been spoken to as Jenny had. Jenny, on the other hand, was like a frail flower. Too much wind would blow it away whereas Alicia was like a piece of granite. A hurricane couldn't stay that girl from a course once she had made up her mind to it. Sally wondered what Alicia would say or do once she finally made her grand entrance. She was sure that Alicia would make some scene. She only hoped this girl sitting next to her was up to the confrontation that was sure to arise. But as Sally looked at the girl before her, trying so hard to be the gracious hostess in the face of these rude slurs, she was convinced that Travis had made the right choice. So like Ellen. Small but determined. Sally knew her good friend would have approved of Jenny.

Sally watched as one by one Jenny brought each member seated before her into a discussion that they loved. She was enchanting these southern belles as surely as if she possessed a true southern drawl instead of the precise British speech.

"Mrs. Jacobson, did I hear you say you won an award for your cornbread at some type of fair?" Jenny asked a small woman of indiscriminate age.

"Why, yes. They say my cornbread will melt in your mouth," the woman answered, beaming.

"Well, I would love to have the recipe, but if it's a secret, I would surely appreciate your advice on baking mine," Jenny said sweetly.

The woman smiled as she leaned forward to take Jenny's hand in hers. "My dear, it would be my pleasure to show you." Turning to the woman who sat on the other side of Sally, Minna Jacobson asked, "Twyla, could you show her how you make your hot apple cobbler? Travis always loved it so."

Twyla sat up straighter, pleased that she would be included, and turned to Jenny. "Why, my dear Jenni-

338

fer, Travis is positively mad for my cobbler. I'll be happy to show you how it's made, if you like. It always made me so happy to see him take seconds on it."

Sally sat back noting the women were now firmly behind Jenny. The girl was doing a splendid job of making everyone feel they were helping her be a good wife to the man most of them wanted for their own daughters.

The discussions were going smoothly when Sally noticed Jenny stiffen. Nothing too apparent, but Sally's maternal instinct was at a high where Jenny was concerned. The girl's eyes riveted on something behind Sally. Looking down, Sally saw Jenny clasp her hands together to still their shaking. As unobtrusively as she could, Sally turned to see the reason for the girl's upset. All she could see were the colonel and Katherine Colby. She knew Jenny was related to these two and could not fathom the distress that girl was obviously suffering. What was going on here? she wondered.

While Jenny was enchanting the good ladies of Charleston, Travis was in the middle of a great debate of the 1816 tariff. The view was that the congress in Washington had imposed the tariff on goods coming from England to ensure that Northern manufacturers would have a continued high earning capability. Since the South relied heavily on England for manufactured goods, the South felt they were paying the tariffs to the North. The divisions that would one day cause a great war were begun at barbecues and parties around the South that summer of 1818.

Travis watched as Colonel Colby and Sir Reginald joined their exchange, and as one of the neighbors made some remark about northerns trying to wipe the South's economic base out from under them, Sir Reginald stepped forward.

"My good man, the tariffs paid by England are just as severe. Why, we can send goods to any country except the Colonies, at half the cost. I know that our two countries have been at odds in the past, but please see it from our point of view. We are continuing to deliver the goods you so desperately need at a rather high cost to us." His smugness was ingratiating.

A neighbor who had lost his son in 1813, during the most recent English-American conflict, spoke up, "Well, sir, I just want to say that I don't rightly see what England's doin' for us. They still make a profit. After all, when all the smoke's gone, we are the ones paying your portion. If you really want to help, pay a higher price for our cotton. As it is, we are being eaten alive." He turned and walked away, his proud southern heritage showing in every step. Several others left the group at the same time. Old wounds were hard to heal.

Travis was concerned about the way some of his neighbors and friends still disliked and distrusted the English. It wasn't just Sir Reginald. It was Jenny and what effect her birthplace would have on his neighbors. He decided he had left her long enough and went to her.

Approaching the little group of women, an amused smile played on his lips. There sat Jenny, surrounded by some of the most purebred of his acquaintances. Jenny had a small girl on her lap, and a little boy was staring up at her as she told the children and the ladies a story.

Sally saw Travis and motioned him to come sit by her, but when he sat down, she leaned over to him and whispered, "Walk with me. My leg has stiffened up."

"Of course. Here, let me help you up," Travis said with a twinkle in his eye.

"I'm not that old, you young scalawag," she said while she tapped his shoulder lightly with her cane.

They walked as far as the oak trees lining the drive. Sally stopped and looked back on the scene of Jenny and the children.

"What's going on here, Travis? That child is afraid of something."

"What do you mean, Sally? Did something happen?" Travis asked with immediate concern.

"Oh!" She chuckled. "Plenty happened, but she got through it fine. Just some young chit you wouldn't have given the time of day to bared her fangs, but we managed to clip them." The old woman smiled when she thought of them storming off in a huff.

"Sally, what is the matter? You sound so mysterious."

"I can't put my finger on it," she remarked. And then she turned to him, asking point-blank, "What do you know of this girl?"

Travis was immediately on the defensive and bristled, saying, "What do you mean?"

"Oh, settle down. You don't have to protect your wife from me." She looked back at Jenny. "The child is frightened of the colonel, that's plain, but she seems ill at ease in what should be familiar social surroundings."

Travis debated with himself the wisdom of confiding in his old friend, then realized she was the closest thing to a mother he had, and he could tell her things he couldn't anyone else.

"Sally, I trust you, and I need someone to talk to." He waited for her understanding gaze to focus once more on him. "Jenny is not the Lady Elaine Seaton. She took the lady's identity when the *Himes* went

341

down, taking the lady with it. I don't know why she took that identity, but I believe she is afraid of that man." Travis indicated Reginald. "He knows she is not Lady Elaine but for some reason has gone along with the charade."

Sally turned to stare at Reginald and then back at Jenny who was unaware of Sir Reginald's eyes on her. Sally shook as though she had a chill.

"Are you all right? Do you want to go back?" he asked.

"No!" She turned and looked directly into the black eyes in front of her. Grabbing Travis's arm, she squeezed it to make him understand the urgency in her plea. "Travis, you watch that man and keep Jenny away from him. I fear I detect evil around him. Try to find out why he's staying here."

"All right," he said, then turned to stare at the Englishman and also felt some sort of foreboding where he was concerned. "Let's go join my wife. I think dinner is about to be served." He helped Sally back to her chair.

As he seated Sally, again by Jenny, he noticed a carriage coming up the drive. He turned to Jenny when she started to stand and said, "A late arrival. I'll go. You stay here with Sally." He kissed her cheek and walked briskly to greet his new guests.

He stepped up to the door of the carriage as Oscar stepped down. "Oscar! I'm glad you came. I was beginning to think you were going to miss the party."

Oscar attempted a smile then turned to give a hand to his wife.

Travis saw her and rushed to take her other hand. "Pansy, you look wonderful. I'm glad you made it back in time for the party."

Pansy Shealy scowled at Travis. "Don't you be polite to me, you ungrateful man you. How could you

342

go and get married while I was out of town and to a perfect stranger at that?" The perky little woman stamped her foot in vexation at the man she had thought of as a brother for so many years.

Travis tried to silence her, saying, "Pansy, please," he pleaded. "Not here. Come with me." He led Oscar and Pansy to the front parlor and closed the doors behind them.

"Pansy, listen to me before you berate me so," he said pleading for her understanding.

Pansy looked up at him, then lowered her eyes and walked to the window, asking, "Which one is she?"

Travis came up behind her and pointed Jenny out of the crowd.

"She's very pretty, Travis," she said without looking at him.

"Pansy, I'm sure that after you meet her you will understand, but I must ask a favor of you," he said in a careful tone.

Turning to him, Pansy cocked her head and asked, "What kind of favor?"

He looked at Oscar and got no help. "Pansy, I don't want people to know when Jenny and I got married. Can I count on you to keep the knowledge to yourself? You'll understand when I tell you. Jenny is with child."

As this was a surprise to Oscar also, Travis went on to explain: "We fell in love on the *Sea Breeze*. Only my damn stubbornness kept me from admitting that fact until much later. Jenny haunted me with memories that made me go mad with longing but still I resisted. Jenny is the most wonderful woman I've ever known. She's kind, sweet, and decent. I couldn't bear it if she were hurt because of my obstinacy. I'm sure you will agree."

Pansy walked up and put her hand on Travis's arm,

saying, "All right, Travis. I can see you do love her. I'll keep your secret." She raised up and kissed his cheek. "I still think I deserve some consideration." She smiled sweetly at him, continuing, "After all, if I hadn't given you all those silly women to compare her with, you might still be a lonely man. I'm happy for you, Travis. I think you'll make a fine papa for your child." She walked back to stand beside Oscar. "I'm only sorry I was delayed in Savannah and couldn't be here to give her some moral support, but my father had a runaway on his hands and was out scouring the area, and I didn't want to leave mama alone. Actually there have been several runaways these past months, but I'm sure you're not interested in the matters of the family right now. Now," she said, starting to walk to the door, "I think I would like to meet the woman who has finally hooked you."

Travis smiled at her in relief. "Of course. I'll take you to her."

Before Travis got to the door, Oscar halted him, saying, "Pansy, could you go by yourself? I have something to discuss with Travis. We won't be long."

Pansy knew what they had to discuss and quickly said, "Of course. I'll see you two later."

Travis closed the doors and turned to Oscar. "What's the matter, Oscar? You've acted funny since you arrived."

Oscar turned to the mantle, saying, "Sit down, Travis."

Taking a seat, Travis felt a foreboding. "This is serious, isn't it?"

Turning around to stare into Travis's eyes, Oscar stated, "Yes. Someone else has turned up missing."

"Who?"

"Alicia Adams."

Travis was stunned. He hadn't even realized she

hadn't come to the party. "How do you know she's disappeared?"

Oscar lit a cigar, blowing the smoke out in a blue haze and watched it drift away. Turning his attention back to Travis, he said, "Her parents reported it this morning. She didn't come home yesterday. That's why I'm late. I had some things to check out."

"Have you any leads?"

Turning back to the mantle, Oscar looked up at the portrait of Ellen Gardiner. "Travis, I have one lead that I must check out." Pain reflected from his eyes when he turned back to Travis.

"Is there—anything—I can help with?"

"Yes." Oscar looked away with obvious uneasiness. "Travis, did you see Alicia on Thursday?"

Thinking back to the confrontation with Alicia outside of Madam LaFarrier's shop, Travis answered, "Yes. I saw her in Charleston."

"Did you two have a scene on Meeting Street?"

"I don't think you could call it a scene. She was upset when I introduced Jenny to her as my wife, but the whole encounter only lasted, at the most, five minutes."

Oscar looked at Travis with the pain again on his face as he said, "Travis, believe me when I say this is not my idea. But," he said, taking a deep breath before continuing, "did you have any reason to harm Alicia?"

Travis stood up abruptly. "For God's sake, Oscar, you know me. I would never harm her. She's a pain in the butt, but I would never do anything to hurt her."

Smiling at his life-long friend, Oscar came up to him, slapping him on the back. "I know you wouldn't. I'm sorry to even bring it up, but I have to check every lead no matter how obscure."

Travis was still upset with his friend's allegations,

345

but on thinking it over, he decided Oscar had to follow every lead and said, "All right, Oscar, but what could have happened to her? She's conniving but I doubt she would do this to her parents."

"I know. Her mother is in hysterics. Said she had gone out at about nine yesterday morning. She had a fitting with Madam LaFarrier. I talked to the madam, and she said Alicia left her shop at ten-thirty. Alicia had picked up a new gown for the barbecue today. Madam said she was very excited about coming." Oscar started toward the door. "I think I heard the dinner bell. Let's go eat some of the famous Gardiner barbecue."

"Oscar, wait a minute." Travis looked at his friend in consternation. "I saw Alicia yesterday morning." At his friend's look, Travis continued: "She came to the Tradd Street house and tried to suggest we have—" He didn't know what to tell Oscar. "Have relations." He quickly hurried on at Oscar's shocked expression. "I knew she had designs on marrying me, but I'm afraid I didn't realize to what lengths she would go to ensure her future. I was finally able to show her of my love for Jenny, and then she left. I think she realized I wasn't interested. Maybe the shame of her actions was too much for her and she just went away for a while?"

"What time did she come to see you?" Oscar asked anxiously.

Thinking back to the time, Travis said, "It was early, about nine or shortly after, I think."

Pulling his hand through his hair, Oscar stated, "This is making absolutely no sense. According to Madam LaFarrier, she was excited about coming here today and that was after you saw her."

Travis thought for a moment. "Maybe she hadn't given up hope for the two of us. She knew Jenny was to have my child. What is going on?"

Oscar looked up to his friend of so many years, saying, "Travis, according to madam, Alicia was coming here to see Jeff, not you."

A look of understanding came over Travis. "So she *had* given up on me but decided Jeff would at least get her the name she so desperately wanted and Moss Grove. It's not very flattering but I believe I'm actually feeling sorry for her. She would have run into another stone wall in Jeff. He's in love with Mary Lou, and I don't think Alicia is one of his favorite people anyway."

Oscar turned away from the look on Travis's face as another lead was given to him. "Travis, do you think she could have gone to Jeff with her idea?"

Knowing his spoken thoughts had given Oscar another lead, Travis tried to quickly assure him otherwise. "Jeff came out here shortly after we arrived yesterday to help with the preparations. He left late last evening to return to Charleston. As no one mentioned seeing Alicia here yesterday, I rather doubt that he had an opportunity to see her."

"All right. Let's leave it for now. I'm sure something will turn up. Alicia is not the sort to go willingly with someone if she didn't want to. Somebody must have heard a ruckus. We'll find her. Let's go join the ladies."

Travis and Oscar came down the steps to the whole assembly talking about Alicia. Travis hurried to Jenny, who was walking with Sally and Pansy.

Jenny saw Travis approach and hurried to meet him, saying, "Travis, we heard about Alicia. What could have happened?"

Travis told them, "Oscar is checking it out. We won't know until all the facts are in."

Sally thumped her cane on a rock, getting Travis's

347

attention. "Travis, this is serious. First the Harmon girl, now Alicia. I'm beginning to think we should all go lock ourselves in our homes."

Travis thought the same but was determined this party not be ruined. "Come on, ladies, and I will escort you to supper."

Sally was not so easily swayed from the topic of conversation and said, "Supper? Travis, one of our oldest families is in trouble. Shouldn't we do something?"

"Everything is being done that can be, Sally. Althea and Thomas are in seclusion, but I'm sure they wouldn't want us to alarm the rest of the guests with undue speculation. Who knows but that Alicia isn't doing something just to get attention."

Sally looked up at him then turned to the worried people around her, saying, "You're right, Travis. Alicia is quite the dramatist. I wouldn't put something like this past her. Now," she said, taking Travis's arm, "I am ready for some of that food."

Jenny was looking around as though seeking someone and asked, "Travis, have you seen Rosalie?"

Travis smiled and pointed to where Darby stood passing out hard candy to all the children. Rosalie was standing beside him with her little hand on his arm, working the hard candy in her mouth. A smile of contentment lit her face when she waved to Jenny.

Turning to the others, Jenny excused herself saying, "If you will excuse me one moment, I'll go see how much she's had."

Sally and Pansy watched Jenny take the child by the hand and walk toward Mammy, who was supervising the buffet table.

Pansy looked up at Travis, noticing the look of love he was bestowing on his wife and noted it held complete happiness. Something she hadn't seen in his face since they had been children. She touched his arm, drawing his attention to her, and said, "Travis, I'm afraid I owe you an apology."

Travis smiled at her. "Pansy, you owe me nothing. You only wanted to see me married and here I am." He spread his arms.

Pansy smiled, saying, "She's lovely and I wish you both happiness." She reached up and kissed his cheek.

Travis spotted the colonel coming toward him with Katherine following closely behind.

"What's this about Miss Adams disappearing, Gardiner?" the fat man demanded.

Travis looked at the man, carefully hiding his disgust and said, "Colby, no one knows what's happened to her. It would be best not to draw any conclusions until we know more."

The colonel acted for all the world like a concerned father. "But, Eudora could be in danger if this keeps up. I demand to know what precautions are being made to protect these ladies."

Travis privately thought that Eudora had nothing to worry about. The only women who had disappeared were beautiful. "Colonel, I really think you are jumping to conclusions. We don't know what has happened to Alicia so I think Eudora will be safe. As for any precautions being taken, you'll have to talk to Judge Shealy. He's in charge of the investigation of this incident."

"If it's not asking too much, I think I should be kept advised as to the investigation. My family is very important to me."

"Of course, colonel." Travis sneered. "We all know how you protect your family."

Colby couldn't miss the implication of Elaine's treatment at his house and again cursed his wife.

"About that, Gardiner. I believe we, all of us, were not at our best. I can only apologize to you for the treatment Elaine received. It seemed the best thing at the time." He laughed and leaned forward. "You know these highborn ladies. They don't know how we pioneers lead our lives. Thought she would get an education on her visit. That's all."

Travis listened to this with an air of disdain marking his features and said nothing.

Colby cleared his throat and extended his hand, saying, "Gardiner, I just want you to know this is a great party. So glad you invited us."

Travis had no choice but to accept the proffered hand. "I'm happy you are enjoying yourself, Colonel." He looked at Katherine, who was glaring at him, and added, "And, Katherine, you look radiant today."

Anyone close simply thought Travis was being a good host. Katherine knew better.

The colonel was puffing out his chest, and with his brown waistcoat, over a red cummerbund, Travis thought he looked like a fat robin.

"If you will excuse me, I believe dinner is being served at the buffet table. Please help yourselves." Nodding to them, Travis turned and walked in the direction he had seen Jenny take.

Watching his retreating figure, Katherine whispered to her husband, "I'm afraid I don't see the logic in this charade, Jules. Why are we here?"

Continuing to smile and puff out his chest, Jules said, "My dear, we are laying the groundwork for our next venture. That peacock Wenthrop may just prove to be our ace in the hole. Yes sir, I do believe all is not lost to us yet."

"Jules, you heard that Shealy woman make reference to Elaine's condition, did you not? What good is she if she's with child?"

"Babies come, my dear, and usually in a girl of Elaine's stature, it only enhances the beauty. We'll simply wait until after she gives birth to the brat." He smiled and nodded to an acquaintance, then said softly, "What I would like to know is the exact date of their marriage. I can't believe they were married before Elaine arrived and lived with us. You can't tell me that Travis Gardiner wouldn't have taken her directly here. And why wouldn't he come to see her if he was her husband? By the way he continually fawns over her, it just doesn't seem right. What has me really curious now is why everyone is calling the chit Jenny and not Elaine." He thought he knew the answer to this puzzle, too, but as it did not affect his motive toward the girl, it really was of no importance other than the fact that Reginald was keeping something from him, if his assumptions turned out to be true.

Katherine's attention was drawn to Eudora, and she picked at her husband's sleeve to gain his attention. "I believe Eudora has set her cap for Sir Reginald, Jules."

Watching his daughter drool over the gentleman in question, Jules scowled. He had been disappointed in Eudora from birth. Her display now only fired the feelings of inadequacy he found in her. If she would just wait, the real thing would be in their grasp. Reginald Wenthrop was a fraud, and Jules only wanted the best from now on. He almost rubbed his hands together as the culmination of his plans were envisioned in his mind.

He looked over at Jenny and gasped when he saw the light-skinned little girl standing beside her. So that's where she ended up. Still within reach, he thought and smiled.

Travis found Jenny filling a plate for Rosalie, indicating this and that dish to the child. Rosalie's eyes were as big as saucers as she accepted something of almost every dish. Jenny laughed when the plate was overflowing.

"Rosalie, you will never be able to eat all of this."

Rosalie carefully took the plate and sat down under a tree and proceeded to take bites of everything.

Mammy walked up to Jenny and put her arm around her shoulders. "Chile, you go and eat somethin'. Mammy will watch out fer dis chile."

Jenny smiled at Mammy, and they both turned to stare in wonder at Rosalie. She had finished most of the food and was working on the rest. Jenny leaned toward Mammy and whispered, "Don't let her overdo or we'll have a sick child on our hands tonight."

"Ah know what ta do if'n she be sick. Let her go now an' you—" She turned to Travis as he took Jenny's arm. "Make dis chile eat!"

Travis stood up straight and said, "Yes, ma'am."

Whispering into Jenny's ear, he said, "Come on before she swats me." He walked along the table holding two plates as Jenny put a little of everything on each platter. Travis indicated the direction, and they walked over to the chairs that were set up under the oak trees.

Between bites, Travis asked, "Are you having a good time?"

"Oh, Travis, it's a wonderful party," Jenny said before she stiffened and lowered her eyes as pain registered in the blue orbs.

"What's the matter?"

Jenny tried to laugh away his concern, but her eyes were drawn back to Eudora, wearing one of her favorite gowns, as she walked by with Reginald.

Travis saw what had alarmed her. "Has he said anything to you?"

Still following the couple with her eyes, Jenny replied, "No, and I still can't figure out what he's up to." She turned back to Travis, adding, "He didn't even act surprised to see me. What I don't understand is why he's here at all. He had to have left England shortly after we did to get here so fast."

"Jenny, don't worry about it. I'll find out what his game is."

Alarm made Jenny's voice squeak when she said, "Travis, please don't. Maybe he'll just go back to England now. Maybe he just saw no need in exposing me. Please just let it be." Jenny knew better but was so frightened that, if confronted, Sir Reginald would tell Travis of her indenture and take her back to England.

Travis noted the fear in his wife's eyes and quickly covered her hand with his, saying, "All right, but I want you to tell me if he tries anything."

Jenny nodded.

The party went on into the night with singing and dancing after dark. Travis took Jenny to bed about midnight as she had fallen asleep with her head on his shoulder. Several guests, including Sally, would spend the night, and Travis left Mammy in charge of their comforts. All in all, everyone had enjoyed the barbecue tremendously.

Chapter Nineteen

After the overnight guests had said their good-byes and departed the next day, Jenny and Travis walked over the grounds watching the cleanup duties of the help. They leaned against a fence looking to the Ashley River.

Travis pulled Jenny into his arms and they stood there, each content and happy.

"Did you enjoy your party, Jenny?"

She turned to him and put her arms around his waist, leaning her head on his chest. "I had a very good time," she lied. How could she tell him of the nightmare that plagued her last night after seeing Reginald? Thinking of it again in the bright morning sunshine did little to stem the terror she had felt. She remembered it clearly:

She had been sitting near a small white cottage by a bright fire that encircled the night in an orange glow. She was holding something. At first she couldn't see what it was that had held her spellbound in the dream. Then, as thundering hooves reverberated through the night air, her dream-self had turned. She was holding a small baby tenderly in her arms. The look of contentment that had been present turned to shocked terror as the horses, pulling a large black carriage, stopped before her. No one was at the driver's seat. The reins were being held aloft by unseen hands. It was as though the ghost of someone she couldn't see commanded the big black horses to stop before her. Moments passed as her dream-self watched the heaving sides of the horses, wondering what apparition would appear from the dark interior of the coach. Heart pounding, she had tightened the hold she had had around the sleeping child. A black-gloved hand was seen first as the doors slowly opened. Then a tall, black leather boot stepped down, and Jenny had screamed as a face, a cruel demented face, stared at her. It was a facsimile of Sir Reginald, only this apparition was ten feet tall, dressed entirely in black, and the eyes that stared down at her were as red and glowing as burning coals of fire. The man said nothing to her as he stared at her terror-filled eyes. Her dream-self was transfixed by the eyes. She couldn't tear herself away from the form before her. An evil smile split the white face, showing blooded teeth and fangs like a wolf. He raised one arm and pointed a crooked forefinger at her. A hissing sound preceeded every word as he spoke.

"You will come with me now, Jennifer," he commanded.

Her dream-self had shrunk over the sleeping child, in a desperate attempt to protect it from the demon before her. "No," she had whispered, still transfixed on the glowing red orbs before her.

The demon had thrown his head back and gave a hauntingly loud laugh that sent spasms of terror through her.

"You have no choice. You belong to me. I will take you like I wanted now that Miles and Elaine are no longer here to interfere. You will crawl to me and beg for me to take you." He reached into his breast pocket and withdrew a blood-smeared paper, waving it before her while he continued: "This paper is your indenture, Jenny. It's quite legal and binding. You belong to me now in lieu of Lady Elaine, in lieu of Sir Miles, in lieu of your murderous father. You belong to *meeeeee*." His words echoed in her brain as he threw his head back and laughed again.

Her heart pounding, she had shaken her head in denial, saying, "No. I belong to Travis now. I'm the mother of his child. He will never let you take me away."

The demon had laughed again, sending cold, piercing, lifeless air across her face. He turned and pointed to the carriage door.

Jenny's eyes had followed to the door as it opened again, showing a man dressed completely in white. It was Travis. He stepped forward to stand beside the demon. His face held no expression, as though he were in some kind of trance. The demon had hissed at him.

"Do you want this servant as your wife and the mother of your child?"

The man Jenny loved had turned his eyes to those of the demon. "No. She has lied to me. I will take the child. You can have the servant."

Her dream-self had screamed in agony, "But you love me, Travis."

The form of her husband had turned to glare at her, saying, "You are a servant to this man. I will never forgive you for lying to me. Give me my child!" He held out his arms to her child.

Her arms released the tight hold on the child. Try as she might to strengthen her hold, a force she was unable to fight lifted the child into the waiting arms of the husband who was now betraying her.

She screamed, "Travis, our child needs a mother. Don't do this. Remember Celeste."

The white form had smiled tenderly to the child, then had turned to a red mist which quickly turned into the form of Alicia Adams. Alicia was dressed completely in red gauze. Her lips were painted blood red as were her cheeks. Her red veil of a gown showed her red nipples through the bodice. Travis had handed their child to this harlot. He had smiled lovingly to the woman. The woman had turned to stare at Jenny with a sneer on her painted lips. Then as Jenny watched in horror, the woman had dropped the child into a black hole to disappear. She then turned to capture Travis's lips with hers.

Jenny had stared at this spectacle in disbelief as the demon picked her up and carried her limp form to the waiting carriage.

It had been at that point in the nightmare that she had awoken in a cold sweat. Travis was beside her, breathing evenly. She had lain beside him the rest of the night, afraid to return to sleep for fear of seeing again the evil that surrounded her dreams.

"Jenny." Travis waited until her head had come up to see her eyes. "You seem tired. Was all the excitement too much for you?"

About to tell him she hadn't slept well, a movement within her made her breath catch in her. "Oh! Travis!" Her eyes were wide with wonderment as she put her hand to rest over her child.

Travis became concerned and said, "What's the matter? Are you all right?"

Jenny's eyes opened wider as a look of astonishment filled her beautiful face. She put Travis's hand to her waist, saying, "Can you feel it?"

"Feel what?" he asked in bewilderment.

"I don't know, but it felt like I had a butterfly in here." She indicated with her hand.

Travis laughed and hugged her. "That's our child, Jenny. It seems he wants to be included in our thoughts."

Jenny smiled back and hugged him again. Here was the way she wanted all her remaining days to be: nestled in his arms and basking in the glow of his love. Travis would protect her, she knew, despite the terror of her dreams.

Chapter Twenty

The days following the barbecue were filled with learning experiences for Jenny. Under Mammy's supervision, Jenny learned how to run a house as big as Moss Grove. She especially liked the doctoring that was required when one of the hands got hurt. Darby showed her how to clean and stitch deep cuts and told her various remedies for different ailments. Mammy called her one afternoon to come help with the birth of a baby.

Jenny stood in awe as the little black head emerged from his mother. She held the child and counted fingers and toes before washing the baby and then wrapping it in a soft woolen blanket and handing him to his mother. She watched as the eager little mouth sought the nipple on his mother's breast until he succeeded and sucked noisily.

"Such a miracle," she said wistfully to Mammy.

Mammy smiled knowingly at her as she washed her hands. "You's goin' ta have a miracle soon 'nough, missy. Y'all bess be larnin' all y'all cain fore y'all be a mama."

Jenny found her experiences at Eden Hall to be useful as her days at Moss Grove progressed. She found the duties as mistress of Moss Grove to be varied and diverse. From planning menus and shopping lists, she progressed to arranging furniture and keeping an intricate set of household books. She found herself in charge of numerous everyday decisions that only someone with the patience of Job could handle. But she loved every moment of this new experience as each day brought new problems and exciting challenges. And each day it became harder and harder to tell Travis the truth.

The day when Madam LaFarrier arrived, followed by four of her assistants with boxes and boxes full of Jenny's new gowns, was a trial for Jenny. Travis had been thankfully absent as Jenny tried on one then another of the gowns, only to find them too tight across the bodice or waist.

The madam clicked her tongue as she walked around Jenny, saying, "Madam Gardinere, I am so sorry to have this happen. I thought I had left enough room but you are, how you say, showing, more than I thought." She turned to a girl and spoke in rapid French. The girl hurried from the room and returned with three boxes that she gave to Jenny. "Madam Gardinere, please accept these gowns. They are of an old fashion but I believe they will—how you say—grow with you."

Jenny opened one of the boxes and shook out an emerald green damask gown. It had short sleeves with a low-cut square neck. The skirt fell from just below the bust to fall in delicate gathers to the floor. She donned the gown and was very pleased to note that it did, indeed, hide her advancing condition and did look rather good on her.

Madam LaFarrier smiled and walked around Jenny, fluffing out the skirt. "This is call the 'Empire' gown. That Marie Antoinette, she change the style and call it the 'directoire' gown, but I like this more full skirt better, no? You will be able to wear it until the wee babe is born, no?"

Jenny thanked the woman and suggested they leave the other gowns as they were, since she was sure they would fit after the baby came.

Travis came in just as the last gown was donned and accepted. He sat down and grinned as the seamstress pulled and fluffed, making references to the way the gown made Jenny's bosom look "*elles sont grande.*"

Even though Jenny spoke no French, she understood what the madam was speaking of and turned beet red, feeling the size of her bosom was none of this woman's business.

Travis knew his wife was uncomfortable and stood up quickly, asking, "Is your business complete, my love?"

"Oh, yes. I'm quite finished," Jenny replied thankfully.

"Well, then, madam, I believe we can go to my office and I will complete our arrangements." Travis bowed and indicated the door.

The madam quickly moved to follow Travis's lead, calling to the girls to go to the wagon and remarking that she would be there presently.

Sitting down at his desk in the study, Travis pulled out a strong box from a locked drawer. Taking a pouch from within, he handed it to Madam LaFarrier and said, "I believe that will cover the costs of the gowns."

The madam hefted the pouch and was only too anxious to see what riches it contained but decided

361

not to show her voracity to this man. "*Merci*, monsieur. I hope the madam is satisfied with the gowns?"

"I'm sure she is, madam. From what I saw, you did an excellent job, as always."

"*Merci*, but I hope you do not take offense that I gave to your lady gowns that were meant for Mademoiselle Adams." The madam shook her head as she continued. "I will never understand why Alicia insisted on those old styles, but since your lady is with child, they will fit her, no?" She turned and walked to the study door.

He sat contemplating her remark before halting her, asking, "Madam, when did Miss Adams order those gowns?"

The woman turned back to stare at him, then said, "Why the day she disappeared. I was paid for them, so I completed them." She saw the unsettled expression on the man's face and said, "Monsieur, I have made gowns for Mademoiselle Adams for many years. Several months ago she ordered the latest fashions from Paris which are scandalous. Then she came that day and ordered the most modest gowns I have sketches for. This has had me puzzled, but maybe she just realized how women of Charleston would look upon her in those rather immodest gowns." The woman wrinkled her nose more for Travis's benefit than from outrageous indignation.

He thanked the woman again but remained seated after the door had closed. He remembered the gown that Alicia had worn that day to the Tradd Street house. It *had* been scandalous. The gown Jenny had on now was very modest. Somehow the two designs did not fit. What was Alicia's game and what had happened to her? Travis couldn't believe she had just gone away. Too many women were turning up missing. What could all this mean? He hated feeling afraid, but without any ideas as to what was happening, he would have to take precautions. One thing he was certain: He would not let Jenny out of his sight. He doubted anyone or anything would happen to her while she was with child, but he would be damned certain nothing could happen, either.

He stood up and walked out of the study and headed toward their bedchamber. He had a sudden need to be with her. To touch her and hold her to his breast.

Jenny was busy hanging up the gowns and putting away the many hats, gloves, and matching shoes. Travis leaned against the doorjamb and watched her as she smoothed a skirt or touched a plume before carefully adding the item to the wardrobe.

"Are you pleased, my love?" he asked quietly.

Jenny turned suddenly, grasping her hand to her heart. "Oh! Travis. You startled me." She laughed to hide the panic that had arisen in her.

He came to her, taking her into his arms before saying, "You've been awfully jumpy lately. Is something the matter?"

She put her head on his chest, trying to steady the rapid beat of her heart. "No. I guess it's just all the excitement, and I've had trouble sleeping lately."

Travis knew of the nightmares that plagued her, but he could never get her to talk about them. He rubbed his hand down her back, wanting only to see her safe and happy. "You are not still worried about the Wenthorp fellow are you?" He felt her tense.

"No. I haven't seen or heard from him since the barbecue. Maybe he went back to England." She prayed, but Travis's next words dashed her hopes.

"I'm afraid he is still here, Jenny. Darby saw him yesterday in Charleston."

"Oh." It sounded more like a squeak than what she

had hoped to pass off as unconcern. She wondered again what he was doing here? This waiting for him to do something was tearing her apart. Not knowing when he would come to take her away or expose her to Travis. Her thoughts were interrupted when Travis stepped back from her and looked at her with a smile.

"Tell you what. Let's have a picnic this afternoon. It's a beautiful day, and I know a secluded spot that will brighten our day."

Thinking this would take her mind off her problems, she readily agreed.

"All right, I'll go tell Mammy to fix us up a hamper and you get ready." He kissed her forehead and quickly left the room. Suddenly he felt alive again. He rubbed his hands together as he thought of the spot he meant to take his beautiful wife.

Jenny stared after him. How would she ever live apart from him again? She shook herself as she made up her mind to live each day as it came. If she dwelled on all the pitfalls that awaited her, she would just wither away instead of basking in Travis's love, as long as it lasted. She threw back her shoulders and prepared for the outing with great care.

They drove slowly along the river road, Travis telling her tales of his boyhood along every spot. He pulled the wagon off the road, and they traveled some distance along a rutted, seldom-used path that was overgrown with weeds. Jenny was in awe of the peace and serenity this spot afforded them.

Travis helped her down and picked up the hamper from the back of the wagon. Jenny walked to the edge of a lovely pond surrounded completely by a deep forest of pines, birch, and ash. She didn't hear Travis when he came to stand behind her.

"This is where Jeff and I spent many a lazy summer afternoon. We'd go skinny-dipping here."

Jenny turned a questioning glance to him, asking, "What's skinny-dipping?"

Travis threw his head back and laughed before leaning down and whispering in her ear. "Remember that secluded beach in Barbados?"

Jenny laughed as they both said in unison, "That's skinny-dipping!"

Travis put his hands on Jenny's shoulders saying, "Wouldn't you like to repeat Barbados now?"

Laughing, she stepped away from him and put her hands on her hips in mock anger demanding, "Are you planning on having your way with me, Mr. Gardiner?"

He pulled her back to him and curled his lip while he replied, "Yes, my dear. You are at my mercy, and I demand a skinny-dip with my wife."

She laughed then lowered her lashes to gaze up at him with a coquettish look, saying, "The last one in has to serve breakfast in bed for a week."

They both rushed to strip the clothes from their bodies, then they slipped together into the icy waters of the pond.

"Who won?" she asked.

Diving under the water and coming up next to her, Travis held her close while sliding his hands up and down her back. "If I have anything to say about it, we both did."

At his touch, Jenny no longer wanted to play. She wanted him to love her, hold her and take away the pain. And he obliged with tenderness and love.

He picked her up and carried her to the lush grass that surrounded the rim of the pond. When he laid her upon the sweet-smelling ground and lay down beside her, he marveled at the perfect texture of her skin, the pink spheres on each breast rose to his touch, the softly rounding belly that held his child. When he

365

placed his hand over the babe, he felt a love for Jenny that he could not describe. An almost physical ache that he had never felt before.

Jenny's hands moved along his body, never tiring of the feel of him beneath her fingers. Opening her eyes, she looked up through the leaves of a giant oak to the blue sky above. It seemed even the heavens were shining upon them and their love. Only one thing marred the perfect happiness she wanted so desperately. But she would not think of him now. Now was only for Travis and this time, this day. Nothing more.

"Jenny, oh, Jenny, I love you so."

It had been no more than a whisper, then he entered her, gently at first, then rising as each reached up and out of themselves to heights beyond mortals, beyond the heavens.

They lay side by side for a time, each lost in their own thoughts. Travis cradled her, wondering why he felt such a nagging doubt all of a sudden. Was it the thought that something might happen to destroy the perfect life he now led, or was it the fact she still had not told him her fears? His lack of knowledge made him impotent to help her. He worried about the nightmares that she was having. He knew Reginald Wenthrop was behind her fears, but how much could he do when he hadn't exposed her. Why hadn't he exposed her? So many questions with no answers.

"Travis, would you do something for me?" she interrupted his reverie to ask.

"Anything."

Sitting up, Jenny drew a finger down his chest before stopping just above his navel. "Would you teach me to swim?"

Travis smiled. "Of course, but maybe we should wait until after the baby comes."

"Why?"

"Because you might take in some water before you learn how to stay up."

"Oh, Travis, I know I'll be all right if you're with me. Please teach me. Please?"

He laughed at her childish begging and slapped playfully at her bottom. "All right, but be warned, wench. I'll not let you go."

"Why, I wouldn't want you to. Ever," she said seriously before pulling Travis with her into the water once again.

She surprised him by being an apt and fearless pupil, and within a short time she was indeed floating and swimming on her own.

Later, while they were eating their picnic lunch, Jenny felt the hairs bristle on her neck. She felt they were being watched. It wasn't the first time this peculiar sensation had disturbed her. Other incidents during the last couple of weeks had made her skin crawl in the same fashion. Nothing she could put her finger on. Once, while she walked out to the stables, she was sure someone was watching, but the feeling left when Darby walked out of the barn with a new horse he had just shod. Another time, when she and Rosalie had been picking peaches, she had suddenly been terrified by a sudden panic at being separated from the little girl. She had laughed it away when, after calling, Rosalie had scampered back to her, but now she wondered.

She turned her head to look around the perimeter of the pond's enclosure. Seeing nothing, she thought maybe her mind was playing tricks on her but the feeling persisted.

Travis watched her, then said, "I think you have had enough fun for one day. Let's get back to Moss Grove."

"Yes, let's." Jenny quickly put the picnic back in

the hamper. The feeling of being watched stayed with her until the wagon started its journey home, and she saw a deer ease its way down to the water's edge for a drink. She relaxed as she thought that it was the deer who had been watching them. She only hoped the deer enjoyed the pond as much as she had.

While Jenny's pregnancy advanced, so did her peace of mind. She was no longer plagued by the recurring nightmares. Reginald had made no attempt to see her, and Travis's attentiveness never wavered, so she was sure he had not been approached by Reginald either.

Travis had decided not to move into Charleston that summer. He felt Jenny needed time to adjust and hoped that the wagging tongues would stop if they were not present.

Jeff and Mary Lou would come to Sunday dinner after church. Jenny enjoyed Mary Lou's company and looked forward to the visits. Mary Lou showed Jenny how to knit little hats and socks for the baby, and Jenny became quite adept at the intricate little garments, and soon the wardrobes of the nursery were filled with her handiwork. The two women would sit in the parlor for hours after dinner and knit by the windows that faced the Ashley.

Travis and Jeff would spend their Sunday afternoons going over accounts or riding in the fields. On the first Sunday after Madam LaFarrier had arrived with Jenny's gowns, Jeff and Travis were riding over the cotton fields when Jeff casually remarked, "Jenny certainly looks good. Marriage must agree with her." He gazed at his brother's happy profile and added, "You don't look to be wasting away either."

"Thanks, little brother."

"I especially like that gown Jenny is wearing. Is it new?" Jeff inquired innocently.

Travis thought back to his conversation with Madam LaFarrier and told Jeff, "That gown and two others like it were made for Alicia before she disappeared. The madam gave them to Jenny instead."

Jeff turned a shocked expression to his brother. "Alicia? Travis, I may be dense, but Alicia certainly wouldn't be caught dead in a dress that didn't show off her figure. That gown Jenny is wearing hides most of everything."

"That's been puzzling me too, Jeff. The last time I saw Alicia, her gown left *nothing* to the imagination."

Jeff looked a little piqued and said, "The last time I saw Alicia was not a very pleasant experience."

"When was that?"

"Right after she saw you, the day she disappeared."

"You saw her that day?"

"Yes. She came to my office and suggested we become—how can I say this—friendly. I guess I wasn't very civil to her. I told her I wouldn't feel comfortable with a woman who showed herself like she did, shall we say, to other men. I explained I liked my women to dress a little more modestly." He thought for a moment then added, "She looked like a whore in the getup she was wearing. Why she thought anything would come of us is beyond me. Alicia and I have been having a running battle of some sort since we were kids. I just sat there looking at her, and I mean looking at her, sort of dumbfounded. It's an experience I hope never to repeat."

Travis had stopped his horse as a look of understanding overcame him. "Oscar said she was speaking of you at Madam LaFarrier's that day. I bet she ordered those gowns as a means to show you she meant business."

369

Jeff shrugged. "I guess since you went and got yourself married she decided to try her luck with me. Not very flattering, I must admit."

"She just wanted Moss Grove, and I'm thoroughly convinced she would try anything to get it."

"Do you think she would be stupid enough to disappear, hoping we would come to her rescue?" Jeff asked.

"I've thought about that Jeff, but Alicia is not the type to play such games. Besides, I don't think she's cunning enough for that to have crossed her mind. If she wanted something she would go directly after it. No, I think something happened to her."

Jeff clenched his fist. "It's maddening to just sit by and not be able to do anything. Oscar has had to give up on the investigation. It's as though Alicia and the Harmon girl just vanished."

"Well," Travis said, "I for one don't believe in goblins and devils. I'm keeping a close watch on Jenny, and I advise you to do the same with Mary Lou."

"Oh, I am. I walk her to and from the school, and I make sure she's locked in tight before I leave her."

They changed the subject to more pleasant topics and traversed the fields of Moss Grove.

Sally Bradshaw became a frequent visitor to Moss Grove in the months following the barbecue, and Jenny was thankful to her for all the stories she told of Travis as a boy. It helped her to understand him and love him all the more.

Jenny was spending a lot of her time decorating the nursery. Mammy had winked at her one day as they stood watching as the servants brought in a crib, rocker, and various other furniture into the room.

"Ah know'd if'n ah took dis heah furniture out of dis heah nursery, one a dem boys would get da hint."

Jenny laughed at the old woman's wisdom as she walked around the now filled nursery. A cradle of old mellowed oak was in the corner. When Jenny touched the side of the cradle, it was set in a gentle swinging motion. She turned as the men brought in a huge chest covered in hand-tooled leather with tarnished brass buckles on the straps.

Mammy clicked her tongue and set about polishing the fittings with gusto.

"What's in there, Mammy?" Jenny asked curiously as she ran her hand over the lid.

"Oh, chile, you must come see. Ah saved all dose baby clothes from da boys and Miss Celeste." She opened the lid to display multitudes of small gowns and blankets that were exquisitely embroidered.

Jenny was thrilled with the find. "Oh, Mammy, they're beautiful."

Mammy picked up a white crocheted blanket with delicate pink roses embroidered around the edges. "Miss Ellen done dis one while she were awaitin' Miss Celeste. For some reason she jes' know'd she be goin' ta have a girl chile."

Jenny spent the rest of the afternoon going through the chest and making notes on what else she would need.

Travis found her sitting on the floor among neatly folded piles of baby clothes. He stood and watched her as she first exclaimed over one piece then another. "Having fun, pet?"

"Oh, Travis, yes." She held up a blue gown of wool. "I can't seem to believe you actually wore these tiny gowns."

He came to sit next to her on the floor. "I told you I was a small baby."

She held up the small item to his chest and giggled in delight.

He could not remember ever being so content in his life as he watched her eyes sparkle. He looked down at the evidence of his deed and placed his hand on her rounding belly. "Has he moved today?"

"I should say he has. Sometimes I believe your son has four feet the way he kicks me."

Concern appeared as he quickly asked, "Are you in pain?"

A look of pure loveliness filled her beautiful face when she related, "Travis, it's so wonderful to know a child is there and kicking his strong healthy legs. It's something I guess you will never know of."

The feeling of dread filled him again as she returned to her task. He knew his life would be over if he lost her. Standing up, he held out his hand to her. "Come with me, little mother. You've been up here long enough, and you have plenty of time yet to finish this labor of love. I want to show you something."

Not hesitating, she went with him while he led her to the small sitting room she loved, off their bedchamber. He indicated the window and stepped aside to let her see. Her eyes swept the fields of once dark green plants and widened at the sight of cotton balls covering each plant in a profusion of beauty.

"Travis, it's beautiful," she said in awe.

He came up and placed his arms around her from the back. "It looks like we'll have another good crop this year."

"It looks almost like a cloud."

Travis laughed. "Wait a couple of weeks and look again.

In the next couple of weeks Travis became busy with the harvest of cotton, corn, and rice, and Jenny barely saw him except when he would come in at night exhausted and dirty. She guarded him like a general, making sure of his comforts.

As he came in one particular night, later than usual, Jenny ordered a bath readied for him in their bedchamber. As he eased his tired body into the hot tub, Jenny came in carrying a heavy tray laden with his supper.

"You shouldn't be carrying that tray, Jenny. Where's Mammy?"

Jenny sat the tray on the table and turned to give him a radiant smile. "I'll have you know, Mr. Gardiner, that while you are in your bath no one will cross that threshold but me." She came up and pecked him on his cheek as she ran her hand in the water to test its warmth. "You just relax. I'll pour you a brandy."

Travis had a wicked grin on his handsome face as he said, "Why don't you pour two and come join me in my tub?"

Shocked, Jenny turned to him, saying, "What would the servants think?"

"Go lock the door and come here."

Jenny thought back to the day on the beach and later to the secluded pond, and quickly succumbed to desire. She walked over to the door, clicking the lock, turned and unbuttoned the front of her gown. Naked, she walked over to the table and poured them a small amount of brandy, then turned and handed him the glasses before sliding into the water across from him. "I must say this new tub is big enough for us both."

With a grin, he leaned forward to trace her lips with his wet finger. "Why do you think I bought it?"

Jenny giggled and felt very sinful as he captured her lips to his. Leaning back, she asked, shyly, "You don't mind that my shape is rather misshapened?"

He stared at her with lowered lashes and said softly, "You have never looked more lovely, Jenny." He pulled her hand, saying, "Come here, wench, and I'll show you what fun it is to make love in a tub."

Later, as they were mopping up the water from around the tub, Travis determined to build a room with a tub that wouldn't splash so much.

Chapter Twenty-one

As the summer ebbed into fall, Jenny was nearing the end of her confinement late into November. She had trouble sleeping, and the simple task of walking was a major event. Mammy and Travis constantly hovered over her, making her nervous and irritable. She hadn't heard anything from Reginald or any of the Colbys since the day of the barbecue, and she rarely thought of them in her anxiety to have and hold her baby in her arms. She was sure she was going to have a son. Probably as big as Travis, she thought privately, since he seemed to kick and punch her with such force as to knock the breath out of her.

She felt Travis stir early one morning and sat up to find him getting dressed in rather shabby attire. "Where are you going so early and dressed like that?"

He came to sit on the side of the bed, taking her hand in his. He loved seeing her fresh from sleep with little crinkles of sleep lines around her eyes. "You aren't going to get up this early, madam. I'm going hunting, and you are going stay put until I return."

"What are you hunting for this early?" She cast a glance to the window and could only see darkness. "It's not even light yet."

"Don't you know what tomorrow is?" he asked surprised.

"Tomorrow?" She looked confused. "What's tomorrow?"

Travis suddenly realized that his English wife wouldn't know about this purely American custom. "Why Jenny, tomorrow is Thanksgiving, and I'm off to get our dinner."

She looked up at him and smiled. "What a lovely sounding holiday. How did it come about?"

Travis sat back, pulling the covers up under Jenny's chin as he did. "Well, if I remember my history lesson correctly, it all started with the first settlers who came over here from England. After they had survived their first year here, they celebrated at the harvest of their crops by having a huge celebration. The governor back then—let me try to remember his name—Berry? Bradley? Bradford, that's it. Anyway, he proclaimed a day of prayer and thanksgiving. My father never let us forget, and so we have our own day of thanksgiving after each year's crops are harvested." He leaned down and kissed her forehead.

"What do we do on Thanksgiving?" she asked.

Travis smiled at the excitement her voice carried. "Well, Jeff and I—he'll be here any minute—go out and hunt for the biggest turkey to be found. Then we'll bring it back to Mammy, and tomorrow she'll prepare the best dinner you've ever had. Tomorrow is a special day. We say our thanks to God for all our blessings throughout the year." His eyes softened as he leaned to kiss her. Drawing back, he smiled. "This year I have a lot to be thankful for. Now you go back to sleep. You were up quite a bit during the night with our child kicking you." He pulled the covers up tighter under her chin before turning to leave.

Jenny looked surprised. "How did you know? I tried to be so quiet."

He laughed as he pulled a sheepskin coat on. "My dear child has a penchant for kicking me in the back."

"You felt him?"

"When you get cold, my dear, you snuggle up to me. With our son, or daughter, between us, I feel him, or her, kick the daylights out of me, and I'm sure you get the brunt of his or her actions."

Jenny leaned back with a smug smile on her face. "You can drop the *or her*, Travis. I've decided we are having a son first."

"Well, I'm glad to hear *you've* decided that. Now we don't have to wonder anymore," Travis said with a grin.

"Oh, it just has to be a boy and a big one from the looks of me." She looked down at her swollen middle and folded her hands over the child she carried, smiling securely in her knowledge.

Travis felt the old fear return as he thought again of the possibility of her dying in giving birth. She was carrying a large child by all indications. She was so small he could only pray that nothing would happen to her.

Jenny watched him finish dressing. He was wearing buckskin breeches with a buckskin jacket over a leather vest. He looked rugged and full of good health. The sheepskin coat added a dash of daring to his ensemble. She thought he looked quite handsome in his getup.

Travis turned before he walked from the room, saying, "We should be back with our turkey by noon if all goes well. I'll send Mammy up to look out for you."

Exasperated, Jenny scowled at him. "Really, Travis, between you and Mammy I haven't had a moment's privacy in months." She pouted which brought a laugh from her husband.

"Jenny, I won't have you pouting like a spoiled child. After the baby comes I plan on doing all the watching over you myself. Until then Mammy can help keep you out of mischief."

"Mischief!" She put her hands out before her. "Just what kind of *mischief* can I get into when I must waddle around like a seal?"

He walked once again to the side of the bed and leaned to kiss her, saying, "Humor me, Jenny. I just want you to be as comfortable as possible and safe from harm."

She looked up into his dark eyes and knew that whatever made him happy, she would do. "All right, I'll behave. Go out and slay a turkey and hurry home."

Travis and Jeff returned at noon with a huge bird in tow. As Jenny had never seen a turkey, she insisted she see this mystical bird for herself, and Mammy helped her to the back where the mighty hunters were showing their prize to some black children in the yard. Rosalie stood next to Travis with pride evident on her shining face.

When Travis saw Jenny standing on the porch, he held up the specimen for her approval.

Jenny thought this the ugliest bird she had ever seen. "You mean we are to eat that ugly creature?" She wrinkled her nose, while Travis turned the bird this way and that.

He looked down at the bird he thought a prize, its head hanging limply to one side, and asked her, "Why, what do you mean? I think he's a rather handsome devil."

Jenny continued to debate the wisdom of eating such a grotesque-looking bird and gave an involuntary shudder.

Mammy hugged her around the shoulders and said, "You jes' wait, Miss Jenny. You ain't never et anythin' ta compare ta turkey on Thanksgivin'."

"If you say so, Mammy," Jenny said as she turned to go back to the parlor and away from the creature.

The next morning Jenny was awakened by the most delicious aromas filtering from the cook house. Her stomach rumbled as the scent made her mouth water. She hurriedly got dressed, with Travis's assistance, and they walked down the stairs together to have coffee and sweet rolls for breakfast. A cheery fire burned in the grate as Jeff, Travis, and Darby regaled her with stories of their boyhood. Jenny laughed and giggled when the indiscretions of Jeff were told, much to his chagrin.

Finally, around noon, Mary Lou arrived with Sally, and the festivities began in earnest. And as the dinner bell resounded throughout the house, Mammy called everyone to dinner, and they all walked to the dining room in high spirits.

Jenny was amazed at the amount of food on the sideboard. The aromas were mixed in a delicious array of spices and sweets and the tantalizing smell of roasted fowl. Mammy came in with the bird on a platter, and its rich brown crust was indeed a sight to behold. All of Jenny's earlier apprehensions at eating the ugly creature vanished as the platter was placed before Travis.

Travis stood at the head of the table and raised his hand. "Dear friends and Jeff and Jenny. It is a custom on this day of thanks for each of us to tell of their own thoughts. Jeff, you go first."

Jeff stood and looked at each one around the table.

"Travis, on this Thanksgiving, I would like to thank God for a brother like you. For raising me with care and love. For friends such as these." He swept a hand around the table. For Mary Lou who has given me so much and to Jenny whose presence here has made Moss Grove so much more than a house. It is now a home again."

Jenny's eyes told him of her thanks for his kindness as Darby rose to tell of his blessings.

"I just want to say thanks for Travis here, who's been a true friend to me for all these years, and you, Jeff, and you, Miss Jenny. I'll spend the rest of me days a sayin' thanks for you all." He sat down as everyone turned to Mary Lou, who told of her thanks that she had come to live in Charleston. Then Sally said how she was just thankful that she had lived long enough to see one of these Gardiner boys married.

Then it was Jenny's turn. She didn't know how to put into words her many thanks to these people who were now her friends and family. How could she thank them for making her a part of this wonderful family? How could she thank Travis for taking her from a nightmare into a dream? "I'm so thankful to you all for making me feel a part of this family in such a special way." She turned to look at the man she loved with all her heart. "And, to you, Travis, for making all my dreams come true."

Travis stood up and held up his goblet. "To all my friends and family, whose love I hold dear, thank you for always being there when I needed you. To Mammy, for always showing me the errors of my ways and then loving me in spite of my shortcomings. To Sally for your guidance and wisdom throughout my life. To Jeff who has made me so proud. To Darby whose friendship and—" He paused and winked at the little man. "*Mulish* interference gave me my own precious love," he finished. He turned to Jenny with love in his eyes. "And to my wife, Jennifer, whose very presence has made my life meaningful. I cannot thank God enough for her. Happy Thanksgiving everyone."

Jenny's eyes were full of tears of happiness as she sipped her wine. She hadn't thought she would ever feel the love and pride she felt at that moment. She watched as Travis carved the big turkey, and the house servants held out dish after dish of delectable items for everyone to spoon onto their plates.

She tasted a bite of the tender, juicy white meat of the bird she had thought so ugly and found it delicious. Cornbread stuffing with bits of oysters and raisins; candied yams that melted in her mouth; cranberry and orange rind relish; gravy with bits of turkey and hard cooked eggs which was generously poured over mashed potatoes. Peas in a cream sauce with bits of celery was a perfect compliment to the rest of the delicious meal. Jenny thought she had never seen such an amount of food.

They all ate, talked, and laughed in happy abandon. As the last bite was eaten, Jenny thought she would surely burst, but Mammy brought in the dessert which was generous pieces of pumpkin pie and strong black coffee. Jenny sat back with a sigh of contentment and realized that this had been the first holiday she had spent with this wonderful family. It was a custom she hoped to repeat for the rest of her life.

Travis finally helped Jenny up from her chair, and they all went into the parlor where Sally, Darby, and Jeff promptly fell asleep in their chairs. Mary Lou walked outside, leaving Jenny and Travis to sit in silence holding each other's hands.

Turning to look at Jenny's contented smile, he

asked, "Did you enjoy your first Thanksgiving dinner, Mistress Gardiner?"

"It was the best *Mr.* Gardiner, but I fear I overdid it. I am so full I could burst." She grimaced.

Travis patted her swollen belly, saying, "I do believe you did, my dear."

Jenny laughed, then said, "This child of yours seems to like his Thanksgiving, too. Feel this." She put his hand to her middle. The babe kicked in little ripples.

Travis moved his hands and felt kicking from the other side. "My dear, our son is a puncher and a kicker."

Jenny sighed. "Sometimes I think I'm having a litter."

"Would you like to go up and rest for awhile?"

"Yes. I think that's what I need."

He pulled her to her feet and hugged her gently, saying, "I love you, you know?"

Jenny closed her eyes and placed her head on his chest answering, "Yes, I know."

While Travis was helping Jenny through the foyer, the door burst open to admit Mary Lou who was visibly shaken.

"Mary Lou, what's the matter?" Travis asked quickly.

"Oh!" She put her hand to her hammering heart. "I—feel so—silly," she stammered.

"What happened?" Jenny asked.

"It was—nothing really." Mary Lou tried to laugh. "I just had a feeling someone was following me or staring at me. I don't know why I'm so scared. I guess I'm just still nervous about those other disappearances."

"Mary Lou, you're perfectly safe on Moss Grove," Travis said, trying to convince her.

"Yes, I guess I just let my imagination run away with me. You two go on. I'll be fine."

"Jeff is in the parlor. I'll be down in a minute after I settle Jenny down," Travis said.

Outside, a man slapped angrily at his horse as he led it away from Moss Grove.

Chapter Twenty-two

As November turned into a memory and December was but a few days along, Jenny was finding it harder every day to get around. She had already outgrown all the gowns that Madam LaFarrier had brought to Moss Grove and was forced to wear Travis's shirts over a skirt that Mammy had split at the waist.

Seeing her slow waddle to the garden one day, Mammy remarked to Travis that she had gotten a lot bigger with this child than was normal. Travis's fears surfaced again, and he became so solicitous to Jenny that he got on her nerves which were stretched to their limits even more than before.

Christmas was but ten days away when Jenny told Travis to go do something, anything but to leave her alone for a few hours. Travis was disinclined to leave her, but Sally, who was there for the holidays, said she would watch over his bride, so he took the opportunity to go into Charleston to do some Christmas shopping of his own.

When they heard the carriage go down the drive,

Jenny turned to Sally and asked, "Did you get them?"

"Yes, dear, but I must say I received several rather penetrating glances."

Jenny laughed and said, "Let's see."

Sally called a servant to fetch the boxes from her room. When the girl left, closing the parlor doors, Sally leaned over to Jenny and said, "Child, it may be none of my business, but what on earth is Travis to do with so many?"

An impish grin filled Jenny's face when she remarked, "Oh, he'll find a use for them, believe me."

"All right, child. It's just been my experience that usually if a man has only one, it hangs around in a wardrobe with very little use." Sally picked up her knitting, missing the expression on Jenny's face when she remembered the first day here at Moss Grove.

Sally looked up with a start upon hearing a pain-filled gasp escape from Jenny's lips and asked hurriedly, "Are you all right, child?"

Jenny's hands had covered the swollen mound of her belly. Her face was white, with lines of pain etched into the fine features. She managed a weak smile before whispering, "It's just the baby. He is getting stronger every day. Sometimes it feels as though he's ripping me apart inside." A fine bead of perspiration appeared over her lip and brow.

Concerned, Sally sat up and reached a hand to her, saying, "Would you like to go to your room to rest?"

"No, I'll be all right. He's settled down already. Besides, I want to see what you brought."

"If you say so, dear, but I'm concerned about you, Jenny. You've gotten very large with this child."

Something Jenny had been thinking about constantly for the last couple of weeks surfaced again at the concern of this gracious woman before her, and she called shyly, "Sally?"

"Yes, child."

"Sally, if anything should happen to me, would you take care of Travis and the baby? I mean, Mammy will do all she can but would you watch out for them?"

Patting her hand as she searched for the right words, she answered, "Jenny, nothing is going to happen to you. The baby will be fine and so will you. Women have been having babies for centuries, and most survive to have more."

Jenny waited for her to continue. When she didn't, Jenny asked again, "Will you?"

After a hesitant pause, Sally knew of nothing else to say except, "Yes, Jenny. If something should happen to you, which I cannot believe, I'll watch your baby and Travis for you. But enough of this. I think I hear the servant coming."

The girl came in bearing three boxes and placed them on the table before the two women. Jenny reached for the top one and, opening it, smiled, then indicated to Sally to open the others. Inside were seven silk smoking jackets of various colors. All with black sashes and lapels.

Sally shook her head wondering why anyone would need, let alone use, so many smoking jackets. "Do they meet with your approval, Jenny?" she asked with a grin on her wrinkled face.

"Sally, they are wonderful, but they need one more little thing to be perfect."

"And what might that be?"

"I want to sew his monogram on the lapels," Jenny wore an expression that bucked no interference.

"But Jenny, that would take you weeks. Christmas is less than a fortnight away."

Leaning over, Jenny rang the bell Mammy had

insisted she use, then sat back to await the big woman's arrival.

Mammy came out of the cook house on the run. When she entered the parlor she was breathless when she asked, "What's y'all need, chile?"

"Mammy, he's gone. Do you have everything ready?"

"Ah be right back." Mammy rushed to get the items required and when she returned, she was followed by five girls from upstairs. They each took a jacket and proceeded to sew. Each talking and laughing and all in all having a wonderful time. Mammy even served hot cocoa and blueberry muffins dripping in fresh churned butter.

Sally was astonished to find that even she was enjoying the afternoon's activities.

Each one of the girls had done a design of their own creation, and they compared and found they liked every one of them. They carefully wrapped each one in its own package, then the gifts were hidden until Christmas Eve when they would be put under the tree.

Jenny thanked everyone and swore each of them to secrecy, then Mammy shooed all the girls back to their normal tasks and left Jenny and Sally by the fireside.

Sally watched as Jenny leaned her head back and placed her hands on the high mound of her belly. Sally liked this girl. Travis was happy, that was for certain. She gazed up at the portrait of her friend Ellen. Ellen, if you could see this, you would be smiling too, she thought.

"What are you smiling at, Sally?" Jenny asked in a soft voice.

"Oh." She laughed at being caught. "Child, I was just thinking that I'm glad I decided to take y'all up on coming here for Christmas. My daughter's home in Savannah is always so cold. At least my feet are warm." She chuckled and winked, which made Jenny smile.

Mammy came to the door with a scowl on her face and said, "Miss Jenny, they be a man at da door. Say he want to see you."

"Who is it, Mammy?" Jenny asked with a feeling of impending doom descending over her.

"It be dat Wenthrop man," Mammy whispered.

A cold chill seemed to penetrate every bone in Jenny's body.

Sally sat up and took Jenny's suddenly bloodless hand, saying, "Tell him to go away, Jenny. He is obviously upsetting you."

Jenny wanted to be able to do just that, but she also wanted to get it over with. The waiting for him to make his move might be over if she just saw him. Somehow she was relieved that he had come and she said, "I had better see what he wants."

Squeezing her hand, Sally asked, "Do you want me to stay with you?"

"No. I had better see him alone." She thought a moment and then said, "But, stay close in case I need you."

"All right, honey. I'll just be in the library across the hall. You just yell and I'll come running." She stood up and held her silver-capped cane like a club to show Jenny she meant business.

Jenny gave her a tentative smile of thanks and leaned back in her chair trying desperately to still the pounding of her heart.

Mammy escorted Reginald into the room, and Jenny watched him, feeling her heart begin to slow its rapid pace as she realized he did not look like the demon of her nightmares.

She indicated the chair Sally had vacated and asked, "What can I do for you, Sir Reginald?"

Reginald felt alive and ready for this encounter. He had been left waiting for so many months. When he had seen Travis and that odd little man going into Charleston, he knew the time was right. He smiled lazily as he tugged at his cravat.

"I thought I would come pay my respects to an *old friend*." He sat back, putting his boots on the hearth as if to warm his feet.

Jenny felt his familiar east in her home unsettling, but managed to say, without too much trembling in her voice, "I have been wondering when you would come. Now what do you want?"

"*Tsk, tsk*, Jenny— or should I call you Elaine?" He winked in a conspiratorial manner which made the tiny hairs on Jenny's neck stand up, while he continued: "Actually, I thought you would be interested to know that I have decided to stay here in the Colonies."

"Why would you think I would care about your plans?"

"My dear, you certainly are not extending much of the famous Gardiner hospitality I have heard so much about." His gaze traveled to her advanced state and a lecherous grin appeared on his thin-featured face. "I see you have been busy since last we spoke. If I had known of your desire for rape I would have used it myself."

"How dare you," Jenny spat at him.

"Come, come, my dear. Surely you don't expect me to believe that a man of Travis Gardiner's stature would marry a common servant unless forced to or— lied to."

When he saw the blood leave her face at his remark, he knew. "So you have lied to the great man, heh?

Wonderful."

A sharp pain made Jenny catch her breath before she said, "Just tell me what you want."

"It's really very simple, my dear. *I* want you to remain Elaine and correspond with Elaine's solicitor from time to time in England."

"Why? Surely *you* could forge papers or letters."

He stood up and walked to the hearth, putting one foot up and pulling some papers from his breast pocket. "It would be better to have *you* sign this. Let's say I'm not ready to let you go just yet." He reached over and gently brushed her cheek with the back of his hand.

Jerking her head away, Jenny tried to sit up a little straighter but gave up at the pain in her lower back. "Don't you even want to know what happened to Elaine?" she asked with a tremor now evident in her voice.

He looked indifferent to her question, then studied his nails as though bored, saying, "I assumed she perished in the shipwreck. It really was a pity. Most of her jewels were on board, and I already checked to see if *you* had managed to save any of them. Such a waste."

"I *assume* you are speaking of the jewels," she said with a sneer.

"Let's just stick to business, shall we?" He held out the papers for her to take. "Sign these like the signature on this bank draft, and then I will leave you."

"You don't need me to sign these. What do you really want?" Jenny was confused at this ruse of his.

Reginald smiled without humor, saying, "Let's just say you really don't have a choice. If you don't sign, I will take you back to England to serve out the remainder of your indenture." He leaned closer. "You do remember that little matter of unfinished business, don't you, Jenny? You see, you still belong to Elaine's estate and I, as executor, would be obliged to see to it that all properties are accounted for."

"Why don't you just try it. My husband would never let you take me away." Jenny said bravely.

"I am afraid your husband has very little to say about such matters. Of course, I could speak to him and—"

"No!" Jenny gasped.

"So, he doesn't know you're not a lady. The great Travis Gardiner has been duped by a servant!" He bent over as laughter filled the room.

Jenny felt the pain of her predicament more fully than ever. She hadn't thought of this aspect of her charade. That people would laugh at Travis and ridicule him for a thick-witted dolt made her cringe in despair. She should have told him before this. Now it was too late.

Reginald sat back down, staring at her with a cruel smile. "It seems I have you in a position of great advantage to me, Jenny. I could ruin your little charade with one word."

"Travis knows I'm not Elaine Seaton. You can't blackmail me with that." She was grasping at straws and knew it was panic that seized her.

Reginald steepled his fingers, contemplating this information, wondering whether or not to believe her. "So, you told him the truth? I wonder." He stood again and walked to a window that overlooked the front of Moss Grove. Slowly, he turned to her and said quietly, "I think you are lying."

She stared at him for a long moment. A moment of doubt and self-recriminations. A moment when she knew she would have to stand up to this man or be forever under his threats. Finally, she said, "Think what you want. I will not be a party to your schemes. Now, if you will excuse me, I am fatigued and need some rest."

"You think to dismiss me so easily? Come, come, my dear. I believe I am holding all the cards in this game."

"What do you hope to accomplish with this ruse?" She only wanted him gone but the need to find out what he was up to became stronger.

Feeling completely in command of this situation, Reginald could see no reason not to tell her of his plans. "Well, my dear, I imagine you would be interested in what I am planning." He returned to the chair, sat down and leaned forward, placing his elbows on this knees. He seemed proud of his deceit as he continued: "Actually, it suits my purposes rather nicely that it is you who survived." He paused as Jenny's brows drew down in contemplation. "You see, I now have the opportunity to sell Eden Hall to Abner Bloodheath. He has wanted the property for some time, but Elaine would not even discuss the matter with him."

Jenny remembered the man from the first day she had been at Eden Hall. Tall, thin and dark, sinister features. He had scorned Elaine when she had refused to sell him her estate. The man had ridiculed her saying she, as a woman, would never be able to handle the running of such a vast estate. Those words, spoken by such a vindictive, unscrupulous, lecherous man had spurred Elaine to become the most enlightened and respected businesswoman in the area. Elaine had proven Abner Bloodheath wrong but in the process had gained an enemy.

Now, as Jenny watched Sir Reginald, she realized that Bloodheath had not given up on his desire to own Eden Hall and that Reginald Wenthrop was just the person to give it to him.

"So, you planned this all before Lady Elaine and I left, didn't you?"

"It really is of no importance now, my dear. I shall have it all before too much longer anyway." He looked at her, showing his lust for just a moment. "Now, I really must be leaving, so no more hedging, Jenny. Just sign the papers."

Jenny could not figure out Reginald's game. Surely he or anyone of a dozen people could forge Elaine's signature. He wanted something else from her. Some act that he could hold against her so she would forever be forced to do his bidding. No! She would not submit to forgery.

She looked up at him with no emotion on her face and asked, "What if I refuse to sign?"

Smiling an evil smile, Reginald played with his rings, then said, "If you don't sign, I will expose you for what you really are. An indentured servant, and as the property of the estate, you will be returned to England and sold with the rest of the possessions. You would lose." He waved his hands about the room. "And I would lose." He leaned forward again. "I think you will see the logic in my proposition. Now, do be a good girl and sign the papers. You can live happily ever after, and I can make my arrangements to return to England and conclude this deal." He saw the stubborn set of her chin and quickly added, "Sign the papers and I will leave you in peace. Or . . ."

The threat in his voice was evident. It would be so easy to do as he demanded. It would solve all her problems if she did as he asked and signed the papers. Or would it? Could she live with the knowledge that by sparing herself she would be shutting out the people who had befriended her? Especially Elaine who had loved Eden Hall. Jenny remembered the fierceness with which Elaine had dealt with Abner Bloodheath that day so long ago. Could she do this to Elaine's memory? Condemn her spirit to forever walk the halls of Bloodheath's property. Thinking of the man made a shiver of fear run up her spine. She could not do this to the woman who had treated her so kindly under questionable circumstances. But, most of all, Jenny realized she could not do this because it was wrong.

Sitting up straighter, she looked at Sir Reginald. A bravado she didn't feel came into her voice when she said, "Sir Reginald, I am afraid I won't be able to sign these."

Thinking he had had her, he was shocked by her pronouncement. "Why you! If you don't sign this I will go straight to your husband and tell him his illustrious wife is no more than an indentured servant. How do you think he will react to that news, Jenny?"

The nightmare returned as she saw Travis condemn her again for lying to him, but somehow she knew, in reality, he would protect her and their unborn child from this man. "I'm sorry but you had better go."

Reginald was livid in his rage. The thought that this impostor would refuse him made the veins in his neck swell and his face turn dark red. He turned to the mantle. He had to think. He walked to the window and looked out, pulling his hand over his eyes. Turning back to her, his eyes suddenly took in her condition again. He had it. "You really made a catch in Travis Gardiner, didn't you? A beautiful home, an obviously doting husband." He turned his brows down and with an even tone he said, "And, a child on the way. It would be a pity if something should—happen to it."

A cold sweat seeped through Jenny's gown as the panic of the nightmare returned, only this time she would not wake up to find Travis's arms around her, calling to her soothingly. An instinct of protectiveness overcame her. She would guard her child like a lioness guarding her cubs. Nothing and no one would harm her child.

"I have to ask you to leave now, Sir Reginald. My husband is due back shortly. Our business is concluded." She paused before adding, "And I would think twice about trying to harm the child of Travis Gardiner. He holds dear that which is his."

Determined to see his goals bear fruit, Reginald took his hat in hand and stood before her with dignity and an all-pervasive expression. "When he finds you are not his possession but the possession of an old estate in England, maybe he will trade his child for you." He put the papers back in his breast pocket, then walked to the door but turned before opening it. "You will sign these papers. Someday you will have something you don't want to lose." He looked again at Jenny's swollen belly.

A mocking laugh was all Jenny heard as the door closed behind him. She knew he had threatened her child. "My God! My baby!" She put her head in her hands and was weeping hysterically when Sally came back in the room and rushed to Jenny's side.

"My dear, what did that man do?"

She couldn't talk about it. She said between sobs, "Get—Mammy. I want—I want to go—to my—my room."

"Of course, dear." Sally rushed to the door and called for the servant.

Coming in at the sound of her mistress's distress, Mammy helped Jenny up the stairs, all the while cooing to her. But Jenny was sobbing uncontrollably, and nothing Mammy said to her made any difference. Mammy took her to the bedchamber, making her as comfortable as she could. "Tell Mammy what happened, honey. Y'all wants me ta go send somebody to fetch Mr. Travis?"

"No, no. Just leave me be." She turned away from the kindness of the woman, wanting only to think about what she could do.

After closing the drapes at the windows, Mammy quietly walked from the room, closing the door behind her.

Sally was standing just outside the door, anxiously awaiting news and asked, "Mammy, is she all right?"

"Ah don' know, Miss Bradshaw." Mammy had a worried expression on her plump face and turned to stare at the closed door. Sobs could be heard from within that broke the big woman's heart. She turned to Sally, saying, "If'n she don' stop pretty soon, she goin' ta drop dat babe and soon."

Starting to pace the floor, Sally wondered what that man could have said or done to cause this type of reaction from the child? "Mammy, what do you know of this Sir Reginald Wenthrop?"

"All ah knows is dat he don' come heah da night Mis'er Travis and Miss Jenny got married. He done said to Mis'er Travis dat he was 'sposed ta be Lady Elaine's feeance."

The two women alternated pacing before the bedchamber for the rest of the afternoon until they heard the front door open and looked down to see Travis coming in with his arms loaded with brightly covored packages, and when he saw Sally on the upstairs landing he whispered, "Where's Jenny?"

Sally looked at the happy expression on his face and said, "In her room."

"Good. I'll go hide these," he said, then started to the back of the house when Sally halted him.

"Travis, wait!" She wrung her hands, loath to tell

him what had happened., "I think you should go to her. She's very upset."

Travis put the packages on a sideboard and ran up the stairs three at a time. "Is she all right?"

Just as he asked, they heard a moan coming from the bedchamber. He reached the door and opened it with such force that the handle hit the wall and cracked the plaster. Kneeling down beside Jenny, he took her cold hand in his. "Jenny, Jenny, is it time?" He brushed the hair from her damp brow, noticing the lines of pain along with her swollen, red-rimmed eyes.

Perspiration had broken out on her brow as she squeezed his hand and nodded, biting her lower lip to silence the scream that threatened to come from within her.

In an anguished voice Travis looked up at Mammy and said, "Mammy, it's time. Send someone to fetch Dr. Clayborne and hurry!"

Mammy raced from the room as fast as her girth would let her, nearly knocking Sally over when they collided in the hall.

"Mammy, is everything all right?" Sally grasped the black woman's arm.

"Miss Bradshaw, could you go tell one of da hands to go fetch Doc Clayborne. An' you tells dem ah said ta hurry. Ah's goin' back ta Miss Jenny." She turned and rushed back into the bedchamber without another word to Sally.

Sally turned and hobbled down the stairs calling to any servant who was near.

Travis was reliving the horrors of the damned when Mammy came back to the room. As another contraction gripped Jenny, he looked up at the woman who had delivered himself, Jeff, and Celeste, and begged her, "Mammy, do something!"

Mammy came to the bed and looked at Jenny,

saying, "Mis'er Travis, you's got ta get out a heah so's ah can take a look."

"Nonsense, Mammy. How do you think she got this way? I'm staying here. Just do what needs to be done."

Mammy was scandalized but did not dare argue with him. His face was one of total concern and fear that Mammy understood only too well. She finished her examination and went to the door. She called for water, sheets, and a bottle of whiskey.

"Whiskey!" Travis exclaimed. "Mammy, you are not giving her whiskey!"

"Da whiskey for you," she stated, then began making her preparations, and after checking Jenny again, turned to Travis, saying, "Mis'er Travis, dis goin' ta take a while. Let me stay wid her 'til dat doctor come. Y'all go an' get drunk."

"I'm staying here. If anything should happen to her I want to be here." He continued to mop Jenny's brow with a damp cloth, his eyes never leaving her pain-filled face.

"Ain't nothin' goin' ta happen ta her. She be healthy, and de babe be only a couple weeks early."

Travis acted like he didn't hear her while he continued to give Jenny encouragement and support when a contraction wracked her body.

Around midnight, when Travis was sure she could stand the pain no longer, Mammy did another examination. She was surprised to see a black-haired baby about to pop out, and she quickly got her supplies together, telling Travis to hold Jenny. She told Jenny to push several times, and before long, Mammy was holding a small but perfectly formed baby boy.

"It be a boy chile!" Mammy's smile was as wide as her face.

Travis leaned closer to Jenny and whispered,

"When you make up your mind on something from now on, I'll believe you. Thank you for my son, Jenny."

Weakly, Jenny smiled up at him, saying, "Go see your son and let me rest."

He kissed her gently on her brow and turned to see his son being held in Mammy's massive arms. He looked so small, but the sounds of anger coming from him testified to his health.

Jenny gave another moan while Travis was gazing at his son, and he and Mammy both looked back as the moan turned into gasping breaths. Travis turned white at the sound. The horrors of his mother's death so shortly after Celeste's birth came back to him.

Mammy turned to him as he stood immobile beside her. "Take dis babe and hold him lak dis," she ordered.

Travis was in a kind of trance, wanting to go to Jenny but uncertain as to what to do with his son who he now cradled in his arms.

Mammy was standing at the end of the bed, effectively concealing Jenny from Travis's view. He heard her gasp and knew this was the end. Tears began to come forth for the first time since he had learned of his father's death.

Mammy yelled, breaking into his grief like a hammer, saying "Push, chile, push!"

The tears that had filled Travis's eyes restricted his view of his son when he heard him cry out. Blinking to clear his vision, he noticed that his son was contentedly sucking on his fist and that the crying was not coming from him. The sound of a lusty cry came again, and Travis looked to Mammy with a confused expression replacing the agony of only moments before.

When she turned to him with a big smile on her fat

face, he knew what he had feared was not to be and she said, "Looky heah, Mis'er Travis. Y'all done got a girl chile too!"

Travis walked slowly toward the woman as she held up a wrinkled pink baby who had a fine mat of silvery blond hair covering its delicate little head. His gaze went from his son back to his daughter, not quite believing what had just taken place.

Singing her praises, Mammy cleaned both the children while Travis knelt beside the bed, taking Jenny's hand in both of his and asking her gently, "How do you feel, Jenny?"

"I'm fine," she said weakly. "Did Mammy say a son?" she added with her eyes closed but a contented smile on her face.

He beamed at her, mopping her brow as he said, "A son and a daughter. It's no wonder you were so big, Jenny. They're beautiful, perfect little replicas of you and me."

She sighed and gave a weak smile.

He leaned over and kissed her brow, whispering, "You've just given me the most perfect Christmas gift." He smiled, noticing she had fallen asleep. Standing up, he went to look at his children. Counting fingers and toes and feeling cocky about his deed, he chucked his son gently under his chin. Then, without warning, his legs seemed to grow weak, as the enormity of Jenny's task hit him like a blow.

Seeing the whiteness return around his lips, Mammy quickly asked, "You all right, Mis'er Travis? You look 'bout ready ta faint dead away."

He looked at her without really seeing her before turning his gaze on his sleeping wife, then he asked Mammy, "Is she *really* all right?"

"She be jes' fine, but ah's not too sure 'bout you. Come on, and let's go tend ta dese babies, and we'll let Miss Jenny rest."

Sally was delighted as she took the blond little girl from Mammy. "Who would have believed that that little girl could deliver not one but two beautiful babies." She looked up at Mammy and asked, "Is she all right, Mammy?"

"She be jes' fine, Miss Bradshaw, but ah's not too sure 'bout Mis'er Travis." She indicated with her hand the man stumbling from the room.

They both laughed as Travis staggered from the bedchamber and lurched to a chair in the hall.

Sally turned to Mammy, placing the little girl back in the spacious arm of Mammy, saying, "You take care of these darlings, and I will take care of that one." She indicated Travis.

Mammy gave a knowing laugh and walked to the nursery, cooing and talking to each child held lovingly in her arms.

Sally walked up to Travis and stood before him, leaning on her cane. "I think this calls for a drink. What do you say, Papa?" She leaned down to get his attention.

Looking up at her with bleary eyes, Travis just sat still.

Grabbing his arms and pulling him to his feet, Sally led him down the stairs, giving him more support than he was giving her. When they walked into the library, they noticed Darby pacing with a large glass of whiskey held in his hand.

"Well, Darby, I think we'll have one of those too?" She winked at the startled expression Darby gave her and led Travis to a settee, handing him the big glass of whiskey that Darby had poured him.

Darby looked from one face to the other then

quickly asked Sally, "Is everything all right?" He didn't like the blank look on his captain's face.

"Everything is just fine, Darby." Sally turned to Travis and said, "Travis, tell Darby what has happened." When Travis didn't respond, she leaned closer and yelled in his ear, "Travis!"

He jumped and stared at her like she had lost her senses, demanding, "Why'd you do that?"

More quietly, Sally indicated Darby and said, "Darby doesn't know your big news, so why don't you tell him?"

"Oh!" Travis responded. Feeling himself revived, he got up, and with his chest out and a big grin on his handsome face, looked down at Darby's concerned expression and said, "Why, Darby, old man, I'm a father."

A smile replaced the concern and confusion of earlier, and Darby shook Travis's hand, pumping it hard, saying, "Why, cap'n, that's the best news ever."

Travis leaned down, and with both hands on his knees, said, "No it isn't, Darby."

"Why, what could be better? Was it a boy?"

"Yes and no, Darby."

"Cap'n, would you just tell me what's got you so excited?" Darby declared with his hands on his hips, not liking all the suspense at his expense.

"Darby, I have a son and—a daughter."

"You don't say." Shocked, Darby's mouth gaped open before he asked, "Is the little lady all right?"

Sally interjected, "She's just fine, Darby. She just fell to sleep. It was quite an ordeal for her, but we were more concerned for the father than the mother. I'm glad he seems to be coming around." Sally held up her glass and continued, saying, "To Jenny!"

"To Jenny," Travis and Darby responded, and they all drank to Jenny, then to the babies, one at a time.

Sally matched them drink for drink until the clock on the mantle struck the hour of two, and she demanded everyone go to bed.

Darby watched Travis help Sally up the staircase, saying his thanks to God for seeing Jenny through this ordeal.

Travis had collapsed on the white canopied bed that had once belonged to Celeste. He awoke with a fuzzy tongue and an aching head. He was at the washbasin when Mammy came in with a coffee tray.

"Y'all sho' done some drinkin' las' night, Mis'er Travis. How you be feelin' dis mornin'?"

"Don't yell, Mammy," he said with a grimace, putting his hands up to his head.

"Heah." She handed him a greenish-looking concoction. "Y'all drink dis up. Darby done say it be da bes' thin' fer you." She wrinkled her nose, wondering if the little man knew what he was doing.

Travis smelled the brew she had handed him. It smelled better than it tasted, but he knew from past experience that it would cure what ailed him. He drank it down, grimacing at the taste, and handed the empty glass back to a thoroughly amused Mammy. She was smiling and humming as she went around the room opening the curtains and straightening the bedcovers.

"How are Jenny and the babies? Can I go in and see them yet?"

"Miss Jenny be jes' fine. It took me an awful long time ta get her ta stay in dat bed. Dat girl wanted ta see dem babies. She said she was goin' ta dem children if'n ah didn't get dem ta her."

"Did Dr. Clayborne ever show up?" Travis picked up a sweet roll from the tray, noticing that Darby's concoction was starting to work its wonders.

"He jes' left. He say dem babies and Miss Jenny be fine. Say dat Miss Jenny is sho' some woman deliverin' dem children wid nary a problem. Why she ready ta get up but old doc, he say she has ta stay in bed for a while. She 'bout ready to jump on old doc, she be so mad. Dat sho' is a woman y'all done got, Mis'er Travis." She shook her head at the memory of Jenny's demanding to know the reason *why* she couldn't get out of bed when she felt perfectly fine.

Travis smiled and said, "I'll go see her. Are the babies with her now?"

"Yes, sir. She be tryin' to nurse, but she don' got nothin' yet. Ah got a girl ta come ta be wet nurse. Ah don' think Miss Jenny goin' ta be able ta feed both. An' you be careful wid her. She probably goin' ta cry and pout alot fer a few days. Most new mamas do. Sometimes dey act real crazy, too."

"I'll be the soul of discretion, Mammy."

He eased open the door and saw Jenny holding one of the babies to her breast, so engrossed in the baby, she didn't hear him come in. He watched quietly as one baby suckled while the other slept peacefully by her side.

Jenny felt the odd sensation of being watched again come over her. She turned with a start, saying, "Oh! Travis, it's you."

Coming into the room to sit next to the bed, he looked at her startled expression and said, "And who else would it be but the proud father and loving husband?"

"Come see, Travis. The boy looks just like you." She pulled the blanket away from the baby's face for him to see.

"And the girl, just like you, but Jenny, we can't call them boy and girl. What names would suit you?" he asked while chucking his son under the chin.

Jenny looked down at the little girl sleeping peacefully beside her. She had a soft white down of hair and long dark brown lashes. Jenny looked up at Travis and with all the tenderness and love for him reflected in her eyes, said quietly, "Travis, if it's all right with you, I would like to name our daughter Celeste."

He looked down at his daughter, noticing her eyes open as though she had responded to the name. He leaned over and kissed Jenny on the forehead before saying, "Jenny, I think I love you more everyday. Thank you. Celeste it will be."

He picked up Celeste and held her tenderly, kissing her cheek and nuzzling her neck before looking back at Jenny. "Now, Mama, what will we call this big strapping son of ours?"

"You name him, Travis?"

"All right. Let's see. How about Grayson Gardiner?" He was watching his son and missed the note of sadness on Jenny's face.

She was thinking of her father. What had become of him? Would he be pleased that her son would forever carry on the Grayson name? Was it something she wanted for her son? Was it a name to be proud of? She did not know the answer, but looking up at Travis's happy face, she knew what to do. "We could call him Gray for short," she said quietly.

"Fine. At least that's out of the way. Now young lady, how are you doing?"

"I'm fine, Travis. I wanted to get out of bed, but Mammy and the doctor won't let me," she said pouting.

"You just stay here until Mammy says you can get up. She's handled a lot of mothers in her time." He patted her leg.

"But Travis, the babies are so far away. They'll be safe in the nursery, won't they?" she asked quickly.

"What a silly question, Jenny. Of course they will be safe. What's troubling you?" He had seen the fright that had preceded her question.

Jenny held her son tightly, feeling tears come to her eyes when she thought of the implication Sir Reginald had hinted. She couldn't tell Travis of his threat. He would surely go to Sir Reginald and possibly find out about the indenture. If she told him about the threat she would have to tell him everything. She couldn't bear to see the look of disgust she was sure would follow her pronouncement. She looked up at his concerned face and said, "It's just that I couldn't bear it if anything should happen to them." She made a show of putting Gray up to her shoulder and patting him on his back.

"Nothing is going to happen to them. I think you're just tired and need some rest. I'll call Mammy to come get the babies and you can take a nap.

"All right, but please watch over them."

"Don't worry, I will. Now you go to sleep. I think I can manage to take the babies back to the nursery myself."

She helped Travis get the babies in each arm and watched as he snuggled both children with ease in his big arms. He will be a wonderful father, she thought. Then she closed her eyes and drifted into a sleep which would again hold the nightmares.

As Travis walked the short distance to the nursery, he thought back to Mammy's conversation with him. He was glad he had been warned about what Mammy called "new mother blues." He attributed Jenny's depression to being this malady, which, according to Mammy, affected many new mothers. Mammy had assured him that this peculiarity would only last a couple of days and that it was expected.

After Travis turned the babies over to Mammy, he walked downstairs to get some breakfast. When he entered the dining room, he noticed Sally sipping a cup of tea. "Good morning, Sally," he said cheerfully.

"Good morning, Papa. How do you feel this morning?" Sally asked with a glint of mischief in her eyes.

"I feel wonderful. I still find it hard to believe that I have two beautiful children let alone a beautiful wife. If someone would have told me a year ago that I would have so much, I would have called them a liar." He smiled as he took a seat across from Sally, continuing, "I'm a lucky man."

Sally had wondered if Jenny had told Travis about her visitor of yesterday. Seeing his good mood, she debated whether or not to tell him herself since he obviously didn't know or understand what had transpired. She came to her decision and said, "Travis, yesterday, before Jenny went into labor, she had a visitor."

"A visitor. Who?"

"That pompous Sir Reginald Wenthrop. I don't know what his game is but he obviously said or did something to upset Jenny."

"What happened?" Travis asked, not liking this bit of information at all.

"I don't know. Jenny asked me to leave them alone for awhile but to stay close in case she needed me. I could hear nothing but when he left I heard the door close and went immediately to see if she was all right. When I returned to the sitting room, she was hysterical. Did you find out anything about him yet?"

"I received some information yesterday while I was in Charleston. It seems this is not Wenthrop's first visit to Charleston like he says. He was here two years

407

ago. He stayed in a waterfront boardinghouse and asked a lot of questions about Colby."

"Colby? I wonder what that scoundrel has to do with all this?" Sally knitted her brow in contemplation.

"From what I can gather, the colonel doesn't know Jenny is not, in truth, his niece. But, he is doing business with Wenthrop. In fact, Wenthrop is staying in Charleston at the colonel's townhouse."

"Travis, why doesn't Jenny just tell you the truth? What could she possibly be trying to protect with this ruse? It's obvious that this Wenthrop fellow has something on her other than her identity. I'm a pretty good judge of character, and I just can't see that beautiful child doing anything criminal or deceitful. But, it's obvious she is scared to death of that man."

Travis had ideas about that but was unsure, so he decided to keep his ideas to himself.

When he didn't respond, Sally asked, "Travis Jenny was so concerned this morning about the safety of the babies, she made Mammy promise to never leave them alone."

Travis looked up sharply and said, "She said as much to me only a while ago." Standing up abruptly, he walked to the window that overlooked the misting Ashley and drew his hand through his hair. "By God, I'll find out about this if it's the last thing I do. If he has threatened her or my children, I will see him rot in hell."

"If I can do anything to help, please just tell me," Sally offered.

Travis turned to give her a tentative smile. He loved this woman who had always done her best to give him guidance without seeming to direct him. "Thanks, Sally. I think the best thing to do right now is to make Jenny feel safe and secure until I can find some way to convince her to tell me what Wenthrop threatened her with."

"All right. I will do whatever I can. But," she said, standing up, "right now I'm going up to see those two darlings of yours." She walked to the door but turned to give Travis a conspiratorial grin, saying, "Maybe Mammy will even let me bathe one of them. She's taken to her old role without a misstep. She's a treasure, Travis."

Travis stood by the window long after Sally had left the room. What could Wenthrop be holding over Jenny's head? Surely she wouldn't care that he knew that she wasn't Elaine but the woman's companion. Something else. He cursed again the slowless of getting information. Four months earlier he had sent a missive to a lawyer in London, requesting information on Wenthrop. Travis knew the man had something on Jenny. Something serious enough to cause nightmares and make her fearful of him and now fearful for her children. God, how he wished she would trust him with her secrets. What could be so terrible that she couldn't tell him?

He put on his jacket and walked out to the stables in search of Darby. Darby might be able to find out more than Travis in certain circles.

Jenny was sitting on a Chippendale chair, close to the fireplace that evening, when Travis walked in and asked her, "Does Mammy know you are out of bed?"

"No and I don't want you to tell her either. I feel perfectly fine, and I just couldn't stand lying in bed one more minute." She saw the concern he directed to her and quickly asked, "Tell me, have you seen the babies this afternoon?"

"I just came from the nursery. Little Celeste is

sleeping soundly while my son is screaming his head off." He smiled at the memory.

"Is he all right? I just fed him so he can't be hungry."

Travis remembered Mammy's saying that Jenny probably wouldn't have enough to feed the two of them but didn't know how she would feel if he told her that so he said, "He's fine. He just didn't like getting his napkin changed. I must say he is a scrapper."

She remembered Thanksgiving day when she heard all the tales of Jeff and his exploits. She hoped her son would be fun-loving like Jeff but tender and caring like his father.

Travis walked over to the table and poured Jenny a small glass of sherry and a whiskey for himself. As he handed the glass to her, he said casually, "I understand you had a visitor yesterday?"

Jenny felt a cold chill run down her spine. "Yes, Sir Reginald came to see me," she whispered, not looking at him.

"What did he want, Jenny?" He was standing by the mantle and peered closely at his wife's face for what seemed hours before she answered.

What could she tell him? That he had threatened her and her children? That he wanted her to falsify papers for him? She looked into his tender, concerned eyes and vowed not to lie to him again. But, knowing him as she did, she knew he would go to Sir Reginald and do something drastic or even, God forbid, criminal if he knew of Reginald's threat. Her mind raced with alternatives to her plight but, as before, she realized Travis could do nothing to help her. She was bound by her father's greed to fulfill the indenture. Legally she was the property of Elaine's estate. She couldn't stand to see the look of disgust that Travis surely would bestow on her if she did tell him the truth.

"Travis, I'm really tired. I think I did overdo today. Would you mind helping me back to bed?"

Sitting his glass down on the table, Travis bent to pick her up in his arms. She curled her arms around his neck, put her head on his shoulder and prayed for herself and her children but most of all to never lose Travis.

He didn't move. Emotions he had never before felt were surging through him: hate, disgust, fear, and a pain that she had not trusted him to tell him the truth. He wanted so much for her to trust him. He would never let that man harm her. "Jenny, I love you so much. I would kill anyone who tried to harm you or our children. You are safe with me. You believe me, don't you?"

She tightened her arms around his neck as she whispered in his ear, "I know you would always try, but some things are beyond anyone's control."

He walked over and gently laid her on the bed. Placing his hands on her shoulders, he waited until her blue eyes were looking into his black ones. "Jenny, I feel there is something you need to tell me. No matter what it is, I will always love you and protect you. I am not afraid of anyone or anything. Nothing, I repeat, nothing will ever take you away from me. I only hope you believe me."

Tears again appeared in her eyes as she threw her arms around his neck and kissed him with trembling lips.

Travis felt a deep tenderness for her and a sadness that overwhelmed him. He gently took her arms away from him, saying, "I had better go to another room to sleep."

"No!" she begged. "Travis, please stay with me."

He looked at her and suddenly felt the pain his

father had felt. He knew he couldn't love her as he wished just yet, but he could spend the nights with her in his arms. Maybe in time she would know of his deep love for her and be able to tell him of the terrors and fears that she alone knew. Or barring her confession, maybe he could find out for himself what Wenthrop had on her and why he was continuing this charade. He didn't know what the future held for them with all the secrets and mistrust between them, but he would stay by her and take it moment by moment.

Chapter Twenty-three

Christmas Eve came with all the excitement and merriment that went with the season. Travis carried Jenny down the stairs, much against her will.

"Honestly, Travis, the way you are carrying on, one would think me an invalid."

He smiled. "You had better take advantage of this while it lasts. Tomorrow I plan on taking you horse back riding in the morning and then pickin' cotton in the afternoon."

She started to laugh, saying, "I don't think I am quite ready for all that just yet. I guess maybe being babied isn't all that bad. In fact, it is really quite nice." She kissed his cheek.

They greeted their guests who were already seated in the dining room and then sat down to a festive meal of turkey, rice gumbo, spinach salad, ambrosia, wine, and good friendship.

Between mouthfuls, Jenny said, "It is a shame Jeff and Mary Lou couldn't join us. I wonder what they are doing today?"

Leaning forward, Travis looked both ways as though not wanting to be overheard, and said loud enough for the whole group to hear, "Jeff took Mary

Lou to Virginia to meet her parents. I think this is getting serious."

Sally whooped for joy, saying, "I'm so happy for them. I think Mary Lou will be perfect for Jeff. It looks like there will be another wedding in this family yet."

After they all swore they were stuffed and couldn't eat another bite, they retired to the parlor where a huge tree had been decorated and piles of gaily wrapped packages lay under the lighted boughs.

As was the custom at Moss Grove, the house servants came into the parlor, each smiling in eager anticipation. Each one of the servants received a present from Travis and Jenny along with a bonus for jobs well done.

Obediah beamed as he withdrew a red livery with shiny brass buttons from his box. "Why Mr. Travis, Miss Jenny, I guess I goin' ta be da bess dressed butler in dese parts. I thank ya." He bowed.

Cecelia, the wet nurse, opened hers to discover a hand mirror with shiny sea shells embedded in the handle. "Oh!" she squealed in delight. "Miss Jenny, you done saw me."

Jenny laughed, "Yes, Cecelia, but it's quite all right. I thought you might want one of your own."

"Oh! I thank y'all so much." She primped and patted her hair that was almost completely hidden by a blue gingham kerchief.

Jenny watched her, all the while remembering seeing her using her mirror much like she was using her own now. Jenny was pleased that she had asked Travis to buy her one.

Mammy held her package until everyone had opened theirs, then she slowly untied the ribbon and pulled off the bright paper. Slowly, she peeked under the lid.

414

Jenny didn't know what was in Mammy's package as Travis had not let her see all the gifts, and she was as excited as Mammy when she said, "Mammy, hurry and open your present." She acted like an excited child.

"Miss Jenny, ah done been shocked afore at what dis boy done brung me. Ah's got ta see furst what's in dis heah box." She looked over the rim into Travis's laughing eyes.

Jenny prompted again, "What is it, Mammy? Hurry and let us see."

"Mis'er Travis done gone an done it again." She shook a plump finger at him then slowly withdrew a pair of vivid red stockings. Snickers and peels of ribald laughter were emitted from the assembly.

Walking over to her, Travis placed his arm across her shoulders, saying, "Mammy, I saw those in a shop in Spain and I said to myself, those would be perfect for Mammy."

She swatted him affectionately as everyone laughed and glanced at everyone else's gifts.

Jenny told Travis to hand her the long box under the tree and called Rosalie over to her, saying, "Rosalie, this is for you from Travis and me. Open it up."

The little girl was obviously not used to receiving presents and fumbled with the ribbon. Jenny helped her and then sat back to watch the little girl's expression.

Slowly, Rosalie opened the lid and then gasped before taking the doll in her arms and asking in a awed voice, "Is this baby for me?"

"Yes, that's your very own baby. You must take care of her and keep her safe," Jenny told the little girl.

Travis noted the way Jenny had said *safe*. He thought it was a peculiar request but was soon bending down to accept a wet kiss from Rosalie.

Mammy gave her orders: "Come on ever'body, let's go ta da kitchen and have our services." She ushered everyone out, leaving the family alone.

Darby took a small box from his coat and handed it to Jenny. "My lady, merry Christmas."

Opening the box, Jenny stiffled a giggle and said, "Darby, I don't know what to say. It's beautiful."

Travis craned his neck to see inside the box. There lay a small snuff box with seed pearls and rhinestones scattered over the lid. He stifled a laugh as Darby handed a similar-sized box to him, but upon opening it, he found a small pouch of his favorite tobacco and said, "Darby, thank you. It's my favorite."

"Aye. I know it is," Darby stated matter-of-factly.

Reaching over, Travis picked up a package for Darby and handed it to the grizzled old man saying, "From Jenny and me. Merry Christmas."

Darby quickly opened the box, and a smile crinkled his good eye. "I'll be." He looked up and favored Jenny with a bow. "Eye patches." He rustled the box as his hand moved the different-colored eye patches around. "I think I'll go show Obediah. I thank ye." He walked purposely from the room, calling out to Obediah.

Tapping Travis on his knee with her cane, Sally asked, "Travis, if you would be so kind as to hand me those two packages there?" She pointed to the designated boxes, thumping her cane when Travis picked up one that didn't belong. "Not that one. *That* one." She pointed again.

Hiding his smile at her excitement, Travis turned and brought her the boxes.

"You keep that one, Travis." She took the bigger of the two and handed it to Jenny, saying, "Merry Christmas from me, you two."

Quickly opening the box Sally had handed to her, Jenny discovered a fur muff that she quickly brought to her cheek, saying, "Sally, it is beautiful. Thank you so very much."

"You are entirely welcome, my dear. No lady should go about with cold hands on these blustery days." Sally turned to Travis, who had just opened his present and laughed. "That's definitely you, Travis."

Looking up, Jenny saw Travis posed with one foot on the hearth, his arm folded over his stomach and a haughty expression on his face. An exquisite hand-carved pipe was placed in his mouth. "Why, you look positively regal, darling."

"It's the pipe. I'm just a backdrop." He walked over and kissed Sally on her wrinkled cheek. "Thanks, Sally. I'll think of you everytime I light up."

"Travis, I believe there is a package for Sally right there." Jenny pointed to the right package.

He picked it up and gave it to Sally, saying, "May you have many more Christmases with us."

Carefully untying the bright green ribbon and folding it neatly, Sally said to Jenny in a conspiratorial manner, "You can save ribbon for years and reuse it, you know."

Travis laughed at Sally's frugality. She had more money than she would ever require.

As Sally slowly opened the lid, a gleam came to her eye. "Why, it's lovely and certainly will be used. Travis, help me put it over my shoulders, would you?"

He leaped to the task as he placed around her shoulders the white wool shawl which had a reflective fiber running through it that caught the candlelight in little sparkles.

"I thank you and my rheumatism thanks you." Sally smiled. She turned her attention back to Travis. "Now that we old ones have given and received, I think we should see what the babies have under the tree. Even though they are safe and snug in their beds, I think Saint Nick has something under there for them."

Travis pulled out the boxes marked for Gray and Celeste and Jenny opened them, exclaiming in wonder, "Sally, when did you find time to do this?" She held up a silver goblet with another in the matching box.

"Actually I still must get their names engraved, but the silversmith was so backed up I just decided to bring them out now. I'll take care of the engraving when I get back. I doubt if the children will be ready for cups for some time to come."

"I'm sure the children will thank you themselves when they learn to talk," Jenny said with her eyes expressing her happiness at Sally's thoughtful gift.

She looked up when Travis placed a small box in her lap. Opening it, she gasped, for inside was a ring. "Oh, my, Travis. It is exquisite. I have never seen anything so beautiful." The candles which adorned the tree made little flickers of light like a thousand stars appear in the huge central sapphire and the many diamonds surrounding it.

Leaning down, Travis took the ring out of the velvet-lined box and on one knee he took Jenny's hand in his and slid the ring on her finger, saying, "Jenny, I love you. Will you be my wife forever?" He smiled as Jenny was still gasping, trying to regain her breath.

For the past two weeks a barrier had stood between them. Nothing she could put her finger on, but it was there. She had sidestepped any references to Reginald or there had been an interruption for which Jenny had been grateful at the time. But, she realized, that unless she told Travis her secrets and let him try to help her, they would never have the marriage she had

418

wished for. Everyday she determined to tell him, but everyday she would see his eyes radiating love for her, and she knew she would surely die if that look ever left him.

As she looked into the black orbs now, she knew she would not tell him tonight. She put a hand on his cheek as she responded to his proposal. "Why Travis, this is the most beautiful thing I have ever seen, and I would be delighted to remain your wife forever." She leaned forward and kissed him, a tear in her eye when she prayed for this to be so.

Thinking this was an appropriate time to retire, Sally stood up, saying, "If you two will excuse me, I believe I shall retire for the evening."

Jenny stretched her hand out as Sally stood up. "Sally, the evening is still young and there are more presents to be opened. Besides, we haven't even had our Christmas toast yet."

Smiling as she leaned down to kiss Jenny on the cheek, Sally said, "No, really. I am tired and I have had quite enough to drink for one Christmas. There are certain times when three is too many, and I believe this is one of those times."

Travis went over to her and gave her a hug. "Good night, Sally and merry Christmas. We'll see you in the morning."

After Sally left, closing the door behind her, Travis looked back at the Christmas tree. "Well, I wonder who Saint Nick left all these presents for?" With a comical expression on his face, he walked over and started heaping boxes at Jenny's feet.

Caught up in the excitement, Jenny began opening the presents. Inside the first box was a smoking jacket cut to fit her. Not saying a word, she opened another, then another. All the boxes contained different colored smoking jackets. She laughed until tears rolled down her cheeks. Unable to speak from laughing so hard, she waved her finger toward the remaining boxes under the tree and then toward Travis to indicate that those were his presents and he should open them.

He broke into a roaring laugh as he opened each one and spread the seven jackets in front of him. He sat down beside Jenny and put his arms around her, and they rocked back and forth in each other's arms, both laughing hysterically.

He finally looked her in the eye and said seriously, "I'll wear mine if you'll wear yours." That started them both laughing again.

Finally, her laughter subsiding, she hugged him tightly, saying, "I love you, Travis. This is the best Christmas I have ever had."

"I enjoyed it, too," he whispered. "I could not have received any better presents than the ones I did this year. Two beautiful children, a loving wife, and seven smoking jackets. I can hardly wait until we test the jackets and see if they work."

She smiled with a sad but gentle smile, understanding what he meant, and she said shyly, "I'm sorry, dear, but I imagine we will have to wait to test them. Remember what the doctor said. Not for a couple of more weeks."

He kissed her and then said, "I understand. Come on. It's getting late. Would you like to walk upstairs or would you prefer to be carried?"

Getting up from the settee, Jenny started to walk toward the door, throwing over her shoulder, "I believe I will walk, thank you."

He started to laugh when he noticed the way she waddled and said, "You walk like you have a pumpkin between your knees. Come on, let me carry you or we will be here the rest of the night walking up the stairs." He picked her up and gave her a kiss before taking her to the bedchamber.

Mammy pronounced Jenny fit three days later, and Jenny relished her new freedom because now she was able to spend as much time as she wanted with the babies.

Travis found her there the day before New Year's Eve. She was bathing Gray in a small tub and singing to him. Travis came up behind her and put his arms around her, saying, "I knew I would find you here."

His voice had startled Gray, and in his excitement, he splashed water on his parents.

"You had better watch out. Gray doesn't like people sneaking up on his mama. Do you, Gray?" She picked the baby up from the tub and placed a thick towel around him.

"Jenny?" he called softly. "How would you like to go into Charleston for New Year's Eve?" he asked while he chucked his son under his chubby little chin.

"I don't want to leave the children, Travis."

"We don't have to. We can bring Mammy and Cecilia with us to watch the babies. We've been invited to Oscar's for a ball, and I would certainly like to show Charleston the most beautiful woman in the area. What do you say? We could have dinner at the Colony House with Jeff and Mary Lou and then go to the ball from there."

Seeing Travis's eager expression, she couldn't disappoint him. "All right, but only if the weather is not nasty. I don't want the children to get sick."

"Don't worry. I'll take care of everything. You just go pack, and Jenny," he said, pausing at the door, "pack that black gown with all those sparkles on it, all right?"

"All right." Jenny turned back to the little boy and

snuggled her nose in his chubby little neck. "Oh, Gray, what am I going to do? I can't go on lying to your father like this." She held the baby close as her torment came forth. "I'm going to have to tell him soon. I can't go on like this. I'm so afraid of losing him and—you." A look of determination came across her tear-streaked face. She walked over and placed Gray in his cradle. As she set the small bed in motion, she looked from her son to her darling daughter, asleep in another cradle. "I'm going to tell him tomorrow night. We will start the new year off with no lies and no secrets between us. Connie always told me the truth shall set you free. Whatever the future holds for me, at least I will be free of the lies. I love you two. Good night."

She left the room feeling the weight of the world had been taken from her shoulders with her decision made.

Chapter Twenty-four

The next day proved to be glorious. The sun was shining, and the pines creaked in the gentle breeze. Travis, Jenny, the babies, and Mammy rode to Charleston in an enclosed carriage. The babies slept peacefully, lulled by the gently swaying coach, all the way to the house on Tradd Street.

When Jenny walked in the doorway, she could smell fresh baked bread filtering throughout the house. "Travis, smell that? It's fresh bread." She turned to look questioningly at him.

"I sent Darby and a couple of servants ahead to get the house ready for us."

Feeling the warmth from the many fires that blazed in each room and the homey comfort of the house, she smiled, saying, "It looks wonderful." She turned to Mammy and said, "I'll go with you to the nursery to get the children settled."

About that time Rosalie came running from the back of the house and said quite authoritatively, "I'll take care of the babies. I've been practicing with my baby." The little girl held the doll in her arms like she had seen Mammy and Jenny do so many times.

Jenny laughed. "All right, young lady. You come with us, and we'll see how much you have learned."

Walking into the parlor, Travis lit his new pipe. He had just taken a seat before the hearth when Darby entered the room, closing the doors to the hall. Travis looked over his shoulder as Darby came closer and asked, "Did you find out anything?"

"Aye, cap'n." He took an envelope out of his pocket and handed it to Travis. "This came for you on a ship that anchored this morning."

Taking the envelope from him, seemingly afraid to open it, Travis held the missive in his hand.

Darby said, "Cap'n, somethin' else. The *Sea Breeze* came in yesterday and I done what you said. From what I could get out of some of the crew, they *are* dealing in slaves just like you thought. They put them off in a cove between here and Savannah. Makes the fact that they had no cargo to unload seem to put the truth to what I was told."

"Anything else?"

"No, cap'n. That's 'bout all. No one seems to know 'bout that man you wanted me to check on."

"All right Darby. Maybe this will give me some answers." Travis tapped the envelope on his desk. "If you don't mind, I think I would like to be alone when I open this."

Darby left the room, closing the door after him.

Taking a deep breath, Travis broke the seal to open the missive. He scanned the page and it did indeed answer many questions. Sir Reginald Wenthrop was a gambler and lost his family fortunes and estates in less than a year. He made his way in society by associating himself with rich gentlemen who enjoyed ordering about another of their peers. Reginald, it seemed, was not adverse to groveling for his keep. He is to marry the Lady Elaine Seaton, a very wealthy widow of one of Reginald's last gambling associates, who had been killed by one Gregory Grayson over a gambling debt.

He put the paper down. Could that be her secret? Her father a murderer?

His contemplation was interrupted when the door knocker sounded on the front door. The knock sounded again, and he got up to see who was invading his privacy now, as the servants must have been busy and didn't hear the summons. He opened the door to Sir Reginald.

"I say there, Gardiner. I just saw some activity here and wondered what was up."

Travis felt anger swell within him but decided to get the fop to talk and asked in a civil tone, "Reginald, won't you come in?"

"Why, thank you. It is a bit nippy, what?"

Travis took Reginald into the parlor and offered him a brandy. He poured, then brought the drink to the settee where Reginald lounged his frame.

Looking up at Travis with an ingratiating expression, Reginald said, "I have been meaning to come by and see you and your lovely wife for some time. As you know, I handled all Lady Elaine's business affairs after her husband's unfortunate accident."

Realizing that Jenny hadn't informed Reginald that he knew she wasn't Elaine, he decided to gain as much information as this fact could garner. "Ah, yes, that accident. Elaine has never been able to tell me about how her first husband died. Could you fill me in?"

Reginald was only too happy to tell this country bumpkin exactly how Miles had died. "It was a tragic loss. Miles was gambling at a club in London. This reprobate, one Gregory Grayson, demanded to be included in our game. The man lost everything, but I presume his greed overcame him, and he put up his daughter as collateral on his bet. He lost and the beautiful daughter became the property, so to speak, of Sir Miles. The man was most distraught over his deed and when Miles exited the hall, the man ran him through."

"What happened to the daughter?"

Gleefully Reginald sat up straighter and said, "She became indentured to Elaine."

Indentured! That was it. Travis was feeling disgust over Jenny's father putting her up for a wager, but he could not condemn the man for killing the swine who would take an innocent girl in such a way. *Indentured!*

Reginald cleared his throat and continued: "Enough of such morbid details. As Elaine's—" He looked up. "But I understand you prefer her middle name of Jennifer, am I correct?"

Travis nodded.

"Yes, well, as I was about to say, as Elaine *Jennifer's* business manager, what I really need is to have these papers signed. Just some authorizations and the like. Since you are now her husband, and legally all belongs to you, you could sign these papers as her husband. As I'm now on my way to an appointment, would you be so kind as to sign these for me now?" He stood up and laid the papers on the table. "I can assure you they are all in order. No need to go over them."

Travis looked at the man and smiled. "I'm afraid I can't sign anything for Elaine, Mr. Wenthrop."

Incredulous, Reginald gaped. "But why ever not?"

"Because Jenny is not the Lady Elaine Seaton. You know this, and I'm curious as to why you would perpetrate the farce."

Reginald turned white. He hadn't believed her when she had told him Gardiner knew the truth. "You mean she *did* tell you?"

"Of course she told me. I am her husband."

"Then I suppose you know she is indentured to Lady Elaine and as such is part of the lady's estate?"

"Yes. I suppose you have something in mind?" he

asked with a sneer of contempt on his lips.

Reginald's mind whirled. He hadn't planned on this. But maybe he could turn this situation around to his advantage. He smiled up at Travis. "I can see you are an astute man, Mr. Gardiner. Let us just say that if we play our cards right, like you Colonials like to say, we could both benefit. The Lady Elaine held title to various estates and enterprises in England. If Jennifer would agree, we could turn these enterprises into cash. That's what some of these papers I have here would do. We could start selling small items at first and then, say in a year or so, could liquidate everything. Of course I would be willing to go fifty-fifty on these profits." He placed an arm across the back of the settee and smugly smiled at Travis before concluding his speech, saying, "I would say, all in all, a very pleasing proposition, wouldn't you?"

Wanting to choke the life out of this man but also wanting to find out more, Travis asked, "And what would happen if I declined your—generous offer?"

A smile lit up Wenthrop's face. He stood up and walked around to the back of the settee, putting it between Travis and himself before saying, "Let us just say that in five years your wife will be a little older, but you should be able to pick up the love and companionship you had lost."

Walking over to pour himself another brandy, Travis said casually, "That sounds like a threat, Wenthrop. Surely you didn't intend that?"

Feeling he was holding all the cards, Reginald became bolder. "Take it for what it is, Gardiner. After all, I believe I have all the cards in this game. Jennifer is bound to fulfill her servitude and I, as the manager of Elaine's estate, am bound to see that all properties owned by the dear lady are accounted for."

Travis, no longer hiding his emotions, asked menacingly, "Do you really think I would give my wife up to you?"

Feeling everything was about to go his way, Reginald became bolder still. "What choice do you have? Either go along with my plans about her playing this farce out or turn her over to me so she can finish out her indenture period."

Travis realized he was on shaky legal ground but was determined that this man would not get his hands on his wife. "What if I offered to buy up her indenture papers?"

"Really, Gardiner, I'm afraid even you would not have the capital for that."

"How much?"

Leaning back, Reginald stated, "One hundred thousand pounds."

"How much was in the pot that her father lost?"

"Not more than five hundred pounds, but her value has increased since then."

Travis could not believe a father would wager a girl like Jenny for five hundred pounds or five million pounds for that matter. What a terrible thing for her to live with.

Turning back to Reginald, Travis stood up straight and stated, "I will give you twenty-five thousand pounds and not a penny more. And, before you speak, let me tell you what will happen if you don't take me up on my offer." He walked up to Wenthrop and stood not a foot from him, looking down at him with a menacing scowl. "If you don't take the money I offer and meet *my* terms, I will go to the constable this very night and swear out a warrant for your arrest on blackmail charges, harassment, and anything I can think of. I know about the threats you made to my wife, and believe me, it would give me immeasurable delight to see you rot in jail. Besides, you seem to forget where you are. My wife was indentured under English law, and around here English law means about as much as a pig in a poke."

Knowing this man meant every word he had spoken, Reginald tried to think. Perspiration appeared on his brow. He started grasping at straws. "Why don't you just do so now? Why pay me anything, unless you are afraid I will take your little wife away from you?"

"I'm not afraid of anything you could possibly try to do to me. I just want you out of Charleston and out of my wife's life."

"What makes you think I will be leaving Charleston? I have come to like it here."

"That's another condition of mine. I will pay you only if you leave Charleston and go back to England. Also, you will publicly acknowledge the death of Lady Elaine Seaton aboard the *Himes*. My wife simply was in a state of shock after the accident and is now of sound mind. No one will care that she is not a titled lady here."

"But," Reginald said, leering, "what would it do to her if everyone knew her as nothing more than a servant?"

Travis thought a moment. Even though Jenny was not at fault in that incidence and was only the victim of her father's greed and that Englishman's lust, the knowledge of her indenture could hurt her if it were known.

He leered at Reginald and said through gritted teeth, "If I so much as hear one word from anyone of that, I will personally seek you out and wring your scrawny neck."

"Now who is blackmailing whom, Gardiner?"

"I'm stating a fact. If you don't believe me," he said, leaning farther forward and making Reginald

429

move back a step, "try me."

Sure that this man meant what he said, Reginald decided to go along with his offer. After all, he would still get what he wanted in the end. "Very well, Gardiner. I think you are making a mistake, but since I seem to be in rather dire financial straights at the moment, I will accept your offer of twenty-five thousand."

"Fine. Meet me tonight at the offices of Simples and Gardiner on Meeting Street at, shall we say, nine-thirty. I will have everything ready at that time."

"I will see you then. Good day, Gardiner." He walked out of the house and stood on the front step putting on his gloves. His back was to the house, and he did not try to hide the self-satisfied smile on his bony face.

"Gardiner, I will have your twenty-five thousand, and I will have your wife as well. It's a good thing I have kept that ruffian under wraps. I think he will come in handy. If what he told me is true, I will have my cake and eat it too!" He laughed as he walked to his carriage down the street.

As Sir Reginald leaned back in the carriage, a smile lit his austere features. He had been down the street as the Gardiners had arrived. He had seen Jenny as she had stood on the curb giving instructions and taking a baby in her arms. She had certainly not lost any beauty with childbirth. She retained the slim figure he had remembered. Her breasts were fuller, but it only added to her beauty. He had been right to await the birth of the brats. Yes, all in all he was pleased with the way his life was going at this moment. He was sure that once he got Jenny away from Gardiner, he could persuade her to go along with the farce. A couple of letters from Elaine to establish her remaining in the Colonies and then they could declare her dead after they had sold off her properties, and he would be rich and in control. His mind went over the various forms of torture that would give him immeasurable pleasure and make Jenny putty in his hands.

His mind went back to the night he had first seen her. Such a vision standing there behind that simp Grayson. He had determined that night, long ago, that he would have her. It caused him a moment's regret that his so-called friend Miles had to be eliminated for him to see his desires met. It had been so easy to blame Grayson. Grayson came up to the two as they had come from the club, pleading and begging for his daughter to be spared. The man had stood dumbfounded as Reginald ran the blade through Miles. He had only to hand the sword to Grayson and yell for help. The man was demented with grief and nary a denial came from his lips. Reginald smiled at the memory. He had no regrets that the man had been hanged for a murder he had never committed. It was just a small step on his road to regain the riches that he felt had been stolen from him. He had had to bow to Miles for too many years to gain entry to the most prestigious of games. Miles had always been most generous with funds *if* Reginald had needed them, but the things Miles had demanded in return for his generosity was something Reginald had never regretted murdering him for. The humiliation Reginald had had to endure made a flash of anger come to him.

"Yes," he said aloud into the empty carriage, "dear Miles is well done. I shan't be the butt of another of his perversions."

The coach pulled up before the colonel's townhouse. When Reginald stepped down from the coach, he noticed a drape pulled away from the front window. As he stared, the drape was hastily replaced. Wondering what was going on, he stepped up to the door and opened it into the gloom of the hall's interior. When he closed the door, the door to the library opened. A man stuck his head out and motioned for Reginald to come in quickly.

Deliberately taking his time removing his cloak and gloves, Reginald straightened the lapels of his jacket and pulled down the silk waist vest, before casually walking into the candlelit interior of the library. How he hated this house. Candlelight in the middle of the day somehow depressed him. The door was quickly closed behind him, and he turned to the man before him.

"Why all the subterfuge? Doesn't anyone know you are here?" he asked the little man before him.

"It's that Cicero. You know he gives me the creeps. Sometimes I feel ready to swoon when he is around."

Reginald gritted his teeth at the effeminate little man. "I take it you acquired the information?"

The man bobbed his head and turned the brim of his tricorn nervously in his long white hands. "They are to be going to the ball tonight at the judge's just like I said they would. The judge received a note yesterday saying they would be there."

Reginald went to a worn velvet settee and spread his bony frame upon it. Looking up at the weasel before him, he casually asked, "What time is this ball to begin?"

"Nine o'clock, milord," the man answered.

"Fine. You have done well, George. It was truly a blessing that Jules was able to acquire someone of your resourcefulness to be in his employ. You have surely proven your worth to me." He stood up and withdrew a small leather pouch from the pocket of his jacket. "I believe this will cover your time."

George's eyes lit up as he tested the weight of the pouch. "Is there anything else you want to know, milord?"

"No, George. Just keep an ear open for any news that the judge is getting close. He has made this matter of the missing women his personal crusade. We must be kept informed of any possible evidence."

"Yes, milord. I'll be sure to keep my ears open. I'll leave now." He moved toward the door. "But, I'll meet you tonight like we arranged."

"Yes, of course, George. See you tonight." Reginald watched the man leave the room, closing the door behind him. By tomorrow he would be on his way back to England to collect the riches that awaited him.

He walked to the window, carefully pulling back a small portion of the heavy velvet drapes, noticing with a grimace the stale, musty smell. All was quiet on the street, but he heard a thumping, scraping sound coming from the room overhead.

Walking to the hall, he noticed Cicero casually walking down the stairs. Looking up at the big black man, Reginald asked, "Is there a problem?"

Cicero looked down his wide nose at this man before him. "No. Jes' had ta knock some sense into one a dem. Dey won't be makin' any mo' noise for a while." It gave him some perverse sense of humor to talk in the thick Negro dialect to this man.

"Fine. I'm going to my room. Call me when the colonel arrives." He proceeded up the stairs and past the door where subtle moans could be heard. Giving the closed door only a perfunctory stare, he proceeded on his way, not giving it another thought.

Travis had spent the time since Reginald's departure in quiet contemplation. He understood Jenny's reluctance to admit her father was responsible for her

433

indenture. But, Jenny, his sweet Jenny, had done nothing wrong. She had been wronged by her father, by Sir Miles, and he was sure by Reginald.

He didn't feel comfortable about this deal he had struck with Wenthrop in buying his wife's freedom when he could just take her away from all this madness.

Again, why couldn't she tell him of her troubles? He could have been prepared for all this. He could have worked something out. He could only hope that tonight's business would see the end of Reginald Wenthrop and the nightmares his wife was having every night.

He heard one of the babies cry upstairs and then silence. He felt uneasy as though an evil still permeated his house. Would this deal silence any future talk that might harm Jenny? He would have to make sure it did. He would tell Jeff the sordid details tonight and ask for his help in securing Jenny's freedom.

With a heavy tread, he walked upstairs in search of Jenny and found her in the nursery with Gray at her breast. She smiled as he came into the room.

"He is going to be as big as you in no time if he keeps eating like this. He never seems to have enough," she stated.

He leaned down and placed a kiss on her forehead, a new compassion for her and what she had endured softening his eyes when he said, "He just likes being with his mama."

Jenny reached up and touched his brow, asking, "Is something wrong? You seem troubled."

He raised his head to look into her beautiful blue eyes. Should he tell her he knew the truth? No, not now. He would wait until this business with Wenthrop was concluded, then they could start anew with the new year. "You are so beautiful. Maybe I'm just jealous of my son."

Looking down at her sleeping son, Jenny said softly, "I imagine we could fix that if you promise to be gentle." A slight blush crept into her cheeks.

"Are you sure? It hasn't been four weeks yet."

"Mammy says I'm fine. The babies were so small, I didn't have any damage." She looked down, becoming embarrassed and added, "Of course, if you would rather not, Travis, I will understand."

"You just come with me."

She put the baby in his cradle and turned to Travis. They looked at each other, hunger and need reflected in their eyes. They walked hand in hand to their bedchamber, each anxious to finally be able to hold the other; each knowing that soon they would have no secrets between them.

Walking over to the bed, Jenny turned down the counterpane. She unbuttoned the front of her gown and let it slide off her shoulders.

When she turned to him, he sucked in his breath. Having the babies had done nothing to diminish her figure. Her breasts were a little fuller and her hips had a more rounded appearance, but she still held the delicate translucence of her skin that he loved.

He hurriedly discarded his own clothes and came to her placing his hands on her shoulders, gliding them up and down her silken arms. His breathing was coming faster to match Jenny's. His lips descended to capture hers. The kiss started out tender and gentle.

It had been so long since she had felt him beneath her fingers. So long since they had stood together, her flesh to his flesh, her passion to his. She climbed to higher and higher realms of ecstasy, clinging to him as their kiss grew in passion.

He picked her up, continuing the kiss, and carried her to the bed where he laid her upon the feather mattress as gently as a caress. He kissed her closed eyelids, then her cheeks, her neck, her breasts, and now her taut belly. She groaned with wanting him, but he continued to hold back, taking his time, sending her from plateau to plateau before placing his hand on the triangle between her legs, making waves of sensation engulf her. Jenny begged him to take her, but still he held back. But when she touched his manhood that stood rigid awaiting its role to unfold, he knew it had to be now. He moved on top of her and gently took her to the height of ecstasy that they had not experienced for so long. They erupted in unison, and the great tingling lasted for a long time afterward.

She clung to him, not wanting to let this moment go. Even though her heart was lighter with the knowledge that she would soon tell him all the things that had haunted her life, she knew that with this knowledge it could change his feelings for her. This could be the last time she would feel him loving her.

He felt the desperation with which she held onto him. What was she thinking? Did she somehow feel that by telling him the truth it would change the way he felt for her? Did she feel that he too would betray her like her father?

Raising his head, he brushed the hair from her forehead in gentle strokes. "I love you." He kissed her tenderly and then lay back with her curled at his side.

She relaxed with his words and felt a contentment that she could only pray would last for the rest of her life. She laid her hand on his chest as she asked, "Are you still jealous of Gray?"

"Poor Gray will have to wait a while before he finds a woman to give him what I have with you. I didn't hurt you, did I?" he asked, suddenly concerned.

Snuggling up closer to him, she purred, "I feel wonderful." She looked to the window and noticed the sun throwing deep shadows in the late afternoon gloom of winter. She slapped playfully at him and stated, "It's getting late and I need a bath."

He slapped her bottom as she presented it rising from the bed and then swung his long legs to the floor. "Good. I'll call Darby to bring the tub and we can take one together."

"That's a delightful idea, only this time you get to mop up the water by yourself." She grinned.

"You've got a deal but wait until you see this tub. I doubt either one of us will be required to mop." He smiled and ruffled her hair.

As Darby lugged the huge tub through the door, Jenny gasped. It was twice the size of the one at Moss Grove, and it took many trips to fill it with hot, steaming water. She almost died of embarrassment when Darby scratched his chin whiskers and stated, "I never seen a tub the likes of this one. You could share a bath with this one."

Travis lowered his head, hiding a smile, and looked at Jenny's scarlet face.

Suddenly it dawned on Darby. His face turned bright red and he immediately started for the door, stumbling in his haste. He stammered. "I—I'll be leaving you now." He closed the door with a slam behind him.

Jenny giggled and then came to stand by the tub, asking, "Travis, wherever did you find such a large tub?"

He came to her and started taking her robe from her shoulders. "You would be mad if you knew, so just say I thought it adequate for our needs."

Glowering at him, she stamped her foot and demanded, "Where did you get this?"

437

He grinned. "All right, Jenny. If you insist on knowing." He nuzzled her neck with his arms around her. "I purchased it from a bawdy house that was being dismantled."

Shocked, Jenny quickly turned to stare up at his amused countenance. "Travis, do you mean people know you bought this?"

"No, my love. Jeff purchased it for me and had it delivered in the dark of night. No one but Jeff knows about it. Besides, if anyone does know, they'll think it's for Jeff and Mary Lou. He'll be the talk of the town."

"Oh! How will I ever face him?" She put her hands up to cover her blushing cheeks.

"Jenny, he bought one for himself, too. He and Mary Lou have set the date of their wedding."

Forgetting her embarrassment, Jenny smiled in genuine pleasure, then she laughed, covering her mouth.

"What's so funny?" Travis asked.

"Oh, Travis. I somehow can't see prim and proper Mary Lou in a tub with Jeff."

As the situation became apparent to Travis, he too doubled over in laughter. Straightening up again, he picked Jenny up and lowered her into the tub. "My dear wife, what people do in the privacy of their bedchambers is no one's business but theirs."

She raised bright, shining eyes to his as she pulled his head down for a kiss. "Why don't you shut up and join me in our private pool?"

Without another word, he disrobed and climbed over the rim into her waiting arms.

Chapter Twenty-five

Travis was dressed and downstairs having a brandy when Darby came into the parlor.

"Cap'n, you sure look the dandy. Plannin' on dancin' the night away?"

"Sure do but I wish Jenny would hurry. We're to meet Jeff and Mary Lou for dinner at seven," he said while pacing the room, more concerned about his impending meeting with Wenthrop than the lateness of the hour.

"I think I hear her comin' now, cap'n."

They turned around and watched as Jenny came down the stairs. Travis gaped and Darby clapped his hands.

"My lady, you look like the *Sea Breeze* on a moonlit night," Darby exclaimed.

"Thank you, Darby." She smiled, knowing it to be the highest compliment Darby could give her. She stood waiting for Travis to say something but he just smiled and stared.

"Well, what do you think?" she asked as she spun around.

Travis thought she looked more beautiful than he had ever seen her. She had braided her hair and wound the braids around her head with the effect of a halo. The gown was black and the neckline was cut low and off her shoulders. It was closely fitted to the waist with a billowing shirt that stood out above the many petticoats underneath.

"Jenny, you will be the envy of every lady in Charleston tonight. You look beautiful. It just needs something." He tilted his head this way and that and then snapped his fingers and withdrew a box from behind his back. "I think these will do nicely." He handed the box to her.

She took it, looking at him with a puzzled expression, and asked, "What's this? Another present?" Travis nodded, and she opened the box slowly. Inside lay a diamond necklace and earbobs. She gasped. "Travis, you shouldn't have. These are too much."

"They belonged to my mother, Jenny, and now to you. Here, let me help you."

He took the necklace and fastened it around her neck.

She took the earbobs and put them on and then ran to the mirror in the hall and turned to see them reflecting the candlelight in sparkling prisms of light.

"Oh, Travis, thank you. I feel like a princess."

"You are a princess, my love." He kissed her shoulder and said, "Shall we go?"

Darby brought a fine, fur-lined cape for Jenny and a cloak for Travis. As they walked down the steps, Darby called after them, "You two have a good time. I'll watch everything here."

They had finished dinner and the ladies had gone to freshen up when Travis leaned toward his brother and whispered, "Jeff, I need a favor."

"What is it, big brother?" Jeff leaned back in his chair with a smile on his handsome face.

"I need for you to do something tonight, and I need your complete silence."

Jeff sat up and, noting the seriousness of his brother, said, "Of course, Travis. What's the matter? Is something wrong at the plantation?"

"No, everything is fine there." Travis quickly went on to explain what he needed and why.

Jeff sat in silence as Travis's story progressed. His face tightened into a mask of anger, before he said, "Why the blackguard. Of course, I will go right now and draw up the papers. You take the ladies to the ball, then meet me at my office." He got up to leave when Travis put a restraining hand on his arm.

"Jeff, I want this to be legally binding. No loopholes." He thought for a moment and then gave an additional instruction to his brother.

The anger momentarily left Jeff's face, then he turned and left Travis to await the ladies.

When Jenny and Mary Lou returned, they found only Travis awaiting them. Travis noted the way Mary Lou's eyes searched the dining hall and felt regret at spoiling her evening. "Mary Lou, I'm afraid Jeff has been called away on business, but he will join you at the ball later. I'll take you two." He looked upon his wife's curious expression. "I'm afraid I will have to leave for a short while myself." He saw panic start in Jenny's eyes and quickly took her shaking hand in his, saying, "I will only be a few minutes, Jenny. I promise."

The two women looked at each other, then Jenny turned back to him and realized he would not leave her unless it was important and gave him a reassuring smile.

They pulled up in front of Oscar's impressive Meeting Street house and heard the strings from numerous violins as they spun their magic upon the night. The house shone with lights, and the festive atmosphere of a party permeated the three people seated in the closed carriage. Travis assisted Mary Lou and Jenny from the interior of the carriage and then, with the air of a cavalier, put an arm out for each of the ladies and walked, between them, up the steps and into the receiving hall.

Pansy and Oscar were receiving their guests and when Pansy's eyes saw the new arrivals, a smile spread across her pert features. "Jenny, Travis. I'm so pleased you could come. Mary Lou, why, where is Jeff?" She craned her neck to see where the scamp was.

Travis bent and kissed her hand, saying, "Pansy, I'm afraid Jeff has been called away on business but he will join us later. I also must absent myself for a short time, but I'm sure the ladies will enjoy the festivities until we return."

Oscar looked concerned and asked, "Travis, is there something I can help with?"

"No, Oscar. Just keep an eye on the ladies for me." At Oscar's continued skepticism, Travis nodded, "I'll explain later."

He saw Pansy pouting and quickly said, "I really am sorry, Pansy, but this simply can't be helped."

She drew Travis and Jenny to a corner where she wouldn't be overheard. "It's just that Oscar and I have an announcement to make, and I so wanted you to be here."

Travis looked surprised. "An announcement?"

She looked from Travis to Jenny and a smile lit up her face. "We are going to have a baby."

Travis couldn't have been more thrilled for them. Oscar and Pansy had been married for five years and they had both despaired of ever having a child of their own.

He hugged her, and then Jenny enfolded her in her arms.

"Pansy, I'm so happy for you. You will have to come out to Moss Grove and practice on the twins." Jenny winked.

Travis walked over and shook Oscar's hand. "My best wishes, Oscar, but we'll talk later. I really must go now."

He led the ladies into the ballroom and saw Sally sitting by a window. He escorted Jenny and Mary Lou to seats next to Sally, the strain of the coming event evident on his face.

Seeing them approach, Sally patted the seat next to her and smiled at the two people she loved. "Well, Travis, you certainly have two beautiful ladies this evening. How did you get so lucky?" She smiled at Jenny and Mary Lou.

"Sally, could you keep an eye on Jenny and Mary Lou for awhile? Jenny will explain."

"No, I wouldn't mind. You go on. It will give me a chance to find out about Gray and Celeste."

He bent and kissed Jenny, each expressing the love they had for the other in their eyes, before he turned and left them. He felt secure in the knowledge that Sally would keep a watchful eye out. He hailed a carriage, unaware of the eyes that watched him from across the street.

Mary Lou was asked to dance by a kindly old gentleman and waltzed across the dance floor.

Jenny had been asked repeatedly to dance but had declined all offers until a man, who looked vaguely familiar to her, approached from across the room.

He bowed politely in front of her and asked, "May I have this dance?"

"I'm sorry but I am waiting for someone," she answered politely but with a nagging suspicion that she had encountered this man before and not under happy circumstances.

The man, dressed in a black waist jacket, black trousers, and ruffled white shirt, bent closer and whispered, "I have news from your husband."

Jenny stood up, and he clumsily waltzed her toward the terrace door.

Sally watched all this with concern on her face. She hadn't been able to hear what the man had whispered to Jenny, but she knew the expression that had registered on Jenny's face was one of fear.

As the couple reached the terrace, Jenny shook herself free of his grasp, somehow repelled by his touch, and asked, "What news do you have from my husband?"

The man looked about him as though to make sure they were not being observed, before saying, "He wants me to bring you to him. Something about a man named Wenthrop."

Her heart pounding so loudly in her ears that she had to move closer to the man to hear him, she whispered, "What about Sir Reginald?"

Looking around again, he grabbed her arm and hissed, "I don't know nothin'. I'm just doin' what I was told."

Jenny noted the way the man's eyes continued to dart around. In his rush, his speech had gone from precise to low country British. She had the same feeling that she had encountered this man before and that the meeting had not been pleasant. Panic rising within her, she asked, "Do I know you?"

The man looked at her and simply said, "Come on. We must hurry."

Sally had followed the pair out to the terrace and had heard this last exchange. What could this mean? She watched as the man put Jenny into a closed

444

carriage and turned it around to drive toward the waterfront. Sally retraced her steps and went to search out Oscar and his advice.

The carriage pulled up in front of an old warehouse on the wharf. The man drew Jenny out of the coach and led her to a side entrance. He took a key from his waistcoat and inserted it into the rusty lock. The door opened on squeaky hinges. There was no light inside, and again Jenny started to feel panic rise within her.

"What are we doing here? It's cold. I don't have a wrap. Where is Travis?" She knew her voice was rising but was unable to stop herself.

The man didn't answer but pushed her through the door. He felt around until he found a lantern, then scratched a match on the rough wall to light it.

As the light spilled into the room, Jenny saw a rat run past her feet and she screamed in terror. The man came up and slapped her hard across the face, hissing, "Don't be makin' no more noise, slut. There won't be any rescue for you this time."

Rubbing her burning cheek, the memories of that night on board the *Sea Breeze* came rushing in on her again. "It's you. Tim Hawkins. How did you—"

"How did I survive in that little boat your lover put me in?" he said, finishing for her. "I drifted in that boat for fifteen days with no food or water. Me tongue was swollen so's I could hardly breath. I only had a few sprinkles of rainwater to keep me from dyin' of thirst. Every minute, I had one thing to cling to, one thing to make me want to live. I kept thinkin' of all the ways I could get you and that cap'n for what you done to me." He sneered into her face with stale breath and eyes that looked crazed. "As soon as that Wenthrop fellow tells me your husband has paid him, I'll get to have you all to meself until the ship sails for England." He touched her shoulder and she cringed

445

from him.

Hawkins smiled and touched her cheeks. "No need to do that. I told you the last time that I'd make it good for you."

"What do you want? I'm sure my husband would pay you for my safe return," Jenny pleaded.

"Oh, he'll pay all right. His first installment is being taken care of right now."

Trying to think above the pounding in her head, she asked, "You said Travis was paying Sir Reginald. What for?"

"Why to keep him from takin' you back to England to finish out your indenture time," he said sneering. "I know'd you was a slut when I first laid eyes on you. Too bad the cap'n ain't as smart as me, huh? He went an' married himself a whore."

"Travis knows!" She felt her heart sink into a void.

"Aye, an' he's willin' to pay twenty-five thousand pounds to Sir Reginald for his silence."

She sat down on a crate and stared at the lantern. "Travis, what have I done to you?" she whispered from her heart. Why hadn't she told him before he had found out himself. How he must hate me, she thought.

Hawkins went to the door and leaned back against it. "I guess you'll just have to wait to be pleasured, *my lady*." Sarcasm reeked with every word he uttered. He was enjoying this immensely.

Jenny didn't give any indication she had heard him. She just sat staring at the lantern. Her will gone and all her dreams for a happy future dashed like the *Himes* upon a sea of utter despair, Jenny wept silently.

Travis was pacing the floor of Jeff's office, glancing

at the clock every few seconds. "Where the hell is he? It's nine-thirty-five. He's late."

"Settle down, Travis. He's not that late and it is New Year's Eve. He may have had trouble getting a carriage." As Travis continued to pace, Jeff rechecked the document he had drawn up, finding it as binding as he could legally make it.

They heard a carriage come to a stop and then start up again. Travis quickly took a chair and steepled his fingers as footsteps were heard on the stairs.

Reginald swept into the office without knocking and casually took off his cloak to drape it over his arm. "So sorry I'm late but I had a devil of a time with my cravat this evening." He smiled at each man as though this were a social engagement.

Jeff stood up from behind his desk, wanting only to get this mincing fop out of his office. "Wenthrop, I'm Jeff Gardiner. Let's get this over with. Here's the document. You sign it and then you'll get your money." Jeff didn't try to hide the loathing he felt for this man.

Travis had not looked at Reginald but continued to steeple and unsteeple his fingers before him.

Still smiling, Reginald casually picked up the paper and scanned its contents, not really caring what it said. He picked up the quill, and after dropping it in the inkwell, scratched his name on the paper.

Noticing the quickness with which Wenthrop signed, Travis asked casually, "Are you sure you can live up to the demands on that document?"

"Demands?" Wenthrop acted annoyed and quickly reread the document. Finally, he said, "Of course. I will be happy to remain in England, and I won't be seeing your lovely wife again. Actually, I'm leaving tonight for England, so you see I'm already living up to my part of the bargain." He continued to smile which made Travis wary. Reginald laughed as if at a private joke, then turned back to Travis. "You may now inform your wife she belongs to you. At least for the next five years," he added with a chuckle.

Travis saw nothing amusing in the situation and nodded to Jeff.

Jeff passed a bank draft across the desk. "Here's your money, Wenthrop. Now get your scaly body out of my office," he said through gritted teeth.

Reginald placed the bank draft in his breast pocket and, nodding to each man, left the office, whistling as he marched down the steps and into the brisk winter's night.

Going to the cabinet behind his desk, Jeff said, "I think we could both use a drink. Awful business," he said while shaking his head.

Travis drank the brandy down in one gulp. "Let's get back to the ladies, Jeff. Besides, I need some fresh air."

"I'm right behind you. Oh! Before we go—" He handed Travis the document Wenthrop had just signed. "Here, you had better keep this. You can burn it for all I care, but it might be wise if you hung on to it for a while."

Travis looked at the paper in disgust and placed it on the table. "You keep this one. Did you draw up the other one I asked you to do?"

Jeff walked to his desk and pulled out the middle drawer. "I think this one is more to your liking." He handed the parchment to his brother and watched the expression on his face turn to amusement.

Leaning over, Travis took the pen and signed his name, then passed the pen to his brother to witness.

Jeff signed and then handed the paper back to Travis.

Folding the paper, Travis said, "Yes. This one I

will keep." He pulled his cloak from the peg next to the door. "Come on. Let's go bring in the new year."

They walked into the cold December night and noted the time was just before ten. Just time enough to join the ladies for a waltz before the new year began.

Sally met them at the door of the ballroom before they had taken off their cloaks. She was wringing a handkerchief in her hands as she nervously approached them. "Travis, something awful has happened. I just know it."

Mary Lou came up to Jeff and she, too, wore a worried expression.

Sally looked at her with a pleading expression but Mary Lou shook her head.

"I've looked everywhere and I can't find her. Her cape is still here in the cloak room."

Travis felt a wave of apprehension at the looks on the two women's faces and asked, "What are you two going on about? Where is Jenny?"

Ready to cry, Sally said, "Travis, I don't know. A gentleman came up and asked her to dance. She declined. Then the man leaned down and whispered something in her ear. I couldn't hear what he said but Jenny was concerned and got up and they danced to the terrace. I followed them but only heard the last of their conversation as they walked away. Then he put her in a carriage."

Travis grabbed Sally by the shoulders, demanding, "Who was this man?"

She began to studder in the wake of Travis's ire. "That's just it—no one—has ever seen him before. Oscar received him and—and—thought he was with another couple—couple that had—come in. He didn't

449

think anything about it—not—not until I told him what had happened to Jenny. Travis, he's out trying to find them now."

Travis couldn't think of anyone but Reginald Wenthrop who would try something like this, and he had been with them. "What did this man look like?"

Sally put her hand to her head and shut her eyes, trying to recall exactly what the man looked like. "He was tall, about your size. His hair was reddish blond and his eyes were—green with yellow in them." She looked up when Travis gasped. "I'm so sorry, Travis. I did try to watch out for her."

He didn't hear her plea as a cold chill ran up his spine. It couldn't be. Tim Hawkins could never have survived. "Did this man have an accent?"

"Yes. British, but from the poor side from what I could hear. Definitely not cultured. Why he had dirt under his fingernails and a spot on his cravat," she said as though that in itself would be enough to place the man as a scoundrel.

"How long have they been gone, and did you see which way they went?" His voice was cold.

"About thirty minutes ago, and they headed toward the waterfront," Sally answered quickly.

Travis looked at Jeff with an expression of fright mixed with determination marking his bearing.

Jeff nodded to the unspoken plea, and they both flew out the door and back into the night.

Tim was getting impatient. "Where the hell is that Wenthrop? He said he wouldn't be very long." He started to pace in front of the door. If Wenthrop didn't show up in a few minutes, he was going to take Jenny anyway. He had waited a long time to have her, and nothing and no one was going to deny him again.

As Jenny became aware of his staring at her, she looked up to see the unmistakable desire and lust on his face. She had to keep him talking or he might not wait to take her. She had to have time and finally asked, "How was it you were rescued?"

Her question seemed to work as his gaze left her to stare into the blackness beyond the circle of yellow light. "I was 'bout gone when I seen sails on the horizon. The ship was far off and didn't look to be comin' my way. I knew I had to signal it someway." He grinned as he relived the scene in his mind. "I had a small magnifying glass in me pocket. Don't know why those arses let me keep it, but I held it just so." He indicated with his hands the way he had accomplished his task. "I started the boat on fire. I figgered if they didn't see the smoke, then I wouldn't need the bloody thing much longer anyways. But they did see it and picked me up. I guess I was sort of dazed for a while but when I come to, Sir Reginald was right beside me. I guess I'd done some talkin' in me sleep, and he figgered I might be the man to help him in his enterprises. He seemed real interested in knowing all about how you was rescued. Anyway, I been busy workin' for him for almost a year now. He pays me well and besides, I get all the girls before anyone else can." He licked his lips in remembrance, then turned to stare at her again.

"You can imagine me surprise when he comes to me and tells me I'm to get you. You! The one me bloods been poundin' for ever since I first seen you come aboard the *Sea Breeze* with your gown wet and clinging to your teats. I tried to get to you before, but you always had all those people around you. Then you got so big with child I figgered I'd have time to wait for me pleasures." He walked up to her and rubbed his thumb up and down her neck. "You look even

451

better than I'd hoped after welpin' the brats. But all this time since the brats were born I been tryin' to get you." He leaned closer to her and shouted in his frustration, "Don't you never do nothin' by yourself?"

Jenny suddenly realized that she had been spared only because of Mammy's and Travis's adamant desire to have her with someone day and night. She remembered the feeling of being without privacy and now blessed them for their vigilance. She also remembered the times when she had felt eyes boring into her only to turn and see no one about. She didn't have time to answer as they heard a carriage pull up in front of the abandoned warehouse.

Opening the door just a crack, Tim saw Sir Reginald and another, smaller man step from the carriage. A big black fellow who was the driver stepped down and was following them into the warehouse.

Jenny's heart started to pound once again in her ears when she saw Sir Reginald come in, followed by the colonel and Cicero.

Reginald looked at her sitting on the crate with her arms wrapped around her, trying to warm herself.

Leaning over to the big black servant, the colonel said something to him and Cicero went back outside.

Turning to Tim, Reginald asked, "I see you managed to get her. Were there any problems?"

"Nay. She followed as meek as a lamb," Tim said while rocking back and forth on his heels, obviously very pleased with himself.

Turning to look upon the woman he had wanted for so long, Reginald said quietly, "Yes, I know how that goes."

At the look of confusion on her face, he laughed. "All this time you were under the mistaken impression that your dear father had done the deed to Miles." He leered at her and leaned closer. "When you walked into the club that night, I knew I would have to have you. Miles was under the same impression and, unluckily for him, he won the most beautiful woman I had ever seen." He raised his hand and rubbed Jenny's cheek.

At his touch, Jenny snapped her head away from him as though burned.

"Be careful Jenny," he warned.

She wanted him to keep talking. So many questions could finally be answered. "You said *mistaken impression*. If my father didn't kill Sir Miles, then who did?"

He turned, putting one elegant hand to his chin, as though making a decision. "I imagine it really doesn't matter now. You should know the truth." He again came to stand beside her. "Miles was going to be selfish with your charms, my dear. He wanted you all to himself. When we came out of the club that night, your father was waiting. He begged and pleaded with Miles to forget the bet and let you come home with him. It really was a disgusting scene. Miles ignored him, and I saw the opportunity I had waited for. Miles had used me as his lackey for years. He knew I had run through my fortune and, in order to live the life of a gentleman, I had had to do his bidding. He never let a chance go by to remind me that he held my life in his hands."

The hatred on his face made a shiver run up Jenny's spine. He was no longer aware of her as his mind relived that night of two years ago.

"As Miles pushed your father from him, I saw my chance and pulled my saber out and ran him through. Miles turned to see what had happened, not quite believing he was dying. The look of surprise on his face as he realized I had run him through is something I shall cherish until my dying day. He had not thought me capable of standing up to him." His eyes again turned to her and the present. "It really was no trouble convincing the authorities that your father had grabbed my saber and done the deed. He was sniveling and talking with incoherent speech. He went with them without a struggle. I assume he went to the gallows the same way. Now, I will have Eden Hall and you, dear Jennifer, for now you will belong to me, body and soul."

Her father had died because of this man. Sir Miles had died because of this man. Jenny knew fear so real and chilling it threatened to overwhelm her as she stared up into the crazed eyes of the murderer before her. She didn't even notice when Cicero returned and threw a scratchy blanket over her shoulders. She was numb with fear.

Anxious to be done with this reunion so he could finally get his hands on the girl and also not liking the way Wenthrop was eyeing her, Tim rubbed his hands together and licked his lips before saying, "Did you get the money?"

Reginald turned to him, saying, "My business with Mr. Gardiner is complete."

Turning to Jenny, he said in a gleeful tone, "You will be pleased to know that you are now indentured to your husband." He laughed. "It's too bad you won't be around to do his bidding."

Tim came closer, asking, "Can I have her now? I done what you said. I didn't touch her, just like you said." He licked his lips again.

So engrossed in his lust, Tim didn't see the shadow of the black man edge up behind him.

Reginald looked at Tim with a sneer on his thin lips and said, "No! You will not touch her. She is far too valuable for the likes of you. You have served me well, Tim, but now I am afraid our business arrangements are at a close."

"Wait one bloody minute. You said I could have her just like them others," Tim said with a scowl.

"All of that has changed, my good fellow. Jenny is mine and no one else's." He looked at the big black man and nodded.

Cicero put his strong hands around Tim's neck and soon had choked the life from him.

Jenny stared at the scene before her in horror. She had never seen anyone die before her eyes. In fascination, she watched Tim's eyes bulge from their sockets, his tongue swell and hang from his gaping mouth. She heard the guttural grunts as his lungs fought for air, until at last he became still and the sounds of life faded from his body. She watched as Cicero dragged the lifeless body of Tim Hawkins into a corner as though he were garbage. All this took but a moment, but the image was burned upon her memory forever.

Reginald turned to the colonel, asking, "Now that he is disposed of, how much do you think we will garner from this shipment?"

The colonel, who had remained silent throughout, looked up at the titled gentleman. "If I had a blue-eyed blonde, I could get one hundred thousand for her. As it is," he said, shrugging his shoulders, "I have ten mulattoes who won't bring in half that much all together."

Reginald looked from the colonel to Jenny, his greed obviously fighting with his lust for her. "Does this blue-eyed blonde have to be a virgin?"

"No. The sultan isn't that particular. He simply likes European or—British women."

Deciding he could have Jenny and the money, he made a decision and said, "Then you can have Jenny when I'm through with her." He smiled at her, thinking of the long voyage before they reached the end of their journey.

Jenny's mind would not accept what these men were saying. This couldn't be happening. She heard Reginald say, "What time does the ship sail?"

The colonel answered, "At midnight, right on schedule."

Turning back to her, Reginald held out his hand, commenting, "That seems appropriate. New Years will bring in riches to us." He smiled as he directed his next statement to Jenny. "Come with me, my dear. We have time before sailing."

Jenny's mind saw Reginald's hand coming toward her. The nightmare was real. The shadows thrown by the lantern made his eyes glow with red highlights. She shrunk away from the hand as she had in the nightmare. He would take her away from Travis and her children. The hand kept coming, growing in her mind. And then she heard something that did not belong in her nightmare. The colonel. He wasn't in her tortured dreams. He was saying something that made Reginald withdraw his hand and spin toward him.

"I'm afraid you have that all wrong, Wenthrop."

The hand came away from her abruptly as Reginald whirled on the colonel. "What do you mean?" he demanded.

The colonel swaggered over to a crate and sat down, crossing his arms in front of him. "I mean, you are of no further use to me. I have run this business quite well for twenty years. I only needed your help to get Gardiner and Jennifer. That's done, so—Godspeed, *Reggie*."

Reginald took a step backward as he saw the gun Colby leveled at him. He put his hands out in front of him as if to ward off the attack and started to plead. "Jules, what are you doing? I can bring in wealth from the sale of Eden Hall. It will take only the papers that Jennifer will sign to accomplish our goals."

Jules sneered at the mincing fop. "You are so ignorant, Reggie. You conceived my rightful ownership of Eden Hall and all other estates of Elaine's when you came to me with your plans. I do research, man! I know that Eden Hall alone is worth a fortune, and I also know that as legal heir of my dear departed niece, I will own it all. I will have riches and a title that you could only wish to acquire. I will take my rightful place as Sir Jules Colby, only living relative of the Lady Elaine Seaton. So you see, Reggie, you really would only complicate matters with your presence."

Reginald turned rigid at the betrayal. "You planned this all along, didn't you?" Memories of Eudora's simpering conversations came back to him in bits and pieces. He had thought her ravings to be connected with marriage to him, but the fragmented bits made more sense. *When I am a lady. . . . England must be beautiful. . . . I can't wait to see it. . . . When I'm a lady.*

"That's right, Reggie. My plans to leave this country had been about complete when you ventured to me with your scheme. I thought how appropriate to return to England as a lord. You see, I really must leave here. I am afraid my greed has been the ruination of my trade. As long as I only took the blacks, nothing was done, but now there have been inquiries into the disappearances of the whites. Taking Jennifer will be the end of my trade for I cannot stay here if Travis Gardiner is breathing down my neck. My plans are to sail tonight with my dear wife and daughter to Eden Hall and all the riches that await me there."

Reginald's eyes shone with hatred. "How do you

plan on proving your claim?"

"My dear, Reggie, you also accomplished that feat for me. Remember the Bible you so expertly forged? That is all the proof I will need." Without further ado, Jules Colby pulled the trigger.

Jenny jumped as the retort resounded in the empty warehouse. She saw Sir Reginald Wenthrop stare blankly at the colonel then at her before crumpling at her feet. A dark splotch of blood stained his otherwise immaculate white shirt front. She screamed in agony at the death and gore around her.

They had been searching the warehouses along the wharf for what seemed an eternity when finally Travis heard a shot. "Over there, Jeff." He indicated with his finger, then jumped from the carriage and detected a light from one of the buildings. They heard Jenny's agonized scream, and Travis ran faster in the direction from which the scream had come. He burst through the door and took in the scene in one sweep of the yellowed circle of light.

Jenny jumped up and ran to him, throwing her arms around him and sobbing. They heard a shot and spun around to see Jeff holding a smoking pistol. They looked in the direction he had fired and saw Cicero standing with eyes wide, holding a knife over his head. He crumpled before he could throw it.

She buried her head in Travis's arms and started shaking uncontrollably as Travis held her to him, asking her, "Are you all right? Did they hurt you?"

Jenny tried desperately to speak between the sobs that racked her body. "No—I—al—right—but the colonel."

Pulling back away from her, Travis asked, "The colonel? Where is he?"

"I'm right here, Gardiner." The colonel stepped into the circle of light, holding a gun on Jenny. "I'm afraid you have stepped in again where you are not wanted. You botched my last deal for this girl. You won't botch this one."

"What are you talking about, Colby?" Travis asked in a firm voice.

"Why I've made a deal for your lovely wife. A very lucrative deal."

"I'm afraid you have it wrong, Colby. My wife belongs to me."

"Are you speaking of her indenture, Gardiner? You see, all you have is a piece of paper. I have sold the real thing, and as I'm the only one holding a loaded gun, I would say *I* have the upper hand. Now if you will hand over the little imposter, we will conclude this business right now."

"Imposter?" Travis paused. "You knew about the charade all along, didn't you?"

"I found out when Reggie came and saw her. Actually I'm rather glad. You see the real Lady Elaine was no relation to me. I was playing a charade of my own." He laughed a wicked laugh. "My sole purpose in agreeing to this whole arrangement was to get Elaine and her servant." He paused and looked at Jenny. "You, my dear, were the real prize. My sources said you were breathtaking, and I'm happy they were proven correct."

Travis was trying to keep him talking as Jeff crept to the darkness surrounding them. "What possible purpose could Jenny serve you now?"

The colonel threw his head back and laughed. "You still don't get it, do you? Why I had this whole town looking under doormats for the boogey man." He stepped closer. "Since you won't be around to repeat this, I suppose I can tell you my little secret."

He turned slightly and said, "Mr. Jeff Gardiner. You may return and stand beside your brother."

Jeff cursed under his breath as he moved to stand beside Jenny.

"Fine. Now that I have all of your attention, I will continue." He walked to the crate Jenny had sat on and put a leg up, holding the gun loosely from his draped arm. "You have all been wondering about these disappearances of the most comely of the young ladies of Charleston?"

Travis looked closely at the colonel. "What do you know about them?"

"I see you still don't grasp the situation, Travis. You see, I have been trafficking slaves from Africa for years."

"I suspected that much, Colby. What does your bringing slaves to Carolina have to do with the disappearances of Alicia Adams and the Harmon girl?"

'Oh, it's much more than that. Why I took a mulatto from right under your nose six years ago."

Travis remembered that girl's disappearance. There had been numerous others but nothing had pointed to Colby. "Exactly what are you trying to say, Colby?"

"If I must spell it out for you—" He took his foot down from the crate and glared at the threesome. "You see, I had full cargoes coming back to the Carolinas. I needed to have some type of cargo to ship to Africa and Asia. On one of my trips aboard, I found that some of the more, shall I say, primarily black nations, were desperately interested in light-skinned beauties, and they were quite willing to pay for these beauties since I was quite willing to obtain them." He turned his hands upward and shrugged his shoulders.

As the enormity of what the colonel had confessed registered, Travis shook with rage. "Are you telling me you sold Alicia as a slave?"

"Actually, Miss Adams never made it to Tangier. She was a handful." As the memory of Alicia came back to him, his eyes took on a glassy quality. "Such a pity. She certainly was a ripe prospect, but her will was just too strong." He seemed to drool when he thought about the money he had lost.

Travis was not about to let this lecherous man get his hands on Jenny. "I'm afraid you won't be taking my wife for your personal gain."

"I'm afraid you have nothing to say about it, Gardiner. You see, I am the one holding the gun." The colonel became bolder at his advantage. "I could have had your sister, too, Gardiner. If that damned horse of hers hadn't spooked at my arrival. As her injuries made her useless for my purposes, she was spared."

As the truth of Celeste's accident was told, Travis was filled with an uncontrollable rage. He remembered Celeste's telling him repeatedly of her suspicion that something or someone had spooked her horse. To finally know that this monster had done the deed was almost more than Travis could bare.

Jeff, sensing Travis's mounting rage and determined not to also lose a brother to this mad man, stepped forward and quickly asked, "How have you managed to get away with all this for so long, Colby?"

"Actually, I've spent most of my efforts obtaining women from outside Charleston. This town holds a shameful lack of beautiful women. I have had to go as far west as Montgomery and as far north as Philadelphia to obtain the beauties my clients demand."

Jenny asked a question that seemed to rile him. "Why did you sell Rosalie? She is a pretty-light skinned mulatto."

The look of rage on his face made Jenny's blood

run cold. "That was Katherine's doings. She denied me her bed and resented my pleasures with my slaves. Rosalie is my child. When Katherine found out, she made the child's life miserable. I saw that the child would grow into a beauty and told Katherine to lay off. She sold the child behind my back. When I saw her at your place the day of the barbecue, I felt better about it. After all, I could just take her when she was old enough, now, couldn't I. Such a pity all the beauty going to waste for now I must leave her here."

Jenny knew only too well the way Katherine could inflict her evil. No wonder Rosalie was hysterical the day they came by the manor on their way to Moss Grove. To think that this man was her father. No matter what happened this night, at least Rosalie would be spared this torture.

Looking down at the lifeless form of Reginald, Colby smiled as he continued: "But this man presented me with the idea of a lifetime. Upon checking into his story of wealth beyond my wildest dreams—" He laughed. "I found that I could easily assume the identity of Elaine's long-lost uncle. I plan on taking Eudora to England and pawning her off on some English lord, preferably a rich one." He nodded to Jenny. "My dear, I believe it is time to meet with George."

Travis's attention came back to Colby. "George who?"

Laughing, Colby looked deeply into Travis's eyes. "George has wanted you for a long time, Gardiner. As a bonus, I may just let him have you before I kill you."

A sickening suspicion overcame both Travis and Jeff as they watched Colby's features. "Who are you talking about, man?"

Colby seemed to be having a grand time making Travis Gardiner squirm. "Why, George has been most helpful to me, Travis. Being a secretary to the judge has helped me immensely. You see, I know, for instance, that Elaine—I mean Jenny—was not wed in Barbados as you told everyone but on the night you spirited her away from Salford Manor: a good three months after the conception of your children. The little bastards are just that—bastards."

Jenny's hand flew to her mouth as the colonel laughed at her beautiful children. "Travis, he is insane," she whispered up to him.

Colby caught her words. "Insane, my dear. Why, who's holding the gun? It's time to go. Come here, Jennifer," he ordered menacingly.

She could feel the tension in Travis as he held her away from Colby. She knew she must save him from the colonel. If she went to the colonel, maybe she could find a way to distract him.

"I said come here, Jennifer," Colby demanded again.

She turned to Travis and gently touched his cheek. Her eyes brimming with tears, she turned and made to move in the colonel's direction.

When she moved, Travis exclaimed, "Over my dead body." He pushed Jenny aside and leaped for the colonel. The gun fired but Travis reached the colonel and sent him flying with one swift punch.

Jeff quickly pounced on the now unconscience Colby as Jenny ran to Travis.

"Travis, oh, Travis, are you hurt?" She searched him for bloodstains.

Holding his side, Travis seemed to stagger. "I think I had better sit down. It seems the bugger shot me." He withdrew his hand from his side, and Jenny saw that his shirt was stained red.

"Travis, he *did* shoot you." She guided him to the crate and took off his cloak, then his waistcoat and shirt. The bullet had entered the side and then exited through his back. "Travis, we have to get you to a doctor."

"Just get me to Darby," he said with a grimace.

She was concerned about his wound. It looked deep, and he was continuing to lose a great amount of blood. She quickly bent and tore a bit off her fine organdy petticoat, tying it securely around Travis's waist. When satisfied that she had bound it as tightly as possible, she looked around her at the carnage and noticed that Jeff had securely tied Colby to a support post. When she turned back to Travis, she noticed his slumped posture and white face. A red stain was seeping through the bandage. She called Jeff to hurry, then she knelt down beside Travis, taking his head on her breast for support.

Chapter Twenty-six

Even though it was New Year's Eve, the streets of Charleston were deserted as Jeff drove Jenny and Travis to the Tradd Street house at breakneck speed. Arriving at the front of the house, Jeff immediately jumped from the carriage and ran into the house, leaving Jenny to remain with Travis, trying to comfort him and tending his wound. Soon Jeff, Darby, and Mammy emerged from the house, Mammy holding up her skirts and praying loudly.

Gingerly, Jeff and Darby carried Travis into the house and up the stairs to his bedchamber. Softly they laid him on the clean counterpane, and then Darby and Mammy cleaned his wound and applied bandages to stop the bleeding.

Jeff and Jenny nervously paced around the bed asking if there were anything they could do and feeling totally helpless in the process.

Eventually, Darby stood up, placing his hands to the small of his back and arching his spine before turning to Jenny and saying, "There, that should take care of him." He smiled, then added, "It wasn't all that serious. It was mainly just a flesh wound."

Trying to reassure Jenny, Mammy added, "Honey, ah seen dese two hurt worst den dat fallin' out a trees or bein' kicked by one a dem ole mules when dey was boys."

Feeling secure that everything was fine, Jeff went over to Jenny and put a consoling arm around her shoulders before telling her, "Jenny, I'm going to leave and go get the constable. When I'm finished at the warehouse, I'll come back. Don't worry. Darby knows what he's talking about. Travis will be up grumbling again in no time." He kissed her cheek and added, "I'll be back as soon as I can."

Travis opened his eyes to see Darby, Mammy, and Jenny bending over him with concerned expressions.

"How do you feel?" Jenny asked.

"Just hunky-dory," he said weakly with a slight grin easing the lines of pain on his face.

Feeling relieved, Darby and Mammy smiled and left the room so the two could be alone.

"Travis, you scared me to death. Promise me you won't do anything so foolish as that again."

"You don't suppose I will have to save you again, do you?" he asked with a look of wonder.

"Don't joke about it, Travis. You could have been killed." She had tears in her eyes when she got up to take his bloodied shirt away.

Seeing the concern on her face, he changed the subject, asking, "Where's Jeff?" He grimaced as he moved to sit up.

"Just be still. Jeff has gone to get the constable. He will come up when he returns."

"Come here, wench," he demanded.

She walked to stand beside him, suddenly feeling nervous.

Travis pulled her down to sit beside him on the bed, making Jenny say hurriedly, "You must be careful not to pull the stitches. You want to get better, don't you?"

Bringing his hand up to touch her cheek, he said quietly, "You are all I need to feel better."

She stared into his eyes. A look of pain crossed her pretty face when she confessed, "I am so sorry you were shot because of me."

He lifted her chin and made her look at him. "Jenny, why couldn't you have told me about your father and being an indentured servant. Don't you trust me?"

Tears again filled her eyes when she told him of her torment. "I thought you would stop loving me if you knew. I thought you would be ashamed of me, and it would change everything we had together." She looked down before continuing, "Travis, for most of my life I have been searching for dreams. As a child, I dreamed of having pretty dresses like the other girls. As a young woman I dreamed of a prince who would take me away from the slums of London to his castle and keep me safe. When I met and married you, I thought all my dreams had come true. Then Sir Reginald came to take away even that dream." She stood up and walked to the window. "I knew if I told you the truth about my past that this dream, too, would end. It has nothing to do with trusting you, Travis. I know you feel it does but—" She turned and walked back to sit

467

beside him." I don't think I could have lived if I had seen the look of shame I was sure you would have felt. You married me without knowing of my past. I felt you would be ashamed of me and demand that I leave your home. That was my nightmare, Travis."

He started to speak but she placed her fingertips to his mouth. "Travis, whether you believe me or not, I was going to tell you all this tonight. I could not go on with Reginald's threats and your misguided love. You have given me so much. I felt I could only give you the truth and my love. I want to tell you everything now." A tear appeared as she bowed her head.

Touching a curl that had come loose above her ear, Travis said, "Jenny, I know all about your father's wager." At her look of shame he begged, "Tell me about it and then we will speak no more of it."

Hesitantly, at first, Jenny related the story of her life from the day her father had taken her from Connie Darrow's until the day Travis had rescued her. When she was about to conclude her story, she told Travis of how Reginald had admitted that he had been the one who had killed Miles, not her father. Her father had died because of Reginald. She told him of the hate she had felt for her father's betrayal; the feeling of shame at being indentured by his greed.

Travis did not interrupt her except to ask a question to clarify a point in his mind. As she concluded her tale, he looked closely at her downturned face. He felt her pain and uncertainty where her father was concerned and said, "Jenny, what your father did to you was wrong, but he did plead for your freedom. In a small way he tried to atone for what he had done to you. Reginald has now paid for the wrongs committed against you and your father. Forgive your father,

Jenny. You won't be happy until you can. I know."

Seeing a tentative smile of understanding appear on her tear-stained face, he changed the subject from her father to something else. "Jenny, this Connie Darrow you speak of means a lot to you, doesn't she?"

A softening came to her face when she said, "She's the only mother I ever had."

He smiled at the look of longing and love she held for the woman and asked, "Would it make you happy if I sent for her and she lived at Moss Grove with us?"

Jenny laughed. "I doubt she would but we could ask. She's a very independent woman, Travis. But—" She leaned and kissed him. "Thank you for thinking of her."

"It's settled then. You write to her and extend the invitation and I will make the arrangements."

The look of tenderness and love she bestowed on him made him forget his wound. He pulled her down beside him and kissed her with all the love he had in his heart. "Jenny, I love you. I love you because you are you. I couldn't care less what you were or how you found yourself in such straights. Right now, you are my wife and the mother of my children. Nothing else matters to me."

Jenny felt all the problems of her past leave her as she snuggled up beside her husband.

They heard footsteps in the hall, and Jenny quickly got up and smoothed her gown, making Travis ask, "Are you afraid, little one?"

"No, Travis, but I'm sure Jeff would be shocked if he walked in and found us like that." She pointed to the bed.

Travis laughed and said, "Want to bet?"

The door opened and Jeff sauntered into the room.

469

He smiled at Jenny and then turned his attention to his brother, taking a chair by the side of the bed. "Well, Travis, I'm glad to see you are still among the living."

"I'm thrilled about that myself. Now, tell me what happened with Colby?"

"Well, it seems the fraud wasn't so cocky when the constable showed up. He sang like a blue jay." Jeff looked at Jenny and winked. "It seems our timing was perfect. The ship that was to take Jenny was due to leave at midnight." He paused then said, "It was the *Sea Breeze*. Quartermaine was arrested, and they found ten light-skinned mulattoes in the hold, chained to the pilings."

"Where in the world did they keep ten women in town until the ship arrived?" Travis asked, knowing the *Sea Breeze* had only been in port since this morning.

"It seems the colonel's townhouse in Charleston was the receiving point. Upstairs there is a room they kept them in."

Jenny remembered the room she had stayed in with a lock on the outside but none on the inside and the pulled drapes that Cicero wouldn't allow her to open. It all made a morbid sense to her now.

At Travis's look of disgust, Jeff continued: "Like he said, the colonel didn't restrict his activities to Charleston. One of the girls was from Wilmington, one from Georgetown, two from Macon, and the others were spread out from Alabama to Ohio. The constable had a report to keep on the lookout for a runaway slave from Savannah who fit one of the girl's descriptions. In fact, from Pansy Shealy's parents' plantation. It was their second in a year. The consta-

470

ble pulled out all the runaways listed, and the colonel has confessed to selling the majority of the women. His main problem was getting greedy and trying to sell white women. If he had let Jenny alone, he probably could have kept up with this *trade* of his for years. Runaways are always a possibility, but too many white women would have eventually destroyed him."

Travis laid his head back, saying, "I can't believe the man. Did you find out what happened to Alicia?"

"Yes," Jeff said, then looked down at his hands. "It seems Quartermaine used the women for his pleasures during the voyage. Alicia jumped overboard one night after she had been used by him."

Jenny put her hand over her mouth to stifle the scream that threatened to come from her.

Looking up at her startled face, Travis said, "Jenny, she is better off than if she had reached her destination." He looked back at Jeff. "What about the Harmon girl?"

"Oscar is sending an agent over to Tangier to try to get her back. Maybe she can be returned, but I wonder about the way she will react after everything she's been through." He shook his head then continued: "There were a couple of others on board the *Sea Breeze* when we got there."

Travis looked back from his wife's slumping shoulders to his brother and asked, "Who else?"

A grin spread across Jeff's handsome face as he motioned for Jenny to sit down beside her husband. "It seems Colby was leaving with this voyage and taking Katherine and Eudora. As the constable will no doubt tell you, he had his hands full of two she-cats with claws bared."

This information perked Jenny's immediate interest, and she urged Jeff to continue. "What happened?"

"Well, it was really a quite a sight, and I'm so glad I was there to witness it." Placing his hand on Jenny's, he continued: "I know you were treated terribly while under the colonel's care. But—" He leaned back and laughed. "You should have seen it. Eudora was trying to explain that she was now a titled lady with wealth and that she would hold title to an old estate in England called Eden Hall."

A look of scorn came to Jenny's pretty face. "They planned all this before I even arrived, when they thought I was Elaine. That's why they treated me so badly: to break my spirit and take over Eden Hall." A chill invaded her as she thought of Travis's beautiful sister. "He planned on taking Celeste the day of her accident, didn't he?"

The guilt that Jeff had experienced everytime someone mentioned his sister's name was now gone. "Yes, Jenny, but thank God he didn't get his hands on her. But, Travis, I did find out that Colby took Lulu. That's why she left Celeste for so long and we never saw her again." He shook his head, then said sadly, "Here all this time I was ready to kill her for disappearing like that and—" He couldn't finish.

He looked down at his hand on Jenny's, then took a deep breath. "They also arrested George. It seems he has been working for Colby for several months. He kept Jules informed as to Oscar's investigation. Oh, that reminds me. Oscar says to thank you."

"Thank me? Thank me for what?" Travis asked curiously.

"For taking him away from a very dull party. He's

down at the wharf taking statements. He says this is one case he wants to be sure of. He'll come by tomorrow to pay his respects in person."

A silence invaded the group as all the implications of this night's business rested heavily on their souls.

Jeff put his hands on his knees and stood up. Reaching inside his breast pocket, he withdrew a paper and handed it to Travis, saying, "This must have fallen from your coat. I found it in the warehouse."

Travis took the proffered paper and smiled. "Thanks, Jeff. I just might need this."

"Anytime. I'll come by to see you later. Mary Lou awaits for the traditional New Year's kiss. If I hurry, I'll still be able to make it before dawn. Happy New Year." He started for the door then stopped and turned around. "Oh, yes. I almost forgot. There is one other thing. Here." He stepped back to the bed and handed something to Travis. "I found this bank draft. It must have fallen out of someone's pocket. I hope the person who lost it won't miss it. Happy New Year again." With a wink he opened the door, stepped out on his way to meet Mary Lou.

Jenny stood and walked again to the window.

Watching her slumped shoulders, Travis called to her quietly, "Come here, Jenny."

She turned to look at him and walked slowly to the side of the bed. She sat in the chair Jeff had just vacated.

Travis took her small hand in his and said, "I hope this is the end of all this mess." He paused and lifted her chin to look into her eyes. "Let me tell you something you obviously don't know about me. I decided a long time ago that I would never marry.

473

Most women of my acquaintance, with the exception of only a few, were frivolous, silly creatures who wanted only fashion and gossip to spend their time. When I found you, it was like a gift from God. I never realized what a lonely, unfulfilled life I had until you came into it." He noticed the relaxing of her features as he put his hand to her cheek. "Jenny, I love you. You have been everything to me. I want us to have a beautiful life together. I want us to grow old and see our children grow and have children of their own."

She smiled and bent to kiss him, then said, "Travis, I promise to never hold anything from you again. I love you so much that I sometimes feel my life would end without your love in return. I now know that you would never forsake me for the past. Let us go into the future together."

Travis tenderly kissed her lips, feeling his life was now complete. They separated reluctantly as a knock sounded on the door.

Upset at all the interruptions, Travis growled, "What do you want now?"

Mammy peeped in the door, then proceeded in, saying, "Why ah sho' is glad ta heah you a bellerin' agin. Y'all must be feelin' better." She grinned.

"I'm fine," Travis said while trying to sit up.

"Dey somebody heah dat wants ta check you out fer demself." She walked back to the door and pulled Rosalie in the room.

She stood looking at Travis with big brown eyes. "You all right, Mr. Travis?" she asked with a scared expression marking her pretty little face.

He smiled at the concern she displayed for him and said, "Rosalie, I'm in the pink. How about you?"

"I'm fine too!" She smiled.

Mammy patted her on the shoulder, saying, "Come on, chile. We better go in an' check on da babies and den you got ta get back ta bed."

Rosalie ran to the side of the bed and leaned over to kiss Travis on the cheek, exclaiming seriously, "I'm so happy you didn't get killed."

Smiling, Travis patted her cheek and whispered, "Me too!"

Mammy pulled a reluctant Rosalie from the room, closing the door behind her.

"I'm so happy she wasn't subjected to Colby's slaving of women," Jenny said with a sigh. She looked away from the closed door, back to Travis. "Should we tell her who her father is?"

"No. At least not until she's much older."

She came back to stand beside her husband and said, "I think you should rest now. I'll sleep in Celeste's room tonight."

When she bent to kiss him, he pulled her down to lie beside him, saying, "No you don't, Jenny. We will never, I repeat never, sleep apart."

"But, Travis, I could hurt you in my sleep. I am going and that is all there is to it." She pulled away from him, saying, "After all, you are in no position to issue orders. You do as I say. It will only be until you're healed. You can't do everything you want to do, you know?"

He grinned at her. "I can do anything I want to, Jenny." He reached over to the bedside table and handed Jenny the paper Jeff had given to him, saying, "Read this and then come to bed."

Jenny opened the official looking document and began to read.

I, Travis Gardiner, having paid the sum of twenty-five thousand pounds, do intend to indenture one, Jennifer Grayson Gardiner to a life of love, happiness, and motherhood. This indenture to last for as long as we both shall live.
Signed: Travis Beauregard Gardiner
Witnessed: Jeffrey Townsend Gardiner.

Jenny leaned down and kissed him as the clock struck on the mantle. This dream was real. Her search was at an end.

RAPTUROUS ROMANCE
by Phoebe Conn

CAPTIVE HEART (1569, $3.95)

Celiese, the lovely slave girl, had been secretly sent in her mistress's place to wed the much-feared Mylan. The handsome warrior would teach her the secrets of passion, and forever possess her CAPTIVE HEART.

LOVE'S ELUSIVE FLAME (1836, $3.95)

Flame was determined to find the man of her dreams, but if Joaquin wanted her completely she would have to be his only woman. He needed her, wanted her, and nothing would stop him once he was touched by LOVE'S ELUSIVE FLAME.

SAVAGE FIRE (1397, $3.75)

Although innocent blonde Elizabeth knew it was wrong to meet the powerful Seneca warrior known as Rising Eagle, she came to him when the sky darkened, and let him teach her the wild, rapturous secrets of love.

ECSTASY'S PARADISE (1460, $3.75)

While escorting Anna Thorson to a loveless marriage, Phillip wondered how he could deliver her to another man's bed when he wanted her to warm his own. Anna, at first angered, found he was the only man she would ever desire.

If you enjoyed this book we have a special offer for you. Become a charter member of the **ZEBRA HISTORICAL ROMANCE HOME SUBSCRIPTION SERVICE** and...

Get a
FREE
Zebra Historical Romance
(A $3.95 value) No Obligation

Now that you have read a Zebra Historical Romance we're sure you'll want more of the passion and sensuality, the desire and dreams and fascinating historical settings that make these novels the favorites of so many women. So we have made arrangements for you to receive a *FREE* book ($3.95 value) and preview 4 brand new Zebra Historical Romances each month.

Join the Zebra
Home Subscription Service—
Free Home Delivery

By joining our Home Subscription Service you'll never have to worry about missing a title. You'll automatically get the romance, the allure, the attraction, that make Zebra Historical Romances so special.

Each month you'll receive 4 brand new Zebra Historical Romance novels as soon as they are published. Look them over *Free* for 10 days. If you're not delighted simply return them and owe nothing. But if you enjoy them as much as we think you will, you'll pay *only* $3.50 each and save 45¢ over the cover price. (You save a total of $1.80 each month.) *There is no shipping and handling charge or other hidden charges.*

——— *Fill Out the Coupon*———

Start your subscription now and start saving. Fill out the coupon and mail it *today*. You'll get your FREE book along with your first month's books to preview.

Mail to: Zebra Home Subscription Service, Inc.

120 Brighton Road
P.O. Box 5214
Clifton, New Jersey 07015-5214

YES. Send me my *FREE* Zebra Historical Romance novel along with my 4 new Zebra Historical Romances to preview. You will bill me only $3.50 each; a total of $14.00 (a $15.80 value—I save $1.80) with *no* shipping or handling charge. I understand that I may look these over FREE for 10 days and return them if I'm not satisfied and owe nothing. Otherwise send me 4 new novels to preview each month as soon as they are published at the same low price. I can always return a shipment and I can cancel this subscription at any time. There is no minimum number of books to purchase. In any event the *FREE* book is mine to keep regardless.

_____

NAME

_____

ADDRESS   APT. NO.

_____

CITY   **STATE**   **ZIP**

_____

SIGNATURE   (if under 18, parent or guardian must sign)